About the Author

Marguerite Kaye writes hot historical romances from her home in cold and usually rainy Scotland. Featuring Regency Rakes, Highlanders and Sheikhs, she has published over fifty books and novellas. When she's not writing she enjoys walking, cycling (but only on the level), gardening (but only what she can eat) and cooking. She also likes to knit and occasionally drink martinis (though not at the same time). Find out more on her website: www.margueritekaye.com

Regency Rogues

Regency Rogues:

Candlelight
Confessions

MARGUERITE KAYE

MILLS & BOON

First Published in Great Britain 2020
By Mills & Boon, an imprint of HarperCollins*Publishers*
1 London Bridge Street, London, SE1 9GF

REGENCY ROGUES: CANDLELIGHT CONFESSIONS © 2020
Harlequin Books S.A.

Outrageous Confessions of Lady Deborah © 2012 Marguerite Kaye
The Beauty Within © 2013 Marguerite Kaye

ISBN: 978-0-263-27950-4

0220

OUTRAGEOUS CONFESSIONS OF LADY DEBORAH

Prologue

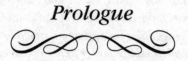

The murals were surprisingly well executed. Whoever had commissioned them certainly had eclectic taste, for Dionysius practiced his arts on one wall, with Sappho adjacent, and a selection of rather graphic and—in his lordship's opinion—physically impossible combinations of male and female were portrayed opposite. Upon the fourth wall was painted a rather interesting triumvirate which Charles Mumford, Third Marquess of Rosevale, would have liked to explore further. His current position, however, made this rather difficult.

'For pity's sake, Bella, have mercy, I beg of you.' The Marquess was a man most unused to pleading. In the normal run of things it was his expectation—indeed, he believed it was his inalienable right—to have his every instruction obeyed instantly. But the situation in which he currently found himself could by no stretch of the imagination be described as normal.

For a start he was trussed like a chicken, bound hand and foot to the ornate canopied bed in the cen-

tre of the room. His shirt having been ripped open and his breeches roughly pulled down, he was also shockingly exposed, excitingly vulnerable, from his neck to his knees.

Then there was the fact that he was being coolly appraised by quite the most exotic and alluring creature he had ever clapped eyes upon. Clad in a black velvet robe with a décolleté so daring it seemed to be held in place only by the sheer power of her considerable will, she was the stuff of every red-blooded man's fantasy. Dark silken tresses tumbled down her back. Her skin was the colour of whipped cream. Her lips were full, painted harlot red. Her countenance sultry. The black stock of the cat-o-nine-tails she stroked was thick and weighty. She was, overall, a perfect combination of the voluptuous and the vicious, which sent the blood surging to the Marquess's most prized piece of anatomy. Charles Mumford groaned. Whether in trepidation or anticipation only he could truly know.

Bella Donna allowed her eyes to wander languidly over the body of her captive. Despite the undoubted fact that he was an insufferable prig, more than deserving of whatever punishment she decided to mete out to him, the Marquess was a prime physical specimen, his lightly muscled body testament to his fondness for the noble art of fencing. A sheen of sweat glistened on his torso as he fought to free himself from his constraints. The muscles in his arms bulged like cords as they strained against the knots she had so expertly tied. A spatter-

ing of dark hair arrowed down from his chest, over the flat plane of his taut belly, and down. Bella's eyes widened as she followed its trail. His reputation was indeed well deserved. She flicked her tongue slowly over her rouged lips. Dispensing punishment did not preclude an element of pleasure. Especially hers.

Bella drew the whip slowly down the Marquess's body, watching his skin quiver as the leather thongs slid over him, giving his twitching member an expert and playful little tug.

His Lordship groaned. 'Devil take you, release me.'

Bella laughed. 'In your world your word may be law, but you are in my world now. The dark and erotic world of the night, where I am queen and you are my subject. I will release you when I have done with you and not before.'

'Curse you, Bella! Deadly Nightshade! You are well named. What have I done to deserve this?'

'You are a man. That is crime enough,' Bella hissed, noting with satisfaction that, despite his pleas, the Marquess's tumescence was burgeoning. She plied her whip once more, a little more decisively this time. A hiss as the leather thongs made contact, raising soft welts on the flesh, made her victim wince, made his jutting shaft stand up proudly. She shuddered with anticipation. They were ready. All three of them.

'Enough talk,' she said, as she hitched up her skirts and prepared to mount him. 'I have a notion for a midnight ride, and I see a stallion champing at the bit. Though I warn you,' she whispered into his ear, as she

*began to sheath the thick pole of his rampant manhood,
'I will not hesitate to use the whip if you cannot maintain the gallop.'*

The author put down her pen with a trembling hand. It
was, she thought, quite the best and most outrageous
scene she had written thus far.

'Goodnight, Bella,' she said as she slipped the sheaf
of parchment into her desk and turned the key in the
lock, 'I look forward to renewing our acquaintance tomorrow.'

Smiling with a satisfaction quite different from
Bella's but no less deep, she snuffed out the candle and
retired to her own rather more spartan bedchamber.

Chapter One

Sussex—February 1817

The mechanism which controlled the huge mantel clock jolted into action, the harsh grating sound shattering the blanket of silence, startling him into dropping his wrench. Elliot Marchmont melted back into the shadows of the elegant drawing room, taking refuge behind the thick damask window hangings. They were dusty. His nose itched. He had to quickly stifle a sneeze. Lady Kinsail, it seemed, was not an overly fastidious housekeeper.

The clock began to chime the hour. One. Two. Three. It was an old piece, Louis Quatorze by the looks of it, with an intricate face showing the phases of the moon as well as the time. Gold in the casing. Diamonds on the display. Valuable. There had been a similar one in a grand house he'd visited while in Lisbon. Elliot's lip curled. He doubted it was still there.

The chimes faded into the night and silence again

reigned. Elliot waited. One minute. Two. Only after five had elapsed did he dare move, for experience had taught him to be cautious while there was still a chance that someone in the household, disturbed by the sound, had awoken. But all was well. The coast was clear.

Outside, thin ribbons of grey cloud scudded over the luminous half-moon like wisps of smoke. Silent and stealthy as a cat, shading the light from his lantern with his kerchief, Elliot made his way over to the wall at the far end of the room on which the portrait was hung. The current Lord Kinsail glowered down at him in the dim light, a jowly man with hooded eyes and a thin mouth.

'Grave-robbing weasel,' Elliot hissed viciously. 'Callous, unfeeling prig.'

The likeness of the government minister who had, some years previously, been responsible for supplying the British army during the Peninsular War—or *not* supplying them, if you asked the man now gazing disdainfully up at him—remained unmoved.

Perched precariously on a flimsy-looking gilded chair, Elliot felt his way carefully round the picture, uttering a small grunt of satisfaction as the mechanism opened with a tiny click. The heavy portrait swung silently back on its hinges. He ducked, only just avoiding being clipped on the jaw by the ormolu corner of the frame.

Getting efficiently down to business, Elliot extracted his selection of picks from the capacious pocket of his greatcoat and carefully placed the wrench he used for leverage. Although the safe was old, the Earl had replaced the original warded lock with a more modern arrangement. Faced with four rather than the standard two separate lever tumblers to manipulate, it took Elliot almost twenty minutes to complete the delicate task. As the last tumbler lifted and the bolt finally slid back he eased open the safe door, breathing a sigh of relief.

Papers tied with ribbon and marked with the Earl's seal were crammed into the small space. Underneath them were a number of leather boxes which Elliot wasted no time in opening, rifling through the contents. The Kinsail jewels were, he noted, of excellent quality, if of surprisingly meagre quantity. The family coffers had obviously been seriously depleted at some point in the past. He shrugged. What these people did with their own property was none of his concern.

The item he was looking for was not in any of the boxes. He paused for a moment, one hand stroking his jawline, the rasp of his stubble audible in the smothering silence. Working his fingers quickly across the back wall of the safe, he found a loose panel which concealed a small recess in which sat a velvet pouch. Elliot's triumphant smile glinted in the moonlight as he unwrapped the prize he sought. The large blue diamond was strangely faceted and rectangular in shape. One hundred carats at least, he guessed, about half the size of the original from which it had been cut.

Slipping it into his pocket along with his picks, Elliot extracted his calling card and placed it carefully in the safe. A creak in the corridor outside made him pause in the act of opening the drawing-room door to make good his escape. It could simply be the sound of the timbers of the old house settling, but he decided not to risk exiting Kinsail Manor the way he had entered—through the basement—since this would require him to traverse the entire house.

Making hastily for the window, he pulled back the leaded glass and, with an agility which would have impressed but not surprised the men who had served under him, former Major Elliot Marchmont leapt on to the sill, grabbed the leaded drain which ran down the side of the building, said a silent prayer to whatever gods protected housebreakers that the pipe would support his muscular frame, and began the treacherous descent.

The stable clock chimed the half-hour as Lady Deborah Napier, Dowager Countess of Kinsail, passed through the side gate leading from the park into the formal gardens. In the time it had taken her to make her usual nightly circuit around the grounds of the Manor the skies had cleared. Shivering, she pulled her mantle around her. Made of turkey-red wool, with a short cape in the style of a man's greatcoat, it served the dual purpose of keeping her warm and disguising the fact that underneath she wore only her nightshift. An incongruous picture she must make, with her hair in its curl papers and her feet clad in hand-knitted stockings and sturdy boots—the staid Jacob, Lord Kinsail, would be appalled to discover that his late cousin's widow was accustomed to roam the grounds in such attire on almost every one of the long, sleepless nights of the annual visit which duty demanded of her.

As she passed through the stableyard, making her way across the grass in order to avoid her boots crunching on the gravel, Deborah smiled to herself. It was a small enough act of subversion when all was said and done, but it amused her none the less. Lord knew there was no love lost between herself and the Earl, who blamed her for everything—her husband's premature death, the debts he'd left behind, the shameful state of his lands and her own woeful failure to provide Jeremy with a son to take them on. Most especially Jacob blamed her for this last fact.

I suppose I should be grateful that he continues to acknowledge me, she mused, for, after all, an heiress whose coffers and womb have both proven ultimately barren is rather a pathetic creature—even if my empty nursery conferred upon Jacob a title he had no right to expect. But, alack, I cannot find it in me to be grateful for being invited to this house. I am, upon each visit, astonished anew that the damned man can think he is conferring a favour by inviting me to spend two torturous weeks in the very place where I spent seven torturous years.

She paused to gaze up at the moon. 'Is it any wonder,' she demanded of it, 'that I cannot find tranquil repose?'

The moon declined to answer and Deborah realised that she'd once again been talking to herself. It was an old habit, cultivated originally in the lonely years she'd spent after Mama and Papa had died, when she had been left largely to her own devices in her aged uncle's house. She had invented a whole schoolroom full of imaginary friends and filled page after page of the notebooks which should have contained her arithmetic with stories to tell them.

Deborah had no idea how long her elderly governess had been watching her from the doorway of the schoolroom that day, as she'd read aloud one of those tales of derring-do, stopping every now and then to consult her invisible companions on a point of plot, but it had been enough for that august lady to declare herself unable to cope with such a precocious child. To Deborah's delight, her governess had left and her uncle had decided to send her off to school.

'Little did she know,' Deborah muttered to herself, 'that she was conferring upon me the happiest five years of my life in all my eight-and-twenty.'

At Miss Kilpatrick's Seminary for Young Ladies, Deborah's stories had made her popular, helping her to overcome her initial shyness and make real friends.

As she'd grown from adolescence to young womanhood, her plots had progressed from pirates and plunder through ghosts and hauntings to tales of handsome knights fearlessly and boldly pursuing beautiful ladies. Love had ever been a theme—even in Deborah's most childish scribblings she had found new families for orphaned babes and reunited long-lost brothers with their loyal sister on a regular basis. But it was romantic love which had dominated her stories those last two years at the seminary—the kind which required her heroes to set out on wildly dangerous journeys and carry out impossible tasks; the kind which had her heroines defy their cruel guardians, risking life and limb and reputation to be with the man of their dreams.

Huddled around the meagre fire in the ladies' sitting room, Deborah had woven her plots, embellishing and embroidering as she narrated to her spellbound audience, so caught up in the worlds and characters she'd created that it had always been a jolt when Miss Kilpatrick had rapped on the door and told them all it was time for bed.

'Some day soon,' she remembered telling her best friend Beatrice, 'that will be us. When we leave here…'

But Bea—pretty, practical, a year older and a decade wiser, the eldest daughter of an extremely wealthy Lancashire mill owner—had laughed. 'Honestly, Deb, it's about time you realised those romances of yours are just make believe. People don't fall in love with one look; even if they did, you can be sure that they'd likely fall out of love again just as fast. I don't want my husband to kiss the hem of my skirt or clutch at his heart every time I walk into a room. I want to know that he'll be there when I need him, that he won't fritter my money away on lost causes and that he won't go off to fight dragons when we've got guests to dinner.'

Bea had married the eldest son of a fellow mill owner less than a year later, whom she'd declared, in one of her frank letters to Deborah, at that time once again incarcerated in her guardian's house, would *do very well*. Deborah's correspondence with her friend—with all of her friends—had been one of the many things Jeremy had taken from her. It was not that he had forbidden her to write, but that she had no longer been able to bear to paint a bright gloss on the dreadful reality of her own marriage. And now, though Jeremy had been dead two years, it was too late.

The melancholy which had been haunting her these last months and which had intensified, as ever, during her annual visit to Kinsail Manor settled upon Deborah like a black cloud. Jeremy's death had been far from the blessed release she had anticipated. Of late, she had come to feel as if she had simply swapped one prison for another. Loneliness yawned like a chasm, but she was afraid to breach it for she could not bear anyone to know the truth—even though that meant eventually the chasm would swallow her up.

She was not happy, but she had no idea what to do to alter that state—or, indeed, if she was now capable of being anything else. Isolated as she was, at least when she was alone she was safe, which was some consolation. No one could harm her. She would not let anyone harm her ever again.

A breeze caught at her mantle, whipping it open. Goosebumps rose on her flesh as the cool night air met her exposed skin. She had been lost in the past for far too long. She would not sleep, of that she was certain, but if she did not get back into the house she would likely catch a cold and that would of a surety not do. It would give Lady Margaret, the Earl's downtrodden wife, whose desperation made her seek any sort of ally, an excuse to beg Deborah to prolong her stay.

Head down, struggling to hold her cloak around her, Deborah made haste towards the side door to the east wing and was directly under the long drawing room when a scuffling noise gave her pause. She had no sooner looked up and caught sight of a dark, menacing figure, seemingly clinging to the sheer wall of the Manor, when it fell backwards towards her.

The bracket holding the drainpipe loosened as he was still some fifteen feet or so from the ground. Deciding not to take a chance on the entire thing coming away from the wall, Elliot let go, trusting that his landing would be cushioned by the grass. He did not expect his fall to be broken by something much softer.

'Oof!'

The female's muffled cry came from underneath him. Her ghostly pale face peered up at him, her eyes wide with shock, her mouth forming a perfect little 'o' shape.

Elliot felt the breath he had knocked out of her caress his cheek before he quickly covered her mouth with his hand. 'Don't be afraid, I mean you no harm, I promise.'

Delicate eyebrows lifted in disbelief. Heavy lids over eyes which were—what colour? Brown? He could not tell in this light. Fair brows. Her hands flailed at his sides. Her body was soft, yielding. He was lying on top of her—quite improperly, he supposed. At the same moment he realised that it was also quite delight-

ful. She seemed to be wearing nothing but a shift beneath her cloak. He could feel the rise and fall of her
breasts against his chest. Her mouth was warm against
his palm. For a second or two he lay there, caught up
in the unexpected pleasure of her physical proximity
before several things occurred to him at once.

She was most likely the Countess of Kinsail.

She would definitely raise the alarm as soon as she
possibly could.

If he was caught he would go to the gallows.

He had to leave. Now!

In one swift movement Elliot rolled on to his feet,
pulling the distracting female with him. Still with one
hand covering her mouth, he put his other around her
waist. A slim waist. And she was tall, too, for a lady.
The Earl was a fortunate man, damn him. 'If I take my
hand away, do you promise not to scream?' he asked,
keeping his voice low.

A lift of those expressive brows and an indignant
look which could mean no or it could mean yes.

Elliot decided to take the risk. 'Did I hurt you? I
wasn't expecting you to be there—as you can imagine,' he said.

'That makes two of us.'

Her voice was husky—but then it would be, for he'd
just knocked the wind out of her. She had an unusual
face, an interesting face, which was much better than
beautiful. A full mouth with rather a cynical twist to
it. No tears nor any sign of hysterics, and her expres-

sion was rather haughty, with a surprising trace of amusement.

Elliot felt the answering tug of his own smile. 'Delightful as it was—for me, at least—I did not intend to use you to soften my landing.'

'I am happy to have been of value.' Deborah looked at him through dazed eyes. 'What on earth were you doing?' she asked, realising as she did so that it was an amazingly foolish question.

But he didn't look like a common housebreaker—not that she knew what housebreakers looked like! She should surely be screaming out for help. Of a certain she should be afraid, for she held his fate in her hands and he must know it, yet she felt none of those things. She felt—a dreadful, shocking realisation, but true—she felt intrigued. And unsettled. The weight of him on top of her. The solid-packed muscle of his extremely male body. The touch of his hand on her mouth.

'What were you doing, halfway up the wall of the Manor?'

Elliot grinned. 'Exactly what you suspect I was doing, I'm afraid, Lady Kinsail.'

Now was definitely the time to cry for help, yet Deborah did not. 'You know me?'

'I know of you.'

'Oh.' Conscious of her curl papers and her nightshift, she struggled to pull her mantle back around her. 'I didn't dress for—I did not expect to meet anyone,' she said, feeling herself flushing, trusting to the gloom that it would go undetected.

'Nor did I.'

The housebreaker chuckled. A low, husky growl of a laugh, distinctively male, it sent shivers over Deborah's skin. He had a striking face, strong-featured, with heavy brows, deep grooves running down the side of his mouth, and eyes which looked as if they had witnessed too much. A fierce face with a discernible undercurrent of danger. Yet those eyes suggested compassion and even more improbably, given the circumstances, integrity. A memorable face, indeed, and an extremely attractive one. She met his gaze and for a few seconds the air seemed to still between them. A connection, a *frisson*, something she could not name, sparked.

'I'm sorry to have alarmed you,' he said finally, 'but if you must blame anyone for my presence here you must blame your husband.'

Deborah began to wonder if perhaps she was dreaming. 'But Jeremy—my husband—is…'

'A most fortunate man,' Elliot said with a twisted smile. 'I must thank you for not calling out. I am in your debt.' He knew he should not, but he could not resist. 'Let me demonstrate my gratitude.' When he pulled her to him she did not resist. The touch of her lips on his was warm, sweet and all too fleeting. He released her extremely reluctantly. 'I must go,' he said roughly. 'And you, madam, must do as you see fit.'

'Wait a minute. I don't even know what your name is.'

The housebreaker laughed again. 'I could tell you, but then I'd have to kill you.'

He was already fleeing across the lawn. Staring after him in utter bemusement, Deborah remained stock still, watching the shadowy figure melt into the darkness. The stable clock chimed the hour. Above her, she could hear the sharper chimes of another clock. Looking up, she saw the window of the long drawing room was wide open. The French clock—it must be that she could hear. She touched her fingers to her mouth where the house-breaker had kissed her. Kissed her! A common thief!

No. Housebreaker he might be, but he was most certainly not common. His voice was that of an educated man. He had an air about him of someone used to command. The greatcoat which enveloped him was of fine wool. And, now she thought about it, his boots were of an excellent cut and highly polished. He smelled of clean linen and fresh air and only very slightly of sweat and leather and horse. She supposed he must have tied his steed up somewhere close by. She listened intently, but could hear nothing save the rustle of the breeze as it tugged at the bare branches of the trees.

She should wake the Earl. At the very least she should alert the servants. Deborah frowned. Whatever the man had stolen must have been concealed about his person, for he'd carried no sackfull of loot. Papers, perhaps? Despite the arduous task of setting Jeremy's estates to rights—a task which his cousin never ceased to complain about—Lord Kinsail continued to play an active role in the government. Was the housebreaker a spy? That certainly made more sense, though the war was so long over there was surely no need for such subterfuge. And he had neither looked nor sounded like a traitor.

Deborah's laugh, quickly stifled, had an unwelcome note of hysteria in it. She had no more idea of what a spy should look like than a housebreaker.

None of it made sense. It occurred to her rather belatedly that the thing which Lord Kinsail would consider made least sense of all was her own presence in the grounds, in her night clothes, at four in the morning. He'd want to know why she'd made no attempt to raise the alarm immediately—what could she say when she didn't know the answer to that question herself? It wasn't as if the thief had threatened her. She hadn't felt scared, exactly, more…what?

The thought of having to suffer Jacob's inquisition made up her mind. She would not give him any more reason to treat her with disdain. In fact, Deborah decided, making her way hurriedly to the side door, the time had come to break free from Lord Kinsail and this blighted place. Small consolation—very small—but her failure to provide Jeremy with an heir had one advantage. She had no real obligation to maintain close ties with his family. Lord Kinsail might grudge her every penny of the miserly widow's portion which he doled out irregularly, and only after several reminders, but she doubted he could ultimately refuse to pay it. In any case, she was determined to find a way to survive without it. This would be her last visit to Kinsail Manor and damn the consequences!

Feeling decidedly better, Deborah fastened the door

carefully behind her and fled up the stairs to her chamber on the third floor. Whatever it was the bold housebreaker had taken would be discovered in the morning. He was already gone, and her rousing the household now would not bring him back.

She yawned heavily as she discarded her mantle and unlaced her muddy boots, pushing them to the back of the cupboard out of sight of the inquisitive maid. Catching a glimpse of herself in the mirror, she made a face. Despite her hair curlers, that look on the housebreaker's face just before he kissed her had been unmistakable. Not that she was by any stretch of the imagination an expert, but she was sure, none the less. He had wanted her.

Heat washed over her. What would it be like to submit to someone like that? Deborah pulled the bedclothes up around her, too beguiled by this thought to notice the cold. Desire. She wrapped her arms around herself, closed her eyes and recalled the velvet touch of his lips on hers. Beneath her palms her nipples budded. Behind her lids wanting flared the colour of crimson. Desire. Sharpened by its very illicitness. Desire of the dark, venal kind which roused Bella Donna, the heroine of the novels which were currently scandalising the *ton*, to shocking heights of passion. Desire such as she had never shared.

Desire. Deborah slipped down into the welcoming dark embrace of the bed, her hands slipping and sliding down over the cotton of her nightdress. And down.

Closing her eyes tighter, she abandoned herself to the imagined caresses of a virile and skilled lover.

She awoke much later in the morning than usual, dragging herself up from the depths of slumber to the hue and cry of a household in a state of pandemonium. Slipping into a thick kerseymere gown, for Kinsail Manor, owing to a combination of its age and its current incumbent's frugality, was an uncomfortably draughty place, Deborah sat at her mirror to take out her curl papers. Her straitened circumstances meant she could not afford the luxury of a personal maid, and, though Lady Kinsail had begged her to make use of her own dear Dorcas, Her Ladyship's 'own dear Dorcas' was in fact an exceedingly dour creature, who believed a widow's hair should be confined under a cap and kept there with a battalion of hairpins—the sharper the better.

Since she had perforce been attending to her own *toilette* for most of her adult life, Deborah made short work of gathering her long flaxen tresses high on her head and arranging her curls in a cluster over one shoulder. Her gown she had fashioned herself, too, in plain blue, with not a trace of the French work, furbelows and frills so beloved of *Ackerman's Repository*.

She had resented her blacks when Jeremy died, resented the way they defined her as his relic, but it had taken her a full six months after the designated year of mourning to cast them off all the same, for she had come to appreciate the anonymity they granted her. It was then she had discovered that she lacked any identity at all to fill the gap. Like the anonymous gowns of blues and browns and greys she now wore, neither fashionable nor utterly dowdy, she felt herself indeterminate, somewhat undefined. Like an abandoned canvas, half painted.

An urgent rap at the door interrupted this chastening thought. 'Please, Your Ladyship, but His Lordship asks you to join him in the long drawing room urgently.' The housemaid, still clad in the brown sack apron she wore to lay the morning fires, was fairly bursting with the important news she had to impart. 'We've all to assemble there,' she informed Deborah as she trotted along the narrow corridor which connected the oldest—and dampest and coldest—wing of Kinsail Manor with the main body of the house, built by Jeremy's great-grandfather. 'The master wants to know if anyone heard or saw him.'

'Heard who?' Deborah asked, knowing full well that the girl could only mean the housebreaker.

She should have woken Jacob, she knew she should have, but she could not find it in her to regret this oversight. If she was honest, there was a bit of her—a tiny, malicious, nothing-to-be-proud-of bit of her—which was actually quite glad. Or, if not glad, at least indifferent. Jacob had taken everything from her that Jeremy had not already extorted. Whatever precious thing had been stolen, she could not care a jot. What was more, she decided on the spur of the moment, she was going to continue to keep her mouth firmly shut. She would not admit to wandering the grounds. She would not provoke one of his sermons. She would not!

'I'm sorry—what were you saying?' Deborah realised the maid had been talking to her while her thoughts had been occupied elsewhere. They were outside the drawing room now. The door stood wide open, revealing the gathered ranks of Lord Kinsail's household. At the head of the room, under his own portrait, stood the man himself.

'Best to go in, My Lady,' the maid whispered. 'We're last to arrive.' She scuttled over to join the rest of the maidservants, who were clustered like a nervy flock of sheep around the housekeeper. Mrs Chambers, a relic from Deborah's days as chatelaine, cast her a disapproving look.

Inured to such treatment, Deborah made her way to the top of the room to join the Earl. The frame of the portrait swung open on its hinge to reveal the safe. Her lips twisted into a bitter smile. Jeremy had shown it to her when they were first married, though in those days it had been concealed behind a portrait of his father.

'Empty coffers,' Jeremy had said to her. 'Though not for much longer—thanks to you, my darling wife.'

The revelation that the terms of her inheritance would force him to wait several years for her to attain her majority and gain the larger part of her fortune had not been the beginning of his change in attitude towards her, but after that he'd ceased to pretend.

She should never have married him. But there was no time for her to become entangled in that morass yet again. Lady Kinsail, even more palely loitering than ever, was seated on a gilt chair almost as frail as herself. Deborah went to her side.

'Cousin Margaret,' she said, squeezing Her Ladyship's cold hand between her own. Though she persistently refused to grant Lord Kinsail the appellation of cousin, she had conceded it to his wife. They were not related, but it rescued them from the hideous social quagmire of having two Countesses of Kinsail in the one household. 'What, pray, has occurred?'

'Oh, Cousin Deborah, such a dreadful thing.' Lady Kinsail's voice was, like her appearance, wraith-like. 'A common housebreaker—'

'No common housebreaker,' her lord interrupted. Under normal circumstances Lord Kinsail's complexion and his temper had a tendency towards the choleric. This morning he resembled an over-ripe tomato. 'I don't know what time you call this, Cousin,' he fumed.

'A quarter after nine, if the clock is to be trusted,' Deborah replied, making a point of arranging her own chair by his wife and shaking out her skirts as she sat down.

'Of course it's to be trusted. It's Louis Quatorze! Say what you like about the French, but they know how to turn out a timepiece,' Lord Kinsail said testily. 'I have it upon good authority that that clock was originally made for the Duc d'Orleans himself.'

'A pity, then,' Deborah said tightly, 'that such an heirloom is no longer in his family. I abhor things being taken from their rightful owners.'

Lord Kinsail was pompous, parsimonious, and so puffed-up with his own conceit that it was a constant surprise to Deborah that he did not explode with a loud pop. But he was no fool.

He narrowed his eyes. 'If you had served my cousin better as a wife, then the estates which you allowed him to bring to ruin upon that ill-fated marriage of yours would not now be my responsibility, but your son's. If you had served my cousin better as a wife, Cousin Deborah, I have no doubt that he would not have felt the need to seek consolation in the gaming houses of St James's, thus ensuring that his successor had hardly a pair of brass farthings to rub together.'

Deborah flinched, annoyed at having exposed herself for, cruel as the remarks were, there was a deep-rooted part of her, quite resistant to all her attempts to eradicate it, which believed them to be true. She had made Jeremy about as bad a wife as it was possible to make. Which did not, however, mean that she had to accept Jacob's condemnation—she was more than capable of condemning herself. And she was damned if she was going to apologise for her remark about the clock!

'Don't let me hold you back any further, Jacob,' she said with a prim smile.

Lord Kinsail glowered, making a point of turning his back on her and clearing his throat noisily before addressing the staff. 'As you know by now, we have suffered a break-in at Kinsail Manor,' he said. 'A most valuable item has been taken from this safe. A safe which, I might add, has one of the most complex of new locks. This was no ordinary robbery. The brazen rogue, a menace to polite society and a plague upon those better off than himself, was no ordinary thief.'

With a flourish, His Lordship produced an object and waved it theatrically in front of his audience. There was a gasp of surprise. Several of the male servants muttered under their breath with relief, for now there could be no question of blame attaching itself to them.

At first Deborah failed to understand the import of the item. A feather. But it was a most distinctive feather—long with a blue-and-green eye. A peacock feather. The man who had dropped from the sky on top of her last night must have been the notorious Peacock!

Good grief! She had encountered the Peacock—or, more accurately, the Peacock had encountered her! Deborah listened with half an ear to Jacob's diatribe against the man's crimes, barely able to assimilate the fact. She watched without surprise as in turn every one of the servants denied hearing or seeing anything out of the ordinary, just as the servants in every one of the Peacock's other scenes of crime had done. No one had ever disturbed him in the act. No one had ever caught so much as a fleeting glance of him leaving. Private investigators, Bow Street Runners—all were completely flummoxed by him. He came and went like a cat in the night. For nigh on two years now, the Peacock had eluded all attempts to capture him. No lock was too complex for the man, no house too secure.

With the room finally empty of staff, Lord Kinsail

turned his attentions back to Deborah. 'And you?' he demanded. 'Did you see anything of the rogue?'

She felt herself flushing. Though God knew she'd had opportunity aplenty, she had never grown accustomed to prevarication. 'Why would I have seen anything?'

'I know all about your midnight rambles,' Lord Kinsail said, making her start. 'Aye, and well might you look guilty. I am not the fool you take me for, Cousin Deborah.' He permitted himself a small smile before continuing. 'My head groom has seen you wandering about the park like a ghost.'

'I have never taken you for a fool, Jacob,' Deborah replied, 'merely as unfeeling. I take the air at night because I have difficulty sleeping in this house.'

'Conscience keeps you awake, no doubt.'

'Memories.'

'Spectres, more like,' Lord Kinsail replied darkly. 'You have not answered my question.'

Deborah bit her lip. She ought to tell him, but she simply could not bring herself to. All her pent-up resentment at his quite unjustified and utterly biased opinion of her, combined with her anger at herself for lacking the willpower to enlighten his ignorance, served to engender a gust of rebelliousness. 'I saw nothing at all.'

'You are positive?'

'Quite. You have not said what was stolen, Jacob.'

'An item of considerable value.'

Alerted by his decidedly cagey look, Deborah raised an enquiring brow. 'Why so close-mouthed? Was it government papers? Goodness, Jacob,' she said in mock horror, 'don't tell me you have you lost some important state secret?'

'The item stolen was of a personal nature. A recent acquisition. I do not care to elaborate,' Lord Kinsail blustered.

'You will have to disclose it to the Bow Street Runners.'

'I intend to have the matter investigated privately. I have no desire at all to have the Kinsail name splashed across the scandal sheets.'

Deborah was intrigued. Jacob was looking acutely uncomfortable. A glance at Margaret told her that Her Ladyship was as much in the dark as she was. She was tempted—extremely tempted—to probe, but her instinct for caution kept her silent. That and the fact that she doubted she would be able to sustain her lie if interrogated further.

The sensible thing to do would be to make good her escape while Jacob was distracted, and Deborah had learned that doing the sensible thing was most often the best.

Getting to her feet, she addressed herself to Lady Kinsail. 'Such a shocking thing to have happened, Cousin Margaret, you must be quite overset and wishing to take to your bed. In the circumstances, I could not bear to be a further burden to you. I think it best that I curtail my visit. I will leave this morning, as soon as it can be arranged.'

'Oh, but Cousin Deborah, there is no need—'

Lord Kinsail interrupted his wife. 'I trust you are not expecting me to foot the bill if you decide to travel post?'

'I shall go on the afternoon stage,' Deborah replied coldly. 'If you can but extend your generosity to providing me with transport to the coaching inn...'

'Cousin Deborah, really, there is no need...' Lady Kinsail said, sounding just a little desperate.

'If that is what Cousin Deborah wants, my dear, then we shall not dissuade her. I shall order the gig.' Lord Kinsail tugged the bell. 'In one hour. I trust you will not keep my horses waiting?'

'I shall make my farewells now to ensure that I do not,' Deborah replied, trying to hide her relief. 'Cousin Margaret.' She pressed Her Ladyship's hand. 'Jacob.' She dropped the most marginal of curtsies. 'I wish you luck with recovering your property. Thank you for your hospitality. I must make haste now if I am to complete my packing in time. Goodbye.'

'Until next year,' Lady Kinsail said faintly.

Deborah paused on the brink of gainsaying her, but once again caution intervened. If there was one thing the Earl loathed more than having his cousin's widow as a house guest, she suspected it would be having his cousin's widow turn down his hospitality.

'So much can happen in a year,' she said enigmatically, and left, closing the door of the long drawing room behind her for what was, she fervently hoped, the very last time.

Chapter Two

London, three weeks later

Elliot stifled a yawn and fished in his waistcoat pocket for his watch. Five minutes off two in the morning and his friend Cunningham was showing no inclination to leave. The atmosphere in the gambling salon of Brooks's was one of intense concentration disturbed only by the chink of coin, the glug of a decanter emptying, the snap of cards and soft murmurings as the stakes were raised. The gamblers were much too hardened to betray anything so crass as emotion as the stack of guineas and promissory notes shifted across the baize from one punter to another.

Some of the cardplayers wore hats to shield their faces. Others tucked the ruffles of their shirt sleeves up under leather cuffs. Elliot, who had been used to gambling with his life for far higher stakes, could not help finding the whole scene slightly risible. He had placed a few desultory bets at faro earlier, more for form's sake than anything, but the last hour and a half had been spent as a spectator.

Restlessly pacing the long room, with its ornately corniced concave ceiling from which a heavy chandelier hung, the candles in it guttering, he called to mind the many similar reception rooms across Europe he had visited. Cards were not the game which had attracted him to such places. In the midst of war, cards were a means for his men to while away the long hours between battles. Civilians didn't understand the boredom of war any more than they understood its visceral thrill. He had no idea why Cunningham could ever have thought he would be amused by a night such as the one they had just spent. Carousing and gambling left Elliot cold. No doubt when Cunningham rose from the tables he would be expecting to indulge in that third most gentlemanly pursuit, whoring—another pastime which held no interest for Elliot. He was a gentleman now, perforce, but he was, first and foremost his own man, and always had been—even in the confines of his uniform. Elliot had had enough.

'I find I have had a surfeit of excitement, my dear Cunningham,' he said, tapping his friend lightly on the shoulder. 'I wish you luck with the cards. And with the ladies.'

'Luck doesn't come into it, Elliot. You of all people should know that. Never met a devil more fortunate with the fairer sex than you.'

'Never confuse success with good fortune, my friend,' Elliot replied with a thin smile. 'I bid you goodnight.'

He collected his hat and gloves and headed out into St James's, doubting he'd be making much use of his new club membership in the future. It was a cold night, dank and foggy, with only a sliver of moon. A house-breaker's kind of night, though it was much too soon to be thinking about that.

Kinsail's diamond had proved rather difficult to dispose of. Elliot's usual fence had refused to have anything to do with such a distinctive stone, forcing him into an unplanned trip to the Low Countries where he had, reluctantly, had it cut and re-faceted before selling it on. The resultant three diamonds had garnered far short, collectively, of what Lord Kinsail was rumoured to have paid for the parent. But then, Kinsail had paid the inflated premium such contraband goods commanded, so Elliot's thief-taker had informed him. More important—far more important—was the price Kinsail was now paying for his dereliction of duty to the British army.

Not that he knew that, of course, any more than he really understood the price paid by that army for his neglect. Men such as Kinsail saw lists demanding horses, mules, surgeons. Other lists requiring field guns, cannons, rifles, vied for their attention, and more often won. But what use was one of the new howitzers when there were no horses to haul it into battle? What use were muskets, Baker rifles, bayonets, when the men who would wield them lay dying on the battlefields for want of a horse and cart to carry them to a field hospital? For want of a surgeon with any experience to tend to them when they got there? What did Kinsail and his like know of the pain and suffering caused by their penny-pinching. The ignorance which led them to put guns before boots and water and bandages?

Elliot cursed, forced his fists to uncurl. Even now, six years later, Henry's face, rigid with pain, haunted him. But what did Kinsail and his like know of that? Nothing. Absolutely nothing. And even if he could, by some miracle, paint the picture for them, it would give them but a moment's pain. Far better to hit them where it hurt—to take from them what they valued and use it to fund what really mattered. Those diamonds, even in their cut-down form, would make an enormous difference. That miserly bastard Kinsail would never know that his jewel had, by the most dubious and complex route, gone some way to make reparation for his war crimes.

As ever, following what he liked to think of as a successful mission, he had scoured the newspapers for word of the robbery, but Lord Kinsail had, unsurprisingly, declined to make public his loss. For perhaps the hundredth time since that night Elliot wondered what, if anything, Lady Kinsail had said about their encounter. For what seemed like the thousandth time the memory of her pressed beneath him flitted unbidden into his mind. The feel of her mouth on his. The soft, husky note to her voice. That face—the haughty, questioning look, the big eyes which had shown not one whit of fear.

He should not have kissed her. He had thought, as he fled the scene of his crime, that she had kissed him back, but had come to believe that mere wish fulfilment. She had simply been too startled to resist. After all, as far as she was concerned he was a thief. But why had she not cried foul?

The bright gas lighting of Pall Mall gave way to the dimmer and appropriately shadier braziers around Covent Garden. Thin as London was of company this early in the year, there seemed to be no shortage of customers for the wretches forced to earn their living on the streets. A scuffle, a loud cry, then a cackle of laughter rent the air as a man was dumped unceremoniously on to the steps of a brothel. Shaking his head at a questioning pock-marked street walker, Elliot pressed a shilling into her filthy hand and made haste across the market square, ignoring her astonished thanks.

The stark contrast between the homes of the gentlemen who frequented the privileged clubs of St James's and the hovels and rookeries which were home to London's whores, whom those same gentlemen would visit later, made him furious. He had seen poorer and he had seen sicker people abroad, but this—this was home, the country he had served for nigh on sixteen years. It shouldn't be like this. Was this what twenty-odd years of war had won them?

In the far corner of the square he spied something which never failed to make him heartsick. Just a man asleep in a doorway, huddled under a worn grey blanket, but the empty, flapping ends of his trousers told their story all too well. The low wooden trolley against which he rested merely confirmed it. To the callused, scarred legacy of guns and gunpowder on his hands would be added the scraping sores caused from having to propel himself about on his makeshift invalid cart. He stank, the perfume of the streets overlaid with gin, but to Elliot what he smelled most of was betrayal.

'May God, if God there be, look down on you, old comrade,' he whispered.

Careful not to disturb the man's gin-fuelled slumber, he slipped a gold coin into the veteran's pocket, along with a card bearing a message and an address. To many, charity was the ultimate insult, but to some—well, it was worth trying. Elliot never gave up trying.

Weary now, he made his way towards Bloomsbury, where he had taken a house. 'The fringes of society,' Cunningham called it, 'full of Cits.' He could not understand Elliot's reluctance to take a house in Mayfair, or even a gentleman's rooms in Albemarle Street, but Elliot had no desire to rub shoulders with the *ton* any more than he desired to settle down, as his sister Elizabeth said he ought. Said so regularly and forcefully, Elliot thought with a smile as he passed through Drury Lane.

They were surprisingly alike, he and his sister. Almost twelve years his junior, Lizzie had been a mere child when Elliot joined the army. He had known her mostly through her letters to him as she was growing up. As their father's health had declined and war kept Elliot abroad, Lizzie had shouldered much of the responsibility for the overseeing of the estate as well as the care of her fast-failing parent. Knowing full well how much her brother's career meant to him, she had refrained from informing him of the true nature of affairs back home until their father's demise had become imminent. Touched by her devotion, Elliot had been impressed and also a little guilt-ridden, though Lizzie herself would have none of that, when he had finally returned for good after Waterloo.

'I have merely done my duty as you did yours. Now you are home the estates are yours, and since Papa has left me more than adequately provided for I intend to enjoy myself,' she'd told him.

She had done so by marrying a rather dour Scot, Alexander Murray, with rather indecent haste, after just three months of mourning. The attachment was of long standing, she had informed her astonished brother, and while her dearest Alex had agreed that she could not marry while her papa was ailing, she'd seen no reason for him to wait now that Papa had no further need of her. Lizzie had emerged from her blacks like a butterfly from a chrysalis—an elegant matron with a sharp mind and a witty tongue, which made her a popular hostess and an adored wife. Matrimony, she informed her brother at regular intervals, was the happiest of states. He must try it for himself.

Russell Square was quiet. Bolting the door behind him, Elliot climbed wearily up to his bedchamber. After tugging off his neckcloth, neatly folding his clothes—an old military habit, impossible to shake—Elliot yawned and climbed thankfully between the cool sheets of his bed. Another hangover from his military days: to have neither warming pan nor fire in the room.

He had no wish to be manacled in wedlock. It was not that he didn't like women. He liked women a lot, and he'd liked a lot of women. But never too much, and never for too long. In the courts of Europe loyalty to one's country came before loyalty to one's spouse. In the courts of Europe the thrill of intrigue and adventure, legitimised by the uncertainty of war, made fidelity of rather less import than variety.

'Living in the moment,' one of his paramours, an Italian countess, had called it. Voluptuous Elena, whose pillow talk had been most enlightening, and whose penchant for making love in the most public of places had added an enticing element of danger to their coupling. That time in the coach, coming back from the Ambassador's party…Elliot laughed softly into the darkness at the memory. It had been later, in another country, in another coach and with another woman—this one rather less inclined to court public exposure—that he had realised how practised had been Elena's manoeuvres. Her ingenious use of the coach straps, for example. He had obviously not been the first and he was without a doubt that he had not been her last.

He wondered what Elena was doing now. And Cecily. And Carmela. And Gisela. And Julieanne. And—what was her name?—oh, yes, Nicolette. He could not forget Nicolette.

Except he could hardly remember what she looked like. And the others, too, seemed to merge and coalesce into one indistinct figure. He missed them all, but did not miss any one in particular. What he really missed was the life, the camaraderie. Not the battles, for the thrill of the charge was paid for in gore and blood. Nor the pitiless reality of war either—the long marches, the endless waiting for supplies which did not come, his men stoically starving, clad in threadbare uniforms, footwear which was more patches than boot. Killing and suffering. Suffering which continued still.

Elliot's fists clenched as he thought of the old soldier in Covent Garden. One of thousands. No, he'd had more than enough of that.

What he missed was the other, secret part of his army career, as a spy behind enemy lines. The excitement of the unknown, pitting his wits against a foe who did not even know of his existence, knowing that before he was ever discovered he would be gone. The transience of it all had made living in the moment the only way to survive. The pulsing, vibrant urgency of taking chance upon chance, the soaring elation of a mission pulled off against the odds. He missed that. The pleasure of sharing flesh with flesh, knowing that, too, was transient. He missed that also. Since coming home he had taken no lover. He would not take a whore, and somehow, in England, taking the wife of another man seemed wrong.

Abstinence had not really troubled him. He had encountered no woman who had stirred him beyond vague interest until his encounter with Lady Kinsail.

Elliot sighed as her face swam into his mind again and his body recalled hers. Between his legs, his shaft stirred. *Dammit,* he would never sleep now! That smile of hers. That mouth. His erection hardened. What would it feel like to have that mouth on him, licking, tasting, sucking, cupping? Elliot closed his eyes and, wrapping his hand around his throbbing girth beneath the sheets, gave himself over to imagining.

Deborah stood undecidedly on the steps of the discreet offices of Freyworth & Sons in Pall Mall. It was early—not long after ten—a pretty day for March, and she longed to stretch her legs and mull over the rather worrying things which Mr Freyworth had said. It was true, her writing had of late become more of a chore than a pleasure, but she had not been aware, until he had pointed it out, that her general ennui had transferred itself on to the page. Stale. That was how her publisher had described her latest book. Knitting her brow, Deborah was forced to acknowledge the truth of what he said. Perhaps her imagination had simply reached its limit?

Across from her lay St James's Park, and a short way to the left was Green Park. There would be daffodils there. Not the sort of freshness Mr Freyworth was demanding, but perhaps they would help inspire her. She could walk over Constitution Hill, then carry on into Hyde Park and watch the riders.

Even at the end, when money had been as scarce as hens' teeth at Kinsail Manor, Jeremy had found the funds to keep his horses. Riding had always been a solace to Deborah, though these days it was, as with most things, a pleasure she could only experience vicariously.

She had no maid to accompany her, which when she was married would have been a heinous crime, but a

combination, she believed, of her widowhood, her im-
poverished state and the bald fact that she possessed
no maid, had allowed her a relative freedom which she
cherished. In fact it was rather her self-possessed air,
the invisible wall which she had built around herself,
which made it only very occasionally necessary for
Deborah to rebuff any man who approached her. For
her charms were not so recondite as she imagined, and
nor was she anywhere near so old, but of this she was
blissfully unaware.

In the Green Park, the fresh grass of the gently rolling meadows made her feel as if she was far from the
metropolis. Her mind wandered from her business meeting back to *that* night, as it had done on countless occasions in the days which had elapsed since. Though
she had scoured both *The Times* and the *Morning Post*
on her visits to Hookham's circulating library in Bond
Street, she had found no mention of the theft from Kinsail Manor. Jacob had been as good as his word.

The shifty-eyed investigator who had come calling
at her lodgings in Hans Town had been equally reticent.
She had absolutely no idea what had been stolen save
that it was small, definitely not papers, and definitely
extremely valuable. *What?* And *why* was Jacob so intent on silence? And *how,* when he was so intent, had
the housebreaker discovered the presence of whatever
it was in the safe when even Jacob's wife had no idea
of its existence?

The housebreaker who had kissed her.

Deborah paused to admire a clump of primroses, but

her gaze blurred as the cheerful yellow flowers were replaced by a fierce countenance in her mind's eye. Try as she might, she had been unable to forget him. Unable and unwilling, if she was honest. In the secret dark of night he came to her and she seldom had the willpower to refuse him. Never, not even in the early days with Jeremy, before they were married, when she had been so naïvely in love, had she felt such a gut-wrenching pull of attraction. *Who and why? And where was he now?* She had no answers, nor likely ever would, but the questions would not quit her mind. His presence had fired her imagination.

Reaching the boundary of the Green Park, she made her way across the busy thoroughfare of Piccadilly towards Hyde Park, with the intention of walking along Rotten Row to the Queen's Gate. Carriages, horses, stray dogs, urchins, crossing sweepers and costermongers made navigating to the other side treacherous at the best of times, but Deborah wove her way through the traffic with her mind fatally focused elsewhere.

The driver of an ale cart swerved to avoid her.

She barely noticed the drayman's cursing, but on the other side of the road Elliot, emerging from Apsley House where he had been petitioning Wellesley—he never could think of him as Wellington—froze. It was her! He was sure of it—though how he could be, when he had not even seen her in daylight, he had no idea.

But it was most definitely Lady Kinsail and she was headed straight for him—or at least for the gates to the park. She was dressed simply—even, to his practised eye, rather dowdily for a countess. The full-length brown pelisse she wore over a taupe walking dress was bereft of trimming, lacking the current fashion for flounces, tassels and ruffles. Her hair, what he could see of it under the shallow poke of her bonnet, was flaxen. She was tall, elegant and slender, just as he remembered. In the bright sunlight, her complexion had a bloom to it, but her expression was the same: challenging, ironic, a little remote. Not a beautiful woman—she was too singular for that—but there was definitely something about her, the very challenge of her detachment, that appealed to him.

He should go. It would be madness to risk being identified. But even as he forced himself to turn away he caught her eye, saw the start of recognition in hers and it was too late.

Elliot, who had in any case always preferred to court trouble than to flee from it, covered the short distance between them in several quick strides. 'Lady Kinsail.' He swept her a bow.

'It *is* you!' Deborah exclaimed. She could feel her colour rising, and wished that the poke of her bonnet were more fashionably high to disguise it. 'The house-breaker. Though I have to say in the light of day you look even less like one than when you—when I…'

'So very kindly broke my fall,' Elliot finished for her. 'For which I am most grateful, believe me.'

Deborah blushed. 'You expressed your gratitude at the time, as I recall.'

'Not as thoroughly as I'd have liked to.'

'I didn't tell,' she blurted out in confusion.

'That I kissed you?'

'No. I mean I didn't report you. I should have. I know I should have. But I didn't.'

'Well, I'll be damned!' Elliot stared at her in astonishment.

Her eyes were coffee brown, almost black, with a sort of hazel or gold colour around the rim of the iris. A strange combination, with that flaxen hair. The pink tip of her tongue flicked out along the full length of her lower lip to moisten it.

He dragged his eyes away. They were in danger of making a show of themselves, standing stock still at the busy entrance gates. Taking her arm, he ushered her into the park. 'Let's find somewhere more private, away from the crowds.'

Deborah tingled where his fingers clasped her arm. It was most—strange. In a nice way. So nice that she allowed herself to be led down one of the more secluded paths without protest.

He was taller than she remembered. In daylight his countenance was swarthy, the colour of one who had spent much time in the sun. The lines around his eyes, too, which gave him that fierce quality, looked as if they came from squinting in bright light. Snatching a glance up at him, she noticed a scar slicing through his left eyebrow, and another, a thin thread on his forehead just below the hairline. A soldier? Certainly it would explain his bearing, the upright stance, the quick stride which even her long legs were struggling to keep up with.

He was exceedingly well dressed, in a rich blue double-breasted tailcoat with brass buttons, and the snowy white of his cravat was carefully tied, enhancing the strong line of his jaw, the tanned complexion. Brown trousers, black boots, a single fob, a beaver hat—though the crown was not tall enough to be truly fashionable. His *toilette* was elegant but simple. Like herself, he eschewed ostentation, though unlike herself his reason did not appear to be lack of funds. Housebreaking must be a lucrative profession.

No, she could not bring herself to believe that he stole in order to dress well. Whatever reason he had for breaking into houses, it was not avarice. It appealed to her sense of irony that the famous Peacock was decidedly no peacock. Maybe his choice of calling card was deliberately self-mocking.

'What is so amusing?' Elliot brought them both to a halt by a rustic bench facing the sun.

'Just an idle thought.'

'We can sit here awhile,' he said, after carefully wiping the wood down with his kerchief. 'As long as the sun prevails we shall not get cold.'

Obediently, Deborah sat down. There were so many things she wanted to ask, but as she stared up at him she was too overwhelmed by the reality of him, which was so much *more* than the memory of him, to order her thoughts properly. 'Are you really the Peacock?'

A word from her in the right ear and he would be dancing on the end of a rope at Tyburn. Though so far she had of her own admission said nothing. 'Yes,' Elliot replied, 'I really am the Peacock.'

'When I saw Jacob holding up the feather I could scarcely believe it.'

It was a small bench. Elliot's knees touched her leg as he angled himself to face her. A spark of awareness shot through him at the contact. He remembered the way she'd felt beneath him. He remembered, too, the things he'd imagined her doing to him since and prayed none of it showed on his face. He had to remind himself that she was married. *Married!* In England, that mattered.

'Why?' he asked abruptly. 'Why did you say nothing to your husband?'

'You mentioned him during our first conversation—if it could be called a conversation,' Deborah said with a frown. 'You said that I must blame him, or some such words. Blame him for what? What has Jeremy to do with your breaking into Kinsail Manor?'

Jeremy! It had slipped his mind, but he remembered now that was the name she'd given Kinsail. 'You mean Jacob, surely?' Elliot said, also frowning. 'Jacob, the Earl of Kinsail. Your husband.'

Her eyes widened with surprise and she burst into a peal of laughter, brimming with amusement like a champagne flute full of bubbles. Then, as if she was quite unused to the sound, she stopped abruptly. 'I am not the current Lady Kinsail. Jacob is my husband's cousin, the Fifth Earl. Jeremy was the fourth.'

'Was? You're a widow?' *She was a widow!*

'Of some two years' standing,' the widow replied.

'I can't tell you how pleased I am to hear that.' The words were out before he could stop them.

'I doubt very much that the pleasure you take from my status could rival mine.'

'That, if you don't mind my saying so, was an even more telling remark than my own.'

Deborah coloured. 'I am aware of that.'

'It was not a love-match, then, I take it?'

'No. Yes. I thought it was. I was just eighteen when we met—my head stuffed full of romantic fancies, as foolish and unworldly as it's possible to imagine a person could be—and Jeremy was…seemed to be…well, he swept me off my feet, to put it in the sort of terms I'd have used myself then,' Deborah said with a twisted smile. 'When Jeremy proposed I thought all my birthdays had come at once. My guardian—my uncle—my parents died when I was very young—was only too glad to be able to wash his hands of me, so we were married three months after we met. I thought myself wildly in love, but it was all a sham. Jeremy was only interested in my money. Pathetic, isn't it? I don't know why I have told you all this, but you did ask.'

'I think it's sad, not pathetic. Were you very unhappy?'

Deborah shrugged. 'I was very naïve and very set upon the match. I was not the only one who suffered as a result. I should never have married him. You know, this is all rather boring. Do you mind if we change the subject?'

Her husband sounded like a complete bastard. Elliot couldn't understand why she was so determined to lay the blame on herself but, much as he wished to probe deeper, her closed look was back. He doubted he would get anywhere. 'I beg your pardon,' he said. 'I didn't mean to upset you.'

'You didn't,' Deborah replied, tilting her chin and sniffing.

He wanted to kiss her then, for that defiant little look. Actually, he'd wanted to kiss her before that. 'You know, you don't look a bit like a dowager,' Elliot said lightly. 'Not a trace of grey hair, you don't dab at your eyes with a black lace kerchief, or sniff at your smelling salts, and I've seen not a trace of an obnoxious little lap dog—unless he's too precious to be allowed outside in the cold. The Dowager Countess of Kinsail.' He shook his head. 'No, it's just not you.'

He was rewarded with a weak smile. 'I prefer not to use the title. It's Deborah Napier. And if I don't look like a dowager you look even less like a housebreaker.'

'Deborah. Now, *that* suits you. I am Elliot Marchmont, known to a very select few as the Peacock.'

'What was it you stole, may I ask? Only Jacob has not let on, for some reason.'

'For a very good reason,' Elliot said drily. 'I suppose there is no harm in telling you, since you already have my fate in your hands. It was a diamond. A large blue diamond, reputedly cut from the original French crown jewels. Kinsail came by it in what one might call a rather roundabout and unorthodox manner.'

'You mean illegally? Jacob?' Deborah squeaked.

'Why do you look so surprised?'

'Because he's a sanctimonious, parsimonious prude who is never happier than when condemning others for lack of principles or morals or—well, anyway—' She broke off, realising she had once again forgotten her golden rule of keeping her feelings strictly under wraps. This man unsettled her. 'How did you know about it?'

'I have my sources.'

'Goodness. Do you mean those people they call fences? The ones who live in the Rookeries?' Deborah asked, using with relish the cant she had only ever written.

'I have to say, for an upstanding member of the aristocracy you seem to have an unhealthy interest in the seamy underbelly of society.'

'I prefer to attribute it to a vivid imagination. Is it true what they say? That there is not a safe in England you cannot break?'

'I have not yet encountered one,' Elliot said, rather taken aback by her reaction, which seemed to be fascination rather than disapproval.

She was sitting on a bench in Hyde Park in broad daylight with the notorious Peacock. She should be calling the authorities. But instead of being in fear for her life she looked intrigued—excited, even. He had the distinct feeling that he had in Deborah Napier, Dowager Countess of Kinsail, met someone almost as subversive as he was himself.

'I wish you would tell me all,' she said, as if to confirm his thoughts. 'Why do you do it? What is it like to pit your wits against the world as you do? Are you ever afraid of being caught?'

She had not asked him what he'd done with the diamond. Surely that was the first question any woman would have asked? But she seemed to have no real interest in the outcome, only the method. Just like him—well, at least in part.

'There's always a chance,' Elliot replied, beguiled by the way her eyes lit up. 'But if it was no risk it would not be worth doing. That is part of it for me—the excitement, knowing that one false move could be an end. There's nothing like it. Not since…'

'The army?'

'How did you know that?'

'The way you walk. The scars on your face.' Deborah touched his brow, felt a jolt at the contact and drew her hand away quickly. 'The first time I met you I thought you were a man used to being in command. Were you a soldier for long?'

'Sixteen years. We ran off when I was just fifteen, me and my school friend Henry. Like you, he was orphaned, only his father had made no provision for him. In the same week he lost his family and his place at school. He was to be apprenticed to a lawyer.' Elliot laughed. 'Henry—a lawyer. Nothing could be more unlikely. He decided he would enlist instead, and I decided to go with him because by then I'd had enough of school and the notion of returning to the family estates and learning from my father how to take up the reins sounded like purgatory. So we ran off together, lied about our ages.'

'What about your parents?'

'My mother was dead. My father was not particularly happy, but we were not yet at war at that point, and I persuaded him that it would be good for me to learn some independence and some discipline. He bought me my first commission. Then the wars with Napoleon came, and by that time I'd discovered I had a talent for soldiering. The army was my family. In a way it was selfish of me, but by that time my loyalty to my men was such that—to be frank—I could not have left while there was a war to be won. To his enormous credit, my father supported me in that. I was a major when I resigned my commission after Waterloo. My only regret is that my father died just six months after I returned home.'

'It must have been very difficult for you to adjust to civilian life after all that time.'

'Yes, it was. Very.' Her perception surprised Elliot. 'People don't really see that.'

'People never do. I was nineteen when I married. When Jeremy died I found I had no idea who I was. Two years later I'm still not sure.'

'I came home to take up the mantle of my family estates, to settle down into the quiet country life I'd joined up to avoid in the first place. Not much more than two years ago and I'm still not sure, either, who I am. I'm not a soldier any more, but I'm pretty damn sure that I'd die of boredom as a country squire.'

'So you've taken up housebreaking instead? Is that it?' Deborah asked, looking amused.

'Partly.'

'I wish I'd thought of something as exciting, but I lack the skills. How came you to acquire them? Is it part of basic army training, lock-picking?'

Elliot laughed. 'No, but the British army is made up almost entirely of volunteers, you know. You'd be astonished at the skills one can learn from the men.'

'Is that how you came about your contacts, too?' Deborah chuckled. 'I do not recall reading in the newspapers that the war against Napoleon was won by fences and pickpockets and the like.'

'The war was won by poor bastards from all walks of life who enlisted because they had the misguided belief that at the end of it they would have made a better life for themselves and their families,' Elliot said grimly. 'The same poor bastards you see begging on the streets now—those of them who made it home.'

'I'm sorry,' Deborah said, taken aback by the sudden change in him. 'I did not mean to make light of it. You must have lost some good friends.'

'Yes.' Surprised by the urge to confide in her, Elliot took a deep breath. 'Sorry.'

'You have no need to be. I should have known better. Time makes no difference with such scars, does it? A year, two—people think you should have forgotten.'

'I won't ever forget.'

'Nor I,' Deborah said softly.

She recognised that tone. And the look in his eyes—

the darkness, suffering, guilt. She wondered what it was that had put it there. It went too deep to be solely down to the horrors of war. But though she was tempted to ask, she did not. Something about him—a shuttered look, a reticence—warned her off. Besides, questions begat questions. She did not wish to reveal why it was she understood him.

'What do you do with your time?' Elliot asked. 'Despite what you said, you don't give the appearance of one who is enjoying her widowhood.'

'I am still becoming accustomed,' Deborah said with a shrug. 'It is not what I expected—not that I was actually planning for it, because Jeremy was only six-and-thirty. I mean, I did not murder him or anything like that.'

'But you thought about it?'

'Well, only by way of diversion when I was…' *Writing my first book,* she had been about to say.

Deborah stared at Elliot, aghast. He was trying not to smile. The corner of his mouth was quivering with the effort of restraining his laughter.

'It's not funny. That was a shocking thing to make me say,' she said, trying to hide the quiver in her own voice.

'I did not *make* you say anything.'

'You know, I wish you would take me with you,' Deborah said impulsively.

'I'm sorry?'

'Just once. I wish I could accompany you—the Peacock. It would be—I don't know—marvellous.' *And perhaps inspiring,* Deborah thought.

Elliot burst out laughing. 'Marvellous! I've heard my escapades described in many ways, but marvellous has never been one of them. You are the most original woman I have ever met.'

'Yes? I take that as a huge compliment, I think. Have you met many women?'

'Many. They've asked me many things, too,' Elliot said wickedly. 'But not one of them has shown an interest in housebreaking.'

'Well, I am very interested in housebreaking,' Deborah said, trying not to think about the many voluptuous and experienced women Elliot had met. 'Will you consider it?'

'Consider—good God. You are not serious?'

She could not quite believe it herself, but it seemed she was. For one night, she would step out of her shadow, cast off the ghosts which haunted her and act as boldly as her literary alter ego. In fact, she would *be* Bella. It was perfect. Just exactly the boost her writing needed to stop it from stagnating.

Deborah's eyes positively sparkled. 'You have no idea how much,' she said.

Elliot seemed to find her enthusiasm amusing. He was laughing—a deep, gruff sound which shivered over her skin. She found herself staring at his mouth. His knee pressed into her thigh through the cambric of her dress. Little ripples of heat spread from the contact. Up.

'Will you take me?' she asked, half-joking, half-something else she chose not to acknowledge.

Elliot couldn't take his eyes off her mouth. She smelled of spring and flowers and something more elusive. He leaned closer. There were just the tiniest traces of lines around her eyes. He'd thought her three- or four-and-twenty, but she must be older. That darkness that lurked at the back of her eyes was experience. She was a widow. He couldn't possibly kiss her here, in the park. But she was a widow. So not married. Or not any more. He wanted to kiss her. He wanted to do a lot more than that.

'Elliot, will you take me?'

She was serious! He sat back, blinked, pulled his hat from his head, looked at it, put it back again. 'Don't be ridiculous.'

'It's not ridiculous,' Deborah said, too taken up with the outrageous idea to care how wild it sounded, to notice the reckless edge to her voice. This was what she wanted. This was what she'd been waiting for. Excitement—enough to jolt her out of her melancholy. And experience. The authenticity it would lend to her story would give Bella Donna a new lease of life. 'Please, Elliot.'

Her hand was on his coat sleeve. Her gloves were worn. His own were new. He hated wearing gloves. He wanted to feel her skin. 'No,' he said, shaking her hand away. 'I could not possibly...'

'Why not? Are you afraid I would mess things up

for you? I would not, I promise, I would do only as you instructed.'

For a few wild seconds he imagined it—the pair of them in cahoots. Her presence would lend a wholly new edge to the thrill of the escapade. What the devil was he thinking? 'Madness,' Elliot exclaimed, leaping to his feet. 'You don't know what you're asking. To risk the gallows...'

'It would not come to that. It never has yet—you are too clever for that.' She couldn't understand why, but she *had* to persuade him. 'Please. My life is so—you have no idea. I can't explain, but if I could just—I want to feel alive!'

Elliot had no difficulty in recognising that particular sentiment. It was still madness and he still had no intention of agreeing, but he couldn't help empathising with what she said. 'Deborah, it's impossible,' he said gently.

'It's not.' Desperation made her ruthless. 'I want to come with you the next time. In fact, I am determined to come with you; if you do not agree I will inform upon you.'

This he had not anticipated. God dammit, he couldn't help admire her daring. She must want this very badly. He wondered why. That fatal curiosity of his. Elliot tried valiantly to stifle it. 'You would be unwise to do so. By your silence, you have already implicated yourself. I could say that you were my accomplice.'

'Oh!' The wounded look Deborah gave him was almost comical. The resolute set to her mouth which followed, the straightening of her shoulders, was not. 'It is a risk I'm prepared to take.'

'It seems to me that you're prepared to take a great many risks.'

'You think so? You don't know me very well.'

The light went out of her so quickly it was almost like looking at a different person. One minute she was sparkling, the next bleak. He recognised the edge of desperation which made her reckless. She was a fascinating mixture.

It would be madness to consider doing as she asked. He was only thinking about it because he wanted her. He wanted her a lot. And she wanted him too—though she would no more acknowledge it than her real reasons for wishing to break into a house with him. If he did not take her, what then? He could not possibly be considering this.

Slowly, he began to shake his head.

'No! Please, don't say no. I mean it, Elliot—if you say no I will inform on you.'

Really, he could not imagine a more original female. She was quite as ruthless in her own way as he was. Elliot's smile was a slow curl, just the one side of his mouth. His finger traced her determinedly set lips. The pulse at her throat fluttered. He felt the shallow intake of her breath, but she did not flinch. Ridiculous, but what he thought he saw in her was a kindred spirit. One who stood on the edge of society. It was absolute madness even to be considering doing as she asked.

'You won't persuade me with threats,' he said softly. 'If I take you, it will be because I want to.'

The words made Deborah shiver. Did he want her? Want *her*? No one had ever wanted her like that. 'And do you—want me?' she asked. Because it was exactly what Bella Donna would have said, and because if she let herself think like Deborah she'd turn tail and flee and regret it for the rest of her days, and she was sick, sick, sick of regrets.

Looking round swiftly to check they were quite alone, Elliot pulled her to him, a dark glint in his eyes. 'You are playing a very dangerous game, Deborah Napier. I would advise you to have a care. For if you dance with the devil you are likely to get burnt. You may come with me, but only if you promise to do exactly as I say.'

'You mean it!' *Oh, God, he meant it!* She would be a housebreaker. A thief!

Since this rather vital aspect hadn't actually occurred to her until now, Deborah wavered. But her failing to take part would not avert the crime. And if their victim was like Jacob most likely he would deserve it anyway, or could easily afford the loss. And Bella needed this, and she needed Bella, and Elliot was waiting for an answer. She would never get another chance. Never!

'I promise,' she said. 'I'll do exactly as you say.'

'Then prove it. Kiss me,' Elliot said audaciously, not thinking for a moment that she would.

But she did. Without giving herself time to think, her heart hammering against her breast, Deborah stood on tiptoe, pulled his head down to hers, and did as she was bid. Right there in Hyde Park, in the middle of the day, she kissed him.

Chapter Three

She meant it as a kiss to seal their bargain, but as soon as her lips touched his memories, real and imagined, made the taste of him headily familiar. Elliot's hands settled on her hips, pulling her closer. Deborah linked her gloved hands around his neck, enjoying the lean length of his body hard against hers, just as before, in the dark of night, when he had landed on top of her.

His lips were warm on hers, every bit as sinfully delicious as she'd imagined, coaxing her mouth to flower open beneath his, teasing her lips into compliance, heating her gently, delicately, until his tongue touched hers. She shuddered, felt rather than heard his sharp intake of breath. The kiss deepened, darkened, and Deborah forgot all about her surroundings as Elliot's mouth claimed hers, as he pulled her into the hard warmth of his body, so close that she could feel the fob of his watch pressing into her stomach, smell the starch on his neckcloth.

It was a kiss like none she had ever tasted, heated by the bargain it concluded, fired by the very illicitness of their kissing here in a public space, where at any moment they could be discovered. She could not have imagined, could not have dreamed, that kissing—just kissing—could arouse her in this way. She had not thought it possible—had not even attributed such an awakening to Bella Donna.

The clop of a horse passing on the other side of the high hedge penetrated the hazy mists of her desire-fuelled mind. Deborah wrenched herself free even as Elliot released her. They stared at each other, breathing heavily. He tugged at his neckcloth as if it were constricting him. Her gloved hand touched her lips. They felt swollen.

Elliot picked his hat up from the ground where it had fallen, striving for a nonchalance he was far from feeling. The reality of Deborah Napier's kisses made a poor shadow of his fantasies. It was complete folly, unbelievably risky, but if this intriguing creature wanted to join forces with his alter ego he could not refuse her.

He wanted her. He wasn't sure what he was going to do about that, but he was sure he wanted to do something. Not that that was why he was going to agree to this madness. He was doing it for her. To relieve the darkness behind those beguiling eyes. To release her, if only temporarily, from the emotional embargo she seemed to have placed upon herself. That was the only reason. The main one, certainly.

'Are you quite sure you want to do this?' he asked.

Still dazed and confused by the delights of lip on lip, tongue on tongue, struggling to tamp down the shocking and wholly new passion which their kiss had lit, Deborah was not at first sure what he was asking. Then the meaning of his question sank home, and she smiled. It was not the tight, polite smile behind which she usually hid, but a wide, true smile which lit her eyes, wiping the haughty expression from her face and with it several years.

'Oh, yes,' she said, 'I'm sure.'

A week went by before she heard from him again. A week when sanity took hold in the light of day and Deborah wondered what on earth had possessed her to suggest this wild escapade.

Housebreaking and stealing—the simple fact that they were illegal should be suffice to prevent her even contemplating them. Her conscience told her so several times a day, her head warned her of the possible consequences, yet her heart would listen to none of it. Whether she accompanied him or not, the Peacock would commit the crime. He was never caught. And even if she was discovered, there was the sad, indisputable fact, that she couldn't make herself see the difference between the prison she already inhabited and gaol, no matter how often she told herself there was an enormous difference.

Had her doubts been more constant they would have prevailed, but the problem was they were fickle things, dissolving whenever she took up her pen, or played out her encounter with Elliot again, or with the coming of dusk. Excitement took hold of her then. Jagged and dangerous like one of the saw-toothed swords she had seen in an exhibition at Bullock's Museum in Piccadilly, it was fatally enticing. For the first time in a very long time, she really *wanted* something.

She knew what she contemplated was reckless beyond belief, but still the logic of this failed to take root. She wanted the visceral thrill. She wanted to feel her blood coursing through her veins. She wanted to feel alive. And besides, she owed it to Bella, whose existence had seen her through the darkest of days, to gild her latest story with as much authenticity as possible.

In truth, when Deborah's heart quailed at the prospect of aiding and abetting the Peacock, it was Bella's ruthless courage which bolstered her. It was through Bella's eyes that she peered out into the dimly lit street from her drawing-room window some eight days after that encounter in the park, her heart fluttering with fear—not of what was to come, but of what she would feel if Elliot did not turn up.

His promise, so reluctantly given, could so easily be reneged upon. She knew nothing of him, after all, and despite his having surrendered his name, she had made no enquiries, having neither trusted friends nor trusted servants. Had he been similarly reticent? It hadn't occurred to her until now that he might ask about her, though it should have. Jeremy's title meant nothing to her; the penurious state in which he had left her made it easy for her to fade into the background of a society she had never really been permitted to inhabit even when he was alive, but she was still, unfortunately, the

Dowager Countess of Kinsail. And though Jeremy had been gone two years, the scandal of his debts, his premature death, were not so easily buried as his corpse.

Deborah clenched her fists inside the pockets of the greatcoat she wore. Elliot would not judge her. It wasn't possible—no one knew the murky details of her marriage. He would come. He had given his word and he had not the look of a man who would break a promise. Casting a quick glance out at the empty street, she retrieved the note from behind the clock, scanning the terse content by the light of the single candle.

It is set for tonight. I will call for you at fifteen minutes past midnight. If you have changed your mind, send word with the boy.

No signature. No address. The boy referred to was the street urchin who had delivered the note earlier in the day. Surely, surely, surely, if Elliot Marchmont had reservations about her, he would not have sent such a note? After all, even if she did know where he lived— which she did not—she was hardly likely to come hammering on his door, demanding that he fulfil his promise. It had been a test, this silence, a test of trust, and she had not failed. He would come, she told herself. He cared naught for her past, and why should he? Besides, she thought defiantly, returning to her vigil at the window, it was not Deborah, Dowager Countess of Kinsail, who would be his aider and abettor, any more than it was Elliot Marchmont who would commit the crime. Tonight it was the Peacock and Bella Donna.

She smiled into the darkness and let go the last of

her doubts as the clock chimed the hour. Midnight. The witching hour. The hour of transformations and magic. Bella's hour. Deborah's reservations must bide their time until morning.

She was waiting for him on the doorstep. He saw the pale glimmer of her hair, stark against the dark of her clothing, as he rounded the corner. Elliot was not sure whether to be glad or sorry. No, that was a lie, he knew perfectly well how he felt, and it was the direct opposite of what he *ought* to. Something like a ripple shimmered through his blood as he strode quickly across the street. Reckless, foolish, crazy as it was to be taking her with him, it was what he wanted. It wasn't just that he was curious, and it wasn't just that he desired her either—not wholly, though that was part of it. He didn't know what it was. The unknown, maybe? Something different? Something more? He didn't care. What mattered now, at this moment, was that she was here and her very presence made everything sharper, more attenuated.

She was wearing some sort of greatcoat. Her smile was tremulous. No gloves. Her hands, when he took them in his, were icy. 'It's not too late, you can still change your mind,' Elliot said softly, but Deborah shook her head, gave him that look, that haughty, determined one. Did she know what a challenge it was? He doubted it. 'Are you sure?'

'You sound as if you're the one who's having second thoughts.'

'I should be, but I'm not,' Elliot replied.

Looking up at him, Deborah felt that kick-in-the-stomach pull of attraction. He was not handsome, his face was too hard for that, but he was charismatic. She pulled her hand from his. 'Where are we going?'

'You'll see.'

'Have you a carriage? A horse?'

'It's not that far.'

Deborah sucked in her breath. 'You mean we're going to—here, in town? But isn't that...'

'Risky? Wasn't that rather the point?'

She shivered. She had imagined a house like Kinsail Manor. The dark of night. The silence of the country. For a few seconds, reality intruded. Streetlamps. Night watchmen. Late-night revellers. And surely more locks, bolts and servants to contend with.

'Having second thoughts, Lady Kinsail?'

His mocking tone made her stiffen. 'No. And don't call me that.'

'Deborah.'

The way he said her name, giving it a dusky note it had never contained before, made her belly clench. His nearness threatened to overset her. She pushed back her greatcoat in an effort to distract herself. 'What do you think of my clothing? Is it appropriate for a house-breaker?'

The breeches and boots revealed long, long legs. Blood rushed to Elliot's groin. He tried not to imagine what her *derrière* would look like, tried not to picture those fabulous legs wrapped around him. Was she wearing corsets beneath that coat? 'It's very...' Revealing?

Erotic? Stimulating? Dear God! 'Very practical,' he said, dragging his eyes away. 'If I didn't know better, I'd say you'd done this before.'

'I found the clothes in a trunk in the house when I moved in. They must have belonged to the previous tenant. I kept them, but he never came back for them. He must have been quite a small man, for they are a perfect fit, don't you think?'

She pushed the greatcoat further back and posed for his inspection, quite oblivious of the effect her display of leg was having on him. 'I think we had best make tracks,' Elliot said brusquely.

Pulling the greatcoat back around her and jamming her hat on to her head, Deborah hurried after him as he crossed the road. 'Where are we going? What are we going to steal? Whose house is it?' Her questions were breathless for she was struggling to keep pace with him as they skirted the beginnings of the new buildings to the east of Hans Town, avoiding the main thoroughfares, heading towards Hyde Park.

'The less you know the better,' Elliot replied.

Her booted feet stumbled on the mix of cobbles and mud as they wended north along mews and through stables. The houses grew grander as they passed Berkeley Square. Crossing Mount Street and into another mews, Deborah's nerves began to take hold. When Elliot pulled her down a shallow flight of steps and into the shelter of the basement wall, she looked up and up and up at the massive building in front of which they stood, and thought she might actually be sick. 'This is Grosvenor Square,' she whispered.

Elliot nodded. She caught the gleam of his smile and remembered her first impression of him. Dangerous. Her fear was dissipated by anticipation, pounding through her veins in a rush. 'Is this *it?*' she asked, looking with awe at the elegant town house, the rows of windows like blank, sleeping eyes.

'This is your last chance to change your mind. After this there is no going back, do you understand?'

He was standing close enough for her to sense his excitement. It was contagious. Her stomach felt as if it were tied in a knot. Deborah nodded.

Elliot's laugh, the low growl she had first heard in the grounds of Kinsail Manor, quivered over her. 'Very well,' he said, 'now listen very carefully.'

Slowly, methodically, he went over the details of his plan, details she realised he could only have compiled as a result of thorough observation and reconnaissance. He had an impressive eye for minutiae. She understood now why it had taken him over a week to contact her. She listened so carefully she scarcely dared breathe before reciting each step back to him slowly, painstakingly, a frown furrowing her brows, determined to miss nothing, to prove herself worthy.

'Good. You have an excellent memory,' Elliot said, when she had repeated it a second time.

'You are impressively well prepared,' Deborah returned with a grin.

'Know your territory. I've had plenty of practice.'

'Another unexpected bonus of your army training, no doubt. If only they knew.'

'And yet another is that I expect to be obeyed. Remember that.'

He spoke lightly, but she was in no doubt that he meant it, nor in any doubt that he had always achieved absolute obedience. It was not fear of retribution, but implicit trust that would have inspired the same loyalty in his troops which she felt stirring her courage. A determination not to let him down, to live up to the expectations he had of her. 'Understood,' Deborah said, with a mock salute which made him smile.

The watch called the hour from the other side of the mews. Across the way, a candle flame reflected in the dimpled glass of a window pane was snuffed out. Above, the town house was in complete darkness. 'They are early to bed, our occupants,' Elliot whispered. 'And early to rise too.' When he awoke tomorrow, the Minister would be the poorer and the men he had deprived would be his beneficiaries. Justice of the sort which the government seemed incapable of delivering would be served. The glow of satisfaction warmed him. 'Ready?' he asked Deborah.

She nodded. Her eyes glittered in the dim light. He leaned towards her, pressing a swift kiss to her icy lips. 'Let's go.'

Though the lock was easily picked, the door on to the mews was bolted on the inside, as he had expected. The lower windows were barred. The wave of crime which the upright citizens of London blamed on the soldiers they had once revered had weighted the coffers of lock-smiths and ironmongers, who did a roaring trade these days in providing protection against the poor wretches who had perforce resorted to theft. Nodding to Deborah to assume her post as lookout at the top of the steps on to the mews, Elliot untied the length of rope from his waist and attached the little hook which had been made by the regiment's smithy to his own design. The cotton which was wrapped around it muffled the report as the hook found its mark on the first throw. Testing it with a sharp tug, Elliot climbed swiftly to the second floor. The lock on this window gave way to his jemmy. It was the work of moments to pull in the rope, detach the hook, close the window, jump lightly down from the sill and make his way stealthily back down into the bowels of the house.

Deborah was waiting at the door as he slid the bolts back. She slipped silently into the narrow corridor and followed him back through the flagstoned kitchen where the banked fire provided a modicum of light, into the gloom of the servants' staircase and up.

He dared not use his lantern. Behind him, Deborah, obviously as able to see in the dark as he was, did not stumble. He was impressed by her courage and excited by her presence there in his shadow.

The painting was in the study, at the back of the house adjacent to the room he had first entered. 'An early study of Philip the Fourth,' Elliot whispered to Deborah. 'It's bigger than I remember. But then, the last time I saw it, it was hanging in a rather larger house.'

She stared at the decidedly ugly subject, resplendent in black and silver. She could see it was beautifully executed, but she could not like it. 'You said you've seen it before?'

'In Madrid. In the house of one of our senior Spanish allies.'

'Then how did it get here?'

Elliot shrugged. 'Plunder. A gift. A bribe. I don't know,' he said, pressing the button which released the blade of his knife. Quickly, he cut the painting from its heavy frame and rolled it up before handing it to Deborah.

She took it gingerly. 'How did you know where to find it?'

'I have my sources.'

'You said that before.'

He caught her wrist and pulled her close. 'This may well be a game to you, but you have to realise, you're playing with fire. If we are caught…'

'We won't be. You're the Peacock, you never have been yet.'

Her utter confidence in him was flattering, there was no denying it, but a tiny noise outside the door distracted him. Quickly, Elliot pulled Deborah towards the cover of the window curtains. 'Hush!'

His hand covered her mouth. Her back was pressed into his body. Her heart thudded much too loud. She listened hard, but could hear nothing save the rasp of her own breathing, the softer whisper of his. The curtains smelled musty. They waited, motionless, for what seemed like aeons. Her nose tickled. She was acutely conscious of him, tensed behind her. She was inappropriately conscious of her legs, her bottom, her back, moulded against the front of his body. Everything felt stretched, more real, and yet unreal. The air crackled with tension. Between them, an invisible cord of awareness. She had never felt more alive.

She felt him relax before he moved his hand from her mouth. 'What…?'

He turned her around. She caught the gleam of his smile, heard the little huff of his chuckle. 'I thought I heard someone, but it must have been a rat.'

Deborah shuddered. 'I hate rats.' Elliot laughed again. She felt it this time, vibrating in his chest against hers. 'What's so funny?'

'You follow me across London in the middle of the night dressed as a man, break into a house and steal a priceless painting with barely a tremble, but a rat makes you shiver. Would you rather we'd encountered the master of the house? He is a rat of an altogether different order.'

'I'd rather we didn't encounter anyone.'

'Then we should make haste.' From his pocket, Elliot produced the feather and handed it to Deborah. 'My calling card. Will you do the honours?'

She placed it carefully on the ledge of the empty frame. 'You made this seem so easy,' she said.

Elliot, who had been in the process of retrieving his grappling hook from the floor, heard the note of disappointment in her voice. It was ridiculous to add danger to risk, but he sensed it was danger she craved. Hastily, he cut his grappling hook free of its rope and crammed it into his pocket, before securing the long cord by twisting it around the gilded legs of the heavy marble-topped table which filled the window embrasure. 'Give me the painting,' he said.

Deborah handed over the rolled canvas. 'Aren't we going back down the stairs?'

'You'll get a more authentic experience leaving this way. If you dare, that is,' Elliot replied. They were two storeys up, nothing for one so used to shimmying up and down ropes, but as Deborah leaned cautiously out of the window and peered down, he saw the sheer drop through her eyes. 'We'll use the stairs,' he said, making to pull the rope in.

She stayed his hand. 'Absolutely not! You're quite right, what is the use in half an experience?' she said. 'Just show me what to do.'

'You could be badly hurt if you fall.' Elliot was already regretting having teased her. He should have known she would rise to the challenge.

'I could hang if we're caught,' Deborah retorted. 'I'll take my chances.'

She was deliberately courting danger. He recognised that, because he did it so often himself. The tilt of her chin, the determination in her voice made it impossible for him to deny her, much as he knew he ought. She seemed always to have this effect on him. A connection between them crackled and briefly flared. 'Very well,' Elliot said, tearing his eyes away, 'I'll go first, that way

I can catch you if you fall. Watch what I do. Wait until I'm on the ground before you come out.'

A clock chimed in the hallway outside the room, making Deborah jump. 'What if someone comes?'

Elliot picked up her hat and jammed it back on her head. 'They won't. You're perfectly safe, you're with the Peacock, remember? Now pay attention. It's all in the way you hold the rope.'

Deborah watched, heart drumming, as he showed her what to do with her hands and feet. Her palms were damp as she leaned out, seeing him disappear swiftly down, making it seem effortless. It was a long way. If she fell—but she would not fall. She cast another glance over her shoulder at the door. She listened hard, but could hear nothing. The room seemed larger, darker, much more sinister without Elliot's presence. Fear crept stealthily up from her booted feet, winding its way like a vine, making her legs shake, her hands too. The urge to turn tail, to flee out of the door, down the servants' staircase to the kitchen, was almost overwhelming. Only the stronger fear, that without Elliot to guide her she would be lost, overturn something, rouse the household, kept her rooted to the spot. Right at this moment, she effectively held his life in her hands. She would not let him down. *She would not!*

Determination to prove herself worthy uprooted her feet. Deborah's heart still pounded so hard and fast she felt faint, but she bit her lip hard, wiped her damp palms on her breeches and sat gingerly on the edge of the sill.

Elliot was already on the ground, looking up anxiously. She waved. The ground swam. *Don't look down!*

She grasped the rope as he had shown her. She edged out. Her legs dangled in the air. Breathing quickly to still the panic, she floundered for the rope with her feet, found it, gripped it tight between her thighs. Her arms were surely too frail to support her. She dangled, half in, half out of the window, for a dreadful moment. Then she kicked away from the ledge and began to descend. Slowly she went, shakily, her hands burning on the rope, losing it, retrieving it, gripping tighter. Her shoulders ached. Her thighs, too. Down. Slowly down, looking neither up at the window nor towards Elliot. One floor. If she fell now, she would probably survive. A broken limb or so. Small consolation. Don't think about falling. Down. Her arms felt as if they would part company with her shoulders. Thank heavens she wore breeches. Even so, she would be bruised. Down.

'Not far to go now. Hold on.'

Elliot's voice sounded strained, for the first time that night. Deborah risked a downward glance. Her foot dangled about a yard from his upturned face. Relieved and triumphant, she grinned. 'Did you think I would fall on you? As you did at Kinsail Manor?'

Elliot grabbed her ankle. 'It crossed my mind!'

She covered the final few feet quickly, safe in the knowledge that he had her. If he had not held her when she landed, she would have sunk to the cobbles, for her legs felt as if the bones had been removed. 'Sorry.' She clutched at Elliot's coat. 'I just need…'

Anxiously casting a glance to the end of the mews where the rumbling of a carriage slowed, Elliot put his arm around her waist. 'We must make haste. If anyone comes—that rope is rather a giveaway, I'm afraid.'

Guiltily, Deborah realised she hadn't even closed over the window. It gaped, wide and betraying, the rope hanging like a declaration. 'I'm fine,' she said, straightening, ignoring the pain shooting through her legs and taking a stumbling step towards the other end of the mews. Gritting her teeth, she forced herself to walk.

'Not too fast, or we will draw unwanted attention. Push your hat down over your face.' Elliot caught up with her, put his arm through hers. His grip tightened.

They walked together back to Hans Town through streets blanketed in silence. Now that it was over, Elliot was astounded at himself for placing Deborah in such danger. 'I should not have brought you.'

She turned the key in her door and pushed it open. 'Don't say that. I'm glad you did, Elliot. It was wonderful. Please don't say you regret it.'

'I would be lying if I did,' he replied gruffly.

She was safe home and it was over. Deborah was awed by her own daring, filled with an exuberance that made her want to clap her hands with glee. 'I can't believe we did it,' she said. 'We really did it. We really did!' She felt buoyant, her delight fizzing, bubbling over, making her want to laugh so much that she had to stifle the sound with her hand.

Plucking Deborah's hand from her mouth, Elliot pressed his lips to the palm. Her presence had added spice to the whole venture, there was no denying it. Her daring roused him. Her excitement, too. He licked the raw, slightly swollen pad of her thumb where the rope had chafed. He felt the intake of her breath. She leaned into him. His exhilaration sharpened and focused into desire, like molten metal poured into the mould of a blade. He pulled her roughly into his arms and took possession of her mouth.

It was a kiss without finesse. A hard, dangerous and demanding kiss. For a moment Deborah did not respond, shocked by the rawness of his barely leashed passion. This was not the Elliot she had kissed before, but some other, more feral creature of the night. As she was, tonight. Just for tonight.

But his ardour, the very unstoppableness of it, unleashed her inhibitions. As Elliot pressed her against her own front door, feverishly seeking the soft flesh concealed beneath the constricting layers of her clothing, Deborah kissed him back. Her tongue clashed with his, her mouth opened to him and she returned his kiss with a fervour that cut them both free of thought and control. Where he led she followed. When he kissed her more deeply, his tongue penetrating, thrusting, she kissed him back, her tongue duelling with his, her lips clinging.

Never, ever, not even in her darkest fantasies, had Deborah been kissed like this. Never had she kissed like this. Not even Bella had kissed like this, for Bella was at heart a creature driven by colder, darker motives than plain passion. Deborah's kisses, like Elliot's, were pure passion in that moment, wild and fierce, abandoned kisses, transporting them both to a place which was all red velvet and raw silk.

His mouth plundered hers, but she did not feel conquered, incited instead to return pressure for pressure, by doing so asking for more, and still more. Nothing mattered, save that she have more. It was as if everything that had transpired this night had been arrowing to this moment, as if all she had experienced had by some process of alchemy transformed itself into this white-hot lust, must culminate in this rushing, tumbling, headlong flight to fulfilment.

She moaned in frustration as Elliot's seeking fingers found only layers of clothing and buttons. He fumbled for the latch and they tumbled together into the dark seclusion of the narrow hallway, still kissing.

The back of her legs encountered the hall table. The candlestick atop it fell over. He wrested her greatcoat to the floor, his own following. Her hat and his, too, her hair unfurling. She curled her fingers into the soft silk of his skin, on the nape of his neck above his neckcloth. Warm skin. He smelled of sweat and soap. Salty and tangy. Irreducibly male.

The rasp of his chin on the soft skin of her face reminded her of the stinging sensation of the rough rope chafing her legs. She was burning between her thighs, but it had nothing to do with the descent. She wanted him there. Touching her. Plunging into her. Shocking images, vivid in their clarity despite her lack of experience, filled Deborah's mind, making her moan. The solid ridge of his shaft was hard against her belly. Powerful. Fierce. Like the rest of him, incredibly, intensely male. Man. Elliot was all man. And such a man. She moaned again as he ground his hips against hers.

Elliot's breath came in harsh gasps. Under her coat, Deborah wore a shirt. No waistcoat. And no corsets. Oh God, no corsets. Her nipples thrust at him through the linen. He cupped one of her breasts, his thumb stroking the delightfully hard nub, relishing the way it made her quiver, made the blood pulse in his already aching groin. Her kisses were like molten silver, burning and searing. His knees bumped against the legs of some sort of table. He picked her up, placed her on to it, spreading her legs, one hand in the heavy fall of her hair, the other on her breast, cupping, stroking, moulding. He wanted to feel her flesh. Tugging the shirt from her breeches he nudged between her legs, wrapping them around his thighs, dipping his head to taste the hard peaks of her nipple.

Her heels dug into his buttocks; her fingers plucked ineffectually at the big silver buttons of his coat. The table shook. It was just the right height to allow him to slide into her, thrusting into the welcoming heat, the slick tightness of her that would envelop him. He was so hard, the release would be spectacular. He had known it would be like this. He had known it! He put his hands around the curve of her bottom to pull her closer. She was still trying to free his coat buttons. Impatiently, Elliot yanked them open.

The crushed canvas fell on to the floor. 'Damn!'

'What? What was that?' Deborah was hazily aware

of a pain in her back. She tried to sit up and whatever she was perched on rocked violently. She was sitting on a table!

'The painting,' Elliot muttered. 'I dropped it. I can't see a damn thing.'

She seemed to have lost a good many of her clothes. And the painting, which they had risked life and limb for, was on the floor somewhere. Deborah slithered back down to reality considerably more quickly than she had slithered down the rope not long before. The candle she'd left for her return was on the floor somewhere, too. It would be easier to fetch another from the parlour. 'Just a minute,' she muttered, stumbling down the hallway, feeling her way to the door, trying to tuck her shirt back into her breeches at the same time.

Lighting the candle from the still-smouldering embers of the parlour fire, she studiously avoided looking in the mirror above the mantel as she did so, having no wish to see her shame confirmed in her wanton reflection. Concentrating on trying to get her breathing back under control, she made her way back to the hallway. Elliot was as dishevelled as she. Clothes awry. Neckcloth untied. His lips looked frayed. Such kisses! Deborah held the candle aloft, well away from her own face, turning her gaze to the floor. 'Here it is.' The canvas had rolled under the table. She picked it up and handed it to him, embarrassed in the frail light, mortified by her behaviour in the dark. She had more or less ravaged the man. Savaged him more like, for she clearly remembered biting into him, her nails tearing at his skin. *Oh God!*

Elliot made no attempt to look at the painting. He wished to hell he'd let the bloody thing lie. Another minute of those kisses of hers and he wouldn't have given a damn. Looking at her now though, seeing the way she avoided his gaze, he knew the chances of him having another minute of her kisses were almost nil. Whatever had caused her to let go that iron control of hers was now firmly leashed.

And it was probably just as well. He, who prided himself on his finesse, had all but ravished her in the hallway, for God's sake! To say nothing of the fact that in their lust they had forgotten all about the extremely valuable painting they had stolen. A painting which was now looking rather the worse for wear. A wholly inappropriate desire to laugh took hold of him. He struggled, but could not stifle it. 'I'm sorry,' Elliot said helplessly, 'it's just—well, ludicrous. I assure you I didn't plan it. The last bit, I mean—at least not like that. Only you were so—and I was so—and there was the painting abandoned on the floor, after we went to such extremes to get it.'

To his surprise Deborah's face lightened. She did not smile back, but she looked as if she might. 'Is it always like this? After you have committed a crime, I mean? Is it always so—so intoxicating? Inflaming?' she asked, daring to meet his gaze now.

'I don't know, I've never had an accomplice before.'

'The painting—it's not damaged, is it?' Deborah asked anxiously.

Elliot unrolled the canvas and shook his head. 'See for yourself.' She came closer to inspect it. Her hair was perfectly straight, hanging well past her shoulders. If he looked, he would see the outline of her breasts under her shirt, for she had not put her coat back on. With a huge effort of restraint, he stopped himself.

'Such an ugly man,' Deborah said softly after a while of staring at the portrait. 'I would not like to have this on my wall. Is it valuable?'

'It's by Velázquez. I should hope so.'

'Will you sell it, then?'

Elliot began to roll the canvas back up, carefully this time. 'Yes,' he said tersely, 'I'll sell it.'

Deborah opened her mouth to ask what he did with the money, then thought better of it. Tiredness washed over her. Her shoulders began to ache. Anticlimax in every sense weighed like a heavy blanket, muffling her. 'It's late,' she said wearily.

'Yes.' Elliot hesitated. He was edgy with frustration. She had been so aroused, he was sure he could easily rekindle the flame between them, but something held him back. *Is it always like this?* 'It wasn't the housebreaking that made me turn to you like that,' he said, running his hand down the smooth cap of her hair, 'it was you. Ever since we met, I've wanted you. You must know that, Deborah.'

She jerked her head away. 'It will be light soon.'

'I see.' He didn't see at all. Rebuffed, puzzled by

the extreme swing in her mood, and too tired in the anticlimax to make sense of it, Elliot picked his hat up and, shrugging into his greatcoat, tucked the painting into a large inside pocket. 'Did it work?' he asked. 'Did it do as you hoped, banish the black clouds, make you feel alive?'

Deborah smiled tremulously. 'While it lasted. I shall keep a look out for reports of our heinous crime.'

'And paste them in a keepsake book?'

'Something like that.'

He kissed the fluttering pulse on her wrist, telling himself that her vulnerability was simply exhaustion. 'Goodnight, Deborah.'

She swallowed the lump in her throat. 'Goodbye, Elliot. Be safe.'

The door closed softly behind him. The parlour clock struck three. Only three. Wearily, Deborah picked up her man's coat and made her way up the creaky wooden stairs to her bed.

Outside, Elliot made his way home by a circuitous route through alleys and mews. She was like a chameleon, changing so quickly that he could not keep up with her. Her kisses. He groaned and the muscles in his stomach contracted. Such a delightful mixture of raw passion and innocence. Hot, burning kisses that even now made his blood surge and pound, yet they were neither knowing nor experienced. Deborah kissed with the savagery of a lion cub.

Elliot stood in the shadow of a stable building as the watch passed by, informing the empty street that all was well. It had frightened her, her passion; she had been far too eager to blame it on the extraordinary circumstances, as if by doing so she could distance herself from it. What kind of marriage had she had with that bastard of a fortune hunter?

He stepped out of the mews and made his way across Russell Square, letting himself in silently. A candle stood ready in the hall, reminding him of the clatter of the candlestick from the table at Deborah's house. The evening had been full of surprises. He should not have allowed her to come down that rope, but the sight of her dangling over him had been…

Mounting the stairs, he tried to put if from his mind. He was exhausted. Carefully stashing the painting, he willed himself to think of the chain of events he must set in train to dispose of it, but as he climbed into bed, the memory of Deborah—her mouth, her hands, her breasts, those long legs, that pert *derrière*—climbed in with him. He was hard. Persistently hard. Lying back against the cool sheets, Elliot surrendered to the inevitable.

Chapter Four

Deborah jerked awake, exhausted from lurid dreams in which she was always in the wrong place, with the wrong person, in the wrong attire, at the wrong time. Dreams in which she was endlessly chasing the shadow of the man who had made a shadow of her. Dreams in which no one could see her, no one would acknowledge her, in which she existed only to herself. When she spoke, the words were soundless. Time and again, she tumbled into the room where *he* was, only to have Jeremy look straight through her.

In her dreams, she was sick from her failures, sick from knowing that no matter how hard she tried, she would fail again. The familiar weight of that failure made the physical effort of rising from her bed a mammoth task. No amount of telling herself that it was just a dream, nor any reminder that it had no basis in reality, could shift that lumpen, leaden feeling, for the truth was that Deborah believed she *had* failed, and it *had* been her fault.

Long experience had shown her that hiding under the covers and willing fresh dreamless sleep had no effect whatsoever, save to nourish the headache which lurked just under the base of her skull. Slowly, with the care of a very old woman afraid of breaking brittle bones, Deborah climbed out of bed and went through her morning ablutions, blanking her mind against the lingering coils of her monochrome nightmares, forcibly filling her head with colourful images from her adventures last night.

She winced as she soothed a cooling lotion on the chafe marks at her knees and thighs, but as she folded away the male clothing she had worn, out of sight of the daily help, her mood slowly lifted. By the time she sat down to take coffee at her desk, she was smiling to herself. Bella Donna, that vengeful, voluptuous creature of the night, would not be confined to history after all. At last, after several barren months, she had her inspiration for the next story.

What would Elliot think if he knew he was her muse? Deborah paused in the act of sharpening her pen as a lurid image of herself atop the hall table, her legs entwined around him, flooded her body with heat. Closing her eyes, shuddering at the memory of his lips, his hands, the rough grate of his jaw on her skin, she was astounded at the speed and intensity of her arousal. Had the painting not fallen, had she not fetched a light and broken the mood, she would have given herself to him. As she recalled raking her nails on his skin, urgently pressing herself against the hard length of his manhood, she turned cold. What on earth had come over her?

It would be a salve, to persuade herself that she had become so caught up in Bella Donna's character as to have forgotten her own, but it would not be the truth. Bella Donna took her pleasures in a calculated way. Bella Donna used and discarded men as she used and discarded her various guises when she had no further use for them. Last night, Deborah had wanted, needed, desired with a purity of feeling which left no room for anything else. It frightened her. The intensity of her feelings, her lack of control, terrified her. She did not want any of it.

Ever since we met, I've wanted you, Elliot had said. But the circumstances in which they met were coloured each time by danger. It was surely that which made him want her, as it made her want him? Only the thrill of defying the rules, the edge which recklessness and daring gave to fear, could explain the strength of their mutual desire in its wake. Nothing else, surely, could explain why she had forgotten all the inhibitions her marriage had taught her and allowed an instinct she hadn't known she possessed to drive her.

No, last night, she had not been Bella Donna, but neither had she been Deborah. She could not reconcile that vivid, bold creature with the one sitting at her desk in her grey gown in her equally grey life. But then, wasn't that what she had wanted from last night's adventure? To shed her skin, to step out of the tedium of her day-today existence, to escape from herself for a few hours? She had certainly achieved it beyond her expectations.

Now, though, she must get back to reality, which might very well be grey by comparison, but at least it was safe. Never mind that it was unexciting, unadventurous and above all lonely. She was used to being lonely. Most of her married life she had been lonely. And lost. And hurt. She would do well to remember how quickly the bride with stardust in her eyes had become the hated wife.

Now she was no longer a victim of her own gullibility. She was not the source of every disappointment, the cause of every misfortune. She need not hide from her friends for fear they discover her unhappiness. She need not pretend to herself that she was anything other than miserable. Guilt and insecurity need no more drive her actions than that most cruel emotion of all, love. Her life might be bland, but it was her own. Safe from feeling, maybe, but it was also safe from pain. She intended always to be safe from now on. Whatever had come over her last night, the person she had been was not the real Deborah. The experience had been a release. Cathartic. An antidote, a dose of danger to counteract the malaise of boredom. That was all, and it was over now.

Resolutely, Deborah picked up her pen. *It was past midnight when Bella Donna made her way stealthily out into the night dressed in male attire, on a mission which would scandalise the* ton *and throw her into the orbit of the most dangerous and devastatingly attractive man in all of England,* she wrote.

* * *

'You look tired, Elliot.' Elizabeth Murray drew her brother a quizzical look.

The resemblance between the siblings was striking enough to make their relationship obvious. The same dark, deep-set eyes, the same black hair, the same clear, penetrating gaze which tended to make its object wonder what secrets they had inadvertently revealed. Though Lizzie's complexion was olive rather than tanned, and her features softer, she had some of her brother's intensity and all of his charm, a combination which her friends found fascinating, her husband alluring and her critics intimidating.

'Burning the candle at both ends?' she asked with a smile, stripping off her lavender-kid gloves and plonking herself without ceremony down on a comfortably shabby chair by the fire.

Elliot grinned. 'Lord, yes, you know me. Dancing 'til four in the morning, paying court to the latest heiress, whose hand I must win if I'm to pay off my gambling debts. Generally acting the gentleman of leisure.'

Lizzie chuckled. 'I am surprised I did not see you in the throng around Marianne Kilwinning. They say she is worth twenty thousand at least.'

Elliot snapped his fingers. 'A paltry sum. Why, I could drop that much and more in a single sitting at White's.'

Lizzie's smile faded. 'I heard that your friend Cunningham lost something near that the other night. I know it is considered the height of fashion, but I cannot help thinking these *gentlemen* could find better things to fritter their money away on.'

'You're not alone in thinking that.'

'Did you speak to Wellington, then?'

'He granted me an audience all right,' Elliot said bitterly, 'but it was the usual story. Other more pressing commitments, a need to invest in the future, resources overstretched, the same platitudes as ever.' He sighed. 'Perhaps I'm being a little unfair. He told me in confidence that he was considering taking up politics again. Were he to be given a Cabinet post, he said he would do all he could, but—oh, I don't know, Lizzie. These men, the same men who have given their health and their youth for their country, they can't wait for all that. They need help now, to feed themselves and their families, not ephemeral promises that help is coming if only they will wait—we had enough of those when we were at war.'

'Henry. I know,' Lizzie said gently, widening her eyes to stop the tears which gathered there from falling as her brother's face took on a bleak look. She hated to cry, and more importantly Elliot hated to have this deepest of wounds touched.

'Henry and hundreds—thousands—of others who were brothers, friends, husbands, fathers. It makes me sick.'

'And Wellington will do nothing?'

'I'm sorry to say it, but at heart he's a traditionalist. He is afraid, like Liverpool and the rest of the Tories, that too many years abroad have radicalised our men.

He thinks that starving them will bring about deference. I think it will have quite the opposite effect and, more importantly, it's bloody unjust. I'm sorry, I shouldn't swear and I didn't mean to bore you.'

'Don't be so *damned* stupid. You neither bore me nor shock me, and you know it. I have no truck with this modern notion that we women have no minds of our own,' Lizzie said tersely.

She was rewarded with a crack of laughter. 'Not something anyone could ever accuse you of,' Elliot replied.

His sister grinned. 'That's what Lady Murray says.'

'Alex's mother is in town? I thought she never left that great big barn of a castle of theirs. Won't she be *afeart that the haggis will go to ground and the bagpipes will stop breeding without her,*' Elliot asked in an appalling attempt to mimic Lady Murray's soft Scottish burr.

'Very amusing,' Lizzie said drily.

'So what momentous event has driven her to visit Sassenach territory, then?' To his astonishment, his sister blushed. 'Lizzie?'

'I'm pregnant,' she said with her usual disregard for polite euphemisms. 'The news that's driven her south is the forthcoming arrival of a potential grandson and heir, if you must know.'

'Elizabeth!' Elliot hauled his sister from her chair and enveloped her in a bear hug. 'That's wonderful news.'

'You're squashing me, Elliot.'

He let her go immediately. 'Did I hurt you? God, I'm sorry, I—'

'Please! Please, please, please don't start telling me to rest, and put my feet up, and wrapping me in shawls and feeding me hot milk,' Lizzie said with a shudder. 'Alex?'

'Poor love, he's over the moon, but when I first told him he started treating me as if I was made of porcelain. Lord, I thought he was going to have me swaddled and coddled to death,' Lizzie said frankly. 'You can have no idea what it took for me to persuade him we could still—' She broke off, colouring a fiery red. 'Well. Anyway. Alex is fine now, but his mother is a different kettle of fish. Or should I say cauldron of porridge? She wants me to go to Scotland. She says that the fey wife in the village has always delivered the Murray heirs.'

'You surely don't intend to go?'

Lizzie's shrug was exactly like her brother's. 'Alex would never say so, but I know it's what he'd prefer. I'm already beginning to show, too. I have no wish to parade about the town with a swollen belly and I've certainly no desire at all to have myself laced into corsets to cover it up, so maybe it's for the best. It's not really a ruin, Alex's castle. Besides, you can't blame him, wanting the bairn to be born in his homeland.'

'Bairn!'

Lizzie laughed. 'Give me a few months up there and I'll be speaking like a native.' She picked up her gloves and began to draw them on. 'I must go, I promised Alex I wouldn't leave him with his mother for too long.' She stood on tiptoe to kiss Elliot's cheek. 'You do look tired. What have you been up to, I wonder? I know you've not been gallivanting, for I've lost count of the number of young ladies who've enquired after my handsome, charming, eligible and most elusive brother. And don't tell me it's because you lack invitations, because I know that's nonsense. What you need is…'

'Lizzie, for the last time, I don't want a wife.'

'I was about to say that what you need is gainful employment,' his sister said, in an offended tone. 'The Marchmont estates aren't enough to keep you occupied, they never were. You need an outlet for all that energy of yours now that you don't have your battalions to order around; you need something to stop you from brooding on incompetence and injustice. I'm not underestimating what you've been through, but it's past, Elliot, and you can't undo it. It's time to move on, put your experience to some use rather than use it to beat yourself up. There, that is frank talking indeed, but if I am to go to Scotland with a clear conscience, I don't have time to tread lightly.'

'Not that you ever do.'

Lizzie chuckled. 'Any more than you do. You don't lack opinions and certainly don't lack a cause. Why don't you go into politics yourself?'

'What?'

'I don't know why you look so surprised,' Lizzie said drily. 'What is the point in you berating the likes of Wellington and all the rest.'

'I hadn't thought.'

'Then think. And when you've concluded that I'm right, think about taking a wife, too.' She tapped his cheek lightly. 'A woman with a bit of gumption, who can force her way past that barricade of charm you arm yourself with. You see how well I know you, brother dear? You don't let people in very easily, do you? I expect the army is responsible for that stiff upper lip and all that—it makes sense in war, but we're at peace now, thank the Lord.' Lizzie nodded decisively. 'Yes. What you need is a woman of character, someone who can stand up to you, not some malleable little thing who would bore you to death before the wedding trip was over, no matter how pretty she was. I shall have to redouble my efforts before I go north, but I am quite set on it, so don't despair,' she said with a bright smile.

'I shall try my very best not to,' Elliot replied, as he opened the door for her.

'I wish you would be serious. I know I've spoken out of turn, but you're clearly not happy. I will fret about you down here all alone when I am up in Scotland.'

'You've got more than enough to worry about. I'm not unhappy, just not quite sure what to do with myself now that I don't have the army. I feel as if I've lost my purpose.'

'Politics will give you that. Will you at least think about what I said?'

'We'll see. Did you come in your carriage?'

Lizzie nodded, deciding against pushing him any further. She was on the step outside when she remembered the package. 'My book!' she declared.

Elliot retrieved the brown-paper parcel from the marble table which sat under the hall mirror. 'What is it?'

'Nothing. It's just a novel. Give me it.'

Intrigued by her cagey look, Elliot held on to the parcel. 'What kind of a novel?'

'I'm not…it's just that—well, Alex doesn't approve.'

'Good Lord, Lizzie, don't tell me you've been browsing in one of those bookseller's back rooms in Covent Garden.'

He meant it as a joke, but, to Elliot's astonishment, Lizzie's face crimsoned. 'And what if I did? Oh, don't look so shocked, it's not *that* kind of book. It's a novel. The latest Bella Donna novel, if you must know.' Seeing her brother's blank look, she sighed. 'The whole *ton* is agog at her exploits, I can't believe you've not heard of her. Bella Donna is the most shocking literary creation, she's a sort of voluptuous sorceress. The stories are quite Gothic, extremely racy and wholly entertaining. I personally see no reason why they should be kept under the counter, nor why I, a married woman, should not read them,' she said darkly. 'If Bella Donna were a man—well, it would be a different story, if you'll forgive the pun. It is the fact that she is a woman who treats—intimacy—exactly like a man that is so shocking. She is quite ruthless, you know, incredibly powerful. I think it would amuse you, I shall send it round once I am done with it if you like.'

'Why not,' Elliot said, surrendering the package, 'it sounds amusing.'

Lizzie chuckled. 'Yes, and now I can tell Alex that

you lent it to *me* if he discovers it. I really must go. You'll come to dinner then, tomorrow? Oh, did I forget to ask you? Never mind, I won't take no for an answer,' she said, turning her back and tripping lightly down the steps to her waiting carriage. 'I promised Alex I'd persuade you to join us. Lord Armstrong will be there—the diplomat. You can talk politics with him.'

Wriggling her fingers at him over her shoulder, Lizzie climbed into her barouche without looking back or giving Elliot a chance to refuse her invitation.

He returned to the parlour, deep in thought. Incorrigible as she was, his sister was all too often right. He could not continue in this mode for much longer. Housebreaking, even if it was for a cause, was hardly a lifelong occupation. And he did need an occupation, though he had always known, as Lizzie herself said, that he was not cut out to play the country gentleman. Perhaps politics was the answer? It was certainly worth considering. Lizzie's ideas usually were. She did not know him as well as she thought, but she knew him better than anyone else.

And a wife—was she right about that, too? Picking up the *Morning Post,* which his man had left, carefully ironed, on his desk, Elliot pondered this question halfheartedly. He hadn't ever seriously considered a wife. As a soldier with an increasingly dangerous sideline in espionage, it would have been irresponsible to marry. Not that that was the reason he hadn't. Such a precarious and transient life hardly lent itself to fidelity, but Lizzie was right, curse her, that was just an excuse.

The fact was, he didn't let people in, he *was* wary of allowing anyone to see past whatever form of veneer he showed them. War made you like that. War taught you how fragile life was. It taught you how easy it was to be crushed by that fragility, too—he'd seen it too many times, written too many letters to grieving widows, listened to the last heartbreaking words of too many of their husbands. Pain like that, he could do without. It could not possibly be worth it.

He sighed. Blast Lizzie for putting such thoughts in his head. If she only knew that he'd been living like a monk since returning to England. What's more, until he'd met Deborah Napier, he had been relatively content to do so. Last night had been so—so bloody amazing! Just thinking about it—oh God, just thinking about it. If only he had not dropped the painting. If only he had not allowed Deborah to go in search of a candle, she would not have found her inhibitions.

'Dammit, what is wrong with me,' Elliot exclaimed, 'England must be full of attractive, available, experienced women looking for nothing more than a little light flirtation and a few indulgent hours in bed.' Except that wasn't what he wanted, not any more. He wanted Deborah. He didn't just want to bed her either, he wanted to understand her. He wanted to know what went on in her head and what had gone on in her past. He wanted to know why it took breaking and entering to release her passion. And he wanted her to release it again.

What was it Lizzie said he needed? *A woman with a bit of gumption, who can force her way past that bar-*

ricade of charm you arm yourself with. A woman of character. Deborah was certainly that. Lizzie would definitely approve. Not that he was in any way seeking her approval. Politics, perhaps he would consider. Marriage—no. But the train of his thoughts disturbed him. Elliot shook out the newspaper, seeking distraction. He found it in the middle pages.

Last night, the Notorious Housebreaker commonly known as the Peacock struck again, this time at the abode of a most Distinguished Member of Parliament who resides in Grosvenor Square. The Villainous Thief has stolen a most valuable painting, the subject of which being a Very Important Personage. Said painting, executed by a Spanish Master, was torn asunder from its frame in the Most Honourable Gentleman's Study. Once again, the Peacock had the effrontery to leave his Calling Card behind, along with the Rope by which he made his escape. Any Member of the Public who saw anything or anyone suspicious is urged to contact the Magistrates at Bow Street.

The portrait of the Very Important Person was currently wrapped in oilskin and safely tucked under the floorboards in Elliot's bedchamber. A certain Spanish official, when approached by way of the intricate web of contacts which Elliot had been careful to maintain from his days in the covert service of the British Government, would most certainly pay a substantial sum for it. Tomorrow, he would set about making the first of those contacts. Today though, he had another alluring, beguiling and altogether intriguing contact to see.

Folding the newspaper into a neat square which would fit into his coat pocket, Elliot loped up the stairs three at a time, calling for his man to fetch his hat and gloves and his groom to have his curricle brought round.

Looking over from her writing desk at the clock, Deborah was astonished to discover that it was well past two. The stack of paper before her bore testament to her labours, the neat lines gradually deteriorating to an unruly scrawl as her pen struggled to keep up with her fevered imagination. She had forgotten what it was like, to be so inspired. It made her realise how much of a chore her books had become. The wisps of this story clung to her like plucking fingers, willing her to pick up her pen once more lest she lose the thread, but she knew that she had reached her limit for today.

Her wrist ached. Her head felt as if it were stuffed with cork. Wiping her ink-stained hands on the equally ink-stained linen smock she wore to protect her gown, Deborah thrust the manuscript into the desk and closed the lid.

Returning from the kitchen, where she had made herself a much-needed pot of tea, she froze on the threshold of the parlour.

Elliot was immaculately turned out, not a crease in his olive-green coat of superfine nor his biscuit-coloured pantaloons. The gloss on his tasselled Hessians showed not a speck of dirt. In contrast, Deborah was horribly conscious of her hair pinned up anyhow under its cap, her work smock, her grubby fingers. *Why did he always have to see her looking at her worst?* And why did he always have to be so much more attractive, every time she saw him? Taller. More muscular—those pantaloons fitted like a second skin. More everything! And why did he have to smile like that? And why, when she was quite resolved to forget all about him, was she so absurdly pleased to see him?

She clutched the tea tray to her chest. 'How on earth did you get in?' The shock of seeing him, as if he had just walked out of Bella's story, combined with the traitorous shiver of simple pleasure which had been her first reaction, made her sound aggressive, but better that, than let him see the effect he had on her.

'It would be a poor Peacock indeed who could not break into a house with such flimsy defences,' Elliot said with a grin, relieving her of the tea tray and giving her no option but to follow him into her own parlour.

'I did not think to see you again.' Deborah sat down on the edge of a chair by the fire. She longed to pour her tea, but was afraid her hands would shake.

Elliot raised a brow. 'Surely you must have known I would call?'

'We said goodbye last night.'

'*You* said goodbye.'

Deborah gazed at him helplessly. He waited for her to say something, but she began measuring leaves from the little wooden caddy. Water splashed as she poured it from the kettle into the pewter teapot. 'I brought only one cup.'

'I hate tea,' Elliot said, sitting himself opposite her.

She poured her drink, took a sip and then a deep breath. 'Why are you here?'

Her antagonism didn't fool him. She was as nervous as a cat, but she hadn't been able wholly to disguise the fact that she was pleased to see him. Elliot handed her the newspaper. 'I thought you might like to see this.'

Deborah scanned the report, her face lightening to a shadow of a smile as she read. 'I woke this morning persuaded that I had imagined the whole episode. I can't quite believe it happened even now, despite seeing it reported in print.'

'Fortunately, there is no indication that anyone knows I had an accomplice, but all the same, you must have a care not to let slip, even inadvertently, anything which might betray you.'

'I won't,' Deborah said, thinking guiltily of the account she had written just this morning of the episode, reassuring herself at the same time that she had changed sufficient details for it not to matter. 'There is nothing to fear, I am sure. You did not strike me as a worrier, Elliot.'

'I am not worried for myself, but for you. I care little for my own safety, but I would rather not have yours on my conscience.'

'You don't. It was I who persuaded you, if you recall.'

'I would never have allowed myself to be persuaded if I had not wanted you with me,' Elliot said with a wry smile. 'How does it feel, to be so vicariously notorious?'

'Vicarious,' Deborah replied pithily. 'I feel as if

it was someone else who clambered down that rope. Though I must confess, my conscience has been bothering me rather belatedly. That painting was very valuable.'

'And you're worried about what I'm going to do with the ill-gotten gains,' Elliot said. 'No, don't look like that, I can't blame you. I'm surprised you haven't asked before.'

'I am ashamed to admit that I most likely did not because I didn't want a reason not to go,' Deborah confessed. She put down her half-drunk cup of tea. 'Why do you do it, Elliot? I mean, I can understand, that it's partly what I wanted—the sheer thrill of it. I can understand, too, that you find civilian life rather boring compared to what you're used to, but—to say that you care little for your own life as you just did—I can't believe that you are hoping to be caught.'

'Of course not. I am bored though, that is a part of it. My sister thinks I need gainful employment and she's probably right,' Elliot said, grimacing.

'Gainful doesn't sound very like you. I didn't know you had a sister. Is she in town?'

'For the moment. Lizzie is married to a dour Scot, who has plans to whisk her away to the Highlands for the birth of their first child.' Elliot grinned, happy to be sidetracked. 'I foresee some epic battles between her and her mother-in-law and I know who I'd put my money on. Lizzie is short of neither opinions nor the will to enforce them.'

'I'd have liked to have a sister,' Deborah said with a

wistful smile. 'I don't have any family. My parents died when I was very young and my uncle, who became my guardian, was a bachelor, very set in his ways. When I came back to live with him after finishing school, he didn't know what to do with me. He didn't like Jeremy, he told me that he was only marrying me for my inheritance, but he didn't make much of an attempt to stop me either. "You must make your own bed, and don't come running to me if you don't like lying in it," he said. Not that I would have,' she concluded, with a twisted little smile.

Did she know how much she had given away with that last little sentence? Elliot wondered, touched by her pride, angry on her behalf at the need for it. 'Is he still alive?'

Deborah shook her head. 'He died five years ago. I rarely saw him once I was married. I often wish I had made more of an effort.' It was surprising how guilty she felt even now, and no amount of telling herself that Uncle Peter had made no effort to keep in touch either made any difference. She had been afraid to let him see her and had kept him at a distance as she kept everyone else. 'I don't know how we came on to this subject,' she said brusquely, 'you cannot possibly be interested in my rather pathetic life.'

'I'm interested in you, Deborah.'

She concentrated on tucking a stray lock of hair back behind her ear, dipping her head to cover the faint traces of colour in her cheeks. 'I can think of any number of topics more interesting.'

Elliot was much inclined to pursue the subject, but his instincts warned him it would be unwise. Teasing out secrets was second nature to him. Knowing when to stop lest he betray just how much he had garnered was a subtle art, but one which he knew he had mastered. Though it had to be said, he admitted wryly to himself, that Deborah was proving to be more of a challenge than any close-mouthed diplomat. 'Why did I invent the Peacock, then? Does that constitute a more interesting topic?'

Deborah nodded. 'Provided it does not also constitute an intrusion. I would like to know, for you puzzle me. Your victims are selected too carefully for them to be random. Do you have some sort of personal grudge against them?'

'What makes you say that?' Elliot asked sharply.

'I don't know.' Deborah frowned. 'I suppose I cannot believe you do it for personal gain and there are too many robberies for it to be simply the thrill of it which drives you. You'd have become bored by now if that was it.'

'You are very perceptive. It is to be hoped that none of the gentlemen at Bow Street has your wit.'

'None of the gentlemen at Bow Street has my inside information. Is it too personal? I will understand if you don't wish to say any more.'

Elliot drummed his fingers on the arm of the chair. His instincts were to confide in her, though common sense told him that by doing so he was taking an unwarrantable risk. Not of deliberate exposure, she would not do that, but an inadvertent comment, a remark let slip in the wrong company—how could he be sure she would not do that?

He just knew. She was as close as a clam and, of her own admission, she lived like a hermit. Besides, he wanted to tell her. He wanted her to know. 'You were right about my victims,' he said. 'They are very carefully selected. All of them were at some point responsible for the supply chain—or lack of it—to the army. Medical supplies, orderlies and doctors, boots, basic rations, horses. Most of all horses. They kept us short of all of those things, because after all, what does an army need to fight except guns? Even if you can't get the guns to the battlefield. Even if you can't get the men wounded by those guns misfiring back to a field hospital. What do they care? They don't,' he said flatly. 'I know they don't because all my letters and protests and reports fell on deaf ears at the time, and now—well, now it is done and everyone wants to forget all about it, so there is even less point in letters and reports and protests.'

'So you take what will hurt them instead.'

'Yes, that's exactly what I do.'

'Did you lose many men because of such shortages?'

'Yes.'

'Friends, too? Forgive me, but it seems to me such a very personal thing you are doing, there must have been someone…'

'There was. My best friend.' Elliot gripped the arms of his chair so tightly that his knuckles showed white.

'Henry,' Deborah said gently. 'I'm so sorry.'

Elliot nodded curtly.

'I truly am sorry, I didn't mean to upset you; you don't need to say any more.'

'I want to,' Elliot said, surprising both of them. 'I want to tell you.' He swallowed repeatedly, cleared his throat. 'We joined up together, Henry and I, I told you that already. We worked our way through the ranks together, though he was much too ill-disciplined to keep his stripes for long. He made it to captain once, but it only lasted about six months. He was a first-class soldier. We always looked out for each other. When I needed an extra pair of hands, I always turned to Henry. He was quick with his fists, but he knew the importance of keeping other things close, which was important in my—my alternative line of business.'

He paused. Across from him, Deborah was gazing at him intently. Would she be shocked? He doubted it, somehow. More likely excited, as she was by the Peacock. That decided him. 'The thing is, I wasn't just a fighting man. There's a reason why the Peacock is so able.' He grinned. 'Actually, it's ironic that the very skills I learned in order to steal secrets are the same ones I use to steal their property now. Most of which, I hasten to add, was stolen in the first place.'

Deborah stared at him in utter astonishment. 'You mean—what you're saying is that you—you *stole?* At our Government's behest? But why? What did you— oh! My God, you were a spy?'

He should have known how she would react. Her eyes were sparkling. Elliot laughed. 'Yes, I was.'

'Good grief! No wonder civilian life bores you. You must tell me—I wish you will tell me—I don't know—anything, all of it—no, I don't expect you can tell me *all* of it. Goodness, what secrets you must know.' Deborah chuckled. 'How horrified the likes of Jacob would be if they knew. You are quite right, Elliot, it is irony past price. *Can* you tell me more? Were you a master of subterfuge?'

Danger, even if it was vicarious, certainly brought her to life. 'I'm afraid it was rather more mundane than that. If anything, I was a master of patience.' He told her a few choice stories because he liked to see her laugh, because he found her laughter infectious, and he told her a few more because returning to the subject in hand was too painful, but he underestimated her.

'He must have been more like a brother than a friend. Henry, I mean,' Deborah said suddenly, interrupting him in the middle of a story. 'What happened?'

'He was wounded in the Pyrenees during the siege on San Sebastian. He took a bullet in the leg, above the knee. It smashed the bone—he'd have lost his leg, but it shouldn't have been fatal. Only they couldn't reach him because there were no carts and no mules.'

'Oh God.' Deborah covered her mouth, her eyes wide with horror.

Elliot's knuckles were white. 'For more than a week, he lay in agony in the blistering sun with his wound festering. He died of a fever a few days after they finally got him to the field hospital. I was with him, at the end, though he hardly recognised me. He died for want of a mule. A mule!' He thumped his fist down hard on the chair. 'But what do those bastards in the War Office with their lists and their budgets know of that? What does it matter, when a man with one leg would have been no bloody use to them anyway? What do they know of the suffering, the agonies that Henry and thousands like him went through, and what do they care now for the survivors?'

'But you care,' Deborah said, shaken by the cold rage. 'You care enough to steal from them, to make reparations for them, is that it?'

'The money goes to a charity which helps the survivors.' Now that he had opened the floodgates his bitter anger, so long pent-up, demanded expression. 'Someone has to help them,' Elliot said furiously. 'While they fought for their country, their country learned how to do very well without them. Now that the Government no longer needs them to surrender their lives, their limbs and their hearts on the battlefield, it has decided it has no need to reward them with employment, back pay, pensions. It is not just the men, it is their widows and children who suffer.'

'I didn't realise,' Deborah said falteringly.

'Few people do. All they see is a beggar. Just another beggar. Proud men, reduced to holding out a cup for alms! Can you imagine what that does to them? No wonder so many cannot face their families. And they are portrayed as deserters, drunkards, criminals.'

The scar which bisected his eyebrow stood out white against his tan. The other one, which followed the hairline of his forehead, seemed to pulse. How many other, invisible scars did he bear? His suffering made hers seem so trite in comparison. The grooves at the side of his mouth were etched deep. His eyes were fierce, hard. Deborah trembled at the sorrow and pain they hid, such depths, which made shallows of her own suffering. 'I just didn't know,' she said simply. 'I am quite ashamed.' The truth was so awful, it made her conscience seem like a paltry consideration. 'I wish now that we had taken more from that house in Grosvenor Square.'

Her vehemence drew a bark of laughter from Elliot. 'Believe me, over the last two years, the Peacock has taken a great deal more.'

'So it is a war of attrition that the Peacock is waging, is that it? And of vengeance?'

Deborah's perception made Elliot deeply uncomfortable. He was not accustomed to thinking about his motivations, never mind discussing them. 'What do you know of vengeance?' he asked roughly.

Enough to recognise it. Deborah hesitated, surprised at the strength of her urge to confide, but the very idea of comparing their causes appalled her. Besides, his voice held an undertone of aggression that warned her to tread lightly. He obviously thought he had said too much already. She could easily empathise with that. 'The painting that we stole,' she said, seeking to lighten the subject, 'you knew about it because of your spying, didn't you?'

'You've no idea how much ransacking and looting

goes on in the higher echelons in wartime. That painting was a bribe.'

To Deborah's relief, some of the grimness left his mouth. She asked him to explain; when he did, she encouraged him to tell her of other bribes, relieved to see the grooves around his mouth relaxing, the sadness leaving his eyes. The battered armchair in which he sat, she had rescued from a lumber room at Kinsail Manor. His legs, in their tight-knit pantaloons, stretched out in front of him. If she reached, she could touch her toe to his Hessian boots.

'I've said too much,' Elliot said, interrupting himself in the middle of a story, realising abruptly how much he had revealed, how little he had talked to anyone of his old life before. It had been too easy to talk to Deborah. He wasn't sure what he thought of that, accustomed as he was to keep his own counsel. His instincts were to retreat. 'I must go,' he said, getting to his feet.

How did he close his expression off like that? Ignoring the flicker of disappointment, Deborah rose, too. 'You have certainly said enough to make me realise how shockingly ignorant I am. I shall not look on those poor souls with their begging bowls in the same way again.'

Outside, it was grown dark. Elliot lit a spill from the fire and began to light the candles on the mantel. 'I'd like to call on you again,' he said.

Deborah bit her lip. It would have been so much easier, had he not chosen to confide in her, if he had not given her so many reasons to wish to know more about him. To like him. In another world, in another life, Elliot was the kind of man she would have...

But there was absolutely no point whatsoever in thinking like that. Slowly, she shook her head. The pang of loss was physical, a pain in her stomach. 'I live a very secluded life.'

'I'm not suggesting we attend Almack's together. We could go for a drive.'

Why did he have to make it so difficult? 'I can't, Elliot. I am perfectly content with my own company.'

'So content that you need to break into houses and climb down ropes to make you feel alive?'

Deborah flinched. 'I thought you understood. That was an escape from reality, merely.'

'I don't understand you.' Elliot cast the spill into the fire. 'One minute, you are hanging on my every word, the next, you imply that you never want to see me again.'

'I'm sorry. I didn't think that you would expect—I never considered us continuing our acquaintance after last night. I should not have encouraged you to confide in me, but I was so caught up in what you said and—I should not have,' Deborah said wretchedly. 'I'm sorry, Elliot.'

'And what about last night? You are sorry about that, too, I suppose? Dammit, I was not imagining it, the strength of attraction between us. Why are you hell bent on ignoring it?' Frustrated and confused, Elliot pulled her roughly towards him. 'You can't deny it! I can feel your heart beating. I can see it in your eyes that you want to kiss me just as much as I want to kiss you.'

'No. Elliot, please…'

He was so sure, so certain that if he could just kiss her, it would rekindle the flame that had flared between them last night, but he had never in his life used persuasion on a woman in that way, and would not do so now. Elliot threw himself away from her. 'I apologise,' he said curtly. 'I have obviously completely misjudged the situation.'

'No,' Deborah whispered, 'it is I who did so. Last night, I gave you to think that I would—when I could not. Cannot. You have nothing to apologise for.'

It went against the grain to leave her like this but she left him no option. 'Your servant, Lady Kinsail.' Elliot sketched a bow.

'Goodbye, Elliot.' He was gone before she had finished saying the words, the front door slamming behind him. Deborah could not resist peering out into the gloom through the window, but he did not look back.

Alone in the parlour, she squared her shoulders. It had cost her dear, not to kiss him. It had cost her even dearer, that look on his face when she behaved so contrarily, but it was for the best. Elliot was not Jeremy, but it made no difference. Never, with Jeremy, had she come close to feeling what Elliot made her feel, but that just made things worse. She did not want to feel anything.

'It's over,' she said to herself, pulling the curtains across the window. It would have been easier, knowing Elliot less, but it was too late for that now. Knowing him better simply made her more certain she was right. But staring into the flames of the fire, Deborah couldn't help wishing that things were different.

Chapter Five

❧

As he walked home from Hans Town, Elliot was angry.
He was hurt, too—at least his pride was hurt, that was
all, he told himself. He was not used to rejection. He did
not understand why Deborah had rejected him, but nor
could he ignore the fact that she had and quite unequivocally. He would not see her again. It didn't matter a
damn that she was the only woman who interested him,
it was over. There were plenty more women in England.

As he changed into evening clothes, a melancholy
seized him. It was not just his pride that was hurt. He
had confided in her. He'd taken his sister's advice and
actually let someone cross the threshold of his feelings.
She'd understood him, too—a little too much for comfort, actually—but she had seemed so sympathetic. The
more he replayed their conversation in his mind, the
more inexplicable he found her behaviour.

Dinner at Lizzie's was a trial. Though he liked Alex,
found the dour Mrs Murray amusing and under normal
circumstances would have enjoyed baiting that wily old

dog Lord Armstrong, Elliot was morose enough for his sister to take him aside and ask him if he was sickening for something. He left the party early.

Impatient with himself as he tossed and turned in a vain effort to sleep, determined not to succumb to the temptation to call on Deborah again in the morning, Elliot decided to pay an overdue visit to his estates in Hampshire. Lizzie was right, he needed an occupation; since he could not, for the moment, contemplate planning another outing for the Peacock, he would interest himself in the running of his lands.

'Well now.' Mr Freyworth, second of the sons for which the publishing house was named, laced his hands together and sat back in his seat. The spectacles which he used for close reading dangled on a chain around his neck. Across from him his client sat, her face as expressionless as ever, and once more Montague Freyworth found himself wondering how such a cold—nay, icy—female could possibly be the authoress of such shocking books. He looked down at the close-written pages before him and tapped one scrawny finger on the topmost. 'Well now,' he said again, 'this is certainly most— I think it would be fair for me to say that it is warmer than your last novel. In fact,' he said with an attempt at humour which did not sit with his sparse, crow-like form, 'I almost expected the paper to burst into flames while I was reading it.'

Deborah smiled tightly. Though her acquaintance with the publisher spanned the four years of Bella's existence, it could not be said that they were any closer than they had been that first day, when she had sat, sick with nerves, in this very seat in this very room, waiting upon his verdict. 'You said you thought that the last book was rather—flat, I believe was your word,' she said carefully.

The publisher nodded. 'Flat. Yes, you are quite correct. Lacking a certain *frisson*. Flat was, I believe, the very word I used.'

'I trust you do not wish to apply it to this story?'

Montague Freyworth's thin mouth stretched into the semblance of a smile. 'Indeed, no. *Indeed,* no. The housebreaking incident is most vividly described.'

He picked up a paper knife, then put it down again. His fingers began to drum on her manuscript which lay on his blotting pad. It was a habit which had often made Deborah grit her teeth, for though she did not mind ink stains or crossings out, she hated to have her original draft, which she thought of as her creation, her child, so roughly manhandled. With difficulty, she resisted the urge to swat her publisher's hand away. 'So you like it? The robbery, I mean.'

'First rate. I must say, Lady Kinsail, absolutely first rate. One could almost believe that you had been there yourself.'

Deborah produced a tinkling laugh that she was relieved to hear sounded almost natural. 'A compliment indeed.' Discomfited, she decided to overlook Mr Freyworth's overt use of her name. It was one of the many unwritten rules which governed their relationship, the pretence of ignorance on his part. Just as she was happy not to acknowledge that the respectable house of Freyworth & Sons made a handsome return on the lurid volumes they printed for her under another publisher's name.

'As I said, it was most enthralling.' Montague Freyworth resumed fiddling with his paper knife. 'The aftermath, now—the scene between Bella Donna and the housebreaker—I think that—'

'What I tried to convey was that for once, Bella was quite carried away by the illicit excitement—the more acute sense of danger. The impulsive way she behaved, it was an outlet for her pent-up feelings.'

Mr Freyworth held up a hand. 'You have no need to explain, madam, I quite understood it. What I was going to say was that I was also rather—forgive me, but this scene too had about it an authenticity which elevates your writing to a new plane.'

'Oh! Oh, I see.' Deborah gazed in confusion down at her gloves.

Across from her, Montague Freyworth was astonished to note a blush staining her pale cheeks. Not such a cold marble statue after all, the Widow Kinsail. Well, well. Mrs Freyworth would gobble up that little snippet. It was she who, unbeknownst to the authoress herself, was responsible for the critical reading of every one of Bella Donna's lurid tales—tales which her husband found not just disturbing, but whose appeal he found incomprehensible. 'What I wanted to say,' Montague said, 'was that I feel the book would benefit from—er—more of such scenes.'

'More?' A hysterical laugh, quickly stifled, escaped from Deborah. 'I thought you were going to ask me to cut it.'

'No, no.' Montague shook his head vehemently, recalling his wife's admonition. 'It is felt—I feel—that is—frankly, my lady—I mean, madam—' He broke off, drumming his grubby fingers on the blotting pad, trying desperately to think of a way of rephrasing Mrs Freyworth's words. *The crime is all very well and good, but what really excites the reader is the aftermath. What I'm saying, Montague, is that the insertion is more interesting than the removal.* He had to concede that his wife had a singular ability to express herself both graphically and succinctly. She was every bit as direct in the sanctity of their bedroom, a fact which was almost entirely responsible for their astonishingly satisfying marital relationship, but there were times—many times—when Montague wished that she would confine her remarks to that chamber.

He sighed heavily and inadvertently caught his client's gaze. He never had been able to decide, in all these years, what colour her eyes were. Was she laughing at him? He narrowed his own uncomplicated blue orbs, but could not be quite sure whether the tilt of her mouth was humour or impatience or simply a tic. She had a way of tilting her chin at him, lifting one brow—there, just like that—that made him feel rather more like an insect she wished to stamp on than he liked. Montague put down his paper knife once more and picked up the manuscript, tying the ribbon which bound it. Handing it back, he saw that it was rather dog-eared and saw, too, from the look of distaste on the Widow Kinsail's face, that she had noticed and didn't like it. The tiny glow of his having irked her gave him the momentum he needed.

'The story needs another felony. And afterwards— well, suffice it to say that you can let that imagination of yours loose on your pen,' he said with something approaching a wink. 'Set the pages aflame, Lady Kinsail, and I am sure that we will run to three, maybe four editions.'

Deborah hesitated, torn between triumph and horror. 'I had not planned…'

'Nonsense! You've done exceeding well with the robbery of that statuette—how hard can it be to dream up another such?' Mr Freyworth got to his feet in an effort to cut short any protestation. 'Think of the returns, madam. Three, four editions I say, and that will be just the start. The interest will generate a demand for the earlier books, too, I am sure of it.'

He was actually rubbing his hands together, Deborah noticed, trying not to laugh, for Mr Freyworth's tall, scrawny frame, the hollowed cheeks, the thin, fluffy covering of black hair through which his skull showed like an egg, combined with the dusty black clothes he wore, made him look like one of the neglected Tower ravens. She held out her hand, tucking her manuscript under the other arm. 'I will attempt to do what you say, sir.'

'I am sure you will not disappoint, madam. I look forward to seeing the results. And if you could perhaps manage to complete the revisions in—say two or three weeks?—then we shall, if we put our minds to it, be able to rush through the first edition in time for Christmas.'

'I hardly think that Bella Donna's exploits will be the most popular of yuletide gifts,' Deborah said with a dry smile.

Montague Freyworth patted her shoulder. 'Now then, my lady, you must allow me to know my business rather better than you. You would be surprised by the number of people who will purchase your little story if it is nicely bound and discreetly marketed. I will not say that you will see it on every drawing-room table, but I will make an informed guess that you will find it in most boudoir cabinets. Good day to you now, madam. And happy writing.'

Rather dazed, Deborah made her way out on to Piccadilly. If what Mr Freyworth said was true, the profits from her pen could free her from the necessity of relying upon her widow's portion. Free her from the last tangible remnants which bound her to Jeremy. Just thinking about the possibility made her realise how much she still resented those ties, despite the knowledge that she was more than deserving of the income which was, after all, originally sourced from her very own inheritance.

Wandering down the busy street, oblivious to the

swarms of traffic heading to the park, for it was the beginning of the Season and approaching the hour for parading, Deborah surrendered herself to the dream of independence. True independence. And all it would take, if Mr Freyworth were to be believed—and why should such an astute businessman lie?—was one more robbery and its aftermath. Surely she could do it?

Three days later, Deborah scrunched up another piece of paper ruined by crossings out and ink blots, with a hole in the middle where she'd pressed her pen too hard in sheer exasperation. She couldn't do it. She just couldn't do it! Throwing the paper ball into the empty hearth with an accuracy born of far too much practice, she pushed back her chair and began to pace the room. Back and forwards she went, between the window and the far wall, a route taken so often that the carpet was beginning to show signs of wear. The familiar litany dogged every step.

Authenticity is the key.

Authenticity will bring you a third edition. A fourth.

Authenticity will bring you independence.

Independence will bring you freedom.

You will be free. Free of the past. Free of Jeremy. Free.

Authenticity will bring freedom.

Elliot is the key to authenticity.

Elliot.

You need Elliot.

You can't do it without Elliot.

He'll most likely be planning another robbery around about now in any case.

And it's for a good cause. The money you give now to every beggarly soldier is a drop in the ocean compared to what his ill-gotten gains can do. You'd be helping save those men and saving yourself.

You need Elliot.

Elliot is the key.

You need Elliot.

You need to see Elliot.

And here, as ever, her mind skittered to a halt. It wasn't that she *needed* to see him, it was that she needed his help. She hadn't missed him. She hadn't been disappointed every time the post brought no word, every time a knock on the door failed to produce him either in person or in the form of a messenger in the three weeks since she had forced him to say goodbye. He'd done what she wanted, he'd taken her at her word. He'd kept away.

So of course she was not looking for an excuse to get in touch with him. Absolutely not! Elliot Marchmont was an extremely attractive and intriguing man, but what she imagined him doing to her in the dark, in the secret of the night, it meant nothing. She knew perfectly well that there was a world of difference between fantasy and reality. She didn't want him. Not really. Not at all!

But she needed him. And unless she did something about it, she would have to pay her annual visit to Kinsail Manor next winter. Oh God no, she just couldn't bear it. Which meant…

With a decisive nod, Deborah resumed her seat and picked up a fresh pen. But having dashed off Elliot's name at the start of her note, she was struck by indecision. Chewing absent-mindedly on the tip of her quill— a disgusting habit she'd never been able to break herself of—she stared blankly at the watercolour landscape which hung on the wall over her desk. It was not just the unequivocal way she had ended their acquaintance, she was horribly conscious of the fact that she would be exploiting his most noble cause to her own ends. She could not, in all conscience, do so without some sort of explanation. Besides, without some sort of explanation, she doubted very much indeed that Elliot would agree.

In fact, the more she pondered it, the more she wondered if Elliot would not—quite justifiably—refuse her request to speak to him. The most likely outcome of her asking him to call on her would be spending the next few days waiting in vain for him to do so, because why would he call when she'd been so determined never to see him again?

Perhaps, then, she should suggest that *she* would call on *him?* It was unconventional, improper even, though she doubted he would be any more bothered by this than she was. But what if he refused her entry to his house? A melodramatic vision of herself pleading on the doorstep with Elliot standing aloof, barring the way, failed to make Deborah smile, for it felt quite possible.

She dropped the pen as her confidence oozed slowly

away. It was a familiar feeling. So many times, in Jeremy's absence, she had rallied herself to try again, or latterly to tell him that she was done with the pretence that was their marriage, that she would not stay, that a separation would make them both less miserable. Every time, every single time, she'd failed, and every defeat crushed her a little further, like a mallet pushing a peg into the ground. Catching sight of her distorted reflection in the window pane, a curled, slumped figure, Deborah sat up straight in her chair. 'Freedom,' she said aloud to rally herself. 'Think of it, Deb, freedom.'

No point in writing. She must leave nothing to chance. She would call on Elliot now. And if he was not at home, she would call again. And if he would not see her, she would refuse to go away until he did. And when he did, she would tell him. Not all, but enough to persuade him, enough to persuade herself, too, of the worthiness of her cause, even if it was a pale shadow of his.

Thus fortified, she ran lightly up the stairs to her bedchamber. Her sad little collection of gowns looked like the washed-out palette an artist would use to paint a November sea, but that could not be helped. Quickly changing into a walking dress and tidying her hair before she could change her mind, Deborah pulled on a pair of boots, tied her bonnet, fastened her pelisse and buttoned her gloves.

Elliot had returned to town in an even more morose mood than the one in which he had departed. Though he had tried to interest himself in the business of his estates, the factor whom Lizzie had trained was extremely efficient and Elliot had been unable to persuade himself that his presence was in any way necessary to the good heart of his land.

Ennui made him irritable and the feeling of unfinished business gnawed at him. No matter how hard he had tried, Deborah kept creeping into his mind and occupying his dreams. Her contradictions fascinated him and his fascination annoyed him. She was intriguing and beguiling, but she was also seriously emotionally repressed and apparently determined to remain so. She was wild and reckless one moment, totally lacking in confidence another. Her kisses were like no kisses he had ever shared, but they were not the kisses of an experienced woman. How could a wanton be an innocent? How could someone so incredibly attractive think herself, as she so patently did, so very ordinary? She was tough and she was fragile. The shadows cast by her past were enormous, but she refused to acknowledge them. She aroused his compassion and his passion. She encouraged his confidences, but would confide nothing willingly in return. It was pointless thinking about her and pointless trying to stop.

In the endless free hours his retreat from town had granted him, Elliot turned all of this over and over in his mind to absolutely no avail. Attempting to divert himself with the question of his future was equally frustrating. He needed to give his life form, but he had no idea what form he wished it to take; the only form which really interested him was Deborah's. There was only one thing for it, Elliot decided, and that was to go back to London and resurrect the Peacock, even if his appeal was, frankly, diminished.

Deborah arrived upon his doorstep the very day he returned. His heart gave a most unexpected little skip at the sight of her standing in his hallway. Telling himself that he could hardly send her about her business without at least granting her a hearing, even if that is what she looked as if she expected him to do, Elliot ushered her into the parlour.

She was out of sorts, nervous, jumping when he closed the door firmly on his over-interested batman, who also served as major-domo. Her eyes were over-bright, her hat askew, as if she had been tugging at the ribbons while she waited. 'Lady Kinsail. This is an unexpected surprise,' Elliot said with a very small bow.

'Deborah. It's Deborah,' she said, flinching at the irony in his tone.

'Won't you sit down?'

'Thank you.' She sat gingerly on the striped sofa. It was a pleasant room. Like Elliot, it was elegant without being ostentatious. Looking up at him through her lashes, she realised she'd forgotten again how tall he was. And the fierce look of him. And the way she liked the fierce look of him. His mouth. The top lip thinner. The grooves at the sides. She'd forgotten how he made her feel. Fluttery and soft and hot. Female.

Afraid that she would lose heart, she launched into speech. 'I know I shouldn't have called unannounced on you like this, but I wanted to see you and I was worried that—I thought if I wrote to you, you might ignore me. I could understand why, after the last time. I was rude, and I was most certain that I—that we should not—there are things—reasons—but that's no excuse. Except I thought it was for the best, and as it turns out—in short, I had to see you.'

Elliot tried hard not to smile at this convoluted speech, tried to hold on to his hurt, tried not to be interested, and failed in every attempt. 'I have been away, visiting my home in the country. If you had called yesterday, you would not have found me.'

'Oh.' The little tug upwards at the corner of his mouth, was it a smile? Deborah tentatively tried one of her own. 'Are you well?' she asked, though it was perfectly obvious that he was. 'You look well,' she added inanely. 'The country air obviously agrees with you.'

'You think so? I confess, I was rather bored.'

'Oh.' Deborah looked down at her hands. She seemed to have pulled off her gloves. There was a bluish tinge on the skin between her thumb and index finger which no amount of scrubbing could remove. 'Your home, I don't think you've mentioned where it is?'

'Hampshire.'

'You have family there? I mean I know that your father passed away and your sister is in town, but you must have other family. Most people do. Except me. But I am not most people.' She was wittering, but as long as she did so, she would be able to postpone having to broach the subject she had come to discuss.

'I have some cousins, but no other close family. It was just me and my factor, who is far too efficient for his own good.'

'You should count yourself lucky, a good factor is worth his weight in gold. I don't know how many times I told Jeremy that that man of his acted as though he was being asked to pay for repairs out of his own pocket. No wonder that we lost every decent tenant we had and the lands went to rack and ruin, but Jeremy didn't seem to care. "I'll be dead before I'll be bankrupt," he used to say, and—' Deborah caught herself up short, colouring deeply. 'Well anyway, you should count yourself lucky.'

'And your husband? Was he right?'

'What? Oh, you mean was he dead before he went bankrupt?' She shook her head. 'You'd think so, to hear his cousin talk, but it was not quite that bad. Most of the land was entailed and could not be sold, and the mortgages were not really—but that is not what I came here to discuss.'

Elliot sat down beside her on the sofa, touched by that heartfelt little speech. Her profligate husband had obviously succeeded in emptying the coffers sufficiently to leave his widow in severely straitened circumstances, and, knowing the current Lord Kinsail's miserly tendencies, it was unlikely that he'd made any attempt to alleviate them. 'I'm glad now I took that blue diamond,' he said impulsively. 'If I'd have known, I'd have taken the family jewels as well and given them to you.'

He said it to make her smile, but Deborah's expression was not amused. 'I want nothing from the Kinsails and I don't want your pity, Elliot.'

Her haughty look was back. She was as prickly as a damned thistle. 'I wish you would tell me what it is you do want from me,' he said, exasperated as much by himself as her abrupt change of mood, 'because I haven't a clue.'

'I need the Peacock,' Deborah blurted out. 'I need to commit another felony.'

The starkness of this statement startled him into laughter and a combination of nerves, and the infectious quality of that rumbling sound which was like a rough caress, made Deborah laugh, too. 'It's not funny.'

'Yes, it is. *I need to commit another felony.* You made it sound as if you'd been prescribed a purgative.'

'Elliot, I am deadly serious.'

His smile faded. 'Categorically, no.'

'Why not?'

'Once was risky. To court such danger a second time would be foolish beyond belief.'

'You have done so countless times.'

'My life is my own to risk.'

'As is mine.'

Elliot launched himself to his feet. 'I don't need an accomplice,' he said through gritted teeth, furious with himself for having hoped that she had called simply because she wanted to see him. Furious at himself for having hoped anything at all when he had quite decided that he would think of her no longer. 'I should have had my man turn you away. I cannot believe you have had the nerve to ask me this after you made it so perfectly clear that you wanted nothing more to do with me.'

'You're angry with me.'

'I'm mad as bloody fire! The last time I saw you, you told me that you were perfectly content with your own company—this, despite the fact that you have admitted several times that you're lonely. You encouraged me into telling you things I've never talked about—and yet you are like a clam. And that night—you kissed me as if you were starved of kisses. If I hadn't dropped that portrait you'd have done a damn sight more than kiss me, but the next day you turn the cold shoulder on me. And now you swan in after almost three weeks of silence and demand—of course I'm angry with you, what did you expect?'

'I shouldn't have asked,' Deborah said miserably.

'No, you should not have.' Elliot kicked at a smouldering log in the grate. Ash floated up from it, marring the polished perfection of his Hessians. He hated losing his temper. He hated that white, pinched look on Deborah's face, and hated himself for having caused it even though she deserved it. He hated himself even more for caring. He dug his hands deep into his pockets and leaned his shoulders against the mantel, warring with the urge to agree with her outrageous request simply because he wanted to.

Deborah twisted her gloves round and round, pulling the worn leather completely out of shape. Seconds stretched and still Elliot said nothing, his expression withdrawn, the lines around his mouth deep grooves.

His anger sapped her will, for it was wholly justified. She was a fool to have come. 'You are quite right, I shouldn't have asked. I beg your pardon, I will go now.'

He watched her get to her feet. He dug his hands deeper into his pockets as she pulled on her gloves. Her hands were shaking. She was biting her lip, unable quite to look him in the eye and he felt like an utter bastard, even though he was right. *He was absolutely right, dammit!*

Deborah got to the door. She was leaving. She was walking away without a fight, even though she had a cause worth fighting for. She was walking away, just as she always did. She hesitated with her hand on the brass door handle. She hadn't even tried to explain. She owed it to herself to at least do that much.

She let go of the latch and turned around. 'You're right,' she said shakily, 'I shouldn't have asked to come with you, but I did none the less because I have a very good reason for doing so. It's not as good a reason as yours. I could lie to you, I could say that it's just because I want to help you fight your battle, but I wouldn't presume, even though I can empathise, and more importantly I *won't* lie to you. If you will do me the courtesy of listening—which is more than I deserve, I know that—then I will explain. If my behaviour has already put me beyond the pale, I'll understand.'

It felt like a victory, simply having had the courage to stand her ground. She was breathing fast, as if she'd been galloping over the Downs, as if she'd been running, and the exhilaration of it was the same, too. She remained where she was, hovering at the door, for the moment not caring what Elliot said, just happy to have spoken up for herself. She was almost surprised when he crossed the room to where she was standing. His nearness made her heart beat even faster. His expression was still grim, but at least he was looking at her and not beyond her.

Their eyes met; for a startling moment all Deborah could think about was kissing him. For a second, an infinitesimal second, she gazed at him, imagining that kiss, dark and hot and velvet. He would thrust his tongue into her mouth, pull her tight against him. It would not be a gentle kiss, no sweetness nor restraint. She would clutch at him, pressing herself shamelessly into the hardness of his chest, his thighs, wanting to be crushed into oblivion. She would kiss him fervently, longingly, as if she would drain him of his strength in order to bolster her own.

Her skin heated. Her breath quickened. She saw it in his eyes, a recognition of the direction her thoughts had taken, and drew herself back, looking away, plucking at her gloves once more. 'Will you allow me to explain, Elliot?'

It had cost her dear, to turn around like that. It had cost him dear to let her go. He was still not sure that he would have, was irked at his relief in not having to, but already his curiosity had begun to subdue his anger. Already, whatever it was about her that plucked a chord in him had overcome his resolution. 'I will listen, but

I make no promises,' Elliot said gruffly, leading her back to the sofa.

Deborah chewed on her lower lip, her thoughts turned inwards. Then she nodded, the way Elliot had noticed she often did when she had come to a decision, and he struggled to contain his smile. She straightened her shoulders, tucking a non-existent strand of hair behind her ear, another endearing habit he'd noticed. She had the look of one preparing for battle. He eased himself back on the sofa a little, because the proximity of his knee to her was distracting. His anger was forgotten. Once more, he was simply intrigued. 'Go on,' he said gently.

'Yes. Yes, I will.' Deborah nodded again. 'You must be aware by now that my circumstances are somewhat straitened.' She spoke quietly, looking not at him, but at her hands. 'My jointure is—well, according to Lord Kinsail it is more than adequate, which perhaps explains his reluctance to pay it regularly.'

'Surely the terms of your husband's will, your marriage settlement…'

'Are not the point, Elliot. The point is that I would prefer not to be beholden in any way to my husband's estate.' Glancing up at him, she realised that her words were very much open to misinterpretation. 'Goodness, don't look like that. I'm not about to suggest that you cut me in on your profits,' she said with a horrified little laugh. 'No, I meant that I—what I am trying to say is that I have found an alternative way to earn my bread. I have taken up writing.'

Whatever he had been expecting, it was not this. Elliot sat bolt upright. 'You write—what, exactly?'

'Books.'

'You never fail to surprise me. What sort of books?'

'Novels. You will not have read any of them, they are not—they are written for—they're not your kind of thing.'

'What kind of thing are they, then?'

'Just stories.'

'For children?'

'Good God, no,' Deborah replied, looking appalled. 'They are sort of adventure stories. Revenge allegories. For adults.'

She was blushing. He tried to snag her gaze, but Deborah remained fascinated by her hands. 'Revenge? I remember now, you told me you recognised vengeance—was that what you meant, that you write about it? Do you not think that is a rather strange topic to choose?'

'It doesn't matter what they are about, save that they are books, that they sell well and that my publisher says that this next one will sell even better. Enough for me to be able to dispense with my jointure.'

'Why would you do that, when it is your legal entitlement?'

'I don't want it. I don't want anything from the Kinsails. That is the point of my writing, to be free.'

'That is an odd choice of word for financial independence.'

Deborah shrugged.

'I still don't understand what this has to do with me.'

'In my latest story, my heroine carries out a robbery and…'

'Wait a minute. You're not telling me that you've put what we did into a book?' Elliot said slowly.

'I know, I should have told you, but…' Deborah twisted her gloves into a tight knot. 'I've changed the details obviously, you need have no fear that there is anything which will betray us. She—my heroine—acts quite alone, and though she does escape by a rope, it is not a portrait, but a statuette she takes.' Her voice faded into a whisper. Put like that, it seemed heinous not to have told him. 'I assure you Elliot, no one would realise—save you, of course, and you are not likely to read it.'

'On the contrary, I shall make a point of doing so.'

'*No!* Good God, no! It's not your sort of thing at all.'

There was no doubt about it now, Deborah was blushing furiously. 'What on earth have you written that you're so embarrassed about?' Elliot asked.

'Nothing! I'm not embarrassed.' Aware that the blush on her cheeks gave lie to her words, she tried to cool them with the backs of her hands. 'I have never told anyone about my work. No one save my publisher knows, and even he pretends to be in ignorance of my real identity.' She risked a look at Elliot, a smile that was almost impish. 'He knows my name full well of course, but he pretends not to. He calls me *madam,*' she said in a fair imitation of Mr Freyworth, 'and only when he is annoyed with me, or very anxious to persuade me of something, does he resort to *my lady.*' Her smile faded. 'He resorted to *my lady* when he read my latest story. He thought my description of the theft had great authenticity. In fact, he liked it so much that he insisted I include another. He told me that such a book would run into several editions. Several, only think of it. I can't tell you how much that would mean to me, Elliot. I tried, I really did try to make something up, but I could not.'

Silence, but this time she had no difficulty in reading the look on his face. He was aghast. 'You don't think it's a good idea,' Deborah said, nodding her head matter of factly, ignoring her sinking heart. 'And you're right. It's not. I should have seen—only I was so very eager to do as he asked because of the sales...'

'You've come here to ask me to take you with the Peacock so you can put it in a book.'

Deborah cringed. 'Yes, yes, I know, when you put it like that...'

'Having already written our first little outing into that same book so successfully that your publisher wants another?'

'Yes.'

'But your imagination has failed you, so you want me—I beg your pardon, the Peacock—to fill in the gaps. Have I that right?'

Deborah nodded mutely.

'And the reason you need to write books in the first place is because you won't take what you're legally entitled to from your dead husband's estate?'

'I won't take it because I don't feel entitled to it.'

'Why not?'

She shouldn't have said that—Elliot was far too perceptive. Deborah stared, wide-eyed, fighting the urge to flee. He wasn't angry any more. He wasn't looking at her in that hard way, though his mouth was still grim. She looked down at her gloves. They were quite ruined.

'Deborah?'

There was a hint of impatience in his voice now. 'I wasn't a very good wife,' she said.

He had to strain to catch her words, and when he did, he almost wished he hadn't, for it was impossible not to be touched by such an admission. Elliot disentangled Deborah's gloves from her fingers. Her hands were icy. He clasped them between his own to warm them. 'From the little you've told me,' he said carefully, 'he wasn't a very good husband.'

'We shouldn't have married. He was only interested in my money, I told you that.'

'It is your money which provides you with your jointure, Deborah.'

'It's not mine, not any more. I don't want it. I don't deserve it. You don't understand.'

'I'm trying to.'

'You can't, Elliot. I can't talk about this. I'm sorry,' she said wretchedly, snatching her hands free of his and scrubbing at her eyes. 'Thank you for your time. It's too much, I understand that, but I appreciate your having listened.' Once again, she made for the door.

'What will you do?'

'Make something up.' Deborah smiled bravely. 'I'm

a writer, it's what we do—invent things. I should go now.' She held out her hand.

Elliot took it, but did not let it go. He felt like a complete heel in the face of such spirit. After all, was she really asking so much? What if he chose one of the safer jobs, one of the ones he'd actually put to the bottom of his list because it would be so boring? Whatever went on between her and her husband, she had obviously suffered. Who could blame her for wishing to sever the ties with his family? Who would not honour her for wishing to be independent? If he managed the risk, would it be so wrong to take her, knowing that by doing so he was helping her fulfil a most worthwhile ambition? She had already proved herself reliable, capable. Wouldn't it be wrong *not* to take her?

'Elliot?'

'Does it really matter so much to you?'

'It's not just about the money. It's freedom, a chance to forget the past. To try to forget the past, at any rate. But it's my past, not yours. I should not have...'

'I'll take you.'

'*Elliot!*' Deborah's smile faded almost immediately. 'No, I can't let you. You're just feeling guilty because I've been so pathetic.'

'It's because you've not been pathetic and it's nothing to do with guilt.'

'I can't let you.'

'I want to.'

'No. You said yourself it would be too risky. What if I did something stupid?'

'You won't. I won't let you,' Elliot said, exasperated by her protestations, for now that he had decided, he had set his heart on it.

'I might, though. What if I cried out, or dropped something, or—?'

'For God's sake, Deborah, I'll take you! I want to take you!' Elliot exclaimed.

Annoyed to discover how much he wanted to, he pulled her towards him. She stumbled and his arms automatically went around her. She smelled of lavender. Her eyes were melting brown. Close up, they were rimmed with gold. A pulse beat wildly at the base of her throat. Her lips were the most seductive pink. He wanted to kiss her. The way she looked at him, she was expecting him to kiss her. Was this why he had agreed to do as she wished, for more of her kisses? No. *No!* There were other reasons. Plenty of reasons, though he couldn't remember them right at this moment, when the softness of her breasts pressed his chest, when he could feel her breath on his mouth.

'I want you.' She had not moved away. She'd made no attempt to free herself. 'I want you to come with me, I mean,' he said raggedly. 'If it means so much to you.'

'Yes.' Deborah's heart beat wildly. She wanted him to kiss her. She was so sure he would kiss her. She touched the scar which sliced his brow. He was so very male, yet it did not frighten her, merely heightened her own sense of being female. Jeremy had never—but Elliot was not Jeremy. 'If you're sure. I won't let you down.'

'I know you won't.' He kissed her then, but it was the

merest touch of his lips before he drew back. 'I don't want there to be any more misunderstandings between us,' he said. 'I did not agree to help you in return for your kisses.' A wicked smile teased the corners of his mouth. 'I do want your kisses, make no mistake about that, but only when you are ready to give them to me.'

Deborah shivered. She wanted to, but she was afraid. But she wanted to, despite the fact that she knew herself lacking in some essential ingredient which made other women desirable. Reluctantly, she stepped clear of Elliot's embrace. 'I understand,' she said tightly.

'Good,' Elliot replied, wondering if *he* did. Until he had met Deborah, he had considered himself rather well versed in the ways of women. Where other men declared roundly that they wished their wives or lovers would simply say what they wanted, Elliot relished feminine subtleties and nuances, the complexities and layers in women's language which made them so very different from his own sex. But Deborah was not so easily read. Had she wanted him to kiss her or not? Did she want him? He had no idea.

'Will you send me a note with the arrangements, as you did last time?' she asked, interrupting this rather frustrating chain of thought.

Elliot nodded. 'In a week or so. I've nothing planned yet, it takes time.'

'I could help you. I could help you with your reconnaissance, and your—whatever it is you do in your planning.'

'To put in your book?' he asked quizzically.

She hadn't been thinking of her book. 'Yes.' Deborah bit her lip. 'No. I mean I would like to with your permission, but that's not why I suggested it. I'd like to help. And I'd like to—to be with you. Because I want to.'

She said it so defiantly, tilted her chin at him in that way she had, that Elliot couldn't help laughing. 'Then I would like that, too,' he said.

'What is it you gentlemen say? We have a deal?'

'We have a deal,' Elliot replied, though he kissed the fingers she held out, rather than shaking them.

Watching from his doorstep as her cab rumbled over the cobbled streets in the direction of Hans Town, he realised that the fog of ennui which had accompanied him like a sodden pack of kit, all the way from London to Hampshire and back again, had now departed along with the bitter taste of rejection. There was no need, yet, to solve the thorny question of the future. Deborah had given him plenty of other things to think about.

She had been most coy with regards to her writing. He wished she could bring herself to confide in him, but he could not see the harm in failing to wait for her to do so. He poured himself a glass of Madeira and took a sip, rolling the wine around his mouth, enjoying the rich, fruity taste of it. It brought back an image, of a night at the royal palace in Lisbon, a ball, a dusky beauty, the scent of bougainvillea. So long ago, he felt as if the memory belonged to another person entirely.

Elliot took another sip of wine. So many times since the war had ended, he had wished himself back in those days, but right now, the present was much more interesting. The past was fading, dimming in comparison to the promise of the next few days. He finished his wine. His hand hovered over the decanter, but he decided against another. He had some digging to do and this kind of digging required a clear head.

Chapter Six

It was too dangerous for them both to reconnoitre, he told her when she suggested it. Though the job was a simple one, Elliot was thorough and Deborah was studious. They were poring over his sketches of the house and grounds together, papers and notes scattered over the polished table in his small dining room, when Lizzie came upon them.

They did not hear her at first; she had waved aside the servant's offer to announce her. Standing in the doorway, she watched them, the flaxen-haired stranger and her brother, looking younger and more carefree than she'd seen him for years. They were seated side by side. Elliot's arm lay on the table, almost but not quite brushing that of his companion. She was reading something, a frown making question marks of her fair brows, so deep in concentration that she didn't notice the way Elliot was looking at her. Lizzie's own brows shot up. She must have made a sound, for Elliot looked around, quickly gathered the scattered papers together and got to his feet.

'Lizzie. I wasn't expecting you.'

'Obviously not,' his sister said archly. 'Am I interrupting?'

'You know perfectly well that you are, else you would have allowed my man to show you into the parlour. Deborah, this is my sister, Mrs Alex Murray. Lizzie, this is Lady Kinsail, the Dowager Lady Kinsail.'

'How do you do?' Lizzie dropped a polite curtsy. *Widow,* she was thinking. *Kinsail. There was a scandal there. I must ask Alex. Not young. Twenty-six, seven? Not beautiful, but memorable.* 'I had no idea you and my brother were acquainted. He goes so little into society, I'm surprised that your paths have crossed.'

'How do you do? I would have known you for Elliot's—Mr Marchmont's sister without an introduction. You are very like.' Deborah eyed Lizzie's carriage dress enviously. Cherry red, with a deep border of black beading, a short velvet jacket with the tightly fitted sleeves finished with the same pattern of beadwork, it was very elegant. And its owner was very perceptive, she thought, tilting her chin under that lady's scrutiny. 'Elliot and I met through my late husband's cousin,' she said. 'Lord Kinsail—the current Lord Kinsail, that is—was of some assistance in a matter concerning the army.' She threw a mischievous look over her shoulder at Elliot, who was ushering them into the parlour, and regretted it instantly when it was intercepted by Lizzie, who was obviously just as sharp as her brother.

'I see.'

'I doubt it,' Elliot said drily. 'I suppose you'll want tea? I'll just go and see to it.'

'Lovely,' Lizzie said, sinking into her favourite sofa and patting the cushion beside her, giving Deborah no option but to sit at her side. 'I don't know if Elliot's told you, but I'm expecting and it's doing horrible things to me. My ankles swell. Do you have children, Lady Kinsail?'

'No. No I was not—we were not—no.'

'I'm sorry. I didn't mean to upset you.'

'It doesn't matter. And it's Deborah, please.'

'Lord, I hope I'm not going to turn into one of those bores who can talk of nothing but babies.' Lizzie cast aside her bonnet with the carelessness of one who had several more. 'I wasn't the least bit interested in them until I started increasing; now I find that little else interests me. It's as well I'm going to Scotland next month, else my reputation for wit will be quite spoiled. What was it that you and my brother were so anxious to hide from me?'

Deborah smiled. 'Your wits have not wandered very far yet. Why don't you ask Elliot?'

'Because he'll tell me to mind my own business, only he won't do it as politely as you. How long have you known him?'

'Not long.'

'He's kept you very quiet.'

'Perhaps because there's nothing to tell.'

Lizzie chuckled. 'Oh, have it your own way. I would

not have brooked any interference in my courtship either.'

'Mrs Murray…'

'Lizzie.'

'We are not—there is nothing of that nature between us. We are merely engaged upon a business venture.'

'Do you really think that? No, for you are blushing. This, let me tell you, is excellent news, for now I will be able to hide myself in the wilds of Scotland without worrying about my brother.'

'You must not be thinking…'

'Oh, don't worry, I shan't say anything,' Lizzie said airily, confining the list of eligibles she had drawn up in her head to the virtual flames. 'Besides, I would not dream of playing the matchmaker for Elliot,' she added, with a fine disregard for the truth.

'I doubt your brother needs anyone's help in attracting female company,' Deborah said.

'Now who is digging? There has been no one since he returned to England, so far as I am aware. Does that answer your question?'

'What question is that?' Elliot asked, kicking a small table into position in front of his sister and placing the tea tray upon it.'

'Deborah was asking me about Scotland,' Lizzie said.

He looked sceptical, but chose not to pursue the matter. Over tea, he watched with interest as Lizzie kept up a polite stream of chatter and gossip. Either Deborah was unaware of the lures being cast, or she was too careful to rise to them, for she expressed nothing other than polite interest in the names Lizzie dropped and claimed not a single one of her impressive list as acquaintances. His sister was baffled and Elliot was amused to see her so, even more amused when Deborah declined the invitation to call.

'I would not dream of intruding, when you will be so busy with your preparations,' she said politely but firmly, equally politely and firmly taking her leave alone.

'Don't hate her,' Elliot said, showing Deborah out. 'She does not mean to be interfering.'

Deborah chuckled. 'She does, but since she does it only because she cares for you, I could not possibly be offended. I liked her.'

'I thought you would,' Elliot said with satisfaction, though he knew Deborah well enough now not to press Lizzie's invitation further. 'Until tomorrow night, then? If you are sure?'

'You know I am.' Deborah's eyes gleamed with excitement. 'Until tomorrow, Elliot.'

She surprised him, standing on tiptoe to kiss his cheek. It was over before he could react and she was gone, tripping lightly down the steps in her faded gown and practical shawl, before he could stop her. Elliot watched her walking across the square. He could tell from the angle of her bonnet that she had her chin up—that haughty, touch-me-not look she used to repel strangers. Her walk was not seductive, but it was very

feminine. Those long legs of hers covered the distance
quickly.

'I like her.' Lizzie joined him on the step. She had
put on her bonnet and was drawing on her gloves while
signalling to her coachman, who had been walking the
horses round the square. 'She's very unusual.'

'Yes.'

'Sad, too. There was gossip about the husband, you
know.'

'What?'

'I wish I could remember. Do you want me to find
out?'

'She'll tell me if she wants me to know.'

Lizzie raised her brows. 'That's not like you.'

'No.'

His sister threw him a look, but said nothing more.

Alone again, Elliot leafed through the plans he and
Deborah had been studying. This last week had flown
by. They had spent hours in each other's company, plot-
ting and scheming. She was more relaxed with him now,
but he was under no illusions. Any edging over the line
from the general to the personal made her tense. She
had a caustic wit, a sharp mind, an eye for detail, a head
for numbers—he knew all those things about her. She'd
written stories as a child. She'd told him some of them
one rainy afternoon, mocking her younger self. He had
the sense not to ask her outright what had changed her
so dramatically, but she had seen the question in his
eyes, clamming up straight away, refusing to recount
any more.

Elliot began methodically to tear up the plans and feed them into the fire. They had served their purpose. Deborah's handwriting was surprisingly bad, an almost illegible scrawl. 'As if your pen cannot keep up with your thoughts,' Elliot had teased her when he'd first seen it and she'd laughed at that, telling him that was exactly it. 'I am amazed that Mr Freyworth can read it sometimes,' she'd said. A rare slip, which Elliot had pounced upon, secreted and used. It had not exactly been taxing, tracing her publisher from that snippet. More difficult was identifying her *nom de plume,* but he had his sources. He always had his sources.

'Though I wish to hell I didn't have to use them,' he exclaimed, casting the last of the paper into the flames. 'Why does she have to be so secretive?'

Why could she not trust him? Why would she not, just once, admit that she wanted to kiss him? Because he knew she did. Attraction crackled like lightning between them all the time, driving him mad with frustration, but he would not surrender to it until she did, he would not! A man had his pride. Though he was tempted, on occasion, to consign his to the flames with the plans.

The simple fact is that he wanted her more than he'd ever wanted any woman. It was because she was so stubborn, he told himself, that's all it was. Elliot used the poker to tamp down the fire. That wasn't all, he knew that, but it was all he was prepared to admit. He had more important matters to focus on right now. Like a housebreaking.

And after that? Elliot placed a fire screen over the hearth. He would think about after that when it happened.

It was twelve miles or more to Richmond. In the dark, travelling across country when they could, in an effort to avoid being noticed, Deborah focused all her attention on simply enjoying the ride. It was the one thing which made her visits to Kinsail Manor tolerable, having the run of the stables, the one privilege she was granted, and one of the things she missed most in London. Tonight, the freedom of her attire and the illicitness of their purpose added a delightful *frisson* to the shivering awareness of the man who rode beside her. Cloaked by the dark, she could admit to herself that Elliot's very presence was arousing. Her blood fizzed and sang in her veins. Her heart beat in time to the thunder of her horse's hooves. She felt truly alive.

Beside her, Elliot felt his mood swing between exhilaration and trepidation. He was as certain as it was possible to be that there were no flaws in their plan. A straightforward break-in, an old-fashioned safe, servants' quarters located in a remote attic, a proprietor forced to retire from Government service because even with the aid of his ear trumpet he could hear nothing quieter than a bellow. Such a simple, failsafe task, that under other circumstances he would have scorned it for the lack of challenge.

As they made their way around the perimeter of a field hedged with hawthorn, Deborah's horse snickered as a rodent of some sort ran across their path. She held it effortlessly back from bolting and Elliot managed to restrain himself just in time from laying his hand on her bridle. She was a consummate horsewoman. When he'd thrown her into the saddle tonight, he'd seen that tinge of anticipation in her face, sensed that edginess in her which was so familiar to him.

His response had been a stab of nerves. Normally, he did not consider failure. Tonight it worried him, the risks he was taking, the safety of the woman by his side, who never gave it a thought. The field gave way to a narrow lane. Soft and muddy from the recent rains, it muffled the sound of their hooves. 'Five minutes and we'll be at the main gate,' Elliot said softly. 'You remember all?'

He caught the flash of Deborah's smile in the gloom. Quietly, but succinctly, she recited the plan. Just before they reached the gatehouse, they came to a halt and dismounted, tethering the horses in the shelter of a line of poplars. 'I don't suppose there's any point in my suggesting you wait here?' he said.

Deborah shrugged out of her greatcoat. Her heart was beginning to beat more erratically. Her excitement had the jagged edge of fear. She'd forgotten that from the first time, but she shook her head at Elliot as she threw her coat over her horse. 'I think you know the answer to that question.'

He caught her hand. Like him, she'd taken off her gloves. Her fingers fluttered in his. 'Deborah, you must promise me, if we are discovered...'

'I am to run as fast as I can without waiting for you,' she said. 'I've already promised. What's wrong—surely the infallible Peacock is not nervous? You said yourself that this was a simple job.'

'I know what I said. But if any harm came to you...' His hands tightened on hers.

'It won't.' Without thinking, she stood on her tiptoes in her topboots and kissed him on the cheek. His skin was cool. He tasted of fresh air and sweat. Alerted by the sharp intake of his breath, she realised her lips had lingered a fraction of a second too long, her body had strayed just a fraction of an inch too close. Awareness flashed, brief as a shooting star. She stepped away. The crack of a branch snapping under her boot made her start, and her start made her realise that fear had the edge. She took a deep breath. Focus. She tucked her hair behind her ear. Focus.

Elliot consulted his pocketwatch. Deborah crammed her hat down over her hair. His expression was remote, closed, intimidating. Intent. Her fear ebbed. 'If things go to plan, we should be back here in under an hour,' he said.

'They will,' Deborah replied, gathering up her courage like petticoats around her. 'Stop worrying.'

He hadn't counted on the dog. How had he missed its existence? Though he'd hardly call the thing a dog. To Elliot's eyes it looked like a rug with paws. In fact, were it not for the high-pitched yapping nose which emitted from somewhere under the heavy fringe of fur, it would have been impossible to tell which end of the creature was which. It came at them from its bed in front of the fire, which had long since died, in the library which also contained the safe. Elliot cursed and made a lunge for it, then cursed again as a pair of extremely sharp incisors sank into the fleshy pad of his thumb. It was Deborah who managed to catch the incensed canine, smothering its yelps with her hat, hugging the wriggling body tight against her, muttering soothing clucking noises that, to Elliot's astonishment, had some sort of mesmerising effect.

One minute, two minutes, three. He counted tensely as they waited, all three of them, behind the window curtains. On five, they moved. His heart was hammering. He dropped a pick. The soft tinkle of thin wire on the boards made Deborah glance towards the door through which they had come. She was struggling with the dog. The lock gave way with a soft click. Though he never hurried, he hurried now, raking through the contents, finding the neat little box of lacquered wood. A quick check inside, then it was tucked into his pocket and they were back out in the long hallway. By the light of the lamp which burned there, he caught a glimpse of Deborah's face. She was biting down on a laugh. Down the stairs, through the baize door, into the kitchens they fled, the dog loosed from her hat now, making energetic attempts to free itself, whimpering and yelping.

'I can't hold it much longer,' Deborah said as they reached the basement window. 'I'm sorry, Elliot, it's more ferret than canine.' She was shaking with muffled laughter now. 'What are we going to do, kidnap it? I doubt anyone in their right mind would pay a ransom for this thing.'

'We'll take it with us part of the way, then release it. It will find its own way back, don't worry.' Elliot climbed out of the window, jumped the three feet to the ground, then held up his hands. The dog, astonished into temporary silence, flopped into them and then bit him again. He cursed under his breath. Two long legs—he tried not to look at those long legs—and Deborah arrived beside him. 'Run,' he said, taking her hand.

They ran at full tilt. At some point before they reached the gate, the dog escaped and fled in the opposite direction, back towards the house, making enough noise to raise the dead. Deborah was flagging, but Elliot pulled her on remorselessly, throwing her into the saddle almost before she had her greatcoat around her. She was off before he had gathered up his own reins, down the path at speed, careless of ruts and rabbit holes.

They were halfway back to town, travelling along the river, before he felt it was safe enough to slow down. Great clouds of steam rose from the flanks of the horses. He could see Deborah's breath. His own chest was heaving. Elliot reined in beside a small boathouse. 'We'll let the horses rest here awhile.'

Deborah dismounted fluidly. 'You'd have thought the hounds of hell were after us,' she said, laughing between trying to catch her breath. Her hat was gone. Her hair rippled like moonlight on the dark wool of her greatcoat.

'I wouldn't call that damned creature a hound, but it was definitely hellish,' Elliot replied, looking ruefully at his bitten thumb.

'So the Peacock is not so infallible after all.'

Her voice was teasing. She was smiling, quite transformed from her daytime self. Elliot felt as Pygmalion must have done, seeing Galatea come to life. 'Flawed,' he said, clutching theatrically at his chest. 'Alack, my feet of clay have been discovered.'

'I think we both have feet of clay.' Deborah looked ruefully down at her mud-clogged boots. A soft breeze fluttered through the willow which wept into the deceptively still waters of the Thames, making her shiver, for she had once again thrown her coat over her horse.

'We can wait in here while the horses cool down.'

Elliot pushed open the door of the boathouse. Inside, it smelled of oiled rope, dried sailcloth and damp wood. He lit the lantern which he always carried with him. The flame cast a soft glow around the narrow building. Through the slats in the wooden floor, they could hear the water shushing against the stilts. The boat, some sort of decorative barge, took up most of the available space. He stepped into it and held out his hand to help her.

Deborah climbed over the wooden edge, sitting down next to him on the cushioned seat built into the stern and it was there, suddenly and indisputably, between them. Awareness. The air resonated with it. Awareness of the kisses they had been avoiding, the desire they had been ignoring. Everything seemed sharpened by it. The smell of the boathouse, the sound of the water, her breathing, her heartbeat, her pulses. Her skin prickled with longing. She had to make a physical effort to keep herself from creeping towards Elliot, close enough to touch. 'May I see our spoils?' Even her voice sounded strange.

The box he placed on his knee was small, like a cigar box, only ornately lacquered, inlaid with gold. 'Japanese,' Elliot said. Deborah's breeches were stretched tight across her legs. Her knee was inches away from his. He concentrated on the box, fiddling with his most delicate pick at the lock, trying not to think about the way her presence intoxicated him. He hadn't planned this, had conscientiously avoided even thinking about afterwards, but now here it was, and it was the same—more—than that first time. Was he imagining that she felt it too, simply because it was what he wanted?

The box opened. Deborah's hair brushed his shoulder as she leaned over to get a closer look and their eyes clashed. Their breath hitched. There was no mistaking it, though they both instantly dropped their gazes to the box. Desire, clear and sharp.

'Are they what we were expecting?' Deborah asked. 'Miniature carvings, you said. Ivory set with precious stones. Unusual, you said.'

'So I was told.'

'By your sources,' she agreed with a quick smile. 'May I see?'

The box was inlaid with velvet. Elliot removed the covering layer of cloth. There were ten figures, set in two rows of five. Deborah picked one out, frowning, turning it over in her hand. A diamond caught the light. Only then did Elliot realise what they had stolen. Deborah's eyes widened as she examined the detailed, highly skilled carving. A woman. Naked. Astride a naked man. 'Good grief,' she exclaimed.

'I was told they were idols,' Elliot said, fascinated by the way her fingers caressed the ivory, tracing the outlines of the figures, trying desperately not to think of those same fingers touching him so intimately.

'I think this one has been broken at some point. See, the woman is not quite fixed.' She pulled gently, and the ivory carvings separated. 'Oh!' The male figure lay on his back in the palm of her hand, quite undamaged and extremely true to nature. She traced the exaggerated length of manhood which had joined the couple with her fingertip and shivered. The expression on the figure's face was not lascivious, but rather ecstatic. The woman, too, now she looked at it.

She picked it up from where it had fallen on the cushion between them and slotted the two back together again. The movement was sleek. She hadn't meant to look at Elliot, but she couldn't stop herself; when she did, her belly clenched at the way his eyes blazed down at her. 'Are they all like this?'

'Variations on a theme,' Elliot said in a voice that sounded strangled.

'Let me see.'

He handed her the box. She ran her fingers over the carvings, an orgy of copulating couples, all created with the same attention to detail as the first. She selected first one, then another, turning them over in her palm, detaching them and then sliding each together, obviously fascinated. Though some of the positions portrayed, in Elliot's opinion, did not merit the challenge of their execution, none was new to him. In fact, the set was actually relatively tame compared to some he had seen.

Deborah, however, seemed to find almost every variation novel. Her face was rapt. He wished she would look at him like that. He wanted her to touch *him*, not some ivory carving. He wanted to slide inside her, certain that they would fit together even more perfectly than the little Japanese idols.

Slotting a female back into position beneath her lover, Deborah shivered again. None of Bella Donna's couplings had the sensual quality portrayed here. Bella's pleasure was to dominate, subjugate, control. But these figures looked as if they were in a state of bliss. 'Do you think—are they all possible?' she asked doubtfully.

Elliot hesitated, taken aback by the innocence of her question. 'Certainly they're all possible. Whether they are all worth the effort is another question.' Deborah stared at him wide-eyed. She seemed more intrigued than shocked. Did she have any idea what an invitation her interest was? 'The set was obviously made as a marriage gift,' Elliot explained.

'I wish someone had given *me* such a gift,' Deborah said. 'Have *you* tried—oh God, don't answer that, I can't believe…'

'Yes, I have. All of them.' Elliot took the ivory from her and put it back in the box, making no attempt to hide the wicked curve to his smile. 'And before you ask, no, I didn't particularly enjoy them all.'

'Oh.'

Elliot pulled her closer. 'But I'd be willing to try them again,' he whispered into her ear, 'just to satisfy your curiosity, you understand. If you wanted me to.' He nibbled on the lobe of her ear, then kissed his way down the column of her neck to the collar of her shirt.

Deborah's heart was racing, a mixture of excitement and fear. *Could she?* She had broken into a house in the middle of the night. She had assisted in a safebreaking and, what's more, she'd managed to shut that damned dog up. She was in an unlocked boathouse in the middle of nowhere with a man she had been fantasising about since first he fell out of the night and landed on top of her. *Could she?*

'Deborah?'

She laughed and threw her arms around his neck. 'Just kiss me, Elliot.'

He pulled her to him and did just that. His lips were like a feather abrading her skin. He pulled her closer and she sighed, letting the tip of her tongue touch his, drinking in the heat, the scent, the reassuringly solid maleness of him. He sank backwards on to the cushioned bench, taking her with him. She lay over him now, her breasts crushed to his chest, the hard length of his erection pressed into the soft flesh of her belly. So hard. So different. Everything about him was so different.

His kiss deepened. She pressed herself into the unyielding strength of his body and kissed him back, relishing the tightening of his hands on her waist, the way his lips clung to hers, his tongue plundered her mouth, relishing the way he was so very male, the way he made her feel so very female. Their kisses were lush, like ripe fruit. Then deeper kisses, edged with desperation.

Elliot pulled her astride him. 'I want to see you,' he said raggedly, running his hand down her arms, tugging at her coat. 'Curves. Skin. So lovely. I want to see.'

Her coat was cast overboard. Elliot's followed. Then his waistcoat. His eyes were hungry on her as he pulled her shirt free of her breeches, his fingers dealing efficiently with the buttons, pulling it over her head, his eyes blazing as he looked, drinking in her naked flesh. The way he looked was unbelievably rousing. His eyes feasted on her, gloried in her, as if he could never have enough of her. It was incredibly empowering, overcoming any trace of embarrassment.

'So much better than dreams,' he said, flattening his palm over her breasts, down the curve of her waist. 'So much better than in your hallway in the dark.' His mouth curved into a sensual smile that made all her muscles clench. 'So very, very lovely.'

He fastened his mouth to her nipple and sucked deep. Jolting heat, like a streak of light connected straight to the fire in her belly, to the tension knotting there, and lower. Elliot growled as she writhed, holding her still, his lips suckling, licking, teasing more and more heat from first one nipple, then the other, until she was in a frenzy of need and want.

Deborah tugged ineffectively at his shirt. Impatiently, he pulled it over his head and cast it aside. She touched him, warm skin, rough hair on his chest arrowing down to the dip of his stomach. His muscles flexed as he breathed, his breathing became shallower, faster, as she touched him, as he touched her, his eyes fierce on hers.

'I want you.'

She did not doubt him. Could not. And she wanted him, too, painfully, achingly, in a quite alien, wholly adult way she could not have imagined. 'Yes,' she said. 'Yes.'

He pulled her to him with a ruthless kiss, rolling her under him, blazing a trail of kisses down to her breasts, then more kisses, licking, rousing kisses, nipping, plucking kisses, until she was so hot she could not bear it, and more kisses, until they were no longer enough.

When he unbuttoned the fall of her breeches, slipping his hand inside, stroking down her belly, she cried out. Down he stroked, to the soft flesh at the top of her thigh, over the curls at the apex, then the other thigh. She moaned again and dug her nails into his back, arching up for him. She was tense, tight, knotted, but she could feel the knot fraying under his insistent caresses, his mouth, his fingers, the scent of him and the weight of him. He shifted slightly, lifted his head from her breast, muffling her instinctive cry of protest with his mouth, a deep plunging kiss, shadowed by the stroking, slipping, sliding plunge of his fingers into the damp, hot flesh of her sex.

The knot inside her tightened. It was not the first time, for she had of necessity learned how to take solitary pleasure, but it had never been like this. This was not just a release. This was no panacea. This was different. Wildly different. A slow climb, the pleasure in the climb itself, so pleasurable that she did not want to reach her destination. Not yet. She clenched and tried to hold on. Not yet. But Elliot's tongue plundered her mouth as his fingers thrust, and stroked and slid. She was slipping.

'Let go,' he said, his voice guttural in her ear, his touch purposeful, stroking harder, faster, until she thought she would die of anticipation, until she could hold on no more and let go, muffling her cries in his shoulder, shaking with the force of her climax, clinging, panting, shocked beyond measure.

Elliot held her fast, a surge of blood making the ache between his legs almost unbearable. Abandonment. Ecstasy. Just exactly as he had imagined, only more. He kissed her hair. She clung to him, burrowing against him, her cheek pressed into his chest. Then her lips on his skin. Then she slipped her hand into the tight space between them and touched him through his breeches. A tentative touch, but enough to make the blood surge. She fumbled with the buttons which fastened his breeches. He yanked them free, wriggled clear of them, kneeling on the floor of the barge beside her to do so.

Deborah pushed herself upright. Elliot was much bigger than what she had seen of Jeremy. And so hard. Jeremy had never been so—he had always had to—but

Elliot's erection seemed to have a life of its own, jutting up, thick and curved. She wanted to touch him, but she was afraid to. When she'd touched Jeremy...

She didn't want to remember. Desperately, Deborah tried to push back the memories, but they were gaining strength now and her courage was wilting as surely as Jeremy's manhood. This was different. Elliot was different, she told herself, but still she couldn't make her hand move towards him. The very fact that she wanted to touch him so much made failure too terrifying to contemplate. Her confidence, the fizz of her climax, the wild excitement of the night fled, leaving her utterly deflated. Deborah edged away, huddling into the corner of the barge. 'I'm sorry. I'm sorry, I just can't.'

The suddenness of her retreat left Elliot stunned. 'Can't?' he repeated, trying to make sense of the word, trying to understand how the flagrant goddess with her pale hair tumbling over full breasts, the nipples rosy, pink as her sex, could be so quickly transformed into this timid creature. 'Did I hurt you? Have I frightened you? I didn't mean...'

'No, it's me. I shouldn't have—I thought I could, but I can't. I'm so sorry, Elliot.'

He was aching with need. She was so hot. So wet. So ready for him. What had he done to deserve that tight white face, the obvious fear in those big eyes? Realising that he was still blatantly hard and pointlessly naked, Elliot scrabbled for his clothes, quickly pulling on his shirt and breeches, handing Deborah hers before sitting down to pull on his boots.

Beside him, Deborah was shaking, struggling into her waistcoat. 'Here, let me,' Elliot said, fastening the buttons. A tear plopped on to his hand. 'Can't you tell me?'

She shook her head.

'I thought you wanted to.'

'I can't.' Deborah sniffed, wiping her eyes on the sleeve of her shirt.

'Will you tell me why?'

'I can't.' Deborah drew a shaky breath. 'I thought I could—but I shouldn't have. I shouldn't have—I should have stopped you, but you made me feel—and then I thought—but I shouldn't have. We should go, before the horses take a chill.' She pushed him aside to drag on her boots, stumbling out of the boat.

'Damn and blast the horses to hell!' Elliot exclaimed, catching her by the shoulders. 'What the hell went on in that marriage of yours to do this to you? Look at you, you're shaking.'

'You're angry. You're right to be angry. It's my fault. I'm sorry.' It had always been her fault. What a fool she was to think that this time would be any different. Another tear slipped down her cheek. Deborah blinked frantically. A storm of emotions was gathering in her breast that she didn't want Elliot to see. She didn't want them to overwhelm her, not like this, so she did the only thing she knew how. She blanked out everything. She pictured herself as a stone, hard and glittering and untouchable. It was difficult, much more difficult than she

remembered, but she'd had years and years of practice.
'We should go.'

'Is that it? You're not even going to explain?'

'I can't. I'm sorry.' Deborah forced open the boat-house door.

'Dammit, stop saying you're sorry.' Elliot stormed out after her. She already had her greatcoat on and was untying her horse. Her face was set. Elliot watched her, fighting a desire to shake the truth out of her, or kiss the truth out of her, or just kiss her. What was going on in that mind of hers? 'Deborah…'

'I just want to go home. Please don't ask me to explain because I can't. It was a mistake. Please, Elliot, just let me go home.'

He had no option but to mount his horse and follow her. They rode in silence all the way back to London. By the time he bid her goodnight, her stony face and determined silence had provoked his temper and roused his pride. He bid her a curt goodbye.

Chapter Seven

Deborah took up her pen early the next morning because she didn't want to think about last night, and because she couldn't stop thinking about last night. She had to finish her book. She eyed the blank page with a weary eye, having dragged herself from her bed, exhausted by dreams of running and falling, falling and running. She had to finish it. Her book meant freedom and freedom meant—she would think about that later.

She worked frantically after that, driven by the vision of liberty. She wrote, laughing as she recalled the dog, transformed in her story to a sleeker, more vicious version of itself. She wrote on the next day, too, and when tiredness made her head ache, her wrist throb, her fingers too numb to keep the quill upright, still she carried on, until she came to what Mr Freyworth called the aftermath and her pen skittered to a halt.

She could not believe it had been her, that abandoned creature in the boathouse. The soaring, falling-apart feeling of her climax still had the power to make her shiver with delight. Bella's climaxes were gloating, triumphal, a powerful metaphor for victory, but that's all they were. Bella might be technically proficient, but she took her pleasure rather clinically. For the first time in their shared history, Deborah felt she had the upper hand.

Elliot would smile at that piece of convoluted logic. Guilt and longing made her close her eyes. For just a moment, Deborah allowed herself the indulgence of conjuring him. The taste of him. The feel of him. The scent of him. The sheer, undeniable maleness of him. The way he looked at her, touched her. For a while, in the boathouse, she had been happy in her own skin, glad to be Deborah, because Elliot desired her. And then she had spoilt it. Most likely ruined it.

How could she have expected anything else, with seven years' worth of failure stacked up against her? But she had. She had believed it would be different, until she allowed Jeremy back into her head. Jeremy had shaped her far too well and, until she broke the mould he had made for her, it would never be different, she realised with a sickening flash of insight. He was dead, but he haunted her still.

Until now, the idea of being emotionally frozen had been an attractive one. Without feelings she could not be hurt. Why was she being so contrary? she wondered, chewing on the end of her quill, because, despite the fact that she knew it would have been disastrous, she couldn't help wishing that she had made love to Elliot.

Made love! What the devil did she know about that!

Nothing—nor was she ever likely to. But she knew enough now to imagine, didn't she? And if she could imagine, then Bella could experience, couldn't she? Deborah took up her pen with renewed determination.

Less than a week later, she delivered the revised manuscript to Mr Freyworth's office and staggered home, numb with tiredness. She went straight to bed, but sleep would not come. She had hoped that allowing Bella to spread her emotional wings would be cathartic. Instead, it seemed to have effected some sort of internal rebellion. The past, which had been kept at bay for two long years, was escaping through the gate which her writing had unwittingly opened. Memories crowded her mind, a host of stalking animals, vying miserably for her attention.

Deborah paced the floor of her darkened bedchamber, the curtains drawn against the afternoon light, her hair in tangled hanks where she had repeatedly twisted it around her fingers. This should be the first day of her freedom, yet Jeremy's ghost was gathering strength, his taunts pounding out a horribly familiar rhythm in her head.

She had misled him. She had ruined him. She was cold. She was so repulsive that she unmanned him. She was not even a woman, but a barren piece of marble. No wonder he took to the tables in search of comfort. No wonder his friends shunned him. He should never have married her. He had never loved her. He despised her. She had ruined his life. He should never have married her. Never have married her. Never.

Deborah threw herself on to the bed and buried her head under the pillow, screwing her eyes tight shut, but Jeremy wouldn't leave her alone. 'It wasn't my fault,' she said aloud, swallowing a sob, but her voice lacked conviction. She curled up into a ball, wrapping her arms tight around her chest, willing the voice to leave her be. She tried to blank her mind. She tried to rock herself to sleep, buried deep under the blankets, but unconsciousness retreated even further. Scenes, long-forgotten scenes, replayed themselves. Snippets of their life together flickered through her mind's eye like the pages of a hellish scrapbook.

Handsome Jeremy sweeping her off her feet. His kisses were chaste. The perfect gentleman, she'd thought him.

Their wedding night. Jeremy's concern for her innocence. He loved her too much to hurt her, he told her. He loved her too much to subject her to base desire, he said.

And there she was, younger and infinitely naïve, plucking up the courage to take the initiative after too many chaste nights, innocently pressing herself against her husband's body. Were she an artist, she could still capture that instinctive flash of revulsion on his face after all this time.

The messy, unsatisfactory fumbles which followed, eventually carrying her over the threshold from maiden to wife, merged and morphed one into the other, none memorable, all unforgettable. Ignorant and embarrassed, still enough in love to deny her disappointment, Deborah watched herself turn again and again from the look of shame on her husband's face as he touched himself.

An angry scene when her uncle refused to advance her inheritance. A furious one later, when Uncle Peter would not be persuaded. Jeremy's wit, which she had loved, turned cruelly upon her. The pain, still raw, of that moment of revelation from which there was no turning back. Not Deborah, but her inheritance. Not love, but money.

Coldness then, months and years of it. Their marriage a stark, barren country neither wished to inhabit. Jeremy never kissed her. He never touched her, save for during those shameful couplings, always in the dark, her on all fours, her husband fumbling first with himself, then her. The undisguised revulsion on his face when she turned around to look at him. After that, she was glad of the dark.

And then the last time. Deborah curled her knees up to her chest, trying to make herself as small as possible. The last time. She closed her eyes, leaning back against the headboard, forcing herself to remember. It came back to her in stark detail, as if it were a play which had been waiting for the curtain to go up.

Jeremy threw himself from the bed, still clad in his shirt, his utter lack of arousal painfully obvious even in the dim light of the bedchamber. Bruised and aching, her flesh cringing at the very notion of trying again, Deborah sat up, forcing herself to smile, a pastiche of allure. She'd wanted him once. If she could want him again, she could make it right.

She'd studied the books she'd discovered hidden behind a rare complete set of the Encyclopédie. *Fascinated and ashamed, she had perused them, learning from the luridly explicit illustrations just how limited her experience was. Telling herself it was worth the mortification to save her marriage, she touched her breasts, mimicking the drawings. Jeremy's face took on a greenish tint before it became an angry red.*

The shock of his fist sent her flying back on to the pillows. Blood stained her fingers when she touched her cheek. 'You hit me.' The words came from far away. This wasn't happening to her. 'What have I done to make you hate me so, Jeremy?'

'You married me.'

'I loved you.'

He gave her a hard look. 'Five years we've been married and you still don't have a clue, do you? You never loved me. Poor little orphan Debbie, you were just desperate for a bit of attention,' Jeremy sneered. 'God, you made it so easy. You more or less pulled the wool over your own eyes.'

'That's not true,' Deborah argued, though what he said had an ominous ring to it. 'I did love you. I thought you loved me.'

'All I ever loved about you was your money.'

'And you've had that, you've had all of it now, even if you did have to wait for my majority. Jeremy...' Deborah plucked at the sheet, willing herself to speak, know-

*ing that if she did not, she never would. 'In all the time
we have been married, things have not been—we have
not been—I've been wondering if this failure of ours
was the reason we have not been blessed with a child.'*

*'Failure!' Jeremy cursed bitterly. 'If there has been
any failing, it has not been for want of trying on my
part. Do you think I enjoy poking away at that soft
flesh of yours?'*

*Deborah shrank at the viciousness of his look, but
five long years of pointed barbs and cutting accusations, five years of blaming herself for failing to arouse
him, five years of guilt and frustration, watching her
romantic dreams fade, seeing herself transformed into
this empty shell—all of this coupled with her new-found
knowledge for the first time made her angry rather than
ashamed. 'I know perfectly well that you don't, you've
made it quite clear from the first. I disgust you, I always have and I want to know why. What is so wrong
with me?'*

*For the tiniest of moments, when she saw that bleak
look on his face, she felt sorry for him. Then his laughter cut through her pity, bitter and sharp. 'I find you
physically repulsive, my dear wife, because that is what
you are. Look at you, playing the harlot in the vain
hope that it will make me want you. The extent of your
naïvety astounds me. Can you not see what is obvious
to half the* ton? *You could never please me, no matter
how many tricks you learned. My tastes are quite beyond your ken, my dear wife. I've never wanted you.
Your only attraction for me was your money and I have*

done with that.' Jeremy pulled on his breeches and gathered up the rest of his clothes. 'I have done with you. I am quite sick of you and the pretence of our marriage.'

'You wish us to separate?' A flicker of hope sprung in Deborah's breast, for it was what she had sadly concluded was the only solution if tonight failed. And tonight had failed spectacularly.

Jeremy laughed again. 'No, that form of satisfaction I will also spare you. I won't give the tabbies any more ammunition. Having the protection of a wife, even one such as you, is still something. Since it is quite obvious that my efforts to overcome my distaste for your flesh are never going to result in an heir—another thing you have denied me—then I see no reason to make any more attempts. I am going back to London now. You can remain here at Kinsail Manor. To be honest, if I never see you again it will be too soon. I wish you joy of your isolation.'

Deborah opened her eyes and found she was rocking herself on the bed, her lashes wet with tears. Her face burned, the kind of burning that comes from cold skin on snow. It was so painful to watch, that little ghost of a person who had been too foolish, too alone, too insecure to stand up for herself. Was she born to be a victim?

But she had struck back, for Bella Donna had been conceived that night, the only child of their barren union. Her birth, several months later, was a small, secret act of revenge to heat the icy wastes of their marriage bed. But Bella Donna was a panacea, not a cure. When Jeremy died, she'd thought that was the solution.

Deborah forced herself to uncurl, getting stiffly to her feet. Her heart was thudding, her body clammy with sweat. Her head ached. She hadn't seen Jeremy again. He had died in his sleep not long after, thanks to a lethal mixture of brandy and laudanum. They told her he'd looked peaceful and she had clung to that, just as she had clung to the certainty that the overdose had been accidental. Whatever his problems, Jeremy would never have shamed the Kinsail name with any hint of suicide. Besides, if he'd meant to kill himself, she was pretty certain he'd have chosen a gun or a riding accident. If there was an explanation for the many contradictions in her husband's behaviour, not least his determination to keep her officially tied to him, he had taken it to his grave.

Night had fallen. With shaking fingers, Deborah eventually managed to strike a light from the tinderbox for her candle. This life she had formed for herself since, it was not really a sanctuary but a cell, and of her own making. A prison, the bars she had erected to protect herself serving only to emphasise her loneliness. She could see that now. Elliot had made her see that and, thanks to Elliot, she was ready to make the first step towards confronting it, too.

Today, she had finished her story. If Mr Freyworth was right, it would give her freedom. The thought kindled warmth in her toes. Perhaps tomorrow she would write to some of her old friends. She was ready now to breach the gap she had allowed her marriage to wedge between them.

And Elliot? Deborah plumped up her pillows and clambered back into bed. *Oh, Elliot.* How she wished she had known him when she was whole. How much she wished she was not broken, but she was. She could patch herself up, and she could try to find some form of contentment, but she could never be anything other than alone. Perhaps the distance of time would make the past fade, but some things would never heal. Her one foray into love had damaged her and the scars were permanent.

The way Elliot had made her feel was beyond anything and far too much. It frightened her, but the idea of losing him from her life for ever frightened her more. She didn't want to retreat back into the gloom in which she existed before she knew him, but tempting, terrifyingly tempting as it was to continue down the path they had taken together in the boathouse, she knew it would be wrong.

She would fail him and then he would have every cause to despise her. She had to find a new path. Surely there must be some way to forge a friendship which was not so intimate? If she could manage to incorporate repaying him for what he had done for her, too, that would be even better. Happily deluding herself by focusing on this knotty problem, Deborah fell asleep.

'You've made up your mind, then? Elizabeth will be pleased.' Alexander Murray swallowed the remnants of his sherry and put the glass back down carefully on the table at his side. His appearance was as reticent as his temper. Neither tall nor short, fat nor thin, his hair was what his doting wife liked to call strawberry blonde and most others would—rather more accurately—describe as ginger. His pale complexion had an unfortunate tendency to freckle in the sun. Alexander was not the kind of man who stood out in a crowd and nor would he wish to.

Despite which, he had a business acumen second to none. In the City, he was known as The Oracle. In the rather more recondite world of Government financing, to which he lent his considerable expertise in considerable secrecy, he was revered. His position as one of the fast-growing Empire's unofficial bankers made Alexander's rather large ears privy to a wealth of information, most of it unwelcome, a very little of it useful, and some of it downright distasteful to his Scots sensibilities. 'I see the Peacock has been up to his tricks again,' he said.

Across from him, Elliot managed to disguise his surprise at the sudden change of subject with a relaxed smile. 'Yes, you have to almost admire the devil. He's clearly smart.'

'More than that. I would say he was driven.'

Elliot raised an enquiring brow. 'Why do you say that?'

'The press concentrate on the crime, of course, but it seems to me that there is a pattern forming in terms of the victims.'

'Really? Do elaborate.'

Alexander beetled his rust-coloured brows. 'They

all are, or were, involved in some way with the armed forces. It strikes me that this Peacock fellow might be a military man with an axe to grind.'

'I see.' Elliot was not one of those fooled by his brother-in-law's unassuming ways but he had, it seemed, underestimated him none the less. 'Have you shared this interesting theory with anyone?'

'Of course not. I have no desire to play the blood-hound,' Alexander said contemptuously.

'Then why are you telling me?'

'You're an ex-soldier, I thought you might have an opinion. Come on, man, don't look so surprised. Your views on how the men were treated are well known. I would imagine you might even be sympathetic to the Peacock's cause.'

'I heartily approve of his choice of victims, if that's what you mean. A more deserving bunch of miscreants I cannot imagine.'

'Aye, but my point is, would a regular soldier know that?' Alex steepled his fingers. 'I mean, some of the things taken—that diamond of Kinsail's, for example,' he said airily, 'you'd need insider information to know it even existed.'

'Insider information which you are obviously privy to,' Elliot said drily. 'I saw no report of a diamond in the newspaper.'

Alexander smiled ruefully. 'No, Kinsail kept that to himself, but it was the Peacock all the same. How would such a fellow come by that kind of information, do you think? If you ask me, this Peacock was involved in espionage.'

Elliot shrugged.

'You worked as a spy for the Government during the war, did you not?'

'What the deuce are you trying to imply?' Elliot asked impatiently.

'Lizzie would break her wee heart if anything happened to you,' Alexander said, his face becoming grim. 'I love that lassie. What she sees in me I don't know, but whatever it is, I'm eternally grateful. I won't have her upset, you understand me?'

'You have no cause to worry.'

'Aye, but I do worry, Elliot,' Alexander said with a sigh. 'I need your word.'

'I've said, you've no cause to worry.'

The basilisk look made Alexander swallow the words of protest he had been about to utter. It was easy to see what it was that had made the man such a fine soldier. 'I'm relieved to hear it. She's fretting about you, you know.'

'She has no reason to. Have you set a date for going north yet? Lizzie tells me that she's set on having that bairn of yours born in the ancestral home.'

'Did she?' Alexander's face softened. 'She's a wee darling, that sister of yours. I'm a lucky man.'

Discovering somewhat to his surprise that he agreed, for domesticity had never appealed to him, Elliot got to his feet to show his brother-in-law to the door. He was restless after his guest left. These last few days, he'd managed to occupy himself with disposing of the ivory figurines, paying overdue calls on friends, attending conscientiously to the little business his efficient bailiff sent his way. Avoiding thinking, in other words, he now admitted to himself as he prowled aimlessly from one room to another. Avoiding thinking, because he didn't know what to think, a state of mind to which he was wholly unaccustomed.

Elliot threw himself into the most uncomfortable chair in his book room and stared at a speck of dust on his Hessians. He still couldn't quite believe what had happened. To be so close. She had been reaching out to touch him. Just thinking about it made him sweat, and he'd thought about it a lot. What the hell had gone wrong? She had been so—and he had been so—*oh God!*

He got to his feet and flicked, unseeing, through the account book which lay open on his desk. It would have been mind-blowing. He drummed his fingers on the desk. He couldn't doubt that she'd wanted him there in the boathouse, he couldn't doubt the passion which flushed her cheeks, her breasts.

Her breasts. Elliot groaned. Dammit! *What the hell had happened in that marriage of hers?* It went against the grain, but he wished he'd asked Lizzie to sniff out the scandal. Ha! As if he'd have listened! The packet of books his source had delivered three days ago remained unopened in the drawer of his nightstand. Deborah's books. Which, despite the odds, he still hoped she'd trust him enough to tell him about herself.

Elliot picked up his letter opener and began methodically to slice through the topmost sheet of paper on the blotting pad. Why was he being so persistent? Why was giving up so impossible to contemplate? Despite the time they had spent together, in many ways Deborah was still an enigma and he was always a man who liked a challenge. Was that it? And if he succeeded in getting her to tell him her story, what then?

He slid the letter opener back into its holder. He didn't know. And he didn't need to think about it, because he hadn't succeeded yet. No point in worrying about the step after the next one, he told himself, blithely ignoring the fact that planning subsequent steps right to an end point had been his lifetime's *modus operandi.* He would give her time to finish that book of hers. She would realise she owed him an explanation. Sooner or later it would dawn on her that if she didn't, he would accuse her of using him merely to get her Peacock story.

Had she? Had she thought to pay him with sex, and then been unable to go through with it? For an appalling moment, Elliot considered this, dismissing it with immense relief. She wasn't capable of such guile. She would come round, he had only to be patient. Until then, what he needed was to do something practical with his time.

Relieved to be spared any further navel-contemplating, Elliot decided to pay a visit to Jackson's Salon in the hope that he would find someone on whom to expend some excess energy.

* * *

He returned two hours later, considerably refreshed, to find Deborah had called. 'I beg your pardon, I know you were not expecting me, but I finished the changes to my book in record time and I had to talk to you.' She smiled nervously.

'I hope you haven't been waiting too long,' Elliot said, ushering her into the parlour, surreptitiously checking his neckcloth, which he had retied without the benefit of a mirror, wondering if his hair was in a similar state of disarray.

'I wasn't sure if you would receive me after—after the last time.' Deborah stood in front of the empty grate. 'I wouldn't blame you if you didn't want to. Only I didn't want you to think—I was worried that you might think that I had—had pursued our acquaintance simply so that I could break into houses with you,' she said in a rush. 'I mean that was the point at first, but I hadn't thought—I didn't mean it to end as it did. And I hoped that despite the fact that I could not—and that I was so stupid—in short, I have come to see if there is a way that we can put that behind us and make a fresh start. If you want to. Though I'll understand if you don't and— and—well, that is all.'

Clearly, she was not ready to explain further. The cost of what she had already said was clear in the way she was clutching at her reticule as if it would save her from drowning. If it had been anyone else, he'd have given up the ghost a long time ago. But there was no one quite like Deborah. Was he prepared to wait? Stupid question. He had no intentions of failing, not now. Elliot disentangled Deborah's reticule from her fingers and took her hands between his. 'I'm happy to make a fresh start, but I won't promise you anything other than that. You must know how much I want you—it was perfectly obvious,' he said with a teasing smile. 'And no matter what convoluted logic is going on in that clever mind of yours, I know that you want me, too.'

'Elliot, I can't…'

His mouth smothered her protests. His lips were gentle, soft, and persuasive. He tugged her closer, so that their interlaced hands were pressed against his chest, and she made no attempt to resist. Warmth and light flooded her.

Elliot released her just as the warmth turned to heat. 'You see,' he said, kissing the tip of her nose, 'you can.'

She could think of nothing to say. Risking a glance at him through her lashes, she caught his smile and couldn't help returning it. She had missed him. She only just caught the words before they betrayed her.

'You look different,' he said.

'A new dress. Do you like it?' The walking dress had been an impulse purchase from Madame LeClerc's in Bond Street, which had cost her a ridiculous amount of her savings. The round gown of primrose-jaconet muslin was simple enough, but the three rows of French work around the hem made it much more fashionable and elegant than anything she had ever worn. The matching spencer was mint green with full puffed sleeves trimmed with satin, and the same satin lined her leghorn bonnet. She was absurdly pleased that Elliot had noticed. She had bought it for herself, because she wished to have some colour in her wardrobe, but she had worn it for him.

He took her hand and bowed over it. 'New gloves, too. You look quite charming.'

Deborah blushed. 'Thank you.'

'I've been sparring. I suspect I look as if I've been dragged through a hedge.'

'A little windswept.' She had missed him. She liked him this way, slightly dishevelled, smelling of clean sweat. Deborah reached up to straighten his neckcloth, then pushed back a lock of black silky hair from his brow, realising too late what she was doing and so deciding to pretend that she hadn't. 'Are you any good— as a boxer, I mean?' She allowed herself a moment to imagine him, stripped to the waist, his torso glistening. She liked that he was so tall. And so solid. Muscle-packed described him perfectly. Everything about him was so very masculine and so very Elliot. And so very, very not Jeremy. 'Have you got—is it science?'

Elliot laughed. 'I'm good enough, but I'm too tall. I spar simply to exercise. In the army, I spent my time breaking up mills rather than taking part in them. When it came to the fancy, Henry was your man.' His smile faded as he realised what he'd said. He never mentioned Henry in casual conversation. He ushered Deborah into a chair and sat down opposite her.

'Actually,' she said, 'I'm pleased you mentioned Henry. I've been thinking about him.'

'And?' Elliot stretched his legs out in front of him, crossing them at the ankles. He wondered what on earth was coming next. Judging by the way Deborah was making a play of untying her bonnet strings, they were getting to the crux of her visit.

'I'm embarrassed at how little I know of the war,' she said, having carefully placed her hat on the floor at her feet. 'The suffering that went on in the battle-fields, the suffering that goes on still, right under our noses. The sheer extent of it all, what your men and their families endured and surrendered so that we could have peace—it's overwhelming. So many men must have gone through what Henry did. Their families and friends and comrades must be struggling with their losses, too.'

Deborah paused, waiting for Elliot to comment, risking a glance at him, but his face was impassive. 'You've made me realise I've been walking about with my eyes closed—well, me and practically everyone else. The press make such a fuss about the begging and the pil-fering, the tavern brawls and the picking of pockets which have increased so dramatically since Waterloo. And housebreaking.' She risked a small smile. 'The reports about the Peacock's activities—they are inter-ested only in the fact that the law has been broken. No one thinks to question why.'

'Except my brother-in-law,' Elliot said drily. 'He was here this morning, subtly warning me off. He's put two and two together and near as dammit made four.'

Deborah's eyes widened. 'What will he do?'

'Oh, there's no need to fear, I gave him short shift and he's no idea of your involvement. Alex won't inform—the last thing he wants is to see me brought to justice, for that would upset Lizzie, and not upsetting Lizzie is all he really cares about.'

'All the same, Elliot, it is surely becoming far too risky for you to continue as the Peacock.'

He shrugged. 'It's more a case of running out of victims, to be honest. I've almost exhausted the list of those who can be held directly accountable. I could always turn Robin Hood, I suppose.' Elliot grinned. 'Steal from the rich to give to the deserving poor. That would certainly give me an occupation for life.'

'If you did that, I suspect your brother-in-law would turn Sheriff of Nottingham,' Deborah said with a chuckle.

She began to twist her gloves between her fingers. 'It's not enough though, is it? However much the Peacock can steal, there have been more than three hundred thousand men demobilised—you see, I do listen. No matter how successful you are, the need will always be too great. Three hundred thousand men, Elliot— it's such an incredible number. And what about the thousands and thousands who did not come home, the thousands more who are too maimed to look for work? Against such a mountainous problem, housebreaking, no matter how successful, can only scratch the surface of need.'

'You put it depressingly well.'

'I'm not trying to make what you've done sound pal-

try,' Deborah said earnestly. 'What you've done is—
is—I can't tell you how much I admire you. You have
made me realise how inward-looking I have allowed my
own life to become. You've made me think and you've
made me want to help. I don't care that you've broken
the law to further your aims, the law deserves to be
broken, if doing so helps just a little.'

Elliot's mouth curled into a smile once more. 'Thank
you,' he said. 'I shall employ you to speak on my behalf
at my trial, should it come to that.'

'I sincerely hope it shall not,' Deborah replied curtly.

'Then we are at one on that,' he said, regretting the
flippant tone immediately as she began to retreat behind
her haughty look. 'I'm sorry, I didn't mean to upset you.'

Deborah studied him for a moment, her lips pursed.
Obviously deciding he passed muster, she gave one of
her serious little nods that always, rather perversely,
made Elliot want to laugh. He refrained and instead
gave her an encouraging look. 'You have a plan for
raising funds without breaking and entering. Go on, I
promise you I'm interested.'

'Very well, then. Pamphlets and preaching are how
philanthropists who aren't housebreakers raise money,
but pamphlets are such dull things and preachers are
generally more worthy than interesting. It is no wonder that they raise more hackles than funds,' Deborah
said caustically. 'I think what we need is a story. A real
story about a real man, something dramatic, not a dull
old piece of polemic. If we could tell people what this
man was really like—funny, brave and flawed—if we

could show, in the language of a novel, what happened to him, how he suffered and died—how could they *not* listen? If we could do that, no one would be able to ignore his legacy.'

Deborah spoke quickly in the rush to make him understand, to share her enthusiasm for her idea, leaning forwards in her seat, her gaze fixed on his. 'I'm talking about Henry's story, Elliot. Henry's bravery, Henry's sacrifices, Henry's life cut tragically short—that's a story that needs to be told, don't you think? I'm a writer, I can tell it, but I need your help. What do you say?' She sat back and tucked a non-existent strand of hair behind her ear, gazing at him expectantly.

'I'm not sure what to say,' Elliot answered, somewhat dazed. 'What exactly are you asking of me?'

'Tell me about Henry. Show me where all the money the Peacock earns goes. Help me to understand what else needs to be done. Help me to reach those who won't or don't listen now. Such a story could make a huge difference, in the right hands. Your hands, for instance.'

'What would I do with it?'

'I don't know,' Deborah said candidly. 'I was hoping that you'd have some ideas.' She grinned. 'I'd rule out becoming a Member of Parliament, though. Frankly, the more I think about it, the less I can see you joining political forces with the likes of Wellington.'

'There we are in complete agreement.' Elliot got to his feet and disentangled Deborah's new gloves from her restlessly twisting fingers, putting them out of reach on the window seat along with her bonnet, which he retrieved from the floor. 'My sister and her husband have been making a concerted effort to introduce me to the many members of the Establishment in their acquaintance, but I'm sorry to say that the more I see of the lot of them, the more I am certain that I don't want to join their club.'

'Despite the fact that there would be a delicious irony in knowing that they had taken a Government spy-turned-housebreaker for one of their own, I think you're right,' Deborah said. 'Elliot, I don't pretend to have a fully formed battle plan, but I do believe that I have the kernel of a very powerful weapon. I want so desperately to help and I believe that doing so will give me a purpose that I lack.'

Deborah fished for her gloves, found her lap empty and began to lace her fingers together instead. 'You see, I am being honest. I cannot pretend to be wholly altruistic.' She had had no intention of saying anything of the ghosts which she had set loose these last few days, so it had taken her unawares, this sudden temptation to speak. But where to begin? And how much could she say, before Elliot began first to pity, then to despise her? She couldn't do it. He was the only person in her life who had no connection with her past and she wanted to keep it that way. 'I have been at a loss, since Jeremy died,' she said awkwardly instead.

'You told me once that you didn't know who you were.'

'Did I?' Deborah grimaced. 'Well, at least I know now who I *don't* want to be. I've had enough of being

Jeremy's widow. And enough of being—of writing the stories I write. It's time for a change.'

'For both of us, you mean?' Elliot said wryly.

Deciding it was wiser not to rise to this bait, Deborah shrugged.

Elliot got to his feet, gazing sightlessly out of the window. 'It's a new approach, there's no doubt about it,' he said. 'Do you really think you can write something which will sell?'

'I have done before. This will certainly be different. I don't know, but I'm willing to try.'

Elliot held up his hands in mock surrender. 'Then so, too, am I,' he said, laughing. 'If only they would allow women into politics, I'd put you forwards. You have most expertly manoeuvred me into a corner.'

'Yes, but is it one from which you wish to escape?'

She was offering him a get-out, but Elliot had already decided not to accept it. Deborah's eyes had a sparkle to them today; there was a vibrancy about her that he hadn't seen in the cold light of day before. It roused him, just as it had when they had broken into houses together. He was touched, too, not so much by what she proposed as by the thoughtfulness and understanding which had led to it. Whether something productive would come of their collaboration he had no idea, but the opportunity it offered to postpone thinking about the future made Elliot more than happy to agree. That, and the rather more enticing opportunity her proposition presented. 'You realise,' he said musingly, 'that we'd be forced into each other's company for significant amounts of time if we're to do this properly?'

Deborah studied her hands. 'I am prepared to suffer for our cause, if you are,' she said lightly.

Suppressing a smile, Elliot tugged on the bell by the fireplace. He was glad he had resisted opening that parcel of books. Relieved he had resisted the temptation to dig into the scandal which Lizzie had hinted surrounded Jeremy's death. Here was the opportunity to persuade Deborah to trust him enough to confide in him herself. 'Champagne,' he ordered the astonished underling who answered the summons. 'Unconventional, I know, in the middle of the day,' he said to Deborah, in response to her raised eyebrow, 'but that seems to me a perfect reason to drink it, for you are the most unconventional female I have ever met.'

Relieving his servant of the tray when he returned a few minutes later, Elliot closed the door firmly behind him. 'Stand up, I have a toast to make.' He handed Deborah a glass full of bubbles. 'To a unique partnership and a most unique woman,' he said, smiling. 'Let us drink to our success. To us.'

His smile was half-mocking, wholly sensual. Their eyes met and locked. A shock of awareness made Deborah's skin prickle. 'To us,' she said. As she touched her glass to Elliot's, she imagined their lips meeting. She sipped and the champagne bubbles tickled her tongue. The fierce force of his gaze made her look up again. The message in those dark eyes reflected her thoughts. Mesmerised, Deborah stepped into his arms.

The touch of his lips on hers made her head spin. Save for that first time in the park, she had never kissed him in daylight before—not properly. It felt different. His mouth was warm on hers, his hands cradled her face, making her feel precious. Their lips clung, then parted. It was the sweetness of it which dazed her. The perfection of it. The completeness, for it was a beginning and an end in itself. She touched Elliot's cheek, rough with the day's growth of stubble. His thumbs stroked the line of her jaw. Their eyes met in a smile which was different, too. Like the kiss, a beginning and an end in itself.

Deborah disengaged herself and Elliot let her go. She lifted her glass again. 'And to Henry,' she said.

'To Henry,' Elliot replied gruffly.

Chapter Eight

The spent the next hour laughing over foolish plans and drinking the champagne. 'I think the bubbles have gone to my head,' Deborah told Elliot as she struggled with her bonnet strings, 'for this ribbon simply refuses to co-operate.'

'Here, let me.'

'Certainly not. Gentlemen don't tie lady's ribbons.'

'No, more often than not they untie them.' Elliot untangled the crushed satin from Deborah's fingers. It hadn't occurred to him that half a bottle of champagne would go to her head, but he was amused and charmed by the effect.

'Have you untied many ribbons?' Deborah asked, grasping Elliot's wrist and quite ruining the bow he had been about to finish.

'A gentleman never discusses such things.'

'You are a spy and a housebreaker, which should pre-clude you from being a gentleman.' Deborah thought this over, frowning. 'But it doesn't. How strange. So, have you known lots and lots of beautiful women?'

'Lots.'

'And drunk champagne with them, in the middle of the afternoon?'

An image of himself, sprawled naked on a bed with satin sheets, popped into Elliot's head. Rose satin. He'd hated those sheets. He couldn't for the life of him remember who they belonged to, though.

'You have!' Deborah exclaimed indignantly.

Despite the champagne, her gaze was remarkably clear-sighted. She would know if he lied. 'I have,' Elliot confessed with a wicked smile, 'but I've never done it with all my clothes on.' He straightened Deborah's bonnet. 'You, madam, have the honour of that first,' he said, planting a kiss on the tip of her nose. 'Though if you were willing, I would of course be more than happy to oblige you by divesting us both of clothes and calling for another bottle.'

'Oh! That was…'

'Outrageous? Shocking? Scandalous?'

'Delightful, is what I was going to say, actually,' Deborah said, turning up her nose, 'but since you obviously didn't mean it, I shan't oblige you now.'

For a startled moment, Elliot was quite speechless. It was her eyes that gave her away, positively dancing with mirth. 'You are a minx, did you know that?'

The low, husky note of his laughter whispered over her skin, making her acutely aware of his masculinity, making her intensely aware of her own femininity.

Deborah's smile wobbled as heat washed over her. Her heart began to beat erratically. Her mouth was dry. She wanted him to kiss her again. She wanted him. The intensity of her wanting made her reach for him. 'Elliot.'

His laughter faded as he caught the hand she held out to him. She saw it in his eyes, the reflection of her desires, and it was the strength of it which brought her to her senses. Too much. 'I think I should go home now.'

Elliot hesitated. His fingers twined with hers. Then he nodded. 'Perhaps you should.' He rang the bell, asked his servant to call a hack, then retrieved her gloves from the window seat and helped her button them. 'I'll call for you tomorrow.'

'Yes.'

'Deborah.' He tilted her chin up, so she could not avoid looking at him. 'Whether we are fully clothed or naked as nature intended, you are the only woman I want to drink champagne with in the middle of the day. Or the middle of the night, for that matter. I promise.'

'Oh.'

'Exactly,' Elliot said, relieved to see that she was smiling again. Quite enchanted, he kissed her. Then he straightened her bonnet again. He would have kissed her again, had not his servant interrupted them with the information that her transport was waiting.

'I thought we'd start at the dispensary in Spitalfields,' Elliot said, extending a hand to help Deborah into his curricle. He picked up the reins and set the horses off at a smart trot. Traffic was light at this time of day, after the rush of morning deliveries, before the modish hour for shopping. 'How is your head today?'

'Much clearer, thank you,' Deborah replied primly, keeping her eyes fixed firmly ahead.

'Don't be embarrassed, you have no need to be.'

'I got hiccups in the hackney on the way home. I am eight and twenty, far beyond the age for hiccups. It was mortifying.'

'I thought you were quite charming, in your cups.'

'I was not in my cups!' Deborah exclaimed indignantly. 'A little half-sprung perhaps, but hardly jug-bitten,' she said, sliding him a mischievous smile.

Elliot gave a shout of laughter. 'How the devil came you to be so familiar with such terms?'

Deborah chuckled. 'I have my sources,' she said, tapping the side of her nose.

'Touché, madame.' She was dressed in one of her older gowns today, of a rather washed-out blue, with a serviceable grey pelisse and plain bonnet. It was practical and wholly appropriate, given their destination, but Elliot was much relieved that her mood was not as sombre as her apparel. This caustic, skittish mix of humour of hers appealed to his own. It pleased him to see that the bluish shadows below her eyes were fading. Just having her at his side pleased him. It wasn't just the nearness of her, her skirts brushing his buckskins, her shoulder brushing his as they turned a corner, it was more than that. It was her, whatever it was that made her Deborah. He liked it.

As they made their way from the town houses and

neatly kept squares of the west to the bustle of Clerken-
well, she began to ply him with questions, scribbling
notes in the book she extracted from a pocket in her
gown with a little silver pencil. Past Moorfields, where
Signor Lunardi's balloon had taken off, the impressive
frontage of the Bethlem Hospital distracted her temporarily, but then she returned to her questions. Those, too,
were in her little notebook, Elliot was amused to see, as
she ticked one off. 'You are nothing if not thorough,' he
said. 'A Bow Street Runner would be impressed with
your preparation.'

'I want to make as good a job of this as I can. Are
you laughing at me?'

'No, truly. I'm impressed.'

'I know how much it matters,' Deborah said.

'To both of us,' Elliot replied. They were past the
coaching inns of Bishopsgate, approaching Spitalfields now. Though the curricle was smart rather than
fashionable, his horses well matched but hardly prime
'uns, they were attracting much interest none the less.
'This place used to be the heart of silk manufacturing,
but most of the work is done in the countryside now.
Cheaper labour, more room for the new machines. You
wouldn't believe it, to look at the rundown state of the
place, but it was thriving not so long ago.'

It was like another world to Deborah. Scantily clad,
filthy children stared out from faces so gaunt their eyes
were made huge. The gutters streamed with effluvia
on which dogs, cats and rats almost as big as the cats
feasted. Raucous cries came from the open door of a gin

house. There were few horses on the road, but a good many hand carts, the men bowed over them as dirty and badly clad as the children. The stench, which had been creeping up on them since Bishopsgate, was eye-watering. The air tasted thick and ripe. In contrast, the streets, the buildings, the people, seemed to be sepia-washed, almost colourless, as if dipped in depression. Appalled, and no little intimidated, Deborah put away her notebook and shuffled a little closer to Elliot.

They skirted round the worst of the rookery. 'The few weavers who are left have moved out of there,' he said as they bypassed Dorset Street. 'A good many of our men have ended up in places like this—in one of the rat-infested lodging houses if they're lucky, sleeping rough if they're not. It's slightly better here, around Christ Church—at least some of the water is clean. Cholera and typhus are rife, though.' He pulled up in front of a large house in significantly better repair than the rest. 'This belonged to one of the richer silk merchants.'

As Elliot bartered with a bold child over the price for the safekeeping of his curricle and pair, Deborah surveyed the building. It was a pleasing but simple edifice of red brick with four windows on either side of the door, nine on the floor above that, and a set of dormers build into the low-pitched roof. The shallow flight of steps were semi-circular, leading up to a plain black-painted door framed by two Doric columns topped with a swan-necked pediment into which was set the institution's motto. *'Nil desperandum,'* she read. She eyed the gleaming windows, the shining brass door fittings and the pristine white steps—such a stark contrast to the streets through which they had just driven. 'It's certainly a shining example of cleanliness, but what is it?'

Elliot rapped on the door. 'It was an army hospital during the last years of the wars. After Waterloo they closed it down, despite the fact that many of the men were still in dire need of medical services—it can take months for the wounds from an amputation to heal properly, sometimes longer if it is aggravated by pressure sores. The men brought any number of recurrent fevers back from Spain and Portugal, too, and some—war is a harsh thing, Deborah. Some men are wounded in the mind. Those poor bastards ended up in Bethlem and places like it.'

The door was opened by a middle-aged man dressed in plain black livery. Despite the wooden peg which formed the lower half of his left leg, his carriage was upright. Seeing Elliot, he stood smartly to attention and saluted. 'Major Marchmont, sir.'

'Good to see you, Sergeant Lyle. This is—'

'Mrs Napier,' Deborah said hurriedly. 'How do you do?'

'Mrs Napier is interested in what you do here, Lyle. I'm just going to show her around, if that's all right?'

'Perfectly, sir. Anything I can do to help, you just give me a shout, I'll be right here. And I'll keep an eye on that gig of yours, too,' the old soldier said, with a meaningful look at the boy holding the reins.

'Lyle was twenty years in the army. He served under

me in Spain. He knew Henry, too, you might want to talk to him at some point,' Elliot said, ushering Deborah towards a heavy green baize door at the back of the hallway.

A volley of noise hit them as he pushed the door open and Deborah stopped on the threshold, staring around her in astonishment. They were in a large room which looked as if it ran the full length of the house. With windows on the three sides which did not adjoin the back of the house, it was bright with the late-morning sunlight and alive with industry.

'Despite what the press will have us believe, what most men want is to work,' Elliot said, raising his voice to compensate for the cacophony of sound. 'For those who have lost limbs, finding work is nigh on impossible simply because they have no access to artificial limbs and bath chairs are quite beyond the means of those who need them most.'

'So you established a workshop to provide what was needed,' Deborah said, looking around her in awe. 'And who better to make such things than those who require them in the first place,' she added, noticing what she had not seen when she first entered the room, that every single one of the workers was an amputee. 'May I take a closer look?'

'Of course you can, but I'll let Captain Symington here do the explaining, since he's the one in charge. How are you, George?'

Captain Symington grinned and punched Elliot on

the shoulder. 'I wondered why we hadn't seen your ugly face for a while,' he said, looking at Deborah.

'This is Mrs Napier. She is interested in the work you do,' Elliot said repressively.

'How do you do, ma'am,' Captain Symington said, making his bow.

'Captain Symington, it is a pleasure.' Deborah said, hesitating to extend her hand, for the captain's right sleeve was empty, but he noticed her unease and extended his left quite naturally.

'Why don't you leave me to show Mrs Napier round?' the captain said to Elliot. 'It's not often we get such charming company, and it's certainly the first time it's come courtesy of you. Go on, leave us to it, that's an order. You don't outrank me here, you know.'

'Deborah?'

'I'll be fine, Elliot.'

He left them reluctantly, for he suspected George's motives, though he could not very well say so without leaving himself open to questions he had no wish to be asked. The charmer was already leaning on Deborah's arm. He could not hear what he was saying, but he was leaning damned close to say it. And Deborah was smiling up at him, laughing, dammit! He had a good mind to warn her.

Elliot sighed and unclenched his fists. What possible harm could come to her in a factory full of men? Several things jumped immediately into his mind. His fists clenched again. He unclenched them again. George would take care of any importunities and, if George importuned, he would take care of George! Dammit, he was making something out of nothing. George was a charmer, but he was a gentleman and played by a gentleman's rules. He would know that Deborah was not— Deborah was—Deborah was not...

Elliot sighed again. Across the room, Deborah had slipped free of George's embrace to inspect one of the new chairs with wheels. Satisfied—or telling himself that he should be—Elliot went in search of Sergeant Lyle.

'It is really most ingenious,' Captain Symington said. 'Try it for yourself.'

Deborah sat gingerly into the movable chair. It was surprisingly comfortable, with a padded leather seat and a rest for her feet, though she had some difficulty arranging her skirts in its narrow confines.

'You see, these two large wheels can be manipulated with a bit of practice, and the little castor on the back gives you balance so that you can propel yourself around without any help.'

Deborah tried to do as he said, but her hands made no impression on the wooden wheels at all. Captain Symington took hold of the little handles set into the back of the chair. 'How long have you known Elliot?' he asked.

Deborah clutched at the arms of the chair as it began to move. It was a most unnerving experience. 'A little while,' she replied.

'And how came you to meet?'

'We had business in common,' she said, just as she had answered Lizzie.

'What does your husband do, Mrs Napier?'

'He is dead, Captain Symington.'

'Ah.'

'I cannot see your face, Captain Symington, but I suspect the quality of that ah.'

He pushed the chair back to the work bench and held out his hand to help her up from it. 'You are quite right, Mrs Napier, I am very curious,' he said with a disarming smile. 'I've not seen Elliot with a female, save that terrifying sister of his, since we came back to England.' Captain Symington frowned. 'He's a good man, you know. I don't know anyone I respect more. This place—it was his idea, by and large, and though the money comes from his mysterious benefactors, the grit and determination to get it off the ground were all Elliot's. He feels guilty for coming through it all unharmed. I've told him all of us feel guilty who've survived, but you know Elliot, he has to take the brunt of it. Did he tell you about…?'

'Henry. Yes, yes, he did.'

'I was there when they brought him into the field hospital—I lost my arm in the same battle. I thought at one point that Elliot was going to go up into the mountains himself, which would have been madness, for not even he could have carried Henry back without help. He was mad with rage. Then when Henry died, he almost stopped speaking. Went about like the walking dead himself.'

'I'm going to write about Henry. That's why I'm here.'

'What do you mean?'

She told him, as they wandered around the workshop, breaking off to admire the workmanship of artificial limbs and the surprising variety of devices which the men had invented to give those like themselves some independence. 'Do you think it will work?' she asked, when they had completed the tour of the school room which took up the second floor.

George Symington shook his head. 'I've no idea, but it's certainly an original notion. May I ask why you're doing this?'

'I want to help.'

'Yes, but it can't just be that. It's a big commitment you're making, if you don't mind my saying so—you must have a more personal reason.'

She had relaxed in his company this last hour, but under the keen scrutiny of his handsome face Deborah drew back. 'It's a cause worthy of significant commitment. I don't need another reason,' she said.

Under that haughty look, Captain Symington flushed, taken aback at the transformation. 'I'll take you back to Elliot,' he said. 'In fact, here he is.' With relief, he saw the major waiting at the foot of the stairs. His farewells were formal, his bow reserved.

'What did you say to George?' Elliot asked, amused and relieved by his friend's obvious retreat.

'I have no idea,' Deborah answered blithely. 'I expect he is just worn out with all my questions.' She tapped her silver pencil on her notebook. 'I still have plenty more—may we visit the dispensary?'

'It's not pleasant.'

'I don't expect it to be, but how can I tell others what I have not seen for myself?'

'Isn't that what writers do, use their imagination?'

'I've done plenty of that, believe me,' Deborah said, thinking of Bella Donna, 'but there are some things best not left to the imagination.'

'Such as housebreaking?'

'And tending the sick.'

'If you're sure,' Elliot said.

'I'm sure,' Deborah replied, taking his arm.

The dispensary took up the second floor and the attics of the main house, with beds for the most serious cases. Though most of the patients were veterans and their families, it was fast becoming a much-needed part of the Spitalfields community. No one was turned away.

After an hour, Deborah was reeling with emotion and information. As they made their way back down the central staircase of the house, she leaned heavily on Elliot's arm. 'I'm sorry, I feel a little faint.'

She staggered, slipped on the marble step and would have fallen had Elliot not caught her. 'Have you eaten today?'

'I forgot. I was so excited about coming here.'

'And last night?'

'I went straight to my bed after I returned from your

house.' She clutched at the ornate wrought-iron banister. 'I'll be fine in a minute. Perhaps a glass of water.'

'You're not drinking the water here.' She was alarmingly pale. Elliot checked his pocket watch. After three and she had eaten nothing since yesterday. He cursed under his breath. 'Have you an ambition to join the patients upstairs?' he said, scooping her into his arms.

'Elliot, put me down, I'm perfectly capable of walking.'

'I know, you are eight and twenty, and more than old enough to do so without help, one would have thought,' he said, ignoring her protest, 'but since you don't seem capable of feeding yourself, I'm not going to trust you to walk. Stop fussing, put your arm around my neck and we'll get along much better. Lyle, is my curricle still intact?'

'It is, Major. Would you be needing a hand there with Mrs Napier?' the sergeant asked, grinning.

'I don't think so. Make your farewells, Deborah. And much as I'm enjoying your wriggling,' Elliot said, lowering his voice for her ears only, 'I'd prefer if you waited until we are alone.'

Blushing, Deborah cast him a fulminating glance. 'Goodbye, Sergeant Lyle. Thank you for your hospitality. I hope the next time I visit that you will spare me some of your time. I would very much like to hear about your experiences. I regret I am not at liberty to do so at present,' she said tightly.

'Major Marchmont knows best, I'm sure, madam,' Sergeant Lyle said, failing to stifle his laugh.

'That was mortifying,' Deborah said, pulling the rug from Elliot's hands to tuck it around her legs herself.

'Think how much more embarrassed you'd have been if you fainted.'

'I never faint.'

'You looked damned close to it there.' Elliot tossed sixpence to his makeshift groom and threw a handful of coppers at the ragged collection of his cohorts, earning himself a cheer. 'You don't look after yourself,' he said, urging the horses into a walk.

'I am perfectly capable—'

'Deborah.'

She folded her arms across her chest. 'What?' she said belligerently.

'Why don't you just sit back and let me look after you?'

'I don't need looking after.'

'You do. And I want to. So why not let me?'

All of a sudden, she felt like crying. Before she could stop it, a tear plopped on to her cheek. She scrubbed it away with her glove. 'I'm sorry. Perhaps I do need something to eat.' Another tear fell, and then another. She turned her face away, desperately trying to compose herself, hoping Elliot hadn't noticed. She cast him a surreptitious glance and her eyes clashed with his. He'd noticed. 'Sorry,' she said again.

He fumbled in his coat pocket and produced a large, pristine white handkerchief. 'Stop apologising, there's no need. It's my fault. The dispensary was too much for you. I shouldn't have taken you there.'

'I insisted that you did.' Deborah mopped her face. Elliot's mouth was set, his brows drawn. His scar showed white. She knew him well enough now to surmise that his anger was turned on himself and not her. Guilt made her confess what she would much rather have kept to herself. 'It wasn't the dispensary. It was just that no one ever offers to look after me. There, that's made me sound quite pathetic.'

'I wish you would not describe yourself so,' Elliot said harshly. 'You are very far from pathetic.'

'Sorry.'

'Stop saying sorry, too.'

'Sorry. I mean—sorry.' Deborah managed a weak smile. 'I promise I'll eat something as soon as I get home.'

'You're not going home yet. I'm taking you to dinner.'

'I'm not dressed for dinner.'

'It's early and I'm not proposing anywhere fashionable. There's an excellent coaching inn at Holborn, the Old Bell, where the food is very good. No, don't bother protesting,' Elliot added. 'Short of grabbing the reins, there is nothing you can do, so save your breath and let me concentrate on my driving. Much as it pains me to admit it, the volume and variety of traffic on London's roads rather tests my handling of the ribbons to its limit. They'd never have me at the Four Horse Club.'

'I think you are being too modest; driving a curricle and pair is not exactly easy. Though I admit, I can't see you in a yellow-and-blue-striped waistcoat, let alone a spotted cravat.'

'God, no, no more can I. How do you know what they wear?'

'Jeremy was a member,' Deborah said shortly. 'Horses were his greatest passion. It was one of the few things we had in common.' She chewed her bottom lip. 'Actually, it might have been the only one.'

She lapsed into silence and the haunted look was back in her eyes and her complexion wan. Compassion and anger kept Elliot quiet, though his grip on the reins tightened enough to make his horses aware of it. Their steps got out of kilter and it took him a few moments to rectify the problem; when he next looked at Deborah, her eyes had drifted closed.

They remained so until he pulled in to courtyard of the Old Bell, when she blinked and looked about her in surprise. 'Are we here already?' She descended shakily, glad of Elliot's arm as his curricle was led efficiently off over the cobbles to the stables.

The inn was large, the original tavern having been much altered, with a two-storey extension built on to the original gable wall, and another, three-storey building at right angles to this, the whole joined on the first floor by a precarious set of galleries.

Elliot steered Deborah to the open door of the main building, where the landlord, in pristine white apron, was waiting for them. 'A private parlour, and the lady will wish to freshen up,' he said. 'Dinner as soon as you can bring it.'

'Certainly, sir. You have timed your visit well, if I may say so; you've just missed the Bristol mail. I have an excellent parlour at the back, away from the noise of the tap room.' The landlord snapped his fingers and ordered a maid to take madam upstairs, and to fetch a jug of hot water, then led Elliot through to a small parlour where a fire was already burning.

Fifteen minutes later, Deborah joined him. The table was already set with pewter plates, a jug of claret and a loaf of bread, still warm from the oven. 'I feel much better, but you're right, I am hungry.'

'There's a white soup, a haunch of venison which I thought you'd prefer to mutton stew, but I wasn't sure, so I ordered the carp in case you fancied fish. There's asparagus and peas, too, and some mushroom fritters. They don't run to much in the way of dessert, but there is a Stilton which the landlord assures me is fine, and—'

'Stop,' Deborah said, laughing, 'you are not feeding an army now. It sounds lovely, Elliot, much better than bread and mousetrap, which is all that I have in my own kitchen,' she added, touched by the care he had taken. 'My mouth is already watering.'

She sat down at the table and took a sip of the wine. The food was excellent and Elliot an attentive host, putting the most succulent morsels on her plate, distracting her with witty anecdotes of make-do meals he had eaten on the campaign trail, so that she partook of every dish and ate far more than she normally would have.

The wheel of Stilton with quince jelly, was served by their host along with a fine port, which Deborah declined. Outside, dusk had fallen. As the door closed behind the landlord, the sound of a horn could be heard, the answering clatter of clogs on wooden boards rushing to the courtyard as a stage coach pulled in.

'Thank you,' Deborah said with a contented sigh. 'That was quite delicious.' The maid who cleared the table had lit the candles. Their reflections flickered in the bevelled glass of the window beneath which the table was set. It was an intimate scene. Domestic.

She and Jeremy had never sat together thus, so comfortably together. The arrival of the port was the signal for Deborah to leave the table, even when they were alone. She propped her chin on her hands, drowsy with the heat and the food and the wine. 'At Kinsail Manor, the dining table seats twenty-four,' she said, half to herself. 'It is so old there are no leafs to be removed and Jeremy was so punctilious about etiquette, he insisted that we sat at opposite ends, even when we were alone. I'd forgotten that. I'd forgotten how fond of pomp and ceremony he was. There was an epergne, a hideous thing, some sort of heirloom, that sat in the middle of the table which made conversation absolutely impossible. I had it removed to a side table once, but Jeremy had it moved back. He couldn't bear anything to be changed in his precious Manor, which was strange, considering how happy he seemed to be to let the place go to rack and ruin. I wondered, after he died, if it was deliberate, you know? A sort of self-inflicted punishment. He let himself go to rack and ruin, too.'

Her eyes were unfocused, lost in the past, but for the first time since he had known her, she seemed contemplative rather than troubled by what she saw. Elliot sipped his port, watching the emotions flitting over her face, almost afraid to move lest he break the mood.

Deborah began to cut the quince jelly which lay untouched on her plate into little cubes, using her left hand to hold the knife, resting her cheek on the other. 'He was indifferent to what we ate, too, provided it was served on the appropriate service with appropriate aplomb. The kitchens at Kinsail Manor are about as far from the dining room as it is possible to be, so whatever we had, it was nearly always cold. I tried to persuade him to have a new kitchen built, but the expense was prohibitive, he said. I suggested we move the dining chamber closer to the kitchen.' She laughed. 'You'd think I'd suggested that I be allowed to cast a vote in an election. He was appalled.' She put her knife down, looking in surprise at the quivering mass of quince she had cut. Her mouth drooped. 'Poor Jeremy. The Manor, the title—they meant so much to him. I wonder how different things would have been, if he'd had an heir.'

She sat up, suddenly conscious of the intensity of Elliot's gaze. He had what she called his fierce look. 'I am become maudlin,' she said, finishing the last of her wine. 'I think it is time I went home.'

'You would have liked children?' Elliot stayed her hand when she would have risen from the table.

'One cannot always have what one would like,' Deborah said lightly, though the lump rose in her throat all the same. She pushed back her chair and busied herself with putting on her bonnet, collecting her gloves and shawl.

'Tomorrow, if you wish, I can take you back to Spitalfields to talk to Lyle.'

'There is no need, I am sure I can get a hackney to take me.'

'You don't need to prove your independence to me. And before you say it, you're not beholden either. Our cause is a joint one, I thought we agreed?'

She opened her mouth to protest, but then thought the better of it and laughed. 'I'm not sure I like your ability to read my mind.'

'I wish I could read it more often.'

His smile was no more than a shadow, a sensuous tilt of his lips, which made her toes curl, her skin flush. Her own was uncertain. She wished she really could read his mind. Did he want to kiss her?

She had her answer when his lips claimed hers. It was the softest of kisses. One of his kisses-for-no-other-purpose-than-kissing kisses. Gentle. Sweet. And over, before it could become more. Elliot straightened her shawl, tucked her hand into the crook of his arm and led her out into the bustling night.

Chapter Nine

'Well?' Deborah hovered in the open doorway. 'Did you read it, or should I go out again? Only if I walk around the square another time your neighbours will think I'm up to something.'

Elliot got up from the seat at her desk and untangled her gloves from her fingers. She was pale, there were circles under her eyes again, testament to the long nights she'd spent with her pen. 'You can stay. I've finished it.'

'Oh.' She sank down suddenly into her chair by the hearth, her knees turned to jelly. She felt sick. She pressed her hands together tight to stop them from shaking. 'And?' Her voice was no more than a whisper.

Elliot sat down opposite, stretching his legs out in front of him. He had been planning on teasing her, but he was no proof against that anxious white face. 'And, I think it's absolutely brilliant,' he said with a grin.

'You're not just saying that because you don't want to offend me?'

'Deborah, it's wonderful. Truly. It's funny and moving and it's angry and it's tragic.'

'And Henry?'

Elliot swallowed hard. 'It was difficult to read. You've captured him so well.'

Deborah got up and caught his hand against her cheek, kneeling at his feet. 'I'm so glad. I wanted so much to get him right.'

'Well, you did.' They stayed in silence for a few moments, Elliot's hand resting on her head. 'The guilt of the survivor—is that what you think I suffer from?'

His eyes were dark, the lines around them etched deep with his frown. Deborah smoothed the scar on his brow. 'Not just you,' she said carefully. 'Almost every man I spoke to felt it to a degree, but I think you suffer from it more because you came through unharmed. You have no scars to show, save these little ones.' She kissed her fingertips and pressed them to the other scar, just below his hairline. 'But it doesn't mean you don't have other scars, which no one can see.'

Except you. The words hung in the air between them, unsaid. These last few weeks had gone by so quickly, he hadn't noticed how far he had dropped his guard, had been aware only that in Deborah's company he could speak his mind without thinking, without worrying that she would be shocked, or wouldn't understand.

'I can change it if it makes you feel uncomfortable,' Deborah said, displaying her ability to read his mind yet again. 'It's not as if Henry's friend is an accurate portrait of you, and it's only a draft. I don't want to upset you.'

Elliot smiled at her. He was always smiling at her.

'No. It was—difficult, but it's too good to change. Actually it's more than good, moving without being mawkish. And the battle scenes, so real without being bloodthirsty. You have a great talent.'

Deborah blushed with pleasure. 'Thank you.' She got to her feet, and paced over to the window. Her eyes were bright when she turned back to him. 'I can't tell you how much it means to me that you like it. Are you *sure* you do?'

Elliot laughed. He seemed to be doing a lot of that lately, too. 'It's perfect, I assure you. I hadn't realised you'd be finished so soon.'

'Well, as I said, it's only a draft, but the sooner the better, surely? I know that there's no immediate worry about funding for the dispensary, for Captain Symington told me that he had several new benefactors to add to the list.'

Deborah arranged her pens in a line on the blotter, her brows drawn together in a deep frown. Though she wanted to tell him, confidences still came so hard to her.

'What is it?' Elliot asked.

'I've something I want to tell you.'

'And you're not sure how to say it.' He led her over to the seat beside the fire. 'You know me well enough by now, surely? Just say it.'

Deborah smiled faintly. 'It's important. To me, anyway.' She plucked at a loose thread on the arm of her chair with her left hand. It came away in her fingers, leaving a tiny hole in the worn damask.

'You've taken off your wedding ring.'

Deborah examined the dent in her finger. The skin was pale, softer than the rest. 'Yesterday. I shall return it to Jacob. It's an heirloom. The only thing I have left of Jeremy's. Jacob will be relieved to have it back, though I doubt his wife will be particularly eager to wear it,' she said drily.

'What made you do it?' Elliot asked, realising as he did so how much he'd disliked that ring.

Deborah began to worry at another loose thread. 'That's what I wanted to tell you. Writing Henry's story has been a very emotional experience for me. Cathartic, I suppose. When I finished the draft, I knew it was good. Much better than anything I've written before. All that emotion. It made me realise how much was missing from my books.' She gave him a strange little smile. 'I appreciate that you haven't asked about them, I know you must have been curious.'

Elliot thought of the brown-paper parcel of books, still neatly wrapped, still sitting on the table by his bedside. 'Curious enough to obtain some copies for myself.'

Deborah's jaw dropped. 'You *knew*? How did you— did you *spy* on me? Have you read them?'

Elliot grinned. 'I have my sources. Of course I didn't spy on you, I just made enquiries. I've had them for weeks, but I haven't read them, I promise. I was waiting for you to tell me.'

'Good grief, how very self-restrained of you.'

Elliot gave a crack of laughter. 'Deborah, our entire relationship has been an exercise of remarkable self-restraint as far as I'm concerned. You know that.'

'Yes,' she whispered. So many times, over these last weeks, a touch, a glance, a brush of lips to cheek, one of those kisses-for-kisses'-sake kisses could have led to more. She knew he wanted her. She knew, too, that he was waiting for some sort of signal from her. Time and again, her desire for him led her to the edge, but her fear of failure kept her teetering there. At times, just looking at him made the muscles in her belly clench and perspiration break out in the small of her back. The silence between them was becoming charged. Deborah returned to her excavation of the arm of the chair. 'I was telling you about my writing.'

Elliot blinked, dragging his mind away from the delightful visions of Deborah naked that it conjured up so easily. 'Yes. So you were. Go on.'

Deborah pulled out another thread. It was longer than the first. She began to twine it round her fingers. 'You know, we both have a secret other, you and I. You have the Peacock and I have—I have Bella Donna.'

'Bella Donna?'

'That's the name of my heroine. It's a joke, really— you know, Deadly Nightshade. Beautiful and toxic. According to Mr Freyworth, my publisher, she is notorious.'

'You are the author of the Bella Donna books?'

'You've heard of them?'

'I've read one. Lizzie lent it to me.'

'Your sister, Lizzie?' Deborah squeaked in horror.

Elliot laughed. 'She is a great admirer of yours— though her husband, apparently, is not.' He shook his head in disbelief. 'I could not imagine you writing romances along the lines of Mrs Burney's, but I did not think your books were the kind that women hid from their husbands.'

'And husbands from their wives, if I am to believe Mr Freyworth,' Deborah said drily. 'Which one did you read? Did you like it?'

'*Hemlock.* I did like it. It was clever and funny, though the humour was very dark.' Elliot uncrossed his ankles and sat up, his expression quite bemused. 'The main thing I liked about it was that it was so subversive. Your Bella is voluptuous, but quite vicious—she really does enjoy humiliating her victims. What on earth made you think of such a female?'

Deborah had wound the thread so tight around her fingers that it was painful. 'Bella Donna is everything I am not, you see,' she said. 'No man can resist her and she is determined to live her life in her own way, even if she has to be cruel. She doesn't care who gets hurt as long as she gets what she wants, but she's not a hard-nosed harlot. She's like a diamond—she glitters and she's infinitely desirable, but she's hard, no one can hurt her. She's invincible.'

'And immensely popular, according to my sister.'

'Even more popular, thanks to the Peacock, if Mr Freyworth is to be believed.'

Elliot grinned. 'I wonder what Lizzie would make of that?'

'Elliot! You would not…'

'God, no, that would set the cat among the pigeons. Alex is already—but I told you that.'

'You're not planning another break-in, are you? Ever since you told me about your brother-in-law's suspicions, I've been worried. I couldn't bear you to be caught.'

'I still have several names on my list.' Elliot frowned. He hadn't actually thought much about the Peacock at all in the last few weeks. 'There is no real risk, Alex won't say anything. You worry too much.'

'Any *you* don't worry at all!' Deborah exclaimed. 'It's dangerous, Elliot.'

'This, coming from you, my two-time aider and abettor,' he teased. 'Wasn't it you who told me that the Peacock was infallible?'

'It's not a laughing matter.'

'I won't tell you anything, then you won't have sleepless nights.'

'Why should it bother me?' Deborah asked caustically. 'It's not my neck that will be stretched.'

'I'm hoping that it won't be mine, either.'

'Are you sure about that? You told me once that you didn't care.'

He had. And he didn't. Then. And now? 'We were talking about you, not me,' Elliot said, mentally shrugging aside the issue of whether or not he had changed. 'Bella Donna, not the Peacock. What made you think of her? When did you start writing?'

Deborah made a face. 'It was at a—a low point in my marriage. There was—I knew we could not—that Jeremy and I—I knew it was over, even though he would not consider a separation. I still don't understand why he wouldn't. The Kinsail name, I suppose.'

'What happened?'

Deborah wrapped her arms around herself. 'It doesn't matter.'

'It obviously does,' Elliot said grimly.

She shook her head. 'What matters is that it made me fight back—through Bella. She was my—my secret weapon. While Bella wreaked revenge, I could just about bear the mess I had made of my life.' Realising that her nails were digging into her skin through her gown, Deborah forced herself to uncross her arms. 'It's not a mess now,' she said awkwardly. 'That's why I'm telling you. To thank you. Bella helped me survive the last years of my marriage, but lately—working with you, writing Henry's story—I've realised how much I've been living through her, hiding behind her. She's not protecting me any more, she's holding me back, and you've helped me realise that. I've decided to kill her off.' She smiled wanly. 'I've promised Mr Freyworth another book in payment for publishing Henry's story. He won't be too pleased when he discovers that it is Bella's final curtain.'

'You know,' Elliot said, getting to his feet, 'you are the most surprising woman I have ever met.' He pulled her from her chair, bowing low over her hand. 'I hardly know what to say, save that I salute you and I thank you for finally confiding in me. It means a lot, truly.' He turned her hand over and kissed her palm. 'All those secrets. You make me feel like an open book.'

'With many blank pages,' Deborah said sarcastically. Relieved to have finally spoken, she was flattered and fluttered by his reaction. The intensity of his gaze made her acutely conscious of her body beneath her new gown. Her palm tingled where his lips had lingered.

Elliot grinned and pushed back her sleeve to kiss her wrist. 'There's something I'm not clear about though,' he said.

'What is that?' Deborah's pulse fluttered under his mouth. Her corsets were laced too tight.

'Bella is such a very experienced woman. Most inventive.' Elliot's smile was wicked. 'I'm wondering where you got your material, because I'm pretty certain that it was not based on first-hand experience.'

Deborah flushed. 'If you must know, I found some books hidden in the library at Kinsail Manor. With pictures. That was the extent of my research.'

Elliot chuckled. 'So resourceful. I should have known.'

'You're not shocked?'

'Did you think I would forbid you to darken my doorstep, condemn you for corrupting the morals of society? That would be a bit rich, coming from a housebreaker, don't you think? I'm not shocked, but I am very, very intrigued. What sort of things does Bella get up to in the other books?'

'Elliot! I can't possibly...'

'What about those ivory figures we stole? Anything like that?'

'You're enjoying this! I should have guessed you would!' Deborah wanted to bite back the smile which plucked at the corners of her mouth in answer to that sensual curl of his lips, but she could not. It was delightful to discover that he found Bella as exciting as she did.

'I am, I admit it.' Elliot tucked Deborah's hair behind her ear, letting his fingers trail down the soft skin of her neck. 'What a vivid imagination you must have. Do you have a favourite—situation?'

Goosebumps rippled where he touched her. There was that tug of awareness between them as she met his eyes, and became conscious of the weight of his hand on her hip. 'How can I? As you pointed out, my experience is rather limited.'

Elliot caught his breath. 'You do realise that is paramount to a challenge?'

'I realise *you* would see it that way,' Deborah said, tilting her chin. '*I* am such an innocent, I meant no such thing.'

'Liar. Have I told you that you're irresistible?'

'Thus your remarkable exercise in constraint?' She could feel the rumble of his laughter vibrating through his chest. The release of her confession was making her reckless. Deborah put her arms around Elliot's neck and nestled closer. 'I think you are confusing me with another.'

'Bella?' Elliot ran his hand up her side, from hip to waist to breast. 'How much of you is in her, I wonder?'

His hand settled on the curve of her breast. He was kissing the pulse at the base of her neck now. 'If I were Bella,' Deborah said, 'what would you do to me?'

'If you were Bella, it would be more a question of what you would do to me,' Elliot said, nuzzling her ear lobe. 'I should warn you, I'm not particularly keen on being tied and bound.'

'Good God, you mean you've actually...' Deborah bit her lip, but she was too fascinated to keep silent. 'Was it—I mean, did you—what did you—I didn't actually think that people—not in real life, I mean.'

Elliot ran his fingers down the sweet curve of her spine. 'You'd be surprised at what goes on behind the closed doors of the most respectable of houses.'

And what had not gone on, Deborah thought grimly. *Don't think about that.* She was Bella. Elliot thought she was Bella. For one last time, she *would* be Bella. 'The doors of this respectable house are closed right now,' she said, garnering her courage.

Elliot tensed. He had waited so long for this moment that he could not allow himself to believe it was happening. Yet she seemed so different today. He kissed her lightly, though even that was enough to send the blood rushing to his groin. 'Did you have any particular goings-on in mind?'

'I rather thought I would leave that up to you.'

'Are you sure?'

She was sure that she wanted him. She stroked the indent on her ring finger. *Don't think.* 'Yes,' she said, 'I am.'

He pulled her roughly to him and kissed her, a brief, savage kiss that left her in no doubt of his need, before scooping her up into his arms. Yanking open the parlour door, he carried her effortlessly up the stairs. When he set her on her feet in her bedchamber, she was breathless, her heart pounding.

Light filtered in through the window, showing up the spartan room, the simple bed with its plain cotton sheets, the polished boards bare save for the one rug beside the bed. Deborah plucked at her gown. When Bella needed to dispense with clothes, she did so miraculously, without the need for description. Should she take it off? Before the reality of the situation could intrude on her fantasy, Elliot pulled her close and she forgot all about such mundane things as undressing as he ran his hands up and down her spine.

'You taste of summer,' he murmured against her mouth. 'The freshness of a morning heady with the promise of heat.' He wanted to plunge into her and drink deep, but he made himself sip until the tip of her tongue touched his, drawing him in, and the heat went straight to his groin.

Elliot shrugged out of his coat, dropping it carelessly on to the floor. He turned Deborah around in his arms and began to unhook her gown, planting more kisses on the skin revealed by each button, turning her back to face him as he drew the long sleeves down over her arms, the bodice over her breasts, then the skirts over her hips. She was blushing, but she watched him intently, as he watched her.

He kissed her neck, her throat, her shoulders, the creases in each elbow, the pulse at each wrist. He kissed the soft mounds of her breasts above her corset. When he turned her round again to undo the laces, he kissed her shoulder blades, the knot of her spine. His waistcoat was hastily discarded before he faced her once more. He kissed her mouth again. He could never have enough of her mouth.

Elliot's kisses made her weak with wanting. The way he looked at her left her in no doubt that her wanting was returned. The way he looked at her made her want him all the more. It was strange. Exciting. She tugged Elliot's shirt free from his corduroys. He yanked it over his head and she inhaled sharply, seeing for the first time in the clear light of day what she had only touched in the dark of night. She touched him hesitantly, running her palms over the span of his shoulders, his chest, feeling the beat of his heart, the smoothness of his skin, the roughness of the smattering of hair which arrowed down to the fastening of his breeches. His nipples hardened, just like hers did. She hadn't known that. The muscles in his back flexed under her touch. She looked up, and met his fierce gaze, and smiled. Then he kissed her again and it was hotter, somehow. More, somehow.

Elliot scattered the pins from her hair over the floor, combing his fingers through the length of it. 'I've imagined this,' he said, kissing the valley between her breasts, 'your hair spread out on the pillow behind you.'

He untied the ribbons of her chemise and pulled it down over her arms, over her breasts. The cotton abraded her nipples, making her stomach clench, making her close her eyes as a shivering heat whispered over her. He lifted her on to the bed and removed her shoes. He untied her garters and removed her stockings. 'The problem with being tied and bound,' he said, cupping her breasts, 'is that it is rather restricting.' His thumbs caressed the hard tips of her nipples as he eased her on to her back. 'But you know, that isn't really a problem if you are content to let someone else provide the entertainment.'

Before she realised what he was doing, he had her first wrist bound, tied with her garter to the cast-iron post. She tried to snatch her other hand away, but he caught it. 'Trust me,' he said, smiling one of his wicked smiles, 'I'll make it worth your while.'

He did not bind her ankles, but left her stretched on the bed, laid open to his gaze. His eyes blazed with desire as he looked at her, stripping her of embarrassment, leaving her naked and hot. The remainder of his clothes were dropped unceremoniously on to the floor. His erection was as thick and hard as she remembered it. She would not be able to touch him if he kept her like this. *Was that good or bad?*

'I don't want you to do anything,' he said, as if he had read her thoughts. He kissed her briefly. 'You know, there were two rather glaring omissions from Bella's experiences in the book I read. Of course, I haven't read them all, but I doubt very much that they were remedied in any of them.'

He lay down on the bed beside her. Long legs, tightly

packed muscles, almost but not quite touching. She had never lain naked like this before. She tried to turn towards him, but her bonds frustrated her. 'What omissions?'

Elliot kissed her again, leaning over her so that his chest brushed against her breasts. 'Poor Bella. I can't help feel that her victories are something of an anticlimax,' he said, trailing his fingers over her breasts, her belly, back up to her breasts. 'She takes so little pleasure from them, you see.' He eased himself a little way down the bed to capture one of her nipples in his mouth.

Deborah shivered. 'You're wrong,' she said, fighting for control, 'in the last book, the one I have just finished…'

'Yes, but you wrote that after you met me,' Elliot said, looking smug.

He turned his attention to her other nipple, licking, sucking, teasing, so that Deborah moaned, arching up from the bed. She wanted to touch him. 'What was the other thing?'

Elliot leaned over her, covering her body with his. It felt so strange. Not frightening. Deeply exciting. Warm skin. Hard muscle. She could feel his erection, reassuringly, enticingly solid against her thigh. What would it be like to have him inside her? Her muscles clenched, making her shiver again.

'The other thing.' Elliot kissed his way down the valley between her breasts. 'The other thing is a kiss.'

His mouth was on her belly now.

'A kiss? Bella has—she has lots of kisses.'

Elliot looked up, his eyes gleaming. 'Not this kind of kiss.' In one fluid movement he slid between her legs, tilted her towards him and covered her sex with his mouth.

Deborah cried out in shock. Elliot kissed her again, then his tongue slid into the crease at the top of her thigh and he kissed her there, too. She whimpered. He kissed the crease at the top of her other thigh. She whimpered again. Then his tongue slid inside her and she cried out.

Elliot's heart began to hammer so hard that he struggled to breath. She was so damp, so hot, so wet. He licked further into her folds and over the swollen nub of her. He slid his finger inside her as he licked, slowly, slowly, feeling her tighten and swell, feeling the corresponding rush of blood to his already hard shaft.

He tried to regulate his breathing, but he couldn't concentrate on it. Deborah was flushed. Her face. Her breasts. Her lids were heavy, almost closed. He slid his fingers higher and licked her. Thrust again and licked. She shuddered. His shaft pulsed in response. He licked. He circled. He sucked. He licked again.

Deborah strained urgently at her ties. His tongue, his fingers, all seemed to collude, to centre, to tighten her deep inside, as if she were being wrung out. Thrust and lick and slide and tighten. Thrust and lick and slide and tighten. She bucked up underneath him and the world exploded, shattered, scattering glittering pieces of her high into the sky as she floated and burned beneath them. She could hear herself crying out far away, a feral, needy sound as she floated and reformed.

She opened her eyes to find him looking at her, the way he looked at her making her shiver again, making her stretch luxuriously under his gaze, flaunting her body sinuously, like Bella did.

Elliot caught his breath. Deborah lay beneath him, eyes heavy and dark, drugged with desire. Hair streaming over the pillow, so much better than he'd imagined. Her nipples were dark pink. The curls which covered her sex were dark blonde. He had never been so hard. He leaned over to untie her wrists and his erection brushed her belly. 'Are you sure? Because if not, you need to say so now.'

Deborah sat up, twining her arms and pressing her body sinuously against him, just as Bella did. Elliot's hands skimmed her back, her bottom, back up to her breasts and he kissed her. Ravaging kisses. He tasted different. Of her, she realised, and it excited her, this most intimate sharing. His erection strained against her belly. His hand cupped her breast and she felt herself gathering anew, her climax building again before it had even ebbed. 'I want you,' she said, knowing that this time she really meant it, even though she was fast realising she had no idea what it meant. 'I want you.'

Her hands fluttered over his skin, sending little jolting shocks with every touch, which connected up, setting a flaring path to the ache of his erection. Elliot was beginning to doubt his ability to retain any sort of control, with his shaft almost screaming its need. Her mouth was hot, her hands needy. She was so delightfully naked. Had it ever been so glorious before, this skin on skin? He couldn't remember. 'Touch me,' he said urgently, 'I want you to touch me.'

She wanted to, but she faltered, her lack of experience detracting from Bella's confidence. As if he read her thoughts, Elliot took her hand and placed it on his shaft. Solid muscle, sheathed in silk. So hard. So potent-looking. She traced the length of it cautiously. Elliot groaned. Deborah snatched her hand back. 'Sorry.'

'No. God, don't be sorry. You have no idea how long I've waited.' Elliot kissed her, wrapping her fingers around his girth, showing her how to stroke him, wondering how much of it he could take before he came. 'This is what you're doing to me,' he said, slipping his finger back inside her and thrusting. 'And this,' he said, sliding up, over, then back inside. 'This is what you do to me.'

She could feel him pulsing under her caress. She stroked him, slowly tracing the path of silken skin to the friction of the tip. Elliot's chest rose and fell sharply. His shaft thickened. The throbbing between her legs began to pulse, like the shaft in her hand. She stroked him again, astounded and enthralled at the way her touch made him respond, marvelling at the solidness of him, the heft of him. So different. So amazingly, delightfully different.

'Deborah, if you keep doing that I don't think I'm going to be able to wait.' Elliot eased her on to her back, his self-control straining as he anticipated the darkly pink folds between her legs closing around him. He could feel her dampness, her heat, could feel the tightening beneath his erection which told him he was only just clinging on.

He entered her slowly. She felt every inch of him as he eased his way in, clinging to him as she did so, shivering as she sheathed him. She could feel the tension in him, too, in his clenched shoulders, the sinews of his arms standing out. He was panting. Beads of sweat on his forehead. His chest heaved. She lay under him, not knowing what to do. Then he tilted her towards him, and she stopped thinking.

His first thrust was pure pleasure. He took that slowly, too, leading her. She learned quickly, thrusting with him the next, finding a rhythm with the next, roused in a whole other way by the clinging of their bodies, her softness giving way to his hardness, yet holding him, melding with him. This time her climax was sudden and violent, a snapping of wires that made her cry out as Elliot thrust high inside her, made her wrap her legs around his waist, dig her nails into his back, arching up against him to hold him higher inside her until with one last deep thrust he came, too, withdrawing at the last possible moment, the force of his release making him cry out.

Deborah opened her eyes reluctantly. She was lying on the same pillow as Elliot. They were all tangled up, too, arms and legs entwined, so she wasn't quite sure who was what. His heart beat against hers. She felt too heavy to move. She had never been held thus. She had never felt like this. Bella had never felt like this. Sated.

Elliot kissed her lingeringly and rolled on to his back. He smelled of sweat and sex. His hair was a wild tangle. She had never seen him look so good. He smiled at her, the curl of his mouth lazy, incredibly sensual. Just thinking about what he could do with that wonderful mouth made her shudder with delight. She couldn't resist running her fingers over the rough hair on his chest, down to the ripple of muscles on his stomach.

'I was right, wasn't I?' he said, catching her hand. 'Now Bella knows something she did not.' He began to work his way along her hand, kissing the tip of each finger.

'You need not look so smug. It is most ungentlemanly of you,' Deborah said, trying not to laugh.

Elliot pulled her on top of him and ran his fingers down her spine, cupping the curve of her bottom. 'You know perfectly well I am not a gentleman. Besides, I have every right to feel smug. There is no mistaking the look of a satisfied woman. You should be feeling rather smug yourself, you know.'

'Should I? Why is that?' Her breasts were pressed into his chest. Her hair trailed over them both. It was delicious, lying on top of him like this.

'Because you have, lying beneath you, one very, very satisfied man.'

Deborah beamed. 'Really?'

'Completely,' Elliot said, kissing her. 'At least,' he said a few moments later, 'I thought I was. Only I find that perhaps…' He moved suggestively underneath her.

'Elliot! So soon?' Deborah exclaimed.

He couldn't help laughing, she seemed so genuinely surprised. 'I do apologise, but you have only yourself to blame, you know. You are a diamond. Infinitely desirable. You said so yourself.'

Bella. Deborah. Bella. Even Elliot had confused her with her creation. Deborah smiled Bella's wicked smile. 'So it is my fault, is it?'

'Completely.'

'Then I suppose it is up to me to take remedial action.'

'I'd say we should make a joint effort.'

She shook her head. 'It occurs to me that there is something else missing from my—Bella's repertoire that we might try.'

'What is that?'

Deborah wriggled down Elliot's body, kissing his chest, his stomach. Her heart pounded at her own daring, but the sense of power, the illusion of Bella, and the headiness of sexual satisfaction gave her confidence. 'I'll show you,' she said, deliberately echoing Elliot's own words, and began to kiss the thick, hard length of his shaft.

'I am supposed to be dining with Alex at his club,' Elliot said sleepily some time later as they lay in the tangle of sheets.

Deborah opened her eyes, surprised to see, through the uncurtained window, that dusk had fallen. Where had the day gone? How could the hours have passed so quickly? What was she doing here, lying naked in bed, with Elliot?

With Elliot! She closed her eyes, then opened them again. He was still naked. She was still naked. *Oh God!*

He smiled at her lazily and kissed the tip of her nose. 'I find the idea of dinner with Alex incredibly unappealing. I want to stay here.' He tucked a long strand of her hair behind her ear. 'What do you say?'

'Say?' Panicked, Deborah pushed him away and sat up abruptly, clutching the sheet around her. She hadn't thought beyond—beyond—she hadn't thought! When Bella was done with a man, she simply donned her clothes and vanished into the night. Or she made *him* do so. When Bella was done with a man, there were no consequences, no repercussions, no discussions, no expectations. There was certainly no suggestion of spending the night together. Had Elliot not realised? Had she not made it clear?

Oh God, she hadn't thought to explain. She had been so—and he had been so—*why* hadn't she thought? 'Why would you want to stay?' she asked agitatedly.

Confused by the edge in her voice, Elliot, too, sat up. 'Well, for a start there is the matter of finding your favourite situation. I am not suggesting that we can exhaust the possibilities in one night, but—'

'Elliot, there can be no question of—of exhausting the possibilities. I'm not Bella. I mean, I *was* Bella when we—when we were...' Deborah clutched at the sheet. 'I told you, I'm going to kill Bella off.'

'Because you no longer need her. I understand that,

but I'm not sure I understand why you're being so…'
Elliot stopped, momentarily at a loss. 'Don't you want
me to spend the night?' he asked, realising as he did
that spending the night, the thing he never did, was precisely the thing he most wanted.

The very idea of Elliot in her bed, sleeping beside
her, waking up beside her, holding her through the
night, making love to her through the night, was exquisite torture. Deborah stared at him, stricken, as the
last remnants of her fantasy dispersed. Elliot wanted
to spend the night with Bella, but Bella was well and
truly gone, and no matter how much Deborah wanted to
spend the night with Elliot, he would not want to spend
the night with her and…

'Deborah?'

If she didn't know him better, she would think him
offended. She didn't want to think about that. About
why he was offended. About what he wanted. She didn't
want to think about what she wanted either, because it
didn't matter. What mattered was making things clear,
which she should have done before, only she had been
so carried away with Bella and Elliot. Especially Elliot.
Oh hell! 'I thought you understood. This afternoon, it
was a—a last performance. Bella's last performance. I
thought you realised that, Elliot. When we were talking about the books. When you were talking about what
Bella liked, what Bella did not know, I thought you
knew that it was just—that it wasn't real.' She felt as
if her skin, her body, was metamorphosing with every
passing moment, from beautiful Bella to disgusting

Deb. Terrified that he witness her transformation, she pulled the sheet up to her neck.

Elliot ran his fingers through his hair, staring at her in consternation. The voluptuous creature who had been lying in his arms only moments before had been replaced by a haughty, icy female who looked like her maiden aunt. 'Are you telling me that you regret this? That you wish it had never happened?'

'I'm saying it won't happen again. I can't have an *affaire* with you. I think you should go.'

Though an *affaire* was what he would have proposed—given the chance—Deborah's out-of-hand rejection made Elliot wonder whether it was what he actually wanted. He hadn't thought beyond this moment, but now that it had happened and it had been all, more than he had dreamed, he was very far from the point where he wanted to make it finite. This realisation confused him. Deborah's dismissal of an offer he hadn't even had a chance to make hurt. Elliot got out of bed and began to pull on his clothes. 'It is customary to await an offer before turning it down,' he said curtly. 'I haven't asked you to be my mistress.'

'Oh. You mean you did understand after all—about Bella?'

Elliot stopped in the middle of buttoning his waistcoat. 'Are you seriously saying that this afternoon, you and I, it won't happen again?' Deborah looked like a trapped animal. He sat down on the bed again and tried to take her hand, but she shrank from him. 'What the hell is wrong?' he snapped, even more offended. 'What have I done to upset you?'

'Nothing! You haven't. I'm sorry. It's my fault.'

'*What* is your fault?'

'This. I shouldn't have—we shouldn't have. Can't we just forget it?' She knew as soon as she spoke the words that they were preposterous. Why hadn't she thought this through? How could she have been so stupid, so incredibly stupid? No wonder Elliot was looking at her as if she had two heads. She had spoilt everything. 'It was a mistake. My mistake. I'm sorry.'

Her utter dejection cut through Elliot's anger. The feisty, sensual woman who had sparred with him, teased him, flirted with him, aroused him and satisfied him beyond anything he had ever known was fled. 'Deborah, I don't know what it is going on in that clever head of yours, but—'

'Nothing. It is nothing, save that I am sorry that you seem to have misunderstood—that I have not made myself clear. Please don't let this spoil things between us, Elliot. I want us to be friends.'

'Cannot friends be lovers?'

'No! No, I can't. It was Bella. I wish now that I had not told you about her,' Deborah said wretchedly.

'For God's sake, I wasn't making love to Bella!' Elliot exclaimed in exasperation.

'Yes, but, Elliot, that's exactly what you were doing.'

He stared at her in silence, quite unable to formulate any meaningful answer to this *non sequitur*. Snatching his coat from the floor, Elliot dragged it on and made for the door. 'I assure you, *I* was under no illusions about who I was making love to. You told me only this afternoon that the time had come for you to stop hiding behind Bella. Are you absolutely sure that is the case? I would think hard about that, if I were you.'

'I am not the only one hiding,' Deborah threw at him, but Elliot closed the door to the bedchamber, making a point of not slamming it. She listened to the sound of his boots on the stairs. The parlour door creaked open as he went in search of his hat and gloves. She heard the sound of the latch on the front door being lifted. There was a pause, as if he was waiting for something, then the soft thud of the door closing and the house was silent.

Deborah curled up into a ball and huddled under the sheets. They smelled of Elliot. And sex. She smelled of Elliot and sex. Despite the misery of his departure, her body still throbbed with satisfaction. It was like a battle which they had both won. The sheer elation of their coupling was so very different to the sense of subjection, latterly the degradation which she had endured in the marital bed with Jeremy. Elliot made her feel powerful. Or was that Bella?

What did it matter? Elliot was gone and Deborah was bereft. He would never understand. She barely understood herself. It had seemed so right to tell him about Bella; she had been so sure she was seeing things clearly for the first time. She would forget all about the past. The future would be filled with new writing, new friends. And Elliot.

Deborah buried her head under the feather pillow.

The very idea of an Elliott-less future made her feel sick. Whichever way she looked at it, it was a colourless wasteland of a place. She couldn't bear it.

She would not have to! She would not! When he thought about it, Elliot would surely understand about Bella. Things between them would go back to how they had been. She would forget all about this afternoon. They both would. *Wouldn't they?*

Deborah groaned. She did not want Elliot to forget, any more than she really wanted to believe that he had been making love to Bella. Had she been hiding? Was she hiding still? She beat her fists on the mattress, furious at her own contrariness. What the devil was going on in her head? She couldn't want him. She couldn't let him see how much she wanted him. She *didn't* want him. It was Bella, not Deborah, and Bella was no more.

Sitting up, she hurled the pillow across the room. *'Devil take it!'* Deborah dropped her head into her hands. She was not in love with Elliot. She could not possibly be in love with him, she *couldn't*. It would be fatal.

Chapter Ten

Elliot sent Alex his excuses as soon as he returned home. Now he sat in his study, staring at the parcel of books sitting on his desk, strangely reluctant to cut the string. What was stopping him? He poured himself a glass of Madeira and stared at that instead. His mind was such a tangle of thoughts, he had no idea how to begin to unravel them. Taking a sip of the wine, he made a face and put it down.

I am not the only one hiding. He had a horrible suspicion that there were uncomfortable truths lurking somewhere under that last remark of hers, but he wasn't at all sure he was ready to confront them. What the hell had happened, there in her bedchamber, afterwards? He racked his brains, but could think of nothing he had said or done. His offer to spend the night had been the trigger, but why?

Why had he offered anyway? He hated to spend the night with his *chères-amies*. He took a sip of the Madeira and made a face. *Chère-amie* no more fitted his idea of Deborah than mistress. *Affaire* seemed such a temporary word. He had always liked that about it. Before.

Elliot picked up his paper knife and cut through the string. Two books, unbound and uncut, lay before him. *Arsenic* and *Wolfsbane.* Deadly poisons. Deadly Nightshade. Deborah. This afternoon, the revelation of her authorship had been exciting. Tonight, he wondered what his reading would tell him about her marriage. Bella wreaked revenge so that her creator could endure the mess she had made of her life. What mess?

He stared at the frontispiece of the first book. He was afraid. He didn't want to pity her. He didn't want to think ill of her. He wanted…

Elliot swore, then took a deep draught of his wine. He didn't know what the hell he wanted any more. With a sigh, he took his knife and began to cut the pages.

He read both books, one after the other, sitting up late by the library fire in his dressing gown. Like the novel Lizzie had lent him, these were *risqué,* funny and savage. Now that he knew she had penned them, he could detect Deborah's caustic wit in almost every paragraph. Her talent was undeniable; the stories were exceedingly well written. That way of hers, of sketching a character in two or three brief sentences, transferred brilliantly to the page. No wonder the books were popular.

He found them—unsettling. He could not at first understand why this was so, for the knowledge that Deborah had written this scene, her pen had described that act, her mind had conjured this twist in the plot, distracted him. His imagination moved seamlessly from Bella to Deborah to Bella.

Elliot frowned. He had been so carried away, he hadn't really thought about the extent to which Deborah had been transformed, in talking about Bella. To the extent where she had forgotten herself, confused herself with her own creation, the woman she said was everything she was not. Bella was Deborah's secret weapon. Did she really believe that? And why?

What the *hell* had gone on in her marriage? Elliot cursed. How many times had he asked himself that? Whatever it was, he had to admire her for the way she had kicked back. No matter how skewed she was emotionally, Bella Donna was a masterful instrument for revenge. But revenge for what?

The clock on the mantel chimed four in the morning. She wasn't going to tell him and he had to know. Elliot's stomach rumbled. He'd missed dinner. He'd call on Lizzie in the morning, he decided, making his way down the back stairs to the kitchen. Knowing his sister, she would already have done some digging. In her own way, she was every bit as devious as he was. There was ham and cheese in the larder. Some rather stale bread went into the frying pan with several eggs. He wolfed all of it down at the scrubbed table, his mind flying in all sorts of different directions, while all the time, at the centre, was Deborah.

I'm not the only one hiding. What *had* she meant by that? He was not hiding behind the Peacock, was he?

Hiding from what? Elliot pushed back his chair and stretched, rolling his shoulders. This afternoon had been so—just so! He grinned. Perfect. Utterly fantastic, just as he had known it would be. It wasn't just the act itself, it was her. The way she talked and teased and challenged him. The way she made him feel. The way she got inside his head and his skin. What it had felt like, being inside her. Joined in body, in mind.

God Almighty, it was as well no one could hear his thoughts! Elliot cast his plate, fork and knife into the basin by the pump beside the dirty skillet. He hadn't thought about the Peacock in weeks, but perhaps it was time for another outing?

He tested himself for the familiar sense of excitement, but found none. He could not tell Deborah, obviously. She would worry. Not that she had a right to worry. Not that he felt himself accountable. But he wouldn't tell her. Because she *would* worry.

I am not the only one hiding. Dammit, why wouldn't it go away? A stupid remark, flung at him merely to hurt him, that was all. What did he care? Elliot picked up the lamp, and made his way back up to the study. He had a housebreaking to arrange.

By dawn, Elliot had done most of the planning and could no longer keep his eyes open. He dragged himself up to bed and slept soundly for five hours. A bath, a shave, a change of clothes, and he was at his sister's house not long after noon, only to discover she was gone out for the day with her mother-in-law and not expected back until after dinner.

He thought of calling in Hans Town, but was loath to do so until he had spoken to Lizzie. Yesterday he had been hurt by Deborah's refusal even to consider an *affaire*. Today, he was inclined to agree with her. He did not want an *affaire*. What, then, did he want? Why did he no longer want what he had? *Was he hiding?*

Out of habit, Elliot sought respite and clarity in exercise. An hour spent in his shirt sleeves and stockinged feet, thumping hell out of the huge punch bag which swung from a hook in Jackson's sparring room, helped. There was something soporific and at the same time liberating about the thwack of his fist on leather scarred with the thwacks of many hundreds of fists. It was like beating down his own resistance.

Bella was Deborah's revenge on her husband. The Peacock was his revenge for Henry. *That* parallel was obvious enough. Deborah had captured Henry's spirit so well in her book, reading her words had reminded him of the Henry who laughed and broke the rules, who was infuriating as well as funny, as foolish sometimes as he was brave. The real Henry, not the crazed creature who had taken up residence in that fetid wreck of a body before he died. The real Henry, who had loved life above all. Was he done with extracting revenge for Henry's death, as Deborah was done with avenging her marriage?

But the Peacock had not been born just for Henry. Elliot needed him. What would Elliot do without him?

He was no politician, but he was a first-class *agent provocateur*. An agitator, who could make politicians act. Was there such a thing? Could he be such a thing? Would it be enough? Whether or not he would miss the excitement of his night-time escapades, tonight would tell. Whether or not something else could replace them...

The punch bag caught Elliot a glancing blow in the midriff as he stood stock still in the sparring room. Something else already had. Someone else. Elliot dropped his head against the leather bag. 'Bloody hell, not that,' he muttered. 'Surely not that?'

Suddenly aware that he was in the middle of Jackson's salon talking to a leather bag filled with sand, he straightened up and looked around, but attention was focused on a sparring match. Elliot groaned. He couldn't be. Dear God, he couldn't be—*could* he?

Why did he have to choose someone so complicated? Not that he'd chosen her. In fact, he'd gone out of his way *not* to choose her. And not that he was, he told himself as he doused his torso in cold water. Not that. Most definitely not that.

For the second day in a row, Elliot returned home in a daze. Slopping wine into a glass, which he then placed on a side table and completely forgot, he slumped down on to the chair in front of his desk. Wasn't it supposed to make you happy? Weren't you supposed to feel like you were walking on air or some such balderdash? Henry, who liked to think of himself as handy with his fives, had once described a mill he'd seen on leave, just before the Battle of Trafalgar. John Gully, unknown and untested, had gone more than sixty rounds before the champion, known as the Game Chicken, had knocked him out. Henry described Gully's bloody visage in gory detail. Elliot thought now that he knew just how the man must have felt. Surely this couldn't be love?

There, he'd let the word loose and the sky hadn't fallen down. Remembering his wine, Elliot retrieved it and took a cautious sip. It tasted the same. Wasn't the world supposed to look different, somehow? 'What do I know?' he said aloud. Putting his glass down on the mantelpiece, he stared at his reflection in the mirror. Hair in disarray. His neckcloth lopsided. Was there a light in his eyes, a sparkle even? Elliot laughed. 'Damned if I can tell!'

Disconsolately, he returned to his desk and retrieved the file from its secret drawer. It was such an easy job, he had no need of any recce. He'd do it tonight. That would tell him something, surely? He looked at his drawings, scanned his notes, waiting for the familiar sense of excitement, but nothing happened.

He remembered the last time. Deborah's clutching that damned dog, trying to stifle her laughter. The sheer exhilaration of their escape, the reckless gallop, the thud of their horses' hooves, the steam of their breath in the cold air, the *frisson* of awareness, knowing she was there at his side. And afterwards in the boathouse...

And yesterday, in her bed. And before that, all the other days. That strange squeezing in his chest when he looked at her—there, he could admit to that now.

The stupid things he saved up to tell her. The things she knew about him that no one else knew. Did all this, then, amount to love? And if it did, even if it did, what did it mean, what could it mean, when she was so patently still living under the cloud of her past?

A soft tap on the door roused him from the mire that this question enveloped him in. 'Mrs Murray called,' his batman said. 'She has returned earlier than expected and asks if you wish to join her for dinner. Her husband and her mother-in-law will not be with her, she said to tell you.'

Elliot grinned. 'That is most fortuitous.' It wasn't as if he'd be picking the lock on the house in Berkeley Square any time before midnight. 'I'll wear the black coat and the grey pantaloons,' he told his man. 'I shall most likely go on to my club. Tell the servants not to wait up.'

Knowing full well that his master never visited his club, his batman gave him a knowing look. 'You need have no fear, I shall make sure you are not seen.'

Quite taken aback by this remark, Elliot could only stare as the servant left the room. He picked up the file on his lap, gave it another quick glance, then cast it on the flames of the fire. It seemed Alex Murray wasn't the only man with suspicions. He'd better make damn sure this next act didn't turn into his final one, if that was the case!

It was a close call. The kind of close call Elliot would have relished, back in the old days. Back in the days

before Deborah. He was careless, quite distracted by
what Lizzie had told him of Jeremy Napier over dinner,
and did not check the rooms on the third floor, or he
would have spotted the light shining through the gap at
the bottom of the door. The general, whose conscience
was not as clean as Elliot believed, was prone to nightmares, and had become a most reluctant sleeper. As the
Peacock's pick slid the last tumbler on the safe's lock
home, a creaking in the hallway outside alerted him.

The old man who peered around the door of the dining room wore only a nightshirt and a cap. He was
frailer than Elliot remembered. His bare feet made him
look vulnerable. Though he had no option but to am-
bush him, covering his toothless mouth with a muf-
fler to stop him from crying out, the ropes he used to
bind his victim to the chair were loosely tied. Still, he
could easily have completed his task, but the contrast
between the brash, muscular general Elliot remembered
and the scrawny man who flailed weakly at his bonds
was too much. Henry would never have approved such
a conquest. Elliot had better uses for his energies. The
thirst for revenge, which had flourished like a weed inside him for years, was already wilting. Now it began
to shrivel. He closed the safe without retrieving what
he had come for, taking care to keep his face out of the
old man's line of sight. The peacock feather remained
tucked inside his pocket.

The night was warm, a light cover of cloud covering the sky as Elliot made his way along Mount Street.
It was late enough to be early. There was no one about

to disturb his thoughts, only the echo of his footsteps to accompany him. Deborah was right. He had been hiding, but he did not need to any more. The Peacock had served his purpose. Like Bella, he would die. And Elliot—Elliot had no desire whatsoever to risk dying with him.

He touched the feather in his pocket. The last one. Perhaps he would keep it as a memento. As the dawn began to filter through the clouds, he turned homewards. He did love Deborah. He *was* in love with her. It was so obvious, he should be laughing at himself for being so blind. There wasn't any other explanation for what he felt. There wasn't any other he wanted now either. He loved her and he was pretty certain that she loved him. If he could only persuade her to let go of the past.

Could he? Would she? His steps faltered. What Lizzie had told him was not common knowledge, but, according to her, it was accepted fact in Jeremy's circles. Deborah had been married for seven years. She must surely know the truth? Yet if she did, why was she so determined to assume so much of the blame for the failure of her marriage? No, it was impossible that she did not know the truth. He simply needed to persuade her that neither shame nor blame attached to her. Why could she not see that for herself?

As he made his way slowly home, his brow furrowed, Elliot veered between anger and pity. The utter misery of two people bound in such a marriage was almost beyond contemplating. Their vows had sentenced them to a lifetime of failure. Sixteen years in the army, where a blind eye was turned to men who took their comforts where they could, had taught him that there were some men as irrevocably inclined to men as he was to women. Unlike many of his fellow officers, Elliot was confident enough in his own sexuality neither to judge nor to feel threatened. Under any other circumstances, what Lizzie had told him of Jeremy would have been of no import.

Save that Jeremy had been married to Deborah. His pretending to love Deborah, marrying her for her money, was bad enough, but to have used her in such a calculating way—no, Elliot could not forgive that. Not that it mattered. What mattered was Deborah, who seemed unable to forgive herself for her husband's rejection. He couldn't understand it.

Deborah had said that she was done with the past, but it was patently untrue. What if she was never done? What then? An abyss opened up under his feet as he contemplated this possibility. Elliot clenched his fists. There could be no more hiding for either of them. He would make her see that. Failure was simply not an option.

Deborah was working—or trying to work—about as successfully as she had tried sleeping, telling herself not to worry and attempting to stop reliving that afternoon of love-making. The page in front of her was not blank, but covered in a hotchpotch of squiggles, blots, tearstains and—she noticed with dismay—Elliot's name. She couldn't stop thinking about him. Thinking about him led to remembering every kiss, every look, every touch. The ecstatic quiver and clutch of her muscles around him as he entered her. The soaring high of her climaxes. The bliss of skin on skin. The scent of him on her. Remembering made the jolt back down to reality so much harder. It made the panic, that he was gone for ever, that she had ruined all, so much more difficult to quell.

She picked up her pen again and stared blindly at the page. She wished he would call. She was not ready to face him. She was terrified he would not call. She wanted—she wanted—she wanted—the one thing she could not have. That much was constant.

A knock on the door made her jump. Leaping to her feet, her stomach a seething mass of nerves, Deborah looked down quickly at her ink-stained pinafore. A glance at her reflection in the hall mirror confirmed the worst. She had a blob of ink on her cheek and her hair looked as if she'd had some sort of fight to the death with curl papers.

Elliot on the other hand looked very Elliot-ish, she thought as she opened the door. His coat was dark blue, not one she had seen him wearing before. His waistcoat was grey, as were his pantaloons. His cravat was more elaborately tied than usual, with a sapphire pin winking discreetly in the folds. She stared up at him wordlessly, caught in the memory of him without any clothes, in her bed, his face taut with desire as she took him into her mouth. Her face flamed.

'May I come in?'

Too embarrassed to meet his eye, Deborah held the door wide and let him precede her into the parlour.

'You've been working,' Elliot said.

Deborah quickly snatched up the smudged, wasted bundle of papers and held them defensively to her chest. Her hands were shaking. He had perfectly good clothes on, she didn't need to keep thinking about what was underneath. 'I wasn't expecting you,' she said, her voice an odd combination of breathless and harsh. It was true and it was a lie. Like everything these days, or so it sometimes felt.

Despite having spent the rest of the night rehearsing every variation on the scene which was about to unfold, Elliot was still lacking a battle plan. He tried in vain to quell the unaccustomed panic which knotted his stomach. The last time he had seen her, Deborah had been naked, flushed from their love-making. Here, in this very room, it had started. The teasing. The kissing. The touching. Their eyes met and Deborah looked away quickly. She was blushing. He was—just thinking about it, and he was—dammit, he shouldn't be thinking about it!

Elliot made to sit down, realised Deborah was still standing, and propped himself up against the mantel instead. His mind went blank. He had a thousand things to say and he couldn't think of one. He nodded at the papers she was holding against her like a shield. 'Bella's final curtain, I take it,' he said. She thrust the bundle into a drawer. 'I read two of your other books,' he told her.

Deborah dropped into her seat at the fireside. 'Which ones?'

Taking his cue from her, Elliot, too, sat down. '*Arsenic* and *Wolfsbane.*'

Were they going to just sit here and make polite conversation about her books? What else was she expecting? 'Did you like them?' Deborah asked. Her voice sounded desperate. She had to calm down.

Elliot nodded. 'It was strange, reading them and knowing that you wrote them. I can see why they are so popular; you are very talented.'

'But you did not like them?'

'Oh, I did. They are clever and exciting and—sad.'

Deborah winced. 'They are supposed to be witty. No one has ever described them as sad, to my knowledge.'

'I have the advantage of knowing the author. I doubt anyone else would see Bella as I do,' Elliot said.

It was the gentle way he spoke, which made the tears clog her throat. Deborah swallowed convulsively. 'How—how do you see Bella?' she asked eventually.

She was as pale as she had been flushed a few moments ago. She looked as if she were bracing herself for a blow. Elliot's heart did its squeezing thing. He hated seeing her like this. 'Bella,' he said, choosing his words with care, 'she doesn't let herself be defeated, does she? But she doesn't win either. She is so intent on playing men at their own games, she doesn't know how to be a woman. That's what is sad.'

Deborah sat slowly back into her chair. 'Oh.'

'I wish you would tell me about it,' Elliot said. 'I wish you would trust me.'

'For God's sake, Elliot, don't you know more than enough already? I can't. I can't talk about it. It's over, Jeremy is dead and buried, surely that's all that matters?'

He got to his feet and pulled her from her chair, holding her tight. 'It's over, but it's not buried. It's still there, hurting you.'

'I still feel so small sometimes,' she whispered. 'When I was married, I used to feel I was shrinking. I used to want to be so small no one could see me.' Deborah drew a shaky breath. It hurt so much, remembering the ghostlike figure she had become. She hated the idea of showing herself thus to Elliot, but she realised now, with a leaden heart, that if she did not he would never understand, and if he did not understand it would always be there between them, a barrier to any sort of friendship. And she so desperately needed any sort of friendship, for she could have nothing else.

'You're right,' she said finally. It was an agony, suffocating the love which had only just put out the first green shoots, but it would be much, much more painful for her to let it bloom. These last two nights, pacing her chamber, she had tried so hard to talk herself out of the truth and failed miserably. She loved him so much. She knew what she had to do, but she so much wished she did not have to. 'You're right,' she said again.

That determined little nod she gave was his undoing. 'I love you so much,' Elliot blurted out. Stark, and to the point, and utterly true. The relief of it. He took the shock on her face as surprise. 'Deborah, I love you,' Elliot said, warming to the task. 'I've never said it before, not to anyone. I've never wanted to, but I think I could get very used to saying it to you. I love you.'

'Elliot!' Deborah stared at him, aghast. The words she most longed to hear, which she had not thought for a moment to hear, for just a few wonderful seconds made her heart soar. Then plummet. 'Oh, Elliot.'

He caught her hand again. 'I know. I know that it's sudden, it's a shock to me, too, but I know it's right. I won't change my mind. I'm absolutely sure, I couldn't be more sure. I know that your marriage still haunts you, but—'

Deborah yanked her hand free. 'Elliot, you have to stop! It doesn't just haunt me, I can't escape it.'

'You can. I can help you. I *know,* you see—'

'You can't help me,' she interrupted, wringing her hands in anguish. 'I wish you could, but you can't, and I can't let you try. I would fail you in the end. Elliot, I could never make you happy.'

'I can't be happy without you.'

'Oh, please, don't say that.' Deborah dug her nails into her palms. 'Listen to me. You need to listen to me. I had no idea that you felt—but it will pass, I know it will pass,' she said fervently, the words she had recited over and over in the night to give her courage, though they failed to convince her. 'You just need to listen.'

Her voice had a feverish quality that worried him. He wanted to pull her into his arms, to kiss away the frown which scarred her brow, to tell her it would be all right, but everything about her—her rigid stance, the clenched fists, the tight white face—warned him against such action. He had waited so long for her to trust him, but it felt all wrong, more like an end than a beginning. He wanted to tell her that he knew. He wanted to smooth the path to her confession, but the very fact that she was finding it so difficult kept him mute. Could Lizzie have been misinformed? Was there some other dark secret he knew nothing about? The optimism which had lightened his step since last night scuttled off like a frightened rabbit. It took all his resolution to remain calm, but he managed to sit down, to cross his ankles in an appearance of negligence. 'I'm listening. Tell me. Take your time.'

'Yes. Yes, I must tell you.' Deborah took a turn around the room, then straightened her shoulders and resumed her seat. 'You know that my marriage to Jeremy wasn't happy. I told you he married me for my money, but that wasn't the only reason. His family are an old and revered one. They pride themselves on having the line passed down through direct heirs. Jeremy needed a son. So when I came along with my fortune and my bloody great wide-eyed innocence, I made it so easy for him. I was so desperate to be loved, you see.'

Her voice began to break, but when Elliot got up to comfort her, she motioned him away. 'No. Stay there. I can't talk if you touch me and I need to explain.'

Elliot sat back down again, feeling as if he were preparing for a battle in which his forces were vastly outnumbered. Was she going to tell him about Jeremy or not? Deborah was twisting his handkerchief round her fingers, but she seemed calmer. Ominously determined. 'Go on,' Elliot said, trying to sound encouraging.

'It was a disaster, right from the wedding night. Jeremy couldn't—he found me repulsive. He—we did not manage to consummate the marriage for some time, and when we did it was a—a painful experience for both of us. I didn't know any better. He could not—when he came to me—which he did at first, as often as he could bear it, for his desire for a son was even stronger than his disgust of me. It was always in the dark. I was not to touch him. I was always—he made me—with my back to him. And he was—he wasn't like you.'

She was blushing deeply, concentrating on her fingers, his handkerchief, but determined to finish, no matter how embarrassing. 'It was awful, but it was my fault. I knew that, I knew that I was just not the sort of woman who could—and the more I worried about it the worse it got. One night I tried. Those books—I wasn't reading them for Bella that first time. I thought if I could—so I—I can't tell you what I did, but it failed. He hit me then, for the first and only time, and I hated him. That's when Bella Donna was born. Poor Jeremy, he was every bit as destroyed by the whole farcical performance as I was. I hated him, but I could not blame him. It was my fault.'

'Your fault!' Unable to contain his outrage, Elliot leapt to his feet.

'Don't be angry, Elliot. I've been angry for years and

it doesn't help. It was wrong of him, I know it was, but if I'd been a better woman, maybe we—I don't know. He tried, you know, in the beginning, he did try to love me, and God knows, so too did I try, but I simply wasn't good enough.'

Staggered by her ignorance, Elliot dragged his fingers through his hair. 'I can't believe—you really didn't know? You had no idea?' He took a deep breath, forcing his fists to unclench. Another deep breath. 'Deborah, it wasn't your fault. My God, I still can't believe—all those years and he didn't tell you. I can't believe no one told you. Kinsail—he must have known.' He took an agitated turn around the room, struggling to find the words. 'You really didn't know?'

'Known what? Elliot, what didn't I know?'

Elliot took another deep breath. Her face, utterly bewildered, nearly set his temper flaring again, but he managed to damp it down. She didn't know. She really didn't know. All those books she had written and she didn't know. It was unbelievable.

'Elliot, you're frightening me. *What* didn't I know?'

'About Jeremy.' He sat down abruptly. He needed to let go of his anger. She had been deceived. It was done. What mattered was explaining. And understanding. He needed to help her. He could help her. He could. Elliot laced his hands together in an unconscious reflection of Deborah's. 'You were right about one thing. Jeremy needed a wife, but not for the reasons you think. Or not only for those.' He sat forwards, leaning his elbows on his knees. 'Look, I want you to know that I haven't been spying on you or sniffing around your past. I wanted you to tell me yourself, but when I realised how I felt about you, I needed to know, so I asked Lizzie. Jeremy was a—a...' Elliot struggled to find the right words.

'Deborah,' he said delicately, 'the fact is that your husband preferred men to women. Not just as friends, but in every way. He'd been having an *affair* with another man. These—these relationships, they are not uncommon, but your husband and his lover were not discreet. The Kinsails obviously put pressure on Jeremy to avoid scandal. I remember you told me how proud your husband was of his heritage. I'm sorry.'

Deborah's pale face turned ashen. 'What do you mean?'

'He married you to protect his name. He used you.' Elliot's hands clenched into fists again as his sympathy for Jeremy's undoubted plight warred with the man's perfidy. 'If only he had confided in you. If he had had the guts to tell you. But to blame you as he obviously did, for failing... To make you think that you were the problem—' He broke off. 'Sorry. That's not helping, I know.'

Deborah was shaking. 'Do you mean that Jeremy— are you saying that my husband—the man who married me—that he loved men?' She shook her head, her expression a heart-wrenching mixture of incomprehension and hurt. 'He wouldn't have—not even Jeremy would have lied to me about such a thing. Someone would have told me, surely? They would not all have—have colluded over such a thing.'

'Deborah, they probably all assumed that you knew.'

'But I didn't,' she said slowly. 'I didn't know. Did Jacob—do you mean that Jacob knew?' Her voice choked. 'He did. Of course he did. All this time. And Margaret, his wife? Surely she did not…'

Elliot's nails dug into the flesh of his palms. 'I don't know,' he said grimly. 'It doesn't matter a damn.'

Deborah clutched at her chair. There was a rushing noise in her ears. 'But it does. Why did no one tell me?' She clutched at her face now. Her fingers were icy. 'All these years, all the things I did to…' She shuddered. 'Oh God.'

'Deborah, it doesn't matter.' Elliot tried to pull her into his arms, but she pulled away.

'Doesn't matter?' She looked at him incredulously. 'Have you any idea of the humiliation that I suffered? To say nothing of the guilt. How could I not have known? How could I have been so *bloody* stupid? Dammit, only the other day I was talking about moving out from the shadows of the past.'

Her voice had an edge of hysteria to it. She was shaking, her teeth were actually chattering, but when Elliot tried again to touch her, she pushed him away. 'Deborah, I love you. Please, listen to me…'

'How can you love me? How could you possibly love me? I'm a dupe. Even the servants must have been laughing at me.'

This was going badly wrong. Elliot tugged ineffectually at his neckcloth. Deborah had retreated so far into herself he doubted he could reach her. All his confidence, the joy of discovering himself in love, was being shred into little pieces in the face of such misery. 'Deborah, I love you,' Elliot said, clinging to the one certainty. 'I really love you. I've never said that before. I've never had the least desire to think it, never mind say it. I love you, and it's not going to go away, what I feel. You could feel it, too, if you would just let go. If you would just believe in yourself a little.'

'Believe in myself?' Deborah exclaimed. 'Seven years I was married and my husband could not bring himself to trust me. For seven years, and two more since I was widowed, not a single soul has thought enough of me to tell me what seems to have been common knowledge.'

'Deborah, Lizzie did not say…'

'What kind of person does that make me,' Deborah swept on, 'that my own husband lied to me about something so—so fundamental? What on earth is there to believe in, save an ability to bring misery to all those I love?'

He needed an answer, but all he could think about, seeing her distraught face, was that he wanted to make it all go away, make it all unsaid. Yet where would that leave them save back at the beginning with it all to say again? Never in his life had he wanted something so much as to take away her pain and never in his life had something seemed so utterly unattainable. Elliot tried to rally himself, to remind himself of the old saying that love could conquer all, but he never did have much faith in old adages. He loved her, his heart was aching with love for her, but even if he could make her listen, make her believe what he felt, what difference would it make? He had thought his revelation would clear the path to a happy future. Instead, he seemed to have placed an insurmountable object in their way. His dejection was all the deeper for the height from which he had fallen.

Elliot picked up his hat and gloves. His feet felt weighted to the ground, his actions felt as if they were happening in slow motion. Already, it seemed as if Deborah was far away, out of his reach. 'I love you,' he said, his voice cracking on the words he believed he was saying for the last time, 'that won't ever change, but until *you* do, then there is no point in my saying any more.' He waited, but she made no move, said no word. He left.

Chapter Eleven

For more than a week, Deborah struggled to come to terms which what had happened, but every time she tried to reconcile her heart and her head, she failed. The truth, stark and terrifying, took stronger and more resolute root the more she tried to shift it. It hurt because it was so painfully clear, like the sun reflected on snow. She was in love with Elliot.

She was in love and had never been so utterly and completely miserable in her life. It tormented her, this love, which she would never be able to tell him. She tormented herself, crying over the sentimental romances she had so formerly despised, deriving small consolation by constructing alternative, unhappy-ever-after endings. She lost hours gazing into space, dreaming up rose-bowered cottages in which she and Elliot could live happily ever after, even though she hated cottages and the notion of Elliot spending the rest of his life contentedly tending their garden made her laugh. Bitterly. In the park, she gazed enviously at couples strolling arm in arm, inventing falsehoods to explain every little sign of affection. If she could not be happy, why then should anyone else?

But such hostility, such railing at the unfairness of it all, such resentment and vitriol, was exhausting and pointless. Weariness and depressions seized her then and finally, in the void created by lethargy, her spirit began to fight its way back. She loved Elliot. She loved him with her blood and bones as well as her heart. Her love for him made a flimsy edifice of what she thought had been love for Jeremy. Her husband had been right. She'd been in love with the idea of love, no more.

Poor Jeremy. If only she could have understood his turmoil, perhaps she would have made him a better wife. If only he could have told her, trusted her with his secret, perhaps then…

Perhaps then what, exactly? Deborah hauled herself out of bed, where she had been languishing, and sat in front of the mirror. 'Honestly,' she said to her wan reflection, 'what do you think you could have done, if you had known? It wouldn't have made him love you.'

There. It was a fact. Elliot was right. There was nothing she could have done to make Jeremy love her.

'I am not a failure.' She tested the words out in no more than a whisper, but they lacked conviction. Because she *had* failed, hadn't she? She had not realised what everyone else had known. Her not knowing had made it impossible for her to console Jeremy. Had, in fact, forced Jeremy into prolonging his attempts to…

Pity enveloped her, followed by guilt. She could have

helped him, consoled him, made his life a little less miserable, if only she had known. But she hadn't known. He hadn't trusted her. Deborah straightened her shoulders and resumed her study of her reflection. 'It wasn't my fault,' she said, and this time her words sounded like the truth. 'I didn't fail, because he made it impossible for me to succeed.'

Jeremy had been ashamed. His repeated failures had made him more ashamed. She could see that. Deborah gave a little nod. 'Yes, I can see that. But he should have told me.' Another little nod. 'It wasn't my fault.' Convincing. 'I am not a failure.' More convincing.

Elliot didn't think she was a failure. 'Elliot,' Deborah said his name, just for the pleasure of it, and smiled. She loved him. For the first time, this gave her a warm glow. The kind of warm glow that she had, until that point, decided was an invention of the Minerva Press. 'I love him.' Utter conviction. Her reflection softened. She took a deep breath. 'And Elliot—Elliot loves me,' she said tremulously. Her smile became positively foolish. Her warm glow spread.

He loved her. She loved him. She was not a failure. It was not her fault. Was it too late? Deborah turned her back on her reflection, her face set in determined lines. The best things were worth fighting for. Elliot was the best thing ever to happen to her, but how—what could she do to persuade him that she had changed her mind? *Had* she changed her mind? All these years of thinking herself unattractive, undesirable, unwomanly— could she put them behind her? She couldn't be sure, but she could try. Weren't some things worth taking a chance on?

'Oh God, not just a chance, but the biggest gamble of my life.' Deborah paced the floor of her bedchamber, her bare feet icy on the boards. She couldn't risk hurting Elliot. She couldn't bear to hurt Elliot. But if Elliot truly did love her as he said, if he felt what she felt, had she not hurt him already? What was worse, taking a chance or not taking a chance?

Stupid question.

It was dawn before she lit upon the solution. The symmetry of it made her smile again. A beginning where it had all begun, except this time there would be two of them committing the crime. It was seditious and daring, it was illegal and it had the added attraction that by breaking the law they would be offending one of Jeremy's closest conspirators beyond any hope of forgiveness. Deborah thumped her fist into her open palm. It was perfect. Her smile faded. If only Elliot could be persuaded.

'He loves me. I love him. There is no question of failure,' she told her mirror confidently. Then she threw on her clothes and made haste down to her parlour. She had plans to make.

Elliot returned home dejected, having waved Lizzie, Alex and their entourage off on their journey north. Their obvious domestic bliss was like a dose of particularly disgusting medicine, except it did him no good.

He told himself that time would heal. Another of those old adages he had no faith in.

Though he had been angry and hurt by Deborah's rejection, he had been sustained, for the first few days, by the hope that she would change her mind. She would see, once she'd had time to think over what he had said, that he was right. She would realise that she loved him as he loved her, and that alone would be enough to change her. But days passed without a word, and his confidence waned. His nights were fraught. When he slept he dreamt, horrible dreams of running, running, and never reaching his destination. He was always losing things in his dreams, too. Packing them in a portmanteau, then discovering that he had not packed them after all. Leaving his valise somewhere, forgetting where. Putting things in the wrong pocket. Leaving them carelessly for someone else to steal. Nothing valuable, never the same things, but the loss was gut-wrenching.

He woke sweating, panting, his heart racing. Despair swamped him. Deborah did not come. Time and again, he set out to persuade her, but each time he changed direction. Having waited all his life to fall in love, he would not compromise it. Instead, he would focus on his future. There was unrest brewing in the country. With help, it could spread. The army had taught him how to lead. The Government had taught the Peacock how to break rules. He simply had to find a way to combine both talents to good effect. He would work out a role for himself. He would find a purpose. It would be enough. Sometimes, he almost believed it. He made plans, lots of plans, sure that one or several of them would be the thing which made him want to get out of bed in the morning.

He sat down by the empty grate, and was wondering how he was to fill the rest of the day when his servant brought him a note which had been delivered by hand. The familiar, untidy scrawl set his heart thudding. Elliot broke the seal.

It is set for tomorrow morning, he read, then paused, frowning. His own words, more or less, he remembered them clearly. The note he had written to Deborah that first time, when they broke into the house in Grosvenor Square. Not exactly what he was expecting, but then Deborah never did anything expected.

I will call for you at nine o'clock. Nine in the morning? What was she planning?

Bring your usual accessories. Daylight robbery?

If you do not wish to take part in this last assignment, send word by the boy. No signature. Elliot turned the single sheet over, but it was blank. Succinct and to the point. What point? For the first time in days, he found himself smiling. The point was that they would be together. He could hope. He could allow himself to hope.

'Will there be any reply, sir, only the boy is waiting?'

'No. Give him a sixpence and send him on his way,' Elliot said, unable to keep from grinning at his batman. *It is set for tomorrow morning.* Whatever *it* was, it was something.

He was waiting on the steps at fifteen minutes to nine. With still five minutes to go before the hour, Elliot had persuaded himself that she was not coming. He ran his fingers through his hair. The effect was to make it look considerably wilder. It needed cutting. He checked his pocket watch for the tenth time, giving it a shake, certain that it had stopped. He was upon the point of setting out for Hans Town on foot when a post-chaise pulled up in front of him and the door opened.

She was wearing her man's clothing. Breeches and boots. Greatcoat. Hat pulled down over her hair. Her smile, in the gloomy light of the carriage, was tremulous. 'You're here,' Deborah said foolishly, unable to say more because just seeing him made her breathless.

Elliot climbed into the chaise and sat down beside her. 'You're here,' he said, equally foolish, equally breathless. The carriage jolted over the cobblestones.

'Did you bring…?'

From the large pocket of his greatcoat, Elliot drew out his box of picks, his wrench. And the peacock feather.

The initial thrill of seeing him had receded. Deborah began to twist at one of the large brass buttons on her greatcoat.

Elliot took her hand, forcing her to relinquish her hold on the button, which she had already loosened. 'I've missed you,' he said.

Her fingers fluttered in his grip. 'I've missed you, too,' she whispered. She risked a glance up at him. His smile was only just perceptible, but it was there. Enough to give her courage. Enough to give her hope. 'Elliot…'

'Deborah?'

She sighed. 'I had a speech, but I don't think I can say it.' She took off her hat, and threw it on to the bench opposite. Then she gave one of her little nods. 'Elliot, I love you.'

He had hoped, from the moment he had read her note, he had hoped that she would be willing to consider the possibility, but he had not allowed himself to dream that she would say it. Just like that. Elliot was dumbfounded.

'I said, I love you.'

'Say it again.'

'I love you, Elliot.'

He tugged at his neckcloth. 'Are you sure?'

Deborah gave a funny little laugh. 'You think I'd be saying it if I was not?' She pressed a quick kiss to the back of his hand. 'I don't blame you for being sceptical.'

'Not sceptical, just scared, if you must know,' Elliot said, too afraid to consider prevaricating. 'I don't think I could bear it if you found you were wrong.'

She had never seen his face so stripped bare. The simple honesty of what he said, even more than his declaration over a week ago, made her realise the depths of his love for her. Almost she told him that she didn't deserve him, realising just in time that what mattered was that he believed she did. 'I know I love you, Elliot,' she said fervently, 'it's the thing I'm most certain of in the world. I promise.' She pressed another kiss on to his hand, then held it tight against her breast, then spoke in a rush, all the things she had planned so carefully tumbling out at once. 'You were right. About Jeremy.

About it not being my fault. About my hiding behind Bella. You were right about all of it, only it was such a shock. It took me days to be able to think straight. I knew I loved you, you see, from before—before we made love—but I thought it was impossible. Only after what you told me, I realised that I could make it possible if I wanted it enough, and I do, Elliot, I want it more than anything. You. Us. Only you have to understand, there are bound to be times when I think I'm not good enough. It's a hard habit to overcome, but what I'm trying to say is, that I want to try. I want to be happy, and I can't be happy without you, and that's worth trying for, isn't it? If it's not too late?'

'Too late?' Elliot tucked her hair behind her ear. Relief was already turning into something he thought might be happiness, spreading like fingers of sunshine from the inside out. 'It could never be too late. I love you. Didn't I tell you that's not going to change?' He swept her into his arms, pulling her across the bench of the carriage and kissing her ruthlessly. 'I love you,' he said, breathing heavily some moments, later. 'You have no idea how much.'

'I do. I do, Elliot. I have every idea.' Deborah clutched at his shoulders, pressing herself into the reassuringly solid bulk of him, kissing him back, deep passionate kisses, desperate, needy kisses. She ached with love for him. Her fingers twined in his hair, roamed restlessly down his back, under his coat, fumbling with the buttons of his waistcoat. Kisses were not enough. She needed him. All of him. Now.

Except that she had a plan, she remembered belatedly as the post-chaise jolted around a bend in the road and began to pick up speed, throwing them both hard back against the squabs. Elliot looked out of the dusty window, surprised to discover that they had left the city far behind. 'Where are we going?'

'Back to where it began. And ended,' Deborah said.

Elliot pulled her into his arms again. 'I'm not much in the mood for riddles. What I'm in the mood for involves you and me and a bed,' he said, slipping his hand under her coat and cupping her breast.

'That is the plan, sort of,' Deborah said, though she was having serious doubts about her ability to wait until then. His thumb was circling her nipple. She couldn't think and she needed to think. With a huge effort, she struggled free of his embrace. 'An hour, not much longer,' she said.

'An hour!' Elliot looked out of the window again. The countryside looked vaguely familiar. He turned back to Deborah, narrowing his eyes. 'Back to where it began, and ended?'

She nodded.

Her eyes were sparkling, that mixture of daring and excitement that sent the blood rushing to his groin. Elliot bit down on his smile. 'Please don't tell me that you plan to break into Kinsail Manor in the middle of the day?'

She nodded again.

'Am I to fall off the drainpipe and into your arms?'

'No.' Deborah began to pluck at the button of her

greatcoat again. 'We are going to make love. In my bed. In the daylight.' The button came away in her fingers. She stared at it in some surprise, before tucking it away in her pocket. 'I don't want there to be any ghosts to come between us,' she said. 'I want you to know I mean it. I love you.'

Elliot couldn't help it, he laughed. 'And you intend to prove it by breaking into your dead husband's home and making love on your marriage bed? That is the most outrageous, outlandish, subversive and utterly perfect plan I have ever heard of in my life. How could I ever doubt you, after this? And if I have to dangle on the end of a hangman's noose, I will take comfort in knowing that you are by my side.'

'Don't be silly, Elliot, they are not actually in residence.'

'That, my love, I had deduced for myself.'

'So you'll do it?'

'I will do anything you ask, provided you kiss me.'

'I don't think I will ever tire of kissing you.'

'Prove it,' Elliot said huskily, as his lips claimed hers.

They left the post-chaise at the Cross Keys, a mile from Kinsail Manor, and completed the journey on foot. It was hot; the sun beamed down from the pale blue summer sky, making their greatcoats look decidedly out of place. Deborah's step was almost a skip as they approached the huge portico which fronted the manor. She could not stop smiling.

'Are you sure the place is empty?' Elliot asked, surveying the shuttered windows doubtfully. 'There must be a skeleton staff in charge?'

'Mrs Chambers, the housekeeper. And she visits her niece on a Wednesday. The rest are either in London or have been paid off.' Deborah grinned. 'Don't worry, I've checked it all most meticulously. I have, after all, been trained by the master.'

'Then let us get on with it,' Elliot said.

'There is no need to hurry. I've told you, Mrs Chambers—'

'I don't give a damn about Mrs Chambers, and there is every need to hurry. I have a burning need to see you naked, my love,' Elliot said wickedly.

'Oh.'

'Precisely.'

The recent loss of his precious blue diamond had not been enough to overcome Lord Kinsail's inherent miserliness. No new bolts had been fitted to protect his property. Picking the two ancient locks which protected the kitchen door was a simple task which Elliot said disparagingly was quite beneath the Peacock.

The house was cold, unmistakably empty. Deborah led the way through the cavernous kitchens, noting without surprise that the ancient range had still not been replaced. The stone stairs which led through the baize door into the main hall were still treacherous. She paused, looking around her, waiting for the ghosts to grab her, but felt only a wild elation, a growing sense of certainty.

Telling Elliot to wait, she went hastily into the dining

room, retrieving two of the best crystal glasses from the cupboard. Their footsteps echoed on the wooden stair-case as they made their way up to the first floor. The master suite was in the east wing. Two doors. Jacob slept in Jeremy's room, she knew that from previous visits, but Cousin Margaret occupied another, in the west wing. The mistress's chamber, in which Deborah had spent almost every night of her marriage, was no longer used.

She paused outside the door. Her mouth was dry. Her hand hovered over the intricate brass handle.

'Deborah, you don't have to…'

'I want to.' She threw the door back and stepped over the threshold. Placing the glasses along with a small bundle on the dressing table, she opened the shutters, filling the room with light. Dust motes danced in the air. The room smelt stuffy, stale, but she could detect no scent of either failure or misery. Hauling the holland covers which shrouded the bed on to the floor, she looked around her, trying to summon up the past, but it eluded her. Here was the bed. There was the connecting door. But the woman who had been Jeremy's wife was not present.

Turning to Elliot, Deborah smiled. 'Now we can make our beginning.' Wrapping her arms around his neck, she stood on tiptoe. 'Make love to me, Elliot. To me. To Deborah. Not to Bella. Make love to me now,' she whispered, then kissed him.

He kissed her back. Slowly. Lovingly. Then deeply and passionately. The kisses that had begun in the post-chaise blossomed in the sunlit room. They kissed and kissed and kissed, then kisses were not enough. Coats, waistcoats and shirts were cast off, scattered across the room as they kissed.

Deborah sank on to the bed and Elliot removed first her boots and breeches then his own. He cupped her breasts, sucking deep on one nipple, then the other, sending white-hot heat down, pooling in her belly. Her hands roamed over his back, his chest, his stomach. They fell back on to the mattress, kissing, touching, stroking. His fingers traced fire in a path along the tender flesh of her thighs. She touched him, shivering with anticipation as she wrapped her fingers around his shaft, potent and thick.

He sank his fingers into her, making her gasp. She could feel herself tightening, clenching. She wanted him inside her, wanted it with a primal urgency that should be shocking, but was exciting. 'Elliot,' she said, closing her eyes, trying to cling to the edge, 'Elliot, I don't think I can wait.'

She felt the rumble of his laughter as he pulled her on top of him. 'That makes two of us.' His eyes were ablaze. He lifted her on to him, guided her down and she moaned harshly as he slid into her, high inside her. Already, she could feel the spiralling. He bucked under her and she clutched at his chest, her hair trailing over his face. He lifted her, slid her back down again on to him and she cried out at the wonder of it, thrust with him this time and again, harder, higher each time until her climax swept her away. The clenching of her muscles around him sent him over the edge and pulsing into her.

Deborah collapsed on to his chest, warmed by the sun, heated by their passion, breathing hard. 'Elliot,' she said, pressing hot, fluttering kisses to his mouth.

'Deborah,' he said, mirroring her action.

'I used to feel so empty, here,' she said, looking round. 'Now I feel—filled.'

Beneath her, Elliot chuckled. 'I hope so.'

'That's not what I meant,' she said, though her eyes were dancing.

He rolled her over, pinning her beneath him. 'Complete. That's what you meant.'

She blinked away a sudden tear. She had cried enough tears here. 'That's exactly what I meant. But there's just one thing missing.' Wriggling out from under him, she quickly untied the bundle she had brought with her and grabbed the crystal glasses. 'It will be warm, I hope you don't mind,' she said, holding the champagne bottle aloft.

'I must congratulate you on your plan,' Elliot replied, taking the bottle from her and popping the cork. 'You seem to have thought of everything.' He handed her a glass. 'To us.'

'To us,' Deborah said. She smiled at him, Bella's wicked smile, but she was under no illusions. It was Deborah who smiled it. 'I sincerely hope that after today, I shall be the only woman you will drink champagne with. Naked, in the middle of the day.'

Elliot took her glass from her and placed it on the

bedside table. 'I can promise you more than that,' he said. 'You, my love, will be the first and only woman that I will drink champagne from. Naked or otherwise. Day or night.'

'What do you mean?'

He tipped her on to her back and straddled her. 'Let me show you,' he said. The contents of his glass made her gasp as he tipped them on to her. Then his lips began to lap the wine from her skin, licking down the valley between her breasts, sipping from the dip of her belly and down.

The sun had moved round to the west wing of the Manor by the time they finished the champagne. 'They'll realise someone has been here,' Elliot said, tying a careless knot in his neckcloth, watching Deborah arrange the empty bottle and glasses neatly on the side table.

'I want him to know and I want them to know it was us,' she said, picking up the parcel from the dressing table. From it she produced a book. *Hemlock.* She laid it in the centre of the bed. On top of it she placed an antique wedding ring. 'Now Jacob will know that I know, he will know who wrote Bella's stories, and he will be far too embarrassed to do anything about any of it,' she said. 'This is where Bella was born, it feels only right that I leave her here.'

Elliot stared down at the book and the ring and the bed. Then he reached into his coat pocket and took out the last feather, laying it on top of the book, weighting it with the ring. 'In that case, it feels only right that the Peacock should die with her.' He pulled Deborah into his arms and kissed her tenderly. 'You are the most extraordinary woman I have ever met.'

Deborah emerged from his embrace ruffled and heated. 'You know,' she said, casting a final look around the room, 'I think I'm beginning to believe you.'

* * * * *

THE BEAUTY WITHIN

For Arianna, who helped me enormously with all things Italian, though any mistakes are all mine. *Grazie mille!*

Prologue

'Absolutely marvellous. A triumph.' Sir Romney Kirn rubbed his meaty hands together enthusiastically, his fingers like plump sausages, as he gazed at the canvas which had just been unveiled to him. 'Quite, quite splendid. I'd say he's done me justice, would not you, my love?'

'Indeed, my dear,' his good lady agreed. 'One would even go so far as to say he has made you more handsome and distinguished than you are in the flesh, if that were possible.'

Sir Romney Kirn was not a man short of flesh, nor much given to modesty. The glow which suffused his already ruddy and bloated face was therefore most likely attributable to a surfeit of port the previous evening. Lady Kirn turned, her corsets creaking disconcertingly, towards the artist responsible for her husband's portrait. 'Your reputation as a genius is well deserved, *signor*,' she said with a simpering little laugh, her eyelashes fluttering alarmingly.

She was clearly smitten, and in front of her husband

to boot. Had she no shame? Giovanni di Matteo sighed. Why did women of a certain age insist on flirting with him? In fact, why did women of all ages feel it necessary to throw themselves at him? He gave the merest hint of a bow, anxious to be gone. 'I am only as good as my subject, my lady.'

It worried him that the lies flowed with such practised ease. The baronet, a bluff man whose interests began and ended with hop farming had, over the course of several sittings, imparted his encyclopaedic knowledge of the crop while he posed, a copy of Adam Smith's *Wealth of Nations* in his hands—a volume which he admitted bluffly had not previously been opened, let alone read. The library which formed the backdrop to the portrait had been purchased as a job lot and had, Giovanni would have been willing to wager, remained entirely unvisited since its installation in the stately home— also recently acquired, following Sir Romney's elevation to the peerage.

Giovanni eyed the glossy canvas with the critical eye his clients sorely lacked. Technically, it was a highly accomplished portrait: the light; the angles; the precise placing of the subject within the composition, Sir Romney being posed in such a way as to minimise his substantial girth and make the most of his weak profile; all were perfect. An excellent likeness, his clients said. They always did, and indeed it was, in as much as it portrayed the baronet exactly as he wished to be seen.

It was Giovanni's business to create the illusion of authority or wealth, sensuality or innocence, charm or intelligence, whichever combination his sitter desired.

Beauty—of a kind. This polished, idealistic portrayal was what his clients sought in a di Matteo. It was what he was famed for, why he was sought after, and yet, at the peak of his success, ten years since arriving in England, the country he had made his home, Giovanni stared with distaste at the canvas and felt like a failure.

It had not always been like this. There had been a time when a blank canvas filled him with excitement. A time when a finished work made him elated, not desolate and drained. Art and sex. He had celebrated one with the other back in those days. Illusions both, like the ones he now painted for a living. Art and sex. For him, they used to be inextricably linked. He had given up the latter. Nowadays, the former left him feeling cold and empty.

'Now then, *signor*, here is the—er—necessary.' Sir Romney handed Giovanni a leather pouch rather in the manner of a criminal bribing a witness.

'Grazie.' He put the fee into the pocket of his coat. It amused him, the way so many of his clients found the act of paying for their portrait distasteful, unwilling to make the connection between the painting and commerce, for beauty ought surely to be priceless.

Refusing the dainty glass of Madeira which Lady Kirn eagerly offered, Giovanni shook hands with Sir Romney and bade the couple farewell. He had an appointment in London tomorrow. Another portrait to paint. Another blank canvas waiting to be filled. Another ego waiting to be massaged. And another pile of gold to add to his coffers, he reminded himself, which was the whole point, after all.

Never again, no matter if he lived to a hundred, would Giovanni have cause to rely on anyone other than himself. Never again would he have to bow to the wishes of another, to shape himself into the form another expected. He would not be his father's heir. He would not be any woman's plaything. Or man's for that matter—for there were many men of a certain type, wealthy and debauched, who liked to call themselves patrons but who were more interested in an artist's body than his body of work. His answer to those proposals had always been succinct—a dagger held threateningly to the throat— and always had the desired effect.

Never again. If he had to prostitute something to maintain his precious independence, then let it be his art and nothing else.

The room rented for the evening by the London Astronomical Society in Lincoln's Inn Fields was already crowded when the young man slipped unnoticed into his seat, anxious to remain inconspicuous. The meetings of this learned body of astronomers and mathematicians were not open to the public, but the way had been paved for his attendance by one of the members, Charles Babbage. The connection had initially been a family one, Mr Babbage's wife, Georgiana, being a remote cousin of Mr Brown, the name by which the young gentleman went by upon occasions such as this, but a shared passion for mathematics had cemented the acquaintance into a somewhat unconventional, some might even say subversive, friendship.

Tonight, the Society's president, John Herschel, was

presenting his paper on double stars which had recently won him a gold medal. Though it was not an area in which the young man held a particular interest, primarily due to the fact that he had no access to a telescope of his own, Mr Brown took notes assiduously. He had not yet given up hope of persuading his father to purchase such an instrument by stressing the educational benefits which young minds, namely the younger siblings so indulged by his parent, could derive from star-gazing. Besides, Mr Herschel's process of deduction based on reason and repeated observation was a technique common to all of the natural philosophies, including Mr Brown's own particular area of interest.

Candles fluttered on the walls of the panelled room, which was dimly lit and stuffy. As the lecture progressed, coats were loosened and the levels of the decanters fell. The erstwhile Mr Brown, however, partook not a drop of wine nor removed his hat, never mind unbuttoned the bone buttons of his over-large frock coat. He was considerably more tender in years than the other members, if appearances were to be believed, with a soft cheek which looked to be untouched by a razor. His hair, what could be seen of it, was dark brown and corkscrew-curled giving him, frankly, a rather effete appearance. His eyes were an unexpected blue, the colour of a summer sea. Wide-spaced and dark-fringed, a close observer would perceive in them a hint of a sparkle, as if he were laughing at his own private joke. Whether from reticence or some other motive, Mr Brown took care not to allow any such close observation, hunching over his notebook, meeting no glances, chewing on his lower lip, shading his face with his hand.

The fingers in which he held his pencil were delicate, though the nails were sadly bitten, the skin around them picked raw and peeling. His slenderness was emphasised by the heavy folds of his dark wool coat. Underdeveloped, he looked to be, or simply under-nourished as studious youths often were, for they neglected to eat. At the Astronomical Society they were accustomed to such types.

As soon as the lecture was over, the applause given and the myriad of questions addressed, Mr Brown got to his feet, huddling into a voluminous black cloak which made him seem even slighter. To a kind enquiry as to whether he had enjoyed the President's lecture he nodded gravely but did not speak, hurrying out of the room ahead of the other attendees, down the shallow steps of the building and into Lincoln's Inn Fields. The gardens across the way loomed, silent and slightly foreboding, the trees dark shapes which logic told him were simply trees but which felt menacing all the same. 'Be a man,' he muttered to himself. The words seemed to amuse him, and his amusement served to banish his trepidation.

The other buildings, once grand town houses, were these days almost all given over to offices of the law. Though it was after ten at night, lights burned in several windows. The shadow of a clerk huddled over his desk could be made out in the nearest basement. Conscious of the lateness of the hour, determinedly ignoring the lurking danger which any sensible person must be aware accompanied the location, the gentleman skirted Covent Garden and made his way towards Drury Lane. It would have been an easy thing to procure a hackney here, but his destination was relatively close, and besides he had no wish to speed his arrival. Head down, keeping the brim of his hat over his face, he passed the brothels and gaming houses. Eschewing the quickest route along Oxford Street, he headed for the genteel streets of Bloomsbury where he allowed his pace to slacken.

A distinct change came over Mr Brown as he neared Lord Henry Armstrong's substantial town house in Cavendish Square. The sparkle left his eyes. His shoulders hunched as if he were retreating into himself. His steps slowed further. A combination of illicit thrill and intellectual stimulation had charged his blood and his brain during the meeting he had attended. Looking up at the tall, shuttered windows of the first-floor drawing room which stared blankly down at him, he felt as if those sensations were literally draining away. Though he fought it, he could not conquer the feeling, not quite of dread but of dejection, which enveloped him. He did not belong here, but there was no escaping the fact that it was his home.

Through the closed drapes of the window on the ground floor to the left-hand side of the door, light glimmered. Lord Armstrong, a distinguished senior diplomat of many years standing who had contrived to retain his post and increased his influence in the newly elected Duke of Wellington's government, was working in his book room. Heart sinking, the young gentleman turned his key in the lock and made his way as silently as he could across the reception hall.

'Cressida, is that you?' the voice boomed.

The Honourable Lady Cressida Armstrong halted in her tracks, one foot on the bottom step of the staircase. She cursed in a most un-ladylike manner under her breath. 'Yes, Father, it is I. Goodnight, Father,' she called, foolishly crossing her fingers behind her back and making for the staircase, diving as fast as she could for the sanctity of her bedchamber before she was discovered.

Chapter One

London—March 1828

The clock in the reception hall downstairs chimed noon. Having spent much of the morning working and re-working a piece which transcribed the basics of her theory on the mathematics of beauty into a form which could be easily understood by the readers of *The Kaleidoscope* journal, Cressie now stared unhappily at her reflection in the tall looking-glass. Had she allowed sufficient time to summon her maid, perhaps her unruly curls would bear less resemblance to a bird's nest, but it was too late now. The morning gown of brown-printed cotton patterned with cream and burnt-orange flashes and trimmed with navy satin ribbon was one of her favourites. The sleeves, contrary to the current fashion, were only slightly puffed, and came down almost to her knuckles, hiding her ink-stained fingers from sight. The skirts were, also contrary to fashion, not quite bell-shaped, and the hem was trimmed with only one flounce. Sombre and serious was the effect she was aiming for. Cressie pulled a face. Washed-out, plain and rather ragged around the edges was what she had achieved. 'As usual,' she muttered, turning away from her reflection with a shrug.

Making her way downstairs, she braced herself for the encounter ahead. Whatever the reason behind her father's request to speak with her, she could be certain it was not going to be a pleasant experience. 'Be a man,' Cressie said to herself with a defiant swish of her skirts as she tapped on the door of the book room. Curtsying briefly, she took a seat in front of the imposing walnut desk. 'Father.'

Lord Henry Armstrong, still handsome at fifty-five years of age, nodded curtly. 'Ah, Cressida, there you are. I had a letter from your stepmother this morning. You may congratulate me. Sir Gilbert Mountjoy has confirmed that she is increasing.'

'Again!' Bella had already produced four boys in eight years, there was surely no need for yet more—and in any event, Cressie had supposed her father to be well past that sort of thing. She screwed up her nose. Not that she wanted to contemplate her father and Bella and *that sort of thing*. She caught his eye and attempted to re-arrange her expression into something more congratulatory. '*Another* half-sibling. How very—agreeable. A sister would make a most pleasant change, would it not?'

Lord Armstrong drummed his fingers on his blotter and glared at his daughter. 'I would hope Bella would have the good sense to produce me another son. Daughters have their uses but it is sons who provide the where-withal to secure the family's position in society.'

He made his children sound like chess pieces in some arrogant game, Cressie thought bitterly, though she chose not to voice it. She knew her father well enough, and this was a mere preamble. If he wanted to speak to her it invariably meant he wanted her to do something for him. Daughters have their uses right enough!

'To the matter in hand,' Lord Armstrong said, bestowing on Cressie the sort of benevolent smile that had averted a hundred diplomatic incidents and placated a myriad of courtiers and officials across Europe. The effect on his daughter was rather the opposite. Whatever he was about to say, she would not like. 'Your stepmother has not been in her customary rude health. The good Sir Gilbert has confined her to bed. It is most inconvenient, for with Bella indisposed, it means Cordelia's coming-out will have to be postponed.'

Cressie's rather stiff smile faded. 'Oh no! Cordelia will be most upset, she has been counting the days. Cannot my Aunt Sophia take Bella's place for the Season?'

'Your aunt is a fine woman and has been an enormous support to me over the years, but she is not as young as she was. If only it were just a question of Cordelia. I have no doubt that your sister will go off quickly, for she's a little beauty. I have Barchester in mind for her, you must know, he has excellent connections. However, it is *not* simply a question of Cordelia, is it? There is your own unmarried state to consider. I had intended that Bella would act as escort for you both this Season. You cannot prevaricate indefinitely, Cressida.'

The veteran diplomat looked meaningfully at his daughter, who wondered rebelliously if her father had any idea of what he'd be up against, trying to coerce Cordelia into wedding a man whose full, gleaming set of teeth owed their existence in his mouth to their removal from the gums of one of his tenants, if rumour was to be believed. 'If Lord Barchester is your ambition for Cordelia,' Cressie said, keeping her eyes fixed on her clasped hands, 'then it is to be hoped that he is more enamoured with her than he was with myself.'

'Hmm.' Lord Armstrong drummed his fingers again. 'That, Cressida, is an excellent point.'

'It is?' Cressie said warily. She was not used to praise of any sort from her father.

'Indeed. You are twenty-eight now.'

'Twenty-six, actually.'

'No matter. The point is you have scared the devil out of every eligible man I've put your way, and the fact is that I intend to put some of them your sister's way. They'll not want you standing beside her like a spectre when I do. As I mentioned earlier, your Aunt Sophia is too advanced in years to adequately present two gals in one Season, so it seems I must choose. Cordelia will likely fly off the shelf. I think my ambitions for you will have to be temporarily put into abeyance. No, do not, I pray, feign disappointment, daughter,' Lord Armstrong added caustically. 'No crocodile tears, I beg you.'

Cressie's clasped hands curled into fists. Over the years, it had become her determined policy never to let her father see how easily he could bruise her feelings. That he still managed to do so was one of the things which vexed her most. She understood him very well yet still, no matter how predictable were his barbs, they

invariably hurt. She had long ceased thinking that he
would ever understand her, far less value her, but somehow she felt compelled to keep trying. Why was it so
difficult to fit her emotions to her understanding! She
sighed. Because he was her father and she loved him,
she supposed. Though she found it very hard to like him.

Lord Armstrong frowned down at the letter from his
spouse. 'Do not, either, delude yourself that you are entirely off the hook. I have another pressing problem that
you can assist me with. Apparently that damned governess of the boys has fled her post. James put a pig's
bladder filled with water in her bed, and the woman left
without giving any notice.' The diplomat gave a bark
of laughter. 'Chip off the old block, young James. We
used to get up to the same jape at Harrow when I was
a stripling.'

'James,' Cressie said feelingly, 'is not *high-spirited*
but utterly spoilt. What's more, where James leads Harry
follows.' She might have known that this would turn out
to be about her father's precious sons. She loved her
half-brothers well enough, even if they were thoroughly
spoilt, but her father's preoccupation with them to the
exclusion of everything, and everyone, else, grated.

'The nub of the matter is that my wife is clearly in
no position to secure a suitable new governess post-
haste, and I myself, it goes without saying, have many
weighty matters of state to attend to. Wellington relies
on me completely, you know.' It was an illusion, Cressie
knew, but she could swear that her father visibly puffed
up as he made this pronouncement. 'However, my boys'
education must not be interrupted,' he continued, 'I have

great plans for all of them. I have pondered on this, and it seems to me that the solution is obvious.'

'It is?' Cressie said doubtfully.

'It certainly is to me. You, Cressida, will be governess to my sons. That way, Cordelia will be able to come out this Season as planned. Placing you in the position of governess removes you most expediently from Cordelia's arena, and spares you from being a burden by making use of that brain you are so proud of. My sons' education will not be jeopardised. With a bit of luck we may even have Cordelia married by the autumn. And there is the added bonus of having you on hand at Killellan Manor while Bella is indisposed, thus providing you with the opportunity to forge a more amenable relationship with your stepmother than hitherto.' Lord Armstrong beamed at his daughter. 'If I say so myself, I have devised a most elegant and satisfactory solution to a potentially difficult situation. Which, one supposes, is why Wellington values my diplomatic skills so highly.'

Cressie's thoughts were, however, far from diplomatic. Presented with what she had no doubt was a *fait accompli*, her instinct was to find some way of sabotaging her father's carefully laid plans. But even as she opened her mouth to protest, it came to her that perhaps she could turn the situation to her advantage.

'You wish me to act as governess?' Her brain worked feverishly. Her brothers were taxing, but if she could manage to teach James and Harry the principles of geometry using the primer she had written, it might provide her publishers with the evidence they needed to commit to a print date. Freyworth and Son had initially

been most enthusiastic when she first visited their offices, and most reassuring on the subject of discretion.
The firm had, Mr Freyworth told her, several lady writers on their books who wished, for various reasons, to
remain anonymous. Surely such practical proof as she
would obtain from successfully instructing her brothers would persuade him that her book really was a vi-
able commercial proposition? Selling her primer would
be the first step to financial independence, which was
the first step towards freedom. And who knew, if she
managed his precious boys better than any of the other
governesses, she might finally gain her father's approbation. Although that, Cressie conceded, was unlikely.

Even more importantly, accepting his proposal meant
that she would not have to spend a seventh Season
mouldering away on the shelf while her father schemed
and plotted an alliance. So far, he had stopped short of
taking out an advertisement on the front page of the
Morning Post along with the intimations of patents
pending, but who knew what he might do if he became
desperate enough. *One daughter, without looks but of
excellent lineage and diplomatic connections, offered
to ambitious man with acceptable pedigree and political aspirations. Tory preferred, but Whig considered.
No tradesmen or time wasters.*

Now she thought of it, it was a distinct possibility for,
as Lord Armstrong never tired of pointing out, she possessed neither the poise nor beauty of any of her other
sisters. That she was the clever one was no consolation
whatsoever to Cressie, when she thought of how incredibly foolishly she had behaved during that fiasco of her

third Season, by surrendering her one marketable asset to Giles Peyton. That she could have been so desperate—Cressie shuddered. Even now, the memory was mortifying. It had been a disaster in every possible way save one—her reputation, if not her hymen, was intact, for her erstwhile lover and intended husband had hastily taken up a commission shortly afterwards, leaving her in sole possession of the unpalatable facts.

In more recent Seasons, her father's attempts to marry her off had smacked of desperation, but he had never once flagged in his manipulations. He thought he was manipulating her now, but if she kept her cards close to her chest, she might just manage to turn the tables. Cressie felt a small glow inside her. Whether it was self-satisfaction or a feeling of empowerment she wasn't sure, but it was a feeling she liked. 'Very well, Father, I will do as you ask and act as governess to the boys.'

She kept her voice carefully restrained, for to hint that she wished to do as he said would be a major tactical error. It seemed she had hit just the right note of reluctant compliance, for Lord Armstrong nodded brusquely. 'Of course they will require a proper male tutor before they go to Harrow, but in the meantime the rudiments of mathematics, Latin and Greek—I believe I can rely on you for those.'

'*Rudiments!*'

Lord Armstrong, seeing that his remark had hit home, smiled. 'I am aware, Cressida, that you consider your erudition rather above the requirements of my sons. It is my fault. I have been an over-indulgent parent,' he said in all sincerity. 'I should have put an end to these studies of yours long ago. I see they have given you a most inflated view of your own intellect. It is no wonder that you have failed to bring any man up to scratch.'

Was it true? Was she conceited?

'Next year,' Lord Armstrong continued inexorably, 'when Cordelia is off my hands, I shall expect you to accept the first offer of marriage I arrange for you. It is your duty, and I expect you to honour it. Do I make myself clear?'

It had always been made abundantly clear to her that, as a daughter, as a mere female, her purpose was to serve, but her father had never before laid it out so clearly and unequivocally.

'Cressida, I asked you a question. Do I make myself clear?'

She hesitated, torn between bitter hurt and impotent fury. Silently, she pledged that she would use this year to find a way, any way save telling him the awful, shameful truth of her dalliance with Giles, of placing herself firmly on the shelf and just as importantly, of establishing herself as an independent and wholly *un*dependent female. Cressie glared at her father. 'You make yourself abundantly clear.'

'Excellent,' Lord Armstrong replied with infuriating calm. 'Now, to other matters. Ah—' he broke off as a tap on the study door heralded the arrival of his butler '—that will be him now.'

'Signor di Matteo awaits his lordship's pleasure,' the butler intoned.

'The portrait-painter fellow,' Lord Armstrong casually informed his daughter, as if this should be the most obvious thing in the world. 'You shall relieve your step-mother of that burden also, Cressida.'

He had obviously walked in on some sort of alter-cation, for the atmosphere in the study fairly crackled with tension as Giovanni entered the room in the portly wake of Lord Armstrong's butler. The manservant, either oblivious to the strained mood or, more likely in the way of English servants, trained to give that impression, announced him and departed, leaving Giovanni alone with the two warring factions. One of them was obviously Lord Armstrong, his client. The other, a female, whose face was lost under a mass of unruly curls, stood with her arms crossed defiantly over her bosom. He could almost taste the pent-up frustration simmering away beneath the surface, could guess too, from the way she veiled her eyes, the vulnerability she was trying to hide. Such a mastery of her emotions was intriguing, for it required, as Giovanni could attest, a lifetime's practice. Whoever she was, she was not your typical simpering English rose.

Giovanni made his perfunctory bow, just low enough and no more, for it was one of the advantages of his success that he no longer had to feign deference. As was his custom, his dress was austere, even severe. His frock coat with its high shawl collar and wide skirts would be the height of fashion were it any colour other than black. Similarly his high-buttoned waistcoat, his stir-rupped trousers and highly polished square-toe shoes, all unrelieved black, making the neat ruffles of his pris-tine shirt and carefully tied cravat gleam an impossible white. It amused him to create an appearance in such stark contrast to the flamboyant and colourful persona his high-born sitters expected of a prestigious artist—and an Italian one at that. He looked as if he were in mourning. There were times, of late, when he felt that he was.

'Signor de Matteo.' Lord Armstrong sketched an even more shallow bow. 'May I present my daughter, Lady Cressida.'

The glance she shot her father was a bitter dart. It was received with a small smile. Whatever had transpired between them was the latest in what Giovanni surmised had been a lifetime of such skirmishes. He made another bow, a little more sincerely this time. Looking into a pair of eyes the azure blue of the Mediterranean Sea in summer, he saw they were overly bright. 'My lady.'

She did not curtsy, but offered her hand to shake, like a gentleman. 'How do you do, *signor*.' A firm clasp she had, though her nails were in an atrocious state, chewed to the quick, the skin bleeding around the edges. She had a pleasant voice, to his ear, the vowels clipped and precise. He had the impression of a fierce intelligence blazing from her eyes under that intense frown, though not beauty. Indeed, her dreadful gown, the way she rounded her posture, curling into herself as she sat down, made it clear that she cultivated plainness. But for all that—or perhaps because of that—he thought she had an interesting face.

Was she to be his subject? A pique of interest flared momentarily but no, the commission was for a portrait of children, and Lady Cressida was most definitely well past her girlhood. A pity, for he would have liked to try to capture the vitality behind the shimmering resentment. She was no empty-headed society beauty, nor appeared to have any aspirations to be depicted as such. He cursed the paradox which made the most interesting of subjects the least inclined to be painted, and the most beautiful subjects the ones he was least inclined to depict. Then he reminded himself that beauty was his business. A fact he was having to remind himself of rather too often.

'Sit, sit.' Lord Armstrong ushered him to a chair and resumed his own seat, surveying him shrewdly from behind the desk. 'I wish you to paint a portrait of my boys. James is eight. Harry six. And the twins, George and Frederick, are five.'

'Four, actually,' the daughter intervened.

Her father waved away her comment. 'Still in short coats, is the important thing. You'll paint them together, as a group.'

It was, Giovanni noted, an instruction rather than a question. 'And the mother too?' he asked. 'That is the usual…'

'Lord, no. Bella's not—no, no, I do not wish my wife depicted.'

'What, then, of their sister?' Giovanni asked, turning towards Lady Cressida.

'Just the boys. I want you to capture their charms,' his lordship said, looking pointedly at his daughter, whom he obviously considered to possess none.

Giovanni repressed a sigh. Another tedious depiction of cherubic children. Sons, but no daughter. The English aristocracy were no different from the Italian in their views in that regard. It was to be a pretty and idealistic portrait totally lacking in any truth, the licit products of Lord Armstrong's loins displayed in the family gallery for posterity. His heart sank. 'You wish me to show your sons as charming,' he repeated fatalistically.

'They *are* charming.' Lord Armstrong frowned. 'Proper manly boys, mind. I want you to show that too, nothing namby-pamby. Now, as to the composition...'

'You may leave that decision with me.' Forced to paint a vision far removed from reality he might be, but his fame had at least allowed him some element of control. As Giovanni had expected, his lordship looked put out. It was all so predictable. 'You may have every confidence in my choice. I presume you have seen my work, my lord?'

'Not seen as such, but I've heard excellent reports of it. I wouldn't have summoned you here if I hadn't.'

This was new. Across from him, he could see that it was news also to Lady Cressida, who looked appalled.

'I fail to see how my being unfamiliar with your work is at all relevant.' Lord Armstrong frowned heavily at his daughter. 'As a diplomat, I have to trust the word of others constantly. If there's a problem in Egypt, or Lisbon, or Madrid, I can't be expected to hotfoot it over there in person. I ask myself, who is the best man for the job, and then I get him to deal with it. It's the same with this portrait. I have taken soundings, sought expert advice. Signor di Matteo was consistently highly recommended—in point of fact,' he said, turning to Giovanni, 'I was told you were the best. Was I misinformed?'

'Certainly, demand for my portraits far outstrips the rate at which I can produce them,' Giovanni replied. Which was true, and ought to cause him a great deal more satisfaction than it did, even if it did not actually answer Lord Armstrong's question. His success was such that he could command an extremely high premium for his portraits, even if that very success felt not like freedom but a prison of his own making. Another thing Giovanni was discovering recently, that success was a double-edged sword. Fame and fortune, while on the one hand securing his independence, had severely compromised his creativity. It was a price worth paying, he told himself every day. No matter that he felt his muse recede ever faster with every passing commission.

His newest patron, however, seemed quite satisfied with his response. To possess what others desired was sufficient for Lord Armstrong, as it was for most of his class.

His lordship got to his feet. 'Then we are agreed.' He held out his hand, and Giovanni stood too, taking it in a firm grip. 'My secretary will handle the—er, commercial details. I look forward to seeing the finished product. I must make my excuses now, for I am expected at Apsley House. There is a chance I may have to accompany Wellington on his trip to St Petersburg. Inconvenient, but when one's country calls, what can one do! I shall leave you in my daughter's charge, *signor*. She will supervise her brothers during the sittings. Anything you need Cressida can provide, since Lady Armstrong, my wife, is currently indisposed.'

With only a curt nod in his daughter's direction, Lord

Armstrong hurried from the room, content that he had in one fell swoop neatly resolved all his domestic problems and could now concentrate his mind fully on the much more important and devilishly tricky matter of how best to address the issue of Greek independence without standing on either Turkish or Russian toes.

Left alone with the artist, Cressida surveyed him properly for the first time. She had been so absorbed in trying to maintain control of her temper that until now she had noted merely that Signor di Matteo's dress was not at all like the peacock she expected, that he was younger than she had surmised from his reputation, and that his English was excellent. What struck her now with some force was that he was starkly and strikingly beautiful. Not merely handsome, but possessing such an ethereal magnetism and sense of physical perfection that she could almost question whether or not he was real.

Aware that she was staring, she took a mental inventory in an attempt to unscramble her reeling senses. High cheekbones and a high brow, the sleek line of his head outlined by the close-cropped cap of raven-black hair. His eyes were dark brown under heavy dark lids. It was a classically proportioned face, albeit vaguely saturnine. The planes of his cheeks were sharp, accentuated by the hollows below. He had a good nose. A near enough perfect nose, in fact. And his mouth—it was wasted on a man, that mouth. Full lips, top and bottom, deeply sensual, sculpted, and at the same time it curved up just enough to make him look as if he was on the verge of a smile, just enough to take the edge off his forbidding expression. Even without measuring the precise angles, Cressie could tell she was looking at the physical embodiment of perfect mathematical beauty. A face which would launch a thousand ships—or flutter a thousand female hearts more likely, she thought cynically. But it was also the epitome of her theory. And at that thought, her heart gave a little unaccustomed flutter.

She was being rude, though, judging from the way Signor di Matteo was returning her gaze. Haughty and at the same time wearily resigned, he was clearly accustomed to being stared at. No wonder, and even less of a surprise was his indifference to her, for he had painted some famous beauties. Unlike her father, Cressie had studied several examples of Signor di Matteo's work in the course of her research for her treatise. Like the man himself, his paintings were perfectly proportioned and classically beautiful. Too perfect, almost. His subjects were portrayed flawlessly and flatteringly. There was, in the small number of portraits she had managed to view, a similarity in the way their faces conformed to an ideal, the result of which was undoubtedly a very accomplished likeness, but also moulded the individual features from a kind of template of beauty. Which was exactly the premise of the theory that Cressie had developed. Beauty could be reduced to a series of mathematical rules. It would be fascinating to see first-hand how Signor di Matteo, the famous artist, set about creating his works.

A famous artist who, Cressie now noted with deep embarrassment, was tapping his fingers impatiently on her father's desk. She flushed. How rude he must think her. 'I trust you have in mind a suitably flattering composition, *signor*. As you will no doubt have noticed, my father dotes on his sons.'

'His *charming* boys.'

Was there just the lightest hint of irony in his voice? Could this artist actually be mocking his patron? 'They *are* very good-looking,' Cressie conceded, 'but they are most certainly *not* charming. In fact, you should know that they have a particular liking for practical jokes. Their governess has recently left without notice as a result of one such, which is why I shall be taking her place, their reputation being—'

'*You!*'

Cressie stiffened. 'As I have already informed my father, I am perfectly capable of teaching the *rudiments* of mathematics.'

'That is not what I meant. It is merely that the Season is almost upon us. I would have thought you would have had parties to attend—but forgive me, it is none of my business.'

'I have already experienced several Seasons, *signor*, and have no wish to endure another. I am six-and-twenty, and quite beyond dances and parties. Not that I ever—but that is of no account.'

'You have no wish to find a husband, then?'

The question was extremely impertinent, but the tone of his voice was not, and Cressie was, in any case, eager to vent her spleen now that the real object of her wrath had departed. 'There are some women whom marriage does not suit. I have concluded I am one of them.' Which was not quite a lie, but more like putting the truth through a prism. 'Until I am at least thirty and saying my prayers, however, my father will not accept that. His gracious permission to excuse me this year is more to do with ensuring I do not intrude on my youngest sister's chances of making an excellent match. Once she is safely betrothed, I am to be wheeled back on to the market. My role as governess is merely a temporary expedient.'

Her frankness had obviously perplexed him. It had taken her aback too. A small frown marred that perfect brow of his, and confusingly there was also a hint of upward tilt of that far too perfect mouth. Was he laughing at her? Cressie bristled. 'It was not my intention to provide you with a source of amusement, *signor.*'

'I am not amused, merely—interested. I have not before met a lady so determined to boast of her unmarried state and the fact that she understands more than the—er—the *rudiments* of mathematics.'

He *was* mocking her. 'Well, now you have.' Indignation and anger made Cressie indiscreet. 'And I do understand *considerably* more than the rudiments, if you must know. In fact, I have published a number of articles on the subject, and even reviewed Mr Lardner's book, *Analytical Treatise on Plane and Spherical Trigonometry.* I have also written a children's geometry primer which a most respected publisher has shown an interest in printing, and I am currently writing a thesis on the mathematics of art.'

So there! Cressie folded her arms over her chest. She had not meant to blurt out quite so much. Having done so, she waited for Signor di Matteo to laugh, but instead he raised his brows and smiled, not a condescending smile, but rather as if he was surprised. His smile made her catch her breath, for it transformed his beauty from that of a haughty statue to something much more human.

'So you are a published author.'

'Under the pseudonym Penthiselea.' Cressie had just betrayed yet another jealously guarded secret without meaning to. What was it about this man? He had her spilling her innermost thoughts like some babbling child.

'Penthiselea. An Amazonian warrior famed for her wisdom. It is most—apt.'

'Yes, yes, but I must urge you to discretion. If my father knew…' Cressie took yet another deep breath. '*Signor*, you must understand that in my position—that is to say—my father thinks that my facility for mathematics is detrimental to his ambition to marry me off, and I must confess that it is my own experience too, by and large. Men do not value intelligence in their wives.'

Signor di Matteo's smile had a cynical twist to it now, his dark eyes seemed distant, turned in on some unpleasant memory. 'Blood and beauty rule supreme, *signorina*,' he said. 'It is the way of the world.'

It was a stark little expression, which said more precisely than she ever could exactly what Cressie herself believed. Beauty was this man's business, but she wondered what he knew of the burden of pedigree. She could not find a way of framing such a personal question without inviting offence.

He put an end to her attempts, with a question of

his own. 'If you are studying the relationship of mathematics to art, you must have read the definitive work by my fellow Italian. I refer to Pacioli, his *De Divina Proportione*?'

Pleased to discover that he was not the type of man to assume her sex prevented her from understanding such an erudite work, Cressie was at the same time distracted by how lovely the title of the book sounded when spoken by a native Italian. 'You have read it?' she asked foolishly, for he obviously had.

'It is a standard text. You agree with what he says, that beauty can be described in the rules of symmetry?'

'And proportion. These are surely the basic rules of any art?'

Signor di Matteo began to prowl restlessly about the room, frowning. 'If painting was simply about getting angles and proportions right, then anyone could be an artist.'

'How did you learn to paint so well?' Cressie countered.

'Study. Of the Old Masters. In the studios as apprentice to other painters. Practice.'

'So it is a skill. A craft, with rules which can be learned. That is exactly my point.'

'And my point is that art is not simply a craft.' There was anger in his tone now.

'I don't understand what I've said to upset you, *signor*. I was paying you a compliment. The primary purpose of art is to adorn, is it not? And if it is to adorn, it must be beautiful. And if it is beautiful, then it must conform to what we know is beautiful—to the mathematical rules of symmetry and proportion which we see in nature, as your countryman Signor Fibonacci has shown us. To be reckoned the best, not only must you have mastered the technical skills of the draughtsman, but you must obviously have the firmest grasp of these underlying rules.'

'So I paint by rote, that is what you are saying?'

'I am saying that you are a master of the rules of nature.'

'Yet nature has created you, my lady, and you hardly conform to those rules. By your process of deduction, you cannot then consider yourself beautiful.'

The cruelty of his words was like a slap in the face. She had been so caught up in propounding her theory that she had unwittingly insulted him, and his response, to turn her own plainness against her, was much more painful than it ought to be. The light of intellectual conviction died from her eyes, and Cressie tumbled back down into harsh reality. Signor di Matteo possessed the kind of looks which made women cast caution to the winds, though most likely the caution they cast was physical rather than intellectual. 'I am perfectly well aware, *signor*, that I am not beautiful.'

'There is beauty in everything if you know how, and where, to look.'

He was standing too close to her. She was acutely aware of his brooding physical presence. Cressie got to her feet, intending to push him out of the way, but he caught hold of her arm. His fingers were long, tanned and quite free of paint, she noted absently. Her head barely reached the broad sweep of his shoulders. This close, there was no mistaking the strength which lurked underneath that lithe exterior. Being so near to him made her breathing erratic. It was embarrassment which was making her hot. Every propriety must be offended. 'What do you think you're doing? Unhand me at once.'

He ignored her, instead tilting her chin up and forcing her to meet his piercing gaze. She could escape quite easily, and yet it did not occur to her. 'It is true,' he said softly, 'that your nose is not perfectly straight and so spoils the symmetry of your profile.'

Cressie glowered. 'I am perfectly aware of that.'

'And your eyes. They are too wide-spaced, and so not in the proportion to your mouth which Pacioli requires.'

One long finger traced the line he mentioned. His own eyes had a rim of gold at the edges. The lashes were black and thick. His touch was doing strange things to her insides. It made her jittery. Nervous. Was he flirting with her? Definitely not. He was merely punishing her for her unintended insult. 'And my ears are out of alignment with my nose, the ratio between my chin and my forehead is wrong,' Cressie said, with an insouciance she most certainly did not feel. 'As for my mouth...'

'As for your mouth...'

Signor di Matteo trailed his finger along the length of her bottom lip. She felt the most absurd urge to taste him. He growled something in Italian. His fingers splayed out over her jaw. He bent his head towards her. He was going to kiss her.

Cressie's heart thudded. He really was going to kiss her. The muscles in her calves tensed in preparation for flight, but she didn't move. His fingers slid along her jaw to tangle in her hair. She watched, urging herself to escape, but at the same time another part of her brain was enthralled, mesmerised, by that perfectly symmetrical face. Let him, she thought. Let him kiss me, if he dares!

His lips hovered a fraction over hers, just long enough for her to have a premonition of melting, a premonition of what it would be like to cede, to unleash whatever it was he kept restrained. Just long enough for Cressie to come to her senses.

She yanked herself free. 'How dare you!' It sounded very unconvincing, even to herself. She was struggling to breathe, praying that the heat which flooded her cheeks, which was surely mortification, was not too apparent. The nerve of him! He was outrageously attractive *and* he obviously knew it. Also, he was Italian. Everyone knew that Italian men were quite unable to control their passions. Obviously, it was not such a cliché as she had thought.

'To return to your point, *signor*, I concede that my mouth is too wide to be considered beautiful,' Cressie said, relieved to hear that her voice sounded almost composed.

'Beauty, Lady Cressida, is not exclusively about symmetry. Your mouth is very beautiful, in my humble opinion.'

Giovanni di Matteo did not look the least abashed. 'You ought not to have kissed me,' Cressie said.

'I did not kiss you. And *you* ought not to have spoken so scathingly of my work, especially since you have never seen it.'

'Do not assume that I am so ignorant as my father. I

have studied it, and I did not speak scathingly! I merely pointed out that you—that painting—that any art—'

'Can be reduced to a set of principles and rules. I *was* listening.' But even as he curled his lip, Giovanni had a horrible suspicion that this wholly unorthodox female had somehow managed to get to the root of his dissatisfaction. In the early days, when he painted for the simple pleasure of creating something unique, he had channelled that tangible connection between canvas and brush and palette and blood and skin and bone, painting from the heart and not the head. It had earned him nothing but mockery from the so-called experts. *Naïve. Emotional. Lacking discipline and finesse.* The words were branded on his heart. He learned to hone his craft, eradicate all emotion from his work. To his eye it rendered it soulless, but it proved immensely popular. The experts acclaimed it, the titled and influential commissioned it. He chose not to disillusion any of them. Giovanni made his bow. 'Much as I have enjoyed our discussion, Lady Cressida, I must go and continue with the more prosaic task of capturing the likeness of my current client. I bid you good day.'

He took her hand, raising it to his lips. As he kissed her fingertips, the spark of awareness took him by surprise. Judging by her shocked expression, he was not the only one affected by it.

Chapter Two

Giovanni leapt down from the gig as it drew to a halt in front of Killellan Manor, the country estate of the Armstrong family, airily dismissing the waiting footman's offer to escort him to the door. He had travelled to Sussex on the mail, which had been met at the nearest posting inn by Lord Armstrong's coachman. It was a cold but clear day, the clouds scudding across the pale blue sky of early spring, encouraged by the brisk March breeze. Pulling his greatcoat more tightly around himself, he stamped his feet in an effort to stimulate the circulation. There were many things about England he admired, but the weather was not one of them.

Lord Armstrong's impressive residence was constructed of grey sandstone. Palladian in style, with the main four-storey building flanked by two wings, the façade which fronted on to the carriage way was marred, in Giovanni's view, by the unnecessary addition of a much later semi-circular portico. Enclosed by the high hedges into which the gates were set, the house looked gloomy and rather forbidding.

Wishing to stretch his legs after the long journey before announcing his presence, Giovanni followed the main path past a high-walled garden and the stable buildings to discover a prospect at the front of the house altogether different and much more pleasing to the eye. Here, manicured lawns edged with bright clumps of daffodils and narcissi stretched down, via a set of wide and shallow stone steps, to a stream which burbled along a pebbled river bed towards a watermill. On the far side of the river, the vista was of gently rolling meadows neatly divided by hedgerows. Despite the fact that the rustic bridge looked rather suspiciously too rustic, he couldn't help but be entranced by this quintessentially English landscape.

'It is a perfect example of what the poet, Mr Blake, calls *England's green and pleasant land*, is it not?'

Giovanni started, for the words came from someone standing immediately behind him. The rush of the water over the pebbles had disguised her approach. 'Lady Cressida. I was thinking almost exactly that, though I am not familiar with the poet, I'm afraid. Unless—could it be William Blake, the artist?'

'He is more known for his verse than his art.'

'That will change. I have seen some of his paintings. They are…' Giovanni struggled to find an appropriate English word to describe the fantastical drawings and watercolours which seemed to explode out of the paper. 'Extraordinary,' he settled on finally and most unsatisfactorily. 'I find them beautiful, but most certainly they would fail your mathematical criteria.'

'And this?' She waved at the landscape. 'Would you consider this beautiful?'

'I suspect your father has invested rather a lot of money to ensure that it is. That bridge, it cannot possibly be as old as it appears.'

'There is also a little artfully ruined folly in the grounds, and you are quite correct, neither are older than I am.'

It had been more than two weeks since their first meeting in London. In the interval, Giovanni had replayed their conversation several times in his head, and that almost-but-not-quite kiss too. It had been a foolish act to take such a liberty with the daughter of the man who was paying his commission, and a man of such palpable influence too. He couldn't understand why he had been so cavalier. Attempting to recreate Lady Cressida feature by feature using charcoal on paper had proved entirely unsatisfactory. He had been unable to capture the elusive quality that had piqued his interest. Now, as she stood before him, the sun shining directly behind her, making a halo of her wild curls, the dark shadows under her startlingly blue eyes, the faintest trace of a frown drawing her brows together giving her a delicate, bruised look, he could see that it was nothing to do with her features but something more complex which drew him to her. It puzzled him, until he realised that her allure was quite basic. He wanted to capture that ambiguity of hers in oils.

'You look tired,' Giovanni said, speaking his thoughts aloud.

'My brothers are—energetic,' Cressie replied. *Ex-*

hausting would be more accurate, but that would sound defeatist. Two weeks of shepherding four small boys intent on making mischief had taken their toll—for the twins, though not formally included in her lessons, insisted on being with their brothers at all times. Until they had become her responsibility, she had been dismissive of Bella's complaints that the boys wore her down to the bone. They were mere children—all they required was sufficient mental stimulation and exercise, Cressie had thought. She realised now that her contempt had been founded on blissful ignorance.

Her evenings had therefore been spent making a guilty effort to become better acquainted with a stepmother who made it plain that her company was welcome only in the absence of any other, for Cordelia had hastened to London the day after Cressie's arrival at Killellan, fearful that either Lord Armstrong or Aunt Sophia might change their minds about her impending coming-out season. Cressie was alone for the first time in the house without any of her sisters for company. She was becoming short-tempered and grumpy with the boys, which in turn made her annoyed with herself, for she wanted to like her brothers as well as love them. She tried not to blame them for the lack of discipline which made them unruly to a fault. Every morning she told herself it was just a matter of trying harder. 'I fear I rather underestimated the effort it takes to keep such active minds and bodies occupied,' she said, smiling wanly at the portrait painter. 'Still, I believe teaching will bring its own reward. At least—I hope it will.'

Giovanni looked sceptical. 'You should demand fair

payment from your father. I think you would be amply rewarded if you did so, if only by his reaction.'

'Goodness, he would be appalled,' Cressie exclaimed. 'The fact is I'm doing this for my own reasons, not merely to accommodate my father.'

'And those reasons are?'

'No concern of yours, Signor de Matteo. You do not like my father much, do you?'

'He reminds me of someone I dislike very much.'

'Who?'

'That is no concern of yours, Lady Cressida.'

'Touché, signor.'

'You do not much like your father either, do you?'

'You ought not to have to ask such a question. And I ought to be able to answer positively.' Cressie grimaced. 'He enjoys making things difficult for me. And I him, if I am honest.'

The mixture of guilt and amusement on her face was endearing. The wind whipped a long lock of hair across her face, and without thinking, Giovanni made to brush it away at the same time as she did. His gloved hand covered her fingers. The contact jolted him into awareness, just as when he had kissed her hand, and the arrested look in her eyes made him aware that she felt it too. Her eyes widened. She shivered. The sun dazzled her eyes, and the moment was gone.

Cressie wrapped her arms around herself as the wind caught her again. She had come out without even a wrap. 'We should go inside,' she said, turning away, thrown off balance not just by the tangle of her gown, which the breeze had blown around her legs, but by her own reaction to Giovanni de Matteo's touch. She was not usually a tactile person, but he made her acutely conscious of her body, and his. She did not want him to see the effect he had on her, though no doubt he had the same effect on every female he encountered. 'I should take you to meet my brothers now. My stepmother does not like me to leave them with the nursery maid for too long.'

'Let them wait a little longer. I would like to see something of the house in order to find a suitable place to set up my easel. Lady Armstrong cannot object to you assisting me, can she? And you, Lady Cressida, you cannot object to my company over your brothers', even if we seem to disagree on almost every subject.'

She couldn't help laughing, and her laughter dispelled her awkwardness. 'After the morning I have had in the schoolroom I assure you I would take almost any company over my brothers', even yours. I most certainly do not object. Come, follow me.'

The portrait gallery ran the full length of the second floor. Light streamed in through windows which looked out over the formal gardens. The paintings were hung in strict ancestral sequence on the long wall opposite. 'I thought you might wish to set up your studio here,' Cressie said.

Giovanni nodded approvingly. 'The light is good.'

'The yellow drawing room and music room are through these doors, but neither are much used for Bella, my stepmother, prefers the smaller salon downstairs, and since Cassie—Cassandra, my second sister—left home some years ago, I doubt anyone has touched the pianoforte, so you will not be disturbed.'

'Except by my subjects.'

'True. I do not know how you prefer to work, whether they must sit still for hours on end, but…'

'That would be to expect the impossible, and in any event not necessary.'

'That is a relief. I was wondering whether I would have to resort to tying them to their chairs. Actually, I confess that I have been wondering whether I must resort to doing just that in order to keep them at their lessons. I had hoped that my primer—' Cressie broke off, tugging at the knot of hair which she had managed to tangle around her index finger, and forced herself to smile brightly. 'My travails as a teacher cannot possibly be of interest to you, *signor.* Let us look at the paintings.'

Though her determination to shoulder the blame for her brothers' failings intrigued him, there was a note in her voice that warned Giovanni off from pursuing the subject. He allowed her to lead him from portrait to portrait, listening while she unravelled for him the complex and many-branched Armstrong family tree, enjoying the cadence of her voice, taking the opportunity to study, not the canvases, but her face as she talked animatedly about the various family members. There was something deep within her that he longed to draw out, to capture. He was certain that beneath the veneer of scientific detachment and tightly held emotions, there was passion. In short, she would make a fascinating subject.

He must find a way of painting her portrait. Not one of his idealised studies, but something with some veracity. He had thought the desire to paint from the heart had died in him, but it seemed it had merely been lying dormant. Lady Cressida Armstrong, of all unlikely people, had awakened his muse.

But tantalising glimpses, mere impressions of her hidden self would not suffice. A certain level of intimacy would be required. In order to paint her he needed to know her—her heart and her mind, though most definitely not her body. Those days were past.

And yet, he could not take his eyes from her body. As she moved to the next painting he noticed how the sunlight, dancing in through the leaded panes in the long windows, framed her dress, which was white cotton, simply made, with a high round neck. The sleeves were wide at the shoulder as was the fashion, tapering down to the wrists, the hem tucked and trimmed with cotton lace. With a draughtsman's eye he noted approvingly how the cut of the gown enhanced her figure—the neat waist, the fullness of her breasts, the curve of her hips. In this light, he could clearly see the shape of her legs outlined against her petticoats. One of her stockings was wrinkled at the ankle. The sash at her waist was tied in a lopsided knot rather than a bow, and the top-most button at her neck was undone. She employed no maid, Giovanni surmised, and she had certainly not taken the time to inspect herself in the mirror. Haste or indifference? Both, he reckoned, though rather more of the latter.

He followed her to the next painting, but the pleasing roundedness of her *fondoschiena*, the tantalising shape of her legs, distracted him. He wanted to smooth out the wrinkle in her stocking. There was something about the fragile bones in a woman's ankle that he had always found erotic. And the swell of a calf. The softness of the flesh at the top of a woman's thighs. He had tasted just enough of her lips to be able to imagine how yielding the rest of her would be.

Giovanni cursed softly under his breath. Sex and art. The desire for both had been latent until he met her. Painting her was a possibility, but as for the other—he was perfectly content in his celibate state, free of bodily needs and the needs of other bodies.

'This is Lady Sophia, my father's sister,' Lady Cressida was saying. 'My Aunt Sophia is—you know, I don't think you've been listening to a word I've said.'

They were standing in front of the portrait of an austere woman who bore a remarkable resemblance to a camel suffering from a severe case of wind. 'Gainsborough,' Giovanni said, recognising the style immediately. 'Your aunt, you were saying.'

'What were you really thinking about?'

'Is there a painting of you among the collection?'

'Only one, in a group portrait with my sisters.'

'Show me.'

The painting had been hung between two doors, in the worst of the light. Lawrence, though not one of his best. There were five girls, the eldest two seated at a sewing table, the younger three at their feet, playing with reels of cotton. 'That is Celia,' Lady Cressida said, pointing to the eldest, a slim young woman with a serious expression and a protective hand on the head of the youngest child. 'Beside her is Cassie. As you can see, she is the beauty of the family. Cordelia, my young-est sister who makes her come out this Season, is very like her. Caroline is beside her, and that is me, the odd one out.'

Giovanni nodded. 'You certainly have very different colouring. What age were you when this was painted?'

'I don't know, eleven or twelve, I think. It was before Celia married and left home.'

'I am surprised that your mother is not in this paint-ing. Lawrence would usually have included the mother in such a composition.'

'She died not long after Cordelia was born. Celia was more of a mother to us than anyone.' Lady Cres-sida's voice was wistful as she reached out to touch her sister's image. 'I haven't seen her for almost ten years. Nor Cassie, for eight.'

'Surely they must visit, or you them?'

'It is a long way to Arabia, *signor*.' Obviously sens-ing his confusion, Lady Cressida hastened to explain. 'Celia married one of my father's diplomatic protégés. They were in Arabia, sent on a mission by the British Ambassador to Egypt, when Celia's husband was mur-dered by rebel tribesmen. I remember it so well, the news being broken to us here at Killellan. We were told that Celia was being held captive in a harem. My father and Cassie and Aunt Sophia went to Arabia to rescue her only to discover that she didn't want to be rescued. Fortunately for Celia, it turned out that her desert prince was hugely influential and fantastically rich, so my fa-ther was happy to hand her over.'

'And your other sister—Cassie, did you say?'

'When she narrowly escaped a most unfortunate connection with a poet, our father packed her off in disgrace to stay with Celia. He should have known that Cassie, a born romantic, would tumble head over heels in love with the exotic East. When he found out that he had lost a second daughter to a desert prince he was furious. But this prince too turned out to have excellent diplomatic connections and was also suitably generous with his riches, so my father magnanimously decided to be reconciled to the idea.'

'Such a colourful history for such a very English family,' Giovanni said drily.

She laughed. 'Indeed! My father decided two sheikhs, no matter how influential, was more than sufficient for any family. I think he fears if any of us visit them, the same fate would befall us, so we must content ourselves with exchanging letters.'

'And are they happy, your sisters?'

'Oh yes, blissfully. They have families of their own now too.' Lady Cressida gazed lovingly at the portrait. 'It is the only thing which makes it bearable, knowing how happy they are. I miss them terribly.'

'But you are not quite alone. You have your stepmother.'

'It is clear you have not been introduced to Bella. My father married her not long after Celia's wedding. I think he assumed Bella would take on Celia's role in looking after us three younger girls as well as providing him with an heir but Bella—well, Bella saw things differently. And once James was born, so too did Papa. His only interest is his male heirs.'

'Sadly, that is the way of the world, Lady Cressida.'

'Cressie. Please call me Cressie, for no one else here does, now Caro has married and Cordelia has gone to London. I am the last of the Armstrong sisters,' she said with a sad little smile. 'I think you have heard more than enough of my family history for one day.'

'It seems to me a shame that there are no other portraits of you. May I ask—would you—I would like to paint you, Lady—Cressie.'

'Paint *me*! Why on earth would you want to do that?'

Her expression almost made him laugh, but the evidence it gave him of her lack of self-worth made him angry. 'An exercise in mathematics,' Giovanni replied, hitting upon an inspired idea. 'I will paint one portrait to your rules, and I will paint another to mine.'

'Two portraits!'

'*Si*. Two.' An idealised Lady Cressida and the real one. For the first time in years, Giovanni felt the unmistakable tingle of certainty. Ambition long subdued began to stir. Though he had no idea as yet what this second portrait would be, he knew at least it would be his. Painted from the heart. 'Two,' Giovanni repeated firmly. 'Thesis and antithesis. What better way for me to provide you with the proof you need for your theory—or the evidence which contradicts it?' he added provocatively, and quite deliberately.

'Thesis and antithesis.' She nodded solemnly. 'An interesting concept, but I don't have the wherewithal to be able to pay you a fee.'

'This is not a commission. It is an experiment.'

'An experiment.'

Her smile informed him that he had chosen exactly the right form of words. 'You understand, it will require us to spend considerable time alone together. I cannot work with any distractions or interruptions,' he added hastily, realising how ambiguous this sounded. 'You will need to find a way of ridding yourself of your charges for a time.'

'Would that I could do so altogether.' Cressie put her hand over her mouth. 'I did not mean that, of course. I will find a way, but I think it would be prudent if we keep our experiment between ourselves, *signor*.' She grinned. 'You and I know that we are conducting research in the name of science, but I do not think Bella would view our being locked away alone together with only an easel for company in quite the same light.'

As Bella Frobisher, Lady Armstrong had been a curvaceous young woman when she first met her future husband, with what his sister, Lady Sophia, called 'fine child-bearing hips'. Those hips had now borne four children, all of them lusty boys, and were, like the rest of Bella's body, looking rather the worse for wear. A naturally indolent temperament, combined with a spouse who made little attempt to hide his indifference to every aspect of her save her ability to breed, led Bella to indulge her sweet tooth to the full. Her curves were now ample enough to undulate, rippling under her gowns in a most disconcerting manner, her condition having forced her to abandon her corsets. At just five-and-thirty, she looked at least ten years older, dressed as she was in a voluminous cherry-red afternoon dress trimmed with quantities of frothy lace which did nothing for her pale complexion. A pretty face with a pair of sparkling brown eyes was just about visible sunk amid an expanse of fat.

Though she had never aspired to being a wit, Bella had been happy to be labelled vivacious, and had always been extremely sociable until her husband made it clear that her lack of political nous made her something of a liability. He summarily replaced her at the head of his political table with his sister and, having made sure that she was impregnated, consigned his wife to the country. Here, Bella had remained, popping out healthy Armstrong boys at regular intervals, taking pleasure in her sons but in very little else. Though she knew it would displease her husband, she longed for this next child to be a daughter, the consolation prize she surely deserved, who would provide her mama with the affection she craved.

Disappointed from a very early stage in her marriage, unable to express her disappointment to the man responsible, Bella had turned her ire instead on his daughters, who made it very easy for her to do so since they made it all too obvious that they thought her a usurper. Her malice had become a habit she did not even contemplate breaking. Pregnant, bloated, lonely and bored, it was hardly surprising, then, that Giovanni, his breathtaking masculine beauty enhanced by the austerity of his black attire, would appear to her like a gift from the gods she thought had abandoned her.

'Lady Armstrong, it is an honour,' he said, bowing

over her dimpled and be-ringed hand as she lay on the *chaise-longue*, 'and a pleasure.'

Bella simpered breathlessly. She had never in all her days seen such a divine specimen of manhood. 'I can tell from your delightful accent that you are Italian.'

'Tuscan,' Cressie said tersely, unaccountably annoyed by the extraordinary effect Giovanni was having on her stepmother. She sat down in a chair opposite and gazed pointedly at Lady Armstrong's prostrate form. 'Are you feeling poorly again? Perhaps we should leave you to take tea alone?'

Flushing, Bella pushed aside the soft cashmere scarf which covered her knees, and struggled upright. 'Thank you, Cressida. I am quite well enough to pour Signor di Matteo a cup of tea. Milk or lemon, *signor*? Neither? Oh well, of course I suppose you Italians do not drink much tea. An English habit I confess I myself am very fond of. Cake? Well then, if you do not, I shall have to eat your slice else cook will be mortally offended, for Cressida, you know, has not a sweet tooth. Perhaps if she did, her temperament might improve somewhat. My stepdaughter is very *serious*, as you will no doubt have gathered by now, *signor*. *Cake* is far too frivolous a thing for Cressida to enjoy. You know, of course, that she is presently acting governess to two of my sons? James and Harry. You will be wishing to know more about them, I dare say, if you are to do justice to my angels.' Finally stopping for breath, Bella beamed and ingested the greater part of a wedge of jam sponge.

'Lord Armstrong informs me that his sons are charming,' Giovanni said into the silence which was broken only by his hostess's munching. She nodded and inhaled another inch or so of cake. Fascinated by the way she managed to consume so much into such a comparatively small mouth, he was momentarily at a loss.

Brushing the crumbs from her fingers, Bella launched once more into speech, this time a eulogy on the many and manifold charms of her dear boys. 'They are so very fond of their little jokes too,' she trilled. 'Cressida claims they lack discipline, but I tell her that it is a question of respect.' Bella cast a malicious smile at her stepdaughter. 'One cannot force-feed such intelligent children a lot of boring facts. Such a method of teaching is all very well for little girls, most likely, but with boys as lively as mine—well, I am not one to criticise, but I do think it was a mistake, not hiring a *qualified* governess to replace dear Miss Meacham.'

'Dear Miss Meacham left because she could no longer tolerate my brothers' so-called liveliness,' Cressie interjected.

'Oh, nonsense. Why must you always put such a negative slant on everything your brothers do? Miss Meacham left because she felt she was not up to the job of tutoring such clever children. "I wish fervently they get what they deserve" is what she said to me when she left, and I heartily agree. I don't know what your father was thinking of, to be perfectly honest, entrusting you with such a role, Cressida. Though perhaps it is more of a question of not knowing *what* role to assign you, since you are plainly unsuited to play the wife. After—how many years is it now, since I launched you?'

'Six.'

Bella shook her head at Giovanni. 'Six years, and despite the best efforts of myself and her father, she has not been able to bring a single man up to scratch,' she said sweetly. 'I am not one to boast, but I had Caroline off my hands with very little fuss, and I have no doubt that Cordelia will go off even more quickly. You have not met Cressida's sisters, but sadly she has none of their looks. Even Celia, the eldest, you know, who lives in Arabia, has her charms, though it was always Cassandra who was the acknowledged beauty. I suppose one plain sister out of five is to be expected. If only she were not such a blue-stocking, I really do believe I could have done *something* with her.' Bella shrugged and smiled sweetly again at Giovanni. 'But she scared them all off.'

Realising that she was in danger of looking like a petulant child, Cressie tried not to glower. The words so closely echoed her father's that she was for a moment convinced he and Bella were conspiring to belittle her. Though Bella had said nothing new, nor indeed anything which Cressie had not already blurted out to Giovanni upon their first meeting, it was embarrassing to have to listen to her character being dissected in such a way. So much for all her attempts to think more kindly of her stepmother. As to what Giovanni must be making of Bella's shocking manners, it didn't bear thinking about.

She put down her tea cup with a crack, determined to turn the conversation to the matter of the portrait, but Bella, having refreshed herself with a cream horn, was not finished. 'I remember now, there was a man your father and I thought might actually make a match of it with you. What was his name, Cressida? Fair hair, very reserved, a *clever* young man? You seemed quite taken with him. I remember saying to your father, she'll surely reel this one in. In fact, as I recall, you actually told us he was going to call, but he never did. He took up a commission shortly after, now I come to think of it. Come now, you must remember him, for it is not as if you were *crushed* by suitors. Oh, what *was* his name?'

She could feel the flush creeping up her neck. Think cold, Cressie told herself. Ice. Snow. But it made no difference. Perspiration prickled in the small of her back. Having taught herself never to think of him, she had persuaded herself that Bella would have forgotten all about…

'Giles!' Bella exclaimed. 'Giles Peyton.'

'Bella, I'm sure that Signor di Matteo…'

'He was actually quite presentable, once one got over his shyness. My lord thought it was a good match. He is not often wrong, but in this instance—the fact is, men do not like clever women. My husband's first wife, Catherine, was reputed to be a bit of a blue-stocking, and look where it got her—five daughters, and dead before the last was out of swaddling. When he asked for my hand, Lord Armstrong told me that it was my being so very *different* from his first wife that appealed to him, which I thought was a lovely compliment. No, men do not like a clever woman. I am sure you agree, *signor*?'

Blithely helping herself to another pastry, Bella looked enquiringly at Giovanni, but before he could speak, Cressie got to her feet. 'Signor di Matteo came here to paint my brothers' portrait, Bella, not to discuss what he finds attractive in a woman.' She swallowed hard. 'I beg your pardon. And yours, Signor di Matteo. If you will excuse me, I have a headache, which is making me forget my manners.'

'I hope you are not thinking of retiring to your room, Cressida. James and Harry...'

'I am perfectly aware of my duties, thank you.'

'If you wish to be excused from dinner, however, I am sure that Signor di Matteo and I can manage quite well without your company.'

'I am sure that you can,' Cressie muttered, wanting only to be gone before she lost her temper completely, or burst into tears. One or other, or more likely both, seemed imminent, and she was determined not to allow Bella the satisfaction of seeing just how upset she was.

But as she turned to go, Giovanni got to his feet. 'I must inform you that you are mistaken on several counts, Lady Armstrong,' he said curtly. 'Firstly, there are many enlightened men, and I include myself among them, who enjoy the company of a clever woman very much. Secondly, I am afraid that I prefer to dine alone when I am working. If I may be excused, I would like the governess to introduce me to her charges.'

With a very Italian click of the heels and a very shallow bow, Giovanni took his leave, took Cressie's arm in an extremely firm grip and marched them both out of the drawing room.

'Lady Cressida. Cressie. Stop. The boys can wait a few moments longer. You are shaking.' Opening a door at random, Giovanni led her into a small room, obviously no longer used for it was musty, the shutters drawn. 'Here, sit down. I am not surprised that you are so upset. Your stepmother's bitterness is exceeded only by her ability to devour cake.'

To his relief, Cressie laughed. 'My sisters and I used to think her the wicked stepmother straight out of a fairytale. I don't know why she hates us so—though my father is right, we have given her little cause to love us.'

'Five daughters, all cleverer than she, and all far more attractive…'

'*Four* of them more attractive.'

'To continue the fairytale metaphor, why are you so determined to be the ugly sister?'

Cressie shrugged. 'Because it's true. Because it's how it has always been. Do you have any brothers or sisters?'

'No.' At least, none who acknowledged him, which amounted to the same thing. 'Why do you ask?'

'I wondered if all families are the same. In mine, we were labelled by my father, pretty much from birth. Celia is the diplomat, Cassie the pretty one, Caroline the dutiful one who can always be depended upon, Cordelia the charming one and I—I am the plain one. Upon occasion I am classed the clever one, but believe me, my father uses that only as an insult. He doesn't see beyond his labels, not even with Celia, whom he was most proud of because of her being so useful to him.'

Giovanni frowned. 'But he does precisely the same to your stepmother. She is the brood mare—it is her only purpose. It is no wonder she feels inferior, and no wonder that she must disguise it by trying always to put you in your place. She is vulgar and brash and lonely, so she takes it out on you and your sisters. It is not excusable, but it is understandable.'

'I hadn't thought—oh, I don't know, perhaps you are right, but I am not feeling particularly charitable towards her at the moment.'

Cressie had been worrying at a loose thread of skin on her pinkie, and now it had started to bleed. Without thinking, Giovanni lifted her hand and dabbed the blood with his fingertip before it could drip on to her gown. He put his finger to his lips and licked off the blood. She made no sound, made no move, only stared at him with those amazingly blue eyes. They reminded him of early morning fishing trips back home in his boyhood, the sea sparkling as his father's boat rocked on the waves. The man he'd thought was his father.

With his hand around her slender wrist, his lips closed around her finger and he sucked gently. Sliding her finger slowly out of his mouth, he allowed his tongue to trail along her palm, let his lips caress the soft pad of her thumb. Desire, a bolt of blood thundered straight to his groin, taking him utterly by surprise. What was he doing?

He jumped to his feet, pulling the skirts of his coat around him to hide his all too obviously inflamed state. 'I was just trying to prevent—I'm sorry, I should not have behaved so—inappropriately,' he said tersely. She should have stopped him! Why had she not stopped him? Because for her, it meant nothing more than he had intended, an instinctive act of kindness to prevent her ruining her gown. And that was all it was. His arousal was merely instinct. He did not really desire her. Not at all.

'It has been a long day,' Giovanni said, forcing a cold little smile. 'With your permission, I think I would like to meet my subjects now, and then I will set up my studio. I will dine there too, if you would be so good as to have some food sent up.'

'You won't change your mind and sup with us?'

She looked so forlorn that he almost surrendered. Giovanni shook his head decisively. 'I told you, when I am working, distractions are unwelcome. I need to concentrate.'

'Yes. Of course. I understand completely,' Cressie said, getting to her feet. 'Painting me would be a distraction too. We should abandon our little experiment.'

'No!' He caught her arm as she turned towards the door. 'I want to paint you, Cressie. I *need* to paint you. To prove you wrong, I mean,' he added. 'To prove that painting is not merely a set of rules, that beauty is in the eye of the artist.' He traced the shape of her face with his finger, from her furrowed brow, down the softness of her cheek to her chin. 'You will help me do that, yes?'

She stared up at him, her eyes unreadable, and then surprised him with a twisted little smile. 'Oh, I doubt very much that you'll be able to make me beautiful. In fact, I shall do my very best to make sure you cannot, for you must know that my theory depends upon it.'

Chapter Three

Cressie stood at the window of the schoolroom at the top of the house, and looked on distractedly as James and Harry laboured at their sums. The twins, George and Frederick, sat at the next desk, busy with their coloured chalks. An unusual silence prevailed. For once, all four boys were behaving themselves, having been promised the treat of afternoon tea with their mama if they did. In the corner of the room, a large pad of paper balanced on his knee, Giovanni worked on the preliminary sketches for their portrait, unheeded by his subjects but not by their sister.

He seemed utterly engrossed in his work, Cressie thought. He would not let her look at the drawings, so she looked instead at him, which was no hardship—he really was quite beautiful, all the more so with the perfection of his profile marred by the frown which emphasised the satyr in his features. That, and the sharpness of his cheekbones, the firm line of his jaw, which contrasted so severely with the fullness of his lips, the thick silkiness of his lashes, made what could have been feminine most decidedly male.

His fingers were long and elegant, almost unmarked by the charcoal he held. Her own hands were dry with chalk dust, her dress rumpled and grubby where Harry had grabbed hold of it. No doubt her hair was in its usual state of disarray. Giovanni's clothes, on the other hand, were immaculate. He had put off his coat and rolled up the sleeves of his shirt most precisely. She could not imagine him dishevelled. His forearms were tanned, covered in silky black hair. Sinewy rather than muscular. He was lithe rather than brawny. Feline? No, that was not the word. He had not the look of a predator, and though there was something innately sensual in his looks, there was also a glistening hardness, like a polished diamond. If it had not been such a cliché, she would have been tempted to call him devilish.

She watched him studying the boys. His gaze was cool, analytical, almost distant. He looked at them as if they were objects rather than people. Her brothers had, when first introduced to Giovanni, been obstreperous, showing off, vying for his attention. His utter indifference to their antics had quite thrown them, so used were they to being petted and spoilt, so sure were they of their place at the centre of the universe. Cressie had had to bite her lip to stop herself laughing. To be ignored was beyond her brothers' ken. She ought to remember how effective a tactic it was.

She turned her gaze to the view from the window. This afternoon, it had been agreed, Giovanni would begin her portrait. Thesis first, he said, an idealised Lady Cressida. How had he put it? A picture-perfect version of the person she presented to the world. She wasn't quite sure what he meant, but it made her uncomfortable, the implication that he could see what others could or would not. Did he sense her frustration with her lot? Or, heaven forefend, her private shame regarding Giles? Did he think her unhappy? *Was* she unhappy? For goodness' sake, it was just a picture, no need to tie herself in knots over it!

Giovanni had earmarked one of the attics for their studio, where the light flooded through the dormer windows until early evening and they could be alone, undisturbed by the household. In order to free her time, Cressie had volunteered to take all four boys every morning, leaving Janey, the nursery maid, in charge in the afternoons, which Bella usually slept through after taking tea. Later today, Giovanni would begin the process of turning Cressie into her own proof, painting her according to the mathematical rules she had studied, representing her theorem on canvas. Her image in oils would be a glossy version of her real self. And the second painting, depicting her alter ego, the private Cressie, would be the companion piece. How would Giovanni depict that version of her, the Cressie he believed she kept tightly buttoned-up inside herself? And were either versions of her image really anything to do with her? Would it be the paintings which were beautiful or the subject, in the eyes of their creator? So excited had she been by the idea of the portraits she had thought of them only in the abstract. But someone—who was it?— claimed that the artist could see into the soul. Giovanni would know the answer, but she would not ask him. She did not want anyone to see into her soul. Not that she believed it was true.

Turning from the window, she caught his unwavering stare. How long had he been looking at her? His hand flew across the paper, capturing what he saw, capturing her, not her brothers. His hand moved, but his gaze did not. The intensity of it made it seem as if they were alone in the schoolroom. Her own hand went self-consciously to her hair. She didn't like being looked at like this. It made her feel—not naked, but stripped. No one looked at her like that, really looked at her. Intimately.

Cressie cleared her throat, making a show of checking the clock on the wall. 'James, Harry, let me see how you have got on with your sums.' Sliding a glance at Giovanni, she saw he had moved to a fresh sheet of paper and was once again sketching the boys. Had she imagined the connection between them? Only now that it was broken did she notice that her heart was hammering, her mouth was dry.

She was being silly. Giovanni was an artist, she was a subject, that was all. He was simply analysing her, dissecting her features, as a scientist would a specimen. Men as beautiful as Giovanni di Matteo were not interested in women as plain as Cressie Armstrong, and Cressie would do well to remember that.

It was warm in the attic, the afternoon sun having heated the airless room. Dust motes floated and eddied in the thermals. Giovanni removed his coat and rolled up the sleeves of his shirt. In front of him, a blank canvas was propped on his easel. Across the room, posed awkwardly on a red velvet chair, was Cressie. He had discovered the chair in another of the attic's warren of rooms and had thought it an ideal symbolic device for his composition. It was formal, functional and yet sensual, a little like the woman perched uncomfortably on it. He smiled at her reassuringly. 'You look like the French queen on her way to the guillotine. I am going to take your likeness, not chop off your head.'

She laughed at that, but it was perfunctory. 'If you take my likeness, then you will have lost, *signor*. I am—'

'If you remind me once more of your lack of beauty, *signorina*, I will be tempted to cut off your head after all.' Giovanni sighed in exasperation. Though he knew exactly how he wished to portray her, she was far too tense for him to begin. 'Come over here, let me explain a little of the process.'

He replaced the canvas with his drawing board, tacking a large sheet of paper to it. Cressie approached cautiously, as if the blank page might attack her. All morning, she had been subdued, almost defensive. 'There is nothing to be afraid of,' he said, drawing her closer.

'I'm not afraid.'

She pouted and crossed her arms. Her buttoned-up look. Or was it buttoned-down? 'I have never come across such a reluctant subject,' Giovanni said. 'You are surely not afraid I will steal your soul?'

'What made you say that?'

She was glaring at him now, which did not at all augur well. 'It is said that a painting reflects the soul in the same way a mirror does. To have your image taken, some say, is to surrender your soul. I meant it as a jest, Cressie. A mathematician such as yourself could not possibly believe such nonsense.'

She stared at the blank sheet of paper, her brow furrowed. 'Was it Holbein? The artist who painted the soul in the eyes, I mean. Was that Holbein? I couldn't remember earlier, in the schoolroom.'

'Hans Holbein the Younger. Is that what you are afraid of, that I will not steal your soul but see into it?'

'Of course not. I don't know why I even mentioned it.' She gave herself a little shake and forced a smile. 'The process. You said you would explain.'

Most of his subjects, especially the women, were only too ready to bare their soul to him, usually as a prelude to the offer to bare their bodies. Cressie, on the other hand, seemed determined to reveal nothing of herself. Her guard was well and truly up, but he knew her well enough now to know how to evade it. Giovanni picked up a piece of charcoal and turned towards the drawing board.

'First, I divide the canvas up into equal segments like this.' He sketched out a grid. 'I want you to be exactly at the centre of the painting, so your face will be dissected by this line, which will run straight down the middle of your body, aligning your profile and your hands which define the thirds into which the portrait will be divided, like this—you see how the proportions are already forming on the vertical?'

He turned from the shapes he had sketched in charcoal to find that Cressie looked confused. 'There is a symmetry in the body, in the way the body can be posed, that is naturally pleasing. If you clasp your hands so, can you not see it, this line?'

Giovanni ran his finger from the top of her head, down the line of her nose, to her mouth. He carried on, ignoring the softness of her lips, tracing the line of her chin, her throat, to where her skin disappeared beneath the neck of her gown. The fabric which formed a barrier made it perfectly acceptable for him to complete his demonstration, he told himself, just tracing the valley between her breasts, the soft swell of her stomach, finally resting his finger on her hands. 'This line…' He cleared his throat, trying to distance himself. 'This line…' he turned towards the paper on the easel once more and picked up the charcoal '…it is the axis for the portrait. And your elbows, they will form the widest point, creating a triangle thus.'

To his relief, Cressie was frowning in concentration, focused on the drawing board, seemingly oblivious to the way his body was reacting to hers. It was because he so habitually avoided human contact, that was all. An instinctive reaction he would not repeat because he would not touch her again. Not more than was strictly necessary.

'Are you always so precise when you are structuring a portrait?' she asked. 'This grid, will you draw it out on the canvas?'

'*Si.* And I will also block out the main shapes, just as I have shown you.' Giovanni guided her back towards the chair, encouraging her to question him, relieved to discover that by distracting her with the technical details of his craft, the various pigments he preferred, the pre-

cise recipe of oils and binding agents he used to create
his paints, he could distract himself too, from his awareness of her as a woman, of himself as a man, which had
no place here in his studio.

Cressie's face, which was quite plain in repose, when
animated was transformed. He fed her facts, drew her
out with questions as to the detail of her theory and
sketched quickly, trying to capture her in charcoal and
when he had, he replaced the paper with his canvas and
repositioned his sitter. This he did quickly lest she remember the purpose of this session and become self-
conscious once again.

'Tell me more of this book you are using to teach
your brothers,' he said as he began to paint in the grid.

'It is a children's introduction to geometry. I am hoping that if I have evidence of its practical application
I will be able to persuade my publisher to print it. At
present, he is unwilling to do so at his own expense, and
I have not the wherewithal to fund it myself. Unfortunately, to date my brothers have not exactly proved to
be the most interested of pupils.'

'It seems to me that your brothers have been raised
to find only themselves of interest.'

Cressie grinned. 'That is a dreadful thing to contemplate, but I am afraid it is quite true. Save for my
father, they have been raised to care for no one's opinion but their own.'

'And your father cares for none but them, you say?'

'Blood and beauty,' Cressie said with a twisted smile.
'Your words, *signor*, and most apt. Your own father—

is he still alive? He must be immensely proud of you and your success.'

'Proud! My father thinks…' Giovanni took a deep breath and unclenched his fists, surprised by the strength of his reaction. He never thought of his father. Not consciously. He had no father worthy of the name. 'What I know from bitter experience is that you might succeed in mollifying your father by doing as he bids, but he will only see it as his right, his due. You cannot make a man such as that proud of you, Cressie. And in the process of trying, you are making yourself thoroughly miserable.'

'I am not miserable. I have no option but to try. I am not like you, free to please myself, I have no independent means, and my one talent is hardly going to support me.'

Her arms were crossed again, she was hugging herself tight across her chest, eyes bright, expression bleak. If her father only knew how unhappy she was—but that was exactly the point, was it not? Lord Armstrong did not care, any more than his own father, Count Fancini, what unhappiness he inflicted on his children in the name of the bloodline. Seeing her like this, knowing she would go on suffering as long as she continued to try to do what she thought she ought, made him furious. 'Why do you pander to them, your father, his wife, his sons! Why do you allow them to trample on you?'

'How dare you! What gives you the right…?'

Cressie jumped up from her seat and tried to push past him, but Giovanni grabbed her by the arms, wishing he could shake some sense into her. Her unruly curls tumbled from the loose knot which held them. 'I am not trying to hurt you, Cressie,' he said, more gently now. 'Quite the reverse. I am actually trying to help. You *are* unhappy, and will only become more so as long as you keep trying to please your father. Trust me on this.'

'Why should I?'

She was right—why should she listen to him when he was not able to explain? Giovanni shook his head. 'I have said too much. I wished merely to discover the person I wish to paint. The person you are, the woman inside here…' he touched her forehead '…and here…' he placed his palm over her heart '…that is who I wish to discover.'

She breathed in sharply. 'You might be disappointed by what you find.'

'I doubt it.' Her eyes were wide open, such a startling colour. Cobalt, ultramarine, Prussian blue, none of those pigments would capture the exact shade. Beneath his hand, he could feel her heart beating. How could he have thought of her face as plain? What was she thinking now, looking at him like that?

Dio! He snatched his hand away from her breast and took a step backwards. '*Mi dispiace.* I am sorry. I should not—but there are such emotions inside you jostling to be heard. I could never be disappointed by what I find in you.'

Cressie flushed, obviously unused to any sort of compliments, never mind such a strange one as he had just paid her. 'Thank you,' she said awkwardly. 'I think we should stop for the day. I must go and see how Bella fares.'

She whisked herself out of the room before he could reply. Giovanni dropped into the chair she had vacated and tugged his neckcloth loose, closing his eyes. It was his own fault, introducing his father to the conversation, but the similarities in their situations were impossible to ignore. Fourteen years since their paths had crossed, his and Count Fancini's. The memory of that last interview at the palazzo in Firenze was still painfully clear. Their voices echoing round the marble chamber as they argued. His footsteps sounding larger than life, walking across the courtyard as he left. The count's cold fury turned to scorn and threats when he realised that his son was not going to bend to his will.

You will come back with your tail between your legs. No one will buy those pretty jottings of yours. Mark my words, you will be back. And I will be waiting.

Giovanni rubbed his eyes with his knuckles. Was the count waiting still? Had word of Giovanni's fame reached him? He cursed and got to his feet. He did not care. Why should he!

Cressie hovered in the doorway at the far end of the gallery, watching Giovanni at work, carefully measuring oil from a glass bottle before mixing it with pigments on his palette. The wooden case which looked like a travelling medicine chest, in which he kept his various binders and oils, stood open on the table beside him. As usual when he worked, he had taken off his coat and rolled up his pristine white shirtsleeves. His waistcoat was grey today, the satin back stretched across his shoulders, displaying the lean lines of him to advantage. As ever, when she saw him, she was struck by the perfection of his physique, and as ever she reminded herself that her reaction was purely aesthetic.

Her gaze drifted down, to the slight curve of his buttocks outlined by his black trousers. For a man so lithe, he was surprisingly shapely. He had the body of one of those statues of Greek athletes. A javelin thrower, perhaps? She would like to see him pose with a spear, muscles tensed, gracefully poised. She would like to be able to capture him in such a pose—simply for the sake of illustrating symmetry. He had the type of body which would appear very much to advantage when naked rather than clothed. Unlike hers.

She placed the backs of her hands on her burning cheeks. Giles, the one man she had seen naked, had looked a little ridiculous and a little threatening, holding himself, so strangely proud of his jutting manhood. He had been so offended when she had been unable to disguise her—how had she felt? Anxious. Ever so slightly hysterical, unable to reconcile the enormity of what she was about to do with the awkward mechanics of the act itself. And they had *both* been awkward. Giles was not nearly as experienced as he had implied. He had not liked her questions, had taken her nervous request for instruction badly, calling her analytical. And unwomanly. That hurt. Still hurt.

All in all, it had been a most lamentable experience for both of them. In fact, with hindsight, she had the distinct impression that Giles would have been much happier if she'd lain back and said nothing at all while he got on with her deflowering. Which was exactly what she did, in the end. And it had been so unrewarding for him that if his pride would have allowed him he would have decided there and then that once was enough. Which was what she decided for herself, in the end.

Though she did not doubt it was mostly her fault, for she had ample proof that she was not the kind of woman men desired, neither could Cressie imagine that Giovanni would be as inept as Giles in the same situation. Those artistic fingers of his were surely incapable of being anything other than expert. And his mouth, the fullness of his lips, the way the top lip bowed. The other day, during the first of their portrait sessions, she had been sure he was going to kiss her. During the second session, she had been even more certain, but again he had not, and since then, he had been almost brusque with her. She was acting like a silly chit, allowing her imagination to take flight like this, imagining Giovanni naked, imagining him touching her in a way Giles never had, in a way no man ever had.

'Cressie?'

She jumped, opened her eyes and guiltily snatched her hand away from her breast. 'Giovanni.'

He smiled. 'I like the way you say my name.'

She was blushing! Lord, it was as well no one, not even the world's most renowned portrait painter, could actually read her thoughts. All the same, she dared not look at him. 'I came to tell you that the boys—they will be here in a moment if you are ready for them.'

He gestured towards the easel, the palette with its oils already mixed. 'As you see, I am prepared.'

'They have been very difficult today. I am not sure

that they will be keen to sit for long.' Cressie fixed her gaze on Giovanni's top waistcoat button. 'I would bribe them with sweetmeats if I had any.'

'There is no need.'

'There is, you have no idea…'

He smiled, and caught a strand of her unruly hair with his finger, pushing it back from her brow. 'Trust me.'

The barest touch, yet she jumped, acutely aware of him, the more so for the shocking nature of her thoughts just moments before. 'I shall go and—if you're ready then, I shall…'

But there was no need. A shout, the stampede of four pairs of feet, followed by the nursery maid's gentle remonstration not to run, wholly ignored, and the four boys were upon them in a tangle of blonde hair, deceptively cherubic faces and chubby limbs. Janey, her mob cap askew, her apron covered in ink, dropped a harassed curtsy. 'I'm sorry, my lady, only the minute you left them alone with me they was like caged animals. Harry broke James's slate, and Freddie got hold of the ink pot and when I tried to take it back from him…'

'There's no need to apologise, Janey, it's not your fault.'

'Them being cooped up because of the rain don't help one little bit, my lady. If only the sun would come out, we could get them to run some of those flitters out of their legs. If you'll excuse me now, I will go and change my apron. It's quite ruined.'

'Now, then,' Giovanni said, when the maid had bustled out of the room, still tutting and shaking her head at the mess of her uniform, 'I have devised a game for the boys to play.'

'A game?' Cressie said. 'But I thought you needed them to sit still for their portrait.'

'The game requires them to be seated. You must trust me, Cressie.'

'You are forever saying that.'

'And today I shall provide you with proof.' Giovanni clapped his hands together to gain the boys' attention, and when this had no effect on the scrapping twins, pulled them bodily apart, dangling one from each hand by the seats of their nankeen breeches. Freddie and George were so astonished that they were silenced. Watching him walk towards the table, effortlessly carrying the boys aloft, Cressie found it difficult not to be impressed. What was that other thing that Greek athletes were so often depicted throwing? A discus. Yes, she was willing to wager that Giovanni would be skilled at that too. Dressed only in one of those little tunics which stopped short at the top of his thighs. When he lunged to make the throw the fabric would ripple, revealing...

'Cressie?'

For the second time that morning, she jumped and blushed.

'You too,' Giovanni said, holding out one of the chairs which stood at the table for her. The boys were already seated, staring at her expectantly.

'I?'

'You are to join in the game, Cressie. You are to sit beside me because I'm the eldest,' James said, casting Harry a superior look.

'I want Cressie to sit beside me because I'm Mama's favourite,' Harry replied, instantly goaded.

'You are not! I'm the favourite because I'm Papa's heir and I shall one day be Lord Armstrong.' James puffed out his chest in a frighteningly good impression of his father. 'Papa says—'

'Do you wish to play the game or not?'

Giovanni did not raise his voice, but he gained the attention of all four boys immediately. He didn't sound angry or flustered but—bored? Cressie hid her grin behind her hands. Indifference, that was the key. Her brothers were hanging on his every word as he handed them pieces of paper and charcoal and explained the rules of his drawing game. They were looking up at him, all four of them, with their mouths wide open, their eyes expectant. It was only when she realised that Giovanni had stopped speaking and was now looking in her direction that Cressie found she really was required to join in. 'I can't draw,' she said nervously.

Giovanni showed his teeth. 'Anyone can draw. It is simply a question of ratio and proportion—you told me so yourself.'

'That is not fair. There is a difference between theory and execution.'

'Interesting. The first time I suggest you test your own theory you start to make excuses. You do not relish being challenged, do you? No, don't deny it—you have already crossed your arms. Next you will glare at me.'

'I won't. I am not so predictable,' she responded, glaring.

'Cressie does that when she's being scolded,' James piped up. 'And when Mama talks to her. And Papa.'

'I do not! Do I?' Cressie turned to her brothers, appalled. When both James and Harry nodded solemnly, she pulled a face, making a show of unfolding her arms. 'That is very rude of me, boys. I hope that you know better than to follow my example.'

James shrugged. 'Mama and Papa aren't ever angry with us. Are you going to play this game or not?'

'You really expect me to draw a horse?' Cressie looked pleadingly at Giovanni.

'I really expect you to *try* to draw a horse,' he replied. 'Whether you will succeed or not—that I will judge when you have all finished. There will be a prize for the best effort. In the meantime, I am going to get on with my own work.'

He pulled the canvas, upon which the portrait of the boys was beginning to take shape, towards him, picked up his brushes and began to paint. All four boys did the same, concentrating hard on their drawings. Cressie stared down at her blank sheet of paper, completely intimidated by it. She couldn't even remember what a horse, that most familiar of animals, looked like. Glancing up, she caught Giovanni's sardonic look and hurriedly picked up her charcoal. It was just a question of ratio and proportion, for goodness' sake. Cressie furrowed her brow and began to make tentative marks on the paper.

An hour and many false starts later, the animal which looked back at her bore no resemblance whatsoever to anything equine. She had tried to draw it side-on and had produced something which looked rather like a hippopotamus on stilts. Her galloping horse was drawn mid-air in an impossible acrobatic leap which made it look as if each of its legs were being pulled towards a different point of the compass. Her rearing horse looked like a lap dog which had been trained to beg for its food, and, having decided that perhaps the legs were the problem, she attempted a horse lying down with its limbs folded under its body. It looked like a cross between a cat and a sheep.

Her final attempt was a horse's face looking straight out of the paper. This drawing had character, there was no denying it. With its toothy grin and long-lashed eyes, it looked very like Aunt Sophia, who in turn looked very like one of the camels which Cressie had ridden on her single visit to Arabia.

'Camels are a kind of horse,' she said to Giovanni as he examined her masterpiece. His mouth twitched, and she forced herself not to fold her arms across her chest. She would *never* fold her arms across her chest again. 'If I had had the benefit of lessons…' She stopped, suddenly remembering that she had. When Mama was alive, there had been a drawing master who had toiled in vain to improve her artistic skills. 'Oh very well, I admit it, it is not just a question of applying rules. I have no talent whatsoever. Are you happy now?'

'Cressie's horse looks like old Aunt Sophia,' Harry said. 'Look, James.'

She hurriedly retrieved the drawing from her brothers. The last thing she needed was for it to find its way into her father's hands. Or worse, into her aunt's. 'Never mind my drawing, since I am obviously not the winner. Let us judge your attempts.'

Freddie and George had each produced a series of round blobs with lines, the same shape they drew for almost everything. Instead of dismissing them, though, Giovanni took the time to praise each and to find individual merit in each too, eventually declaring that they were all so good that they were equal winners, since each was the best in a different way. Such highly competitive children did not usually take to a decision like this, but once again Cressie was surprised to discover them not only compliant but proud and, most importantly, not bickering. Their prize was an individual portrait, swiftly executed, which managed to be both comic and remarkably accurate. A few strokes of Giovanni's charcoal brought James to life as a king, Harry as a general, Freddie as a lion tamer complete with whip, and George, fists raised, as a boxer.

She had thought Giovanni oblivious to her brothers' chatter and boasting as he took their likenesses in the schoolroom and in this make-shift studio. She had been quite wrong, for he had depicted each of them exactly as they most wished to be seen. Looking over Harry's shoulder at his drawing, Cressie was filled with admiration for Giovanni's skill, though the free-form cartoons were nothing like the carefully executed portrait which was emerging from the canvas. These sketches of her brothers were impish, unrestrained, full of movement and humour. For the first time, she had an inkling of the depths of his ability. In the drawings there were no rules, no careful proportion, only a highly evocative image. Admiration ceded to unease. He saw so much. What would he see in her, that she did not wish to have exposed?

Having sent the boys back up to the nursery for their midday meal, Cressie wandered over to stand beside Giovanni in front of the portrait. Here, there were none of the subtly subversive qualities of the charcoal sketches. This painting would be exactly as her father requested, showing his sons only to best advantage. 'There is more truth in those drawings, the work of moments, than in this meticulously assembled canvas,' she said.

'But much more beauty in this painting, yes?'

'So it is a lie, is that what you are saying?'

Giovanni shrugged. 'It is your father's truth. And your stepmother's. It is the truth of what people want to see, what most people do see, for they do not look beyond the first impression.'

'But you do, Giovanni. Why do you not paint it?'

His smile was bitter. 'Because it is more profitable to sell lies. But I will paint the truth when I paint you for a second time. We will continue with the first portrait this afternoon, yes?'

'The portrait which will provide my proof, which is a lie. What am I to make of that for my thesis, I wonder?' Cressie picked up one of the sable brushes from the box which lay open on the table, and stroked the soft bristle over the back of her hand. 'You were very good with my brothers today. They heed you in a way they never listen to me.'

'You think so? Yet they fought for the privilege of

sitting beside you to draw. Stop thinking of them as your father's sons. They are not your rivals—they are just boys.'

'I wish I had been a boy.'

'You think Lord Armstrong will be any less manipulative with his sons than his daughters?'

'He won't force them into marriage.'

'He cannot force you.'

'He can make my life unbearable.'

Giovanni caught the curl which persisted in hanging down over her forehead, and once again brushed it back into place. 'It is you who are doing that, trying to be what you are not, wishing to be who you are not.'

His hand still lay on the nape of her neck. His touch made her skin tingle. She was so conscious of him, her body so aware of his proximity in a way that confused her. 'I wish you would not persist with the notion that I am unhappy, Giovanni.'

He ignored her. 'This afternoon, when you sit for me, I want you to wear something different. Something with a *décolleté*. Whether you accept it or not, you are a woman, not a man, and I wish to paint you as one. Something else you are hiding under those terrible dresses you favour,' he said, tracing the line of her throat with his fingers, brushing lightly over her breasts.

She caught her breath as he touched her, her nipple tightening as he grazed it. Without being conscious of it, she stepped towards him, wanting his hand to cup her, yearning in the purest, most thoughtless of ways, for him to satisfy the craving she had been feeling for days. It was nothing to do with aesthetics, she knew that. It was elemental, purely carnal.

'Curves,' Giovanni said, his hand tightening on her breast just exactly as she hoped. 'You have the most delightful curves. Did you know that this is what your English painter Hogarth called the line of beauty?' His fingers slid down, brushing the underside of her breast, to the indent of her waist and round to rest on the curve of her bottom, and pull her suddenly hard up against him. 'You, Cressie, have the most beautiful line.'

His eyes were dark. She was trembling, and in absolutely no doubt this time that he would kiss her. Nor in any doubt at all about what she wanted. Cressie stood on her tiptoes and lifted her mouth in invitation.

Darkness, a swirling, dangerous darkness, enveloped her as his lips met hers, not gently but passionately, in a hard, hungry kiss that sent her reeling into a hot, heady place, crimson with desire. His fingers tightened, digging into her *derrière* as he pulled her against him, bracing her against the hard muscles of his thighs, his tongue stroking into her mouth, touching hers, sending a pulse of heat through her. She arched against him, angling her mouth against his, the better to taste him, mindlessly opening to him, wantonly kissing him back, every bit as hungry as he. It was as if they had both been wild dogs restrained, now freed to ravage, devour, a bursting open of pent-up passion which she could not believe, now it was released, had ever been contained.

She could feel the hard length of his manhood against her belly. No thought of it being ridiculous, no thought of that other time, when she had stared with analytical interest at Giles, what she wanted from Giovanni was violent, unrestrained and utterly base. She heard herself whimpering as one of his hands left her bottom, then a guttural moan as he covered her breast, stroking her nipple into an aching nub. His kiss deepened as he pushed her against the table, lifting her up on to it. She clutched at him, opening her legs to pull him between them, impatient with the voluminous folds of her gown, desperate to get closer, pulsing with heat and wet with desire, reaching for the thick length of his erection.

Giovanni groaned as her fingers stroked him through the wool of his trousers. She stroked him again. He muttered something in Italian, leaning over her, pressing her down on to the table. She could smell linseed oil from the palette. Something clattered to the floor. His curse was violent this time, as he released her so suddenly that she fell back, her head colliding with the jar which held his paintbrushes.

The sound brought them both to their senses. Cressie scrabbled from the table, shaking out the skirts of her gown, blushing wildly. 'I must go,' she muttered. He tried to stop her, but she shook him off, fleeing from the room in a flutter of muslin.

Giovanni pulled out a chair and sat down heavily. *Inferno!* What was it about her that made it so difficult for him to keep his hands to himself? She was insecure and defensive, and what's more she was abrasive, challenging and she was far too opinionated. Yet she provoked a reaction in him that no woman ever had.

For years he had embraced the cold kiss of chastity with barely any effort. Why did Cressie make him rail against his self-imposed restraint? He should not have kissed her. He should not have touched her at all. Yet when he had—a fire that threatened to be all-consuming, like a blaze ripping through a tinder-dry forest. His instincts had been right. That buttoned-down front she presented to the world masked a smouldering passion. Just thinking about her response, about her mouth on his, the way her lips clung, the way her hands touched him, stroked him—*Dio*, he was hard. Another few minutes and they would have...

'No!' Celibacy was his strength, the cornerstone of his success. He was confusing his desire to paint her with his desire to make love to her. It was an echo, a residue from the past, when art and sex were so inextricably mixed. His desire for her was so strong because his desire to capture her was irresistible. And yet, the Cressie who kissed him was the one he wanted to paint. The one he needed to paint, with a passion equal to the one she had aroused. To show her to herself, and to reflect that back in his art. His true art. To paint from the heart. *That* was what he wanted most passionately of all.

Giovanni jumped to his feet and began to gather together his palette, brushes and knives for cleaning. He must complete the first portrait, without further compromising himself. He must detach himself from the process, and paint Lady Cressida with as much precision as any other professional commission. The terrible drawing she had executed lay before him on the table. Almost persuaded that he had explained the shocking lapse away, Giovanni folded it up and tucked it into his trouser pocket.

Chapter Four

Cressie had decided to take her brothers for a walk through the estate's park since the sun had eventually condescended to show its face. Bella had been taken poorly again and demanded Janey's soothing presence at her bedside. Cressie was glad of the excuse to avoid sitting for Giovanni. She needed time to think.

The grass was damp underfoot, the trees only barely budding, but the sky was a clear, fresh blue above her head. Freddie and George had abandoned their hoops and were perched on the bank of a small stream, peering into the reedy waters in search of tadpoles. Their older brothers had run ahead into the woods, engrossed in some private game of their own. The skirts of Cressie's gown were muddied, her hair a wild tangle, for she had come out without a bonnet in the vain hope that the breeze would clear the jumble of conflicting emotions in her head. Perching on the top of a stone boundary wall, she kept one eye on the twins, trusting that so long as she could hear the elder two shouting to each other they would be perfectly safe.

She must have taken leave of her senses in the gallery this morning. How had it happened? She could not even remember who made the first move towards the other, only that it felt inevitable and irresistible— words that she, a mathematician, a woman who lived by logic, should not even be thinking, let alone acting upon. Never in a thousand years would she have believed that she could have behaved so outrageously. Never before had she lost control in such a way. Making love to Giles had been a very deliberate act. Kissing Giovanni had been elemental.

It was her own fault. Her own fault for having conjured up those shocking images of Giovanni naked, poised with a javelin, clad only in a tunic. It was her own fault for having allowed her thoughts so consistently to dwell on the perfection of his face, on the clean, pure lines of his body. Her own fault for utterly failing to recognise that what she took for analysis and aesthetic appreciation had somehow metamorphosed into lust. Base, animal lust. She should, in all truth, be ashamed of herself.

The breeze ruffled her hair. She swiped a rebellious curl out of her eyes. The movement reminded her that this was what Giovanni had done, just before he had kissed her. Or before she threw herself at him and made it impossible for him not to kiss her. Not that he had resisted. But then why would he, when he must be quite accustomed to women doing exactly that! And now she was behaving just like those females, even though she knew perfectly well she was not, nor could ever be, because she had none of the attractions which went with successful seduction.

So why, then, had he kissed her, and kissed her as if he really had desired her every bit as much as she desired him? Cressie jumped down from the wall and began to make her way towards the twins, who had given up on the search for tadpoles and were now hurrying after their older brothers, intent on joining the game from which they would without doubt be refused entry. 'Let us go and look at the baby sheep,' she said, holding out a hand to each of the boys and leading them towards the far field, where lambs like little woolly puffs of cloud were cavorting while their mothers chewed complacently at the rich green grass.

She helped Freddie and George up on to the wall, keeping a supporting hand around the back of each. In the far corner of the field one black lamb stood alone, not bleating, but watching the others frolic without showing any inclination to join in. It would be too easy to think of herself as the black sheep of the family, but that was exactly how she felt. Even if Giovanni didn't agree in his determination to get under her skin, to discover this mystical person he claimed was the real Cressie. The Cressie he wanted to paint.

And that, of course, was why he'd kissed her, she thought ruefully. He wanted to disconcert her, make her react. It was simply part of his technique, to rouse her in order to incorporate her reaction into his painting. No doubt it was a technique he had deployed many times, and equally doubtless it was a highly successful one, for who could reject the kisses of a man so perfectly irresistible?

The best thing to do would be to pretend it had not

happened. She would not pander to his ego—not that he seemed to wish it. On the contrary, in fact, he was consistently deprecating about his appearance, now she came to think of it.

Lifting the twins down from the wall and calling to Harry and James to join them, Cressie turned back towards the house. She could not resist putting her fingers to her lips. It had been a professional kiss, Giovanni's motives had been purely artistic, but his kiss had been more deliciously decadent than anything she had ever imagined. Professional or no, she could not pretend she had done anything other than relish it. Her reaction had been proof positive. There could be no denying that, since proof was her stock-in-trade.

Cressie entered the attic studio nervously. For over a week she had sat every day while Giovanni worked on her portrait, saying little, barely acknowledging her presence, save to adjust her pose, occasionally to explain a technical point. The atmosphere between them was claustrophobic, tense. He would not allow her to see the painting, *Not until it is finished to my satisfaction*, he had insisted, though he said he was making good progress with it. He had not once made any reference to their kiss. Which was a good thing, she told herself repeatedly, because she had no intention of mentioning it either. He was an artist, she was his sitter. This room, this situation, did not represent real intimacy but rather a form of artistic intensity. Yes, that was it, she decided, satisfied that she had now explained it logically.

She tugged at the neckline of her gown in a vain attempt to make it cover more of her chest. Yesterday Giovanni had reminded her that he wished her to pose in something more revealing. Today she wore an evening dress and felt horribly exposed. Perhaps it was because it was still daylight and the rich crimson velvet gown, with its low *décolleté* and tiny puffed sleeves, showed far more flesh than she was used to displaying. It had belonged to her mother, and was cut in the old-fashioned style made popular by the Emperor Napoleon's wife, Josephine. An overdress of figured black gauze trimmed with gold spangles gave it a decadent appearance. With her corsets much more tightly laced than usual, Cressie's breasts were, to her mind, all too conspicuous, her nipples only just covered. When first she had seen her reflection in the looking-glass she had been shocked by the change in herself, but also by what her reflection said about Mama, whom she had not previously thought of as the kind of woman to wear a gown so obviously designed to seduce.

Cressie's attempt to dress her hair appropriately had not been overly successful. Unwilling to fuel gossip below stairs, she had dismissed her maid once her corsets were laced. What she had intended was a knot in the Grecian style which would complement the dress, but something had gone sadly awry. Very sadly, she thought dejectedly as she put her hand to her coiffure and came away with several hair pins, which she was attempting to replace when Giovanni arrived.

He halted on the threshold, staring at her. She almost crossed her arms over her breasts, but managed to stop herself. 'You said you wanted me to wear something more—but I didn't have anything of my own. Naturally I have evening gowns, but even though I am six and twenty, I am still considered a girl as far as the marriage mart is concerned and so I—so I borrowed this. It was my mother's, but if it's not suitable, I will…' She stuttered to a halt, blushing, as he continued to stare at her. 'I will go and change into something else.'

'No! Cressida, it is *perfecto. Sei bellisima.*'

'Well, it is a very nice gown, I have to agree. I think the fashions of Mama's youth…'

'It is not the gown, it is you.' Giovanni smiled. 'Though the hair—if you will permit me?'

She stood still, hardly daring to breathe as he quickly adjusted her falling tresses. He smelled of fresh soap and turpentine. There was a bluish stubble on his jaw. Why did he have to look so—and why did she have to react so…?

'There! This is inspired.'

He gently pushed her back into the chair and arranged the folds of her gown and then retreated behind his easel, pulling the covering sheet from the canvas. What on earth had she been expecting? That he would fall at her feet, or pull her into his arms, or bury his head in the valley of her really quite impressive bosom? His stubble would be abrasive on her skin. The *décolleté* of Mama's gown was so low that the least movement would expose her nipples to his attentions. Would he use his tongue? 'Oh, dear.'

'Is there something wrong?'

'No, no. It's nothing.'

'The dress is uncomfortable?'

'No. It is just a little—no.'

'You and your mother must share a very similar figure. It fits you perfectly.'

'Does it?' Cressie eyed herself doubtfully.

'You are very similar in looks too, if her portrait in the gallery is a good likeness.'

'You are flattering me today. Am I to be painted blushing with your compliments?'

Giovanni put down his brush. 'You think my compliments are professional artifice?'

Cressie shrugged. 'It doesn't matter, does it, so long as they are effective?'

Anger flashed in his eyes, but it was quickly suppressed. He made a point of focusing on his palette. Cressie fought the urge to pick at her fingers, another habit she was trying to cure herself of since Giovanni had pointed it out to her. 'Is it beautiful?' she asked. 'The picture, I mean. Are you pleased with it?'

He nodded. '*Si*. I am satisfied. It is what I said it would be. It will be finished sufficiently for me to begin the second portrait very soon.'

'Have you decided how I should be depicted?'

'I thought of you as the Amazonian, Penthiselea, since it is your pen name, but as a warrior queen she would traditionally be portrayed with her breast bared...'

'I feel as if my breast is all but bared in this dress. It is verging on the indecent.' Too late, she realised she had drawn his attention to her bosom, which Giovanni was now staring at, his eyes dark with something that did not look at all painterly. He had looked the same when he had kissed her. It made her feel as before, a sort of hot, unspecified anticipation. A hunger. 'I am not so sure that I really am a warrior queen,' Cressie said hurriedly, embarrassed by the turn her thoughts had taken. 'I am not even brave enough to face up to my father, never mind Achilles.'

'You do yourself an injustice! The first time I met you, you had just been facing up to your father—I remember it most clearly, the defiant look on your face when I walked into the room. And despite what you have told me of his attempts to marry you off, you remain stubbornly unwed.'

'I am unwed because I am unasked.' *Give or take one belated proposal offered under duress, that is.* 'You overestimate my charms, as I have several times pointed out.'

'And you are determined to rate yourself even lower than your father does, as I have also several times pointed out. Had you chosen to, I have no doubt that you could have elicited offers from any number of Lord Armstrong's candidates for your hand. But you did not choose to. In fact, I am willing to wager that you were the very opposite of conciliatory. What is the real truth, Cressie? Why are you not married? Was it that man your stepmother mentioned? Did he break your heart?'

Be careful what you wish for, Cressie Armstrong! That would teach her to hope Giovanni would break his silence. 'What about you?' she countered. 'Are you married? Have you ever been in love?'

'No and no. And we were discussing you.'

'*I* was not discussing anyone.'

'Now you sound just like one of your little brothers.' Giovanni laughed. '*Ti ho messo con le spalle al muro.* You don't like having your back against the wall, do you?'

'I do not—I have not—my back against the wall. Why are you suddenly interested in Giles Peyton?'

'I am not, but I am interested in the effect he had on you. I want to understand you better, now that the first portrait is almost complete and my knowledge will not cloud the purity of the image. Do you understand?'

'So this—this interrogation—is just another of your techniques?'

'For the love of God!' Giovanni threw his brush at the easel. It bounced off the wooden strut and landed on the floor. 'There is a woman hidden inside you, a passionate, witty, *interesting* woman. I have seen her, I have touched her, I have kissed her. But you won't admit she exists, never mind set her free.'

He stooped to retrieve his paintbrush. Straightening, he crossed the room to stand before her. 'You think that no one sees you, and yet you want to be seen. You want people to know that there is more to you than mere bloodstock. I can help you, I can show that person, but only if you will let me see her.'

Cressie bit back the automatic denial just in time, forcing herself to consider his words. 'I don't want you to capture my weaknesses, my past mistakes and indiscretions,' she said with difficulty. 'What happened with Giles, it was because I was so young and so naïve and so—I don't know, so desperate to please. But I'm none of those things now, Giovanni.'

'Then show me the real you. Think of this studio as a form of confessional. We are bound by a solemn vow of secrecy. Whatever is said here, remains here. You have my word on it.'

'And if I do confess? Unfortunately you cannot absolve me of my sins.' She hadn't meant to sound so defensive, but she was not at all sure she liked where this conversation was heading. She had never discussed Giles with anyone. She could hardly bring herself to think of it. 'You are offering to play not only the artist but the priest, are you?'

Giovanni stiffened. 'I do not *play* at being an artist.'

'I am not the only one who dislikes having my back against the wall,' Cressie retorted, leaping at the chance to get her own back, for that remark had stung. 'You do play at it, by your own admission. That canvas in front of you, it is not a portrait but an exercise in aesthetics. You have enormous natural talent, I've seen it in those drawings you did of my brothers, but you choose not to use it, and to instead paint what people wish to see. You could be an artist, but you choose to play the painter.'

She wanted only to deflect his questions, but for a moment she thought she had gone too far. Giovanni's mouth tightened, his eyes flashed, darkly threatening, but even as she watched, his anger faded, brought to heel like a disobedient hound. Running his fingers through his short crop of hair, and rubbing his eyes with his knuckles, he smiled wanly. 'You are right. It is what I have built my career on. And it is no longer enough.'

He pulled at his neckcloth, setting the perfect knot awry, and sat down on an ancient chest at right angles to her, throwing up a cloud of dust which clung to his black trousers. It was the first time Cressie had ever seen him dishevelled, the first time she had seen his expression naked, confused. The first time she had seen him look vulnerable. He was resting his chin on his hands, his elbows on his thighs.

Cressie twisted one of the spangles on her overdress round and round, until the thread which held it came loose. 'I'm frightened,' she admitted finally. 'I'm frightened that the person you paint will be a pathetic, unattractive creature.'

The spangle came loose, leaving a tiny hole in the gauze. Cressie stared at it, for she could not bring herself to look at Giovanni. 'You don't understand. How could you, for you cannot possibly have had any problem in attracting women, but—'

His harsh crack of laughter interrupted her, and forced her to look up. 'This,' he said, indicating his face, 'you think this is an asset? You think I like to be fawned over and petted? You think I like it that this perfect profile is the only thing people see?'

'Is that why you won't socialise with us, Bella and I? Why you eat alone, and...'

'Sleep alone. Always. Since—always. There, now you have me confessing to you.' Giovanni got to his feet, catching her hand in his and pulling her with him. 'From the moment I met you, I saw something different in you, Cressie. It's something I can't really explain but I know if I don't capture it I'll regret it for the rest of my life. To capture you, I need to know you. Do you see?'

She was acutely conscious of his body, of his skin,

of his mouth, and just as acutely aware that he had confided in her, in *her*, things that he had not told anyone else. It made him vulnerable and even more enticing, it made her want to hold him tightly, and to kiss him and to beg to know more, to know it all. But she owed him a confidence back in return for his candour, and for that she needed to steel herself.

'Very well, here is the truth of it, if you must have it.' Cressie disengaged herself, making for the dormer window, where she gazed out absently at the view. 'I was in my third Season. Despite what you think Giovanni, I had done my best to make myself—amenable—to the men my father brought forwards. But it didn't work. I was so gauche, and when I wasn't completely tongue-tied I was boring my potential suitors to death by talking endlessly about my studies. Bella is right, you know— no man can abide a blue-stocking.'

'No men of your father's acquaintance perhaps,' Giovanni said sardonically. 'Which says much about Lord Armstrong.'

Cressie smiled weakly. 'Thank you. It does not alter the facts, however. The more I tried, the more I seemed to scare the candidates for my hand away, and the more desperate I became. You have to understand, I have been raised to accept that marriage is not only a duty but my only option. Back then, I did not even consider an alternative. I *had* to make a match. So when Giles came along, and actually showed a modicum of interest in me rather than my family, I managed to persuade myself that he would make a good husband.

'I was not in love with him, but I thought with time—

for that is what my Aunt Sophia counselled, you know, that one grew into affection. Only I suppose that my lack of certainty must have shown—and it was hardly flattering—for just when I began to think of Giles as mine, he began to lose interest. I could not have borne it—or so I believed—to lose him when I had already told my father that I expected Giles to call. I had never seen Father so proud of me before. "That's my girl," he said, "always knew you'd come up trumps in the end." So I—I...' She took a deep breath and dug her nails hard into her palms. 'I thought that if I allowed Giles to make love to me, then he would be obliged to marry me,' she confessed painfully.

Moments passed. Cressie pressed her heated forehead to the cool of the window glass. Running her finger down the pane, she was surprised to discover that it was clean and realised this must be Giovanni's doing, on account of the light. She felt sick, but now that she had started, she had no choice but to finish. 'It was a dreadful thing to do,' she continued, turning back to face him. 'To try to manipulate Giles like that, it was shameful. That my stupidity had quite the opposite effect from the one I intended is my only saving grace. That, and the fact that no one else knows,' she finished with a pathetic attempt at a smile.

'Are you telling me that you gave yourself to this man, and he abandoned you?'

The stark disbelief in his voice made her squirm. 'No, no. Giles was an honourable man. He did offer for me—at least, he said he would marry me, because he ought to—but I knew he didn't mean it. I knew it would be like a death sentence for us both, even worse than having to endure my father's bitter disappointment. I had achieved my goal, and yet I simply couldn't bring myself to accept.'

Cressie dropped her head into her hands. She wouldn't cry, she wouldn't, but the memory of that dreadful scene between her and Giles was a wound that could still inflict much pain. She took another deep breath, muffling her distress by speaking determinedly to her shoes. 'Poor Giles, in a way he was every bit as naïve as I. I tried to make light of it at first you see—during—when—in the bedchamber. I thought to put us both at ease, but I must have sounded like an idiot. And when that did not work, I resorted to asking for instruction, only my questions rather brought Giles's lack of experience to the fore and—I will leave the rest to your imagination, though I doubt very much you can imagine anything so truly awful. Anyway, the net result was that I turned down my only offer of marriage, and Giles left to join the army soon after. I think he was as mortified by the whole episode as I was.'

Cressie forced herself to look up. 'It was a salutary lesson, for I realised I am simply not the kind of woman whom men—who can enjoy that kind of thing. If I could have analysed less and felt more—but that is not in my nature. Logic and facts, supposition and proof, those are the things I am good at. I decided that I would find a way, somehow, to make mathematics rather than matrimony my destiny. You know where you are with formulae.' She straightened her shoulders. 'There you have it, the whole sordid tale. It was some years ago now,' she said firmly. 'I am quite over it.'

'You think so!' Giovanni exclaimed. 'I am not so certain. To think, if the experience had been only a little less unpleasant, you would have married this man, making your father happy and yourself miserable.'

'Why are you so angry?' Cressie's own hackles began to rise. She had never told anyone what had happened between her and Giles. It was shocking and shameful, yet Giovanni seemed only furious. 'According to you, I am miserable anyway. At least if my misguided tactics had resulted in the acquisition of a husband, I would have done my duty.'

'Your duty! It seems to me you do little else. May I remind you that you are currently saving your father the expense and inconvenience of hiring a vastly inferior governess. You are trying at some great personal cost to provide your stepmother with the company he should rightly be providing her with. You have also taken the place of your eldest sister in looking after the youngest two—another duty your father has avoided—and I have no doubt that there are a thousand other things besides. You have nothing to reproach yourself with, Cressie, but what on earth possessed you to give away something so precious to a man you did not even want to marry? That I do not understand.'

When he put it like that, she really didn't know. 'I told you, I was desperate to please both Giles and my father. You have no idea what it was like,' Cressie said wretchedly. 'Bella had just provided my father with a son, and she made it so clear that she wanted me off her hands just as quickly as possible, and back then, Papa—I mean my father, would do anything to please her. You cannot imagine how important having a son and heir is to a man like him.'

'I understand only too well.'

'I don't see how you possibly can.' She could feel the tears welling, but she was determined not to let them fall. She would not pity herself. She most certainly did not want Giovanni's pity. Cressie clenched her fists. 'I surrendered my virtue in the hope of receiving an offer.' She blinked furiously. 'I know, do not tell me because I know, that if I confessed that fact to my father, it would most likely achieve what I most desire, to be taken off the marriage mart, but I could not bear to have him gloat over my being so stupid. I, who foolishly considers herself clever. My actions have already cost me a considerable portion of my self-respect. I could not compound the felony.'

As she rested her head on the dormer window, her hair finally unravelled, tumbling down over her bare shoulders. Giovanni did not speak. The silence felt thick, ominous. In all probability, he was disgusted with her. 'Your assertion that I am unhappy would appear to be well founded after all,' Cressie said, her voice not much more than a whisper. 'But unfortunately I can see no way to improve the situation. I cannot please my father save by marrying, but I am not marriageable and even if I were…' She threw back her head defiantly. 'Even if I were, do you know, I would not! I will not give myself to a man simply to expand to the dynastic web my father is weaving. I don't want to, and I won't!'

A slow handclap made her look up. *'Bravissimo!* This is progress.'

Cressie smiled weakly. 'It doesn't feel like it.' She crossed the room towards him, the train of her mother's gown sweeping behind her on the dusty floorboards. 'Is this the part of my confession where you decide my penance and absolve me of sin?'

Giovanni shook his head, clasping both of her hands between his. 'You have already done far more penance than you deserve. I do not believe you have committed any sin, save the one of allowing people to judge you. It does not matter what they think, your father, your step-mother, that stupid oaf Giles, even your sisters. Only what you think really matters.'

'I don't know what to think any more. I will confess freely to one thing—I am thoroughly confused.'

Giovanni led her gently over to the easel. 'There, you see. This is in fact the woman you thought you wanted to be.'

Cressie was so taken aback by this unexpected revelation that it was a few moments before she could focus on the portrait. Though the lower half of the body was merely outlined, the dress to be painted in later, the face, shoulders and arms were fully realised. She stared at the woman on the canvas who was her, and yet was not. As Giovanni had promised, all the requisite angles and proportions were there. And as he had promised, she looked beautiful, somehow softer and yes, more femi-nine, more alluring than she really was. There was a hint of promise in her eyes, the whisper of a kiss on her lips. This Lady Cressida was the kind of woman a man would fight to marry and boast about bedding.

'What do you think?'

The tone of Giovanni's voice sounded uncharacteristically uncertain. Realising with some surprise that her opinion mattered to him, Cressie eyed the portrait with renewed concentration, endeavouring to see it objectively, trying to recall the exact terms of their challenge. 'As proof of my thesis, it is well-nigh perfect. You have created beauty using nature's formulae,' she said eventually.

'But that is not what I asked.'

'I know.' Cressie peered at the woman in the portrait. 'She is beautiful, but she is not me. I don't mean the way she looks—it is a very good likeness, Giovanni, and the execution is masterful, but...'

'Tell me how it makes you feel.'

'It's strange, but it's as if there are parts of me missing. If art is truth, then this is a lie. Perhaps not a lie but a fib. You have omitted all my faults and implied characteristics I don't possess. There is very little of me behind that face. I look as if I would not say boo to a goose, as my Aunt Sophia would say, but I'm not biddable like that, nor do I recognise that sort of knowing confidence.'

'No, you are none of those things, but you are extremely perceptive. Not many people are capable of such insight. Especially in relation to themselves.'

Cressie circled the portrait, then stood in front of it again, frowning deeply. 'The proportions, the ratios, the angles, everything is perfect, but it is a lie. Mathematics is the purest of truths, its rules are irrefutable, and yet somehow you have refuted them. I don't understand. Is beauty not its own truth, Giovanni?' She whirled around to face him, her skirts catching on the legs of the easel, so that it rocked alarmingly. 'I am *not* this woman. I don't even want to *be* this woman, this simpering, pouting siren.'

'Though she is exactly the kind of woman you claimed you wished you could be, all compliance and conformity? This woman,' Giovanni said contemptuously, 'would have married to please her father without hesitation.'

'I am not that woman!'

'No, you are not. But you are not honest with yourself either. You like to think yourself a rebel, subverting the strictures of your life with little gestures, but your instinct is still to conform, to comply. This painting,' Giovanni said pointedly, forcing her to face the canvas once more, 'is not a complete lie.'

Cressie stared at her portrait afresh, her anger dying as she assimilated the truth of what Giovanni had said, what Giovanni had painted. *'Why, I can smile and murder whiles I smile, and cry content to that which grieves my heart, and wet my cheeks with artificial tears, and frame my face for all occasions,'* she quoted ironically. *'Richard the Third,'* she added, glancing over her shoulder, to where he stood behind her. 'Apt, apparently, but hardly flattering.'

'Nor the whole truth. When I paint you as Penthiselea, I would like you to have your hair completely down.'

'So you have decided that I am to be an Amazon after all?'

He took her hand between his. 'It is certainly true that you are much stronger than you think you are,' he said, kissing her wrist.

His mouth was warm, her pulse flickered beneath his gentle caress. 'And much more inclined to self-deception, if your character assessment is to be believed,' Cressie replied, trying to ignore the way his touch made her so conscious of her body, of the proximity of his. The tension between them altered subtly, from fraught to dangerous.

'I wished to make you feel better about yourself, not worse. I know how deep go the ties that bind us to those whose blood we share. I know how strong is the urge to please them. I know how difficult it is to please oneself in the face of it.' Giovanni touched her hair, running his hand down the wild curls, to rest on the exposed flesh of her shoulder. 'I know what it is to suffer in this way, and I know what it is to escape.'

His other arm slid around her waist, pulling her to him. His eyes were dark, passionately dark, his voice low, mesmerising. There were secrets, painful secrets, hidden behind the words he used, but she was too distracted by his touch, his scent, the nearness of him, the elemental pull of him, to care. Her skin was heated. She could see the quiver of her breasts, rising and falling in the low-cut gown, as her breathing quickened.

Giovanni's fingers trailed down from her shoulder, along the lace at the neckline of her dress, the lightest and most tantalising of touches. 'You are so much more, so very much more than you think you are, Cressie,' he whispered. His lips touched hers. The slightest of kisses, the merest brush of lip on lip. 'Penthiselea, the warrior goddess. Fight for yourself.'

He dipped his head, and began to kiss his way across her *décolleté*. She moaned softly as his lips, his tongue, trailed tiny kisses over the mounds of her breasts, lingering in the depth of her cleavage. His hands cupped her bottom, his fingers kneading her buttocks. She arched against him, lifting her breasts higher for his attentions. The puffed sleeves of her dress slid off her shoulders, and the front of the gown slid over her breasts, just exactly as if it were designed to do so.

'*Sei bellisima,*' Giovanni muttered, and took one of her exposed tight, pink nipples into his mouth. He sucked, and a shot of pure pleasure made her jerk against him. She staggered back against the wall. He sucked again, and cupped her other breast with his hand, teasing the nipple with his thumb. Her belly tightened. An aching throb took hold inside her, an exquisite tensing of all her muscles. '*Sei bellisima,*' Giovanni said again, and she believed him. Not that she was beautiful, but that he thought her so at this moment. His tongue circled her nipple, flicking, licking, his thumb mimicking the movement on her other breast, rousing her into an agony of wanting.

His hand tightened around her bottom, pulling her tight up against him. She could feel his arousal, hard, unmistakably hard, against her belly. She wanted, desperately wanted, to feel him closer. 'Giovanni.' Her voice sounded hoarse. 'Giovanni,' she said, more insistently now. He seemed loath to lift his head from her breasts. She was loath to urge him to do so, except…

'Giovanni!'

His lids were heavy over his eyes. Slashes of colour accentuated the planes of his cheekbones even more than usual. Cressie touched his jaw, running her palm over the slight abrasion of his stubble. 'You want me to stop?' he said, his voice husky.

She shook her head. 'I want you to kiss me.'

His mouth curled into the most sensual of smiles. One hand cupped her breast, the other her bottom. '*Per fortuna*, that is exactly what I would like to do.' His lips touched hers. She opened her mouth to him.

The attic door flew open with a crash. 'Here you both are! I told James this is your secret room, but he didn't believe me,' Harry exclaimed, bursting excitedly into the room. 'You must tell him I was right, Cressie. You must tell him—Cressie, you must come at once.'

'Why? Whatever is the matter?'

'Papa is here.'

Chapter Five

'That was a most meagre dinner, I must say. What was cook thinking of, sending up such a paltry selection of side-dishes? You must have a stern word with her, my dear. It is a question of maintaining standards, don't you know.'

Lord Armstrong shook out the tails of his evening coat and eased himself into a chair by the fire, opposite his wife. They had retired to the formal drawing room after dinner, a large chamber which had lain unused for several months—since his lordship's last visit to his country estate, as a matter of fact. As a result the room was chilly, the air stale. Bella had of late taken to sharing an early supper tray with her stepdaughter, before retiring to her bed almost immediately afterwards, and was struggling to stay awake. Huddled in a large cashmere shawl, obviously horribly uncomfortable in the constraints of her evening gown, Lady Armstrong remonstrated weakly. 'Had we been expecting you, my love, I would have made sure to order a more suitable and substantial dinner.'

'Always be prepared for every possibility,' her husband said bracingly, 'always stay one step ahead of the opposition, and you will never fail.'

'We are your family, not the opposition, and if you had not failed to send us a note apprising us of your imminent arrival, Father, we should not have failed to provide you with a dinner worthy of your elevated status.' Cressie, seated enough of a distance away from the fire to feel distinctly cold, was also feeling distinctly abrasive. Bella's skin had a waxy pallor, she noted. Her cheeks were also unnaturally flushed, and she knew, for her stepmother had confided in her that evening, that her ankles were so swollen as to make her slippers pinch painfully. 'Bella has been most unwell,' she said pointedly. 'She should be in her bed.'

'Nonsense. It does the circulation good to be up and about. It is good for the child too, for you to get some exercise, Bella. I am sure Sir Gilbert Mountjoy did not mean for you to be lolling abed all day.'

'What Sir Gilbert actually said was that Bella needed to rest,' Cressie said pointedly.

Lord Armstrong, who had made a career out of turning the truth in whichever direction most suited him, waved his hand dismissively. 'She has been resting for some weeks now. As I recall, it was in order to allow my wife to rest that I sent you down here, Cressida. I wonder that it has not occurred to you to relieve her of some simple household tasks. Such as the ordering of a decent dinner.'

An angry retort sprang to her lips, but Cressie caught it just in time. It was her father's most successful tactic, to turn the tables on her, and she rarely failed to rise to the bait. But not this time. He was wholly in the wrong, would never admit to being in the wrong, and she would be wasting her time in trying to make him do so. Such a little thing it was in the grand scheme of things, to refuse to be belittled, but she did refuse, and she felt better for it. Taking a leaf from Giovanni's book, for in many aspects her father was every bit as childish as her brothers, she did not deign to reply at all, but got to her feet.

'Where do you think you're going?'

'Though it seems to have slipped your mind, Father, the main reason you *sent me down here* was to act as governess to your sons. I am going to make sure they are abed and settled. They are such very boisterous boys,' she said with a sweet smile, 'that I fear they do not always heed their nursemaid and often refuse to retire when they ought. Perhaps, now you are here, you will wish to assume the duty for yourself? In fact, I wonder it did not occur to you earlier to offer to take my place in reading them their bedtime story. My apologies. I will ensure that I do not usurp you tomorrow.'

'I have no time to be reading stories,' Lord Armstrong said, his eyes narrowing. He was not accustomed to hearing sarcasm in his own household unless it originated from himself, but if he didn't know better he might imagine that Cressida was mocking him.

'Cressie has been very good with the boys, Henry,' Bella said faintly. 'They heed her much more than they do me. Poor little souls, I was worried that I was neglecting them, for I really have been feeling very low, but they seem perfectly happy with their big sister.'

'Why thank you, Bella,' Cressie said, astonished, earning herself a tight little smile.

'Cressie has been most solicitous to me too, Henry,' Bella persisted. 'She has taken all of the household burdens from me, for there have been days when I have been as weak as a kitten, you know. The morning sickness is quite debilitating.'

'Sickness! But you must be well past that stage by now. You are what—five months gone?'

'Indeed, for your last visit here was November.'

Lord Armstrong was rather disconcerted by this embarrassingly personal snippet of information. 'Nonsense, my dear, you are misremembering. I am sure…'

'You were present for a time on Christmas Day. You arrived in time for church, as I recall, and left after dinner. You have not stayed the night here since November. It is no wonder that little Freddie and George were so awkward with you this afternoon—you are quite the stranger to them.'

Once again, Cressie stared in astonishment at her stepmother. She had never once heard Bella speak to Lord Armstrong in such a way. Seeing her father's face, she realised that he was just as taken aback as she, and hid her smile. For the first time in her life, she felt that she and her stepmother were fighting the same corner.

Bella, it seemed, was not quite finished either. 'You will no doubt wish to become reacquainted with your sons, now that you are here,' she said. 'Cressie would appreciate the morning off from teaching, I am sure, if you wish to take the boys out fishing.'

First Cressida had openly mocked him and now Bella

had decided to get uppity. Something was most definitely afoot, Lord Armstrong decided and he was not at all sure he approved of it. 'I would not dream of interrupting their school work. Besides, I am due back in London almost immediately. I am off to St Petersburg with the duke, you know. I may be gone for some months. That is why I am here, to ensure that the appropriate arrangements are in place before I depart.'

'Oh, I see.'

Bella wilted visibly. Had she not been paying close attention, Cressie would have missed the disappointment, so quickly was it erased from her expression. Her stepmother was hurt. It should not have been a blinding revelation, but it was. Bella actually loved her husband. Bella thought he had come to visit her, obviously hoped he had come because he was concerned about her, when all Lord Armstrong was interested in was his *appropriate arrangements*! With a shock, Cressie realised what arrangements he meant. He would be absent for the birth of Bella's child. *His* child!

Forgetting all about her strategy of indifference, she could no longer hold her tongue. 'Father! You cannot go with Wellington. I am sure he will be able to find an able replacement. Bella needs you here.'

'I beg your pardon?'

'Cressie!' Bella exclaimed.

'Bella will not say it, so I will say it for her.'

'Cressida, I beg you will not!'

'She does not wish you to travel so far beyond reach at such an important time.'

'Henry, do not heed her. I am sure I will do perfectly well on my own.'

'You will not be on your own.'

Lord Armstrong got to his feet. He rarely betrayed anger, but Cressie could see, from the rigidity of his posture, that he was having to work extremely hard to hide his feelings. Under any other circumstances, she would have been gleeful, but for now she was simply concerned with trying to make him see the utter selfishness of his behaviour. 'Father, I know it will be a sacrifice, but surely Bella is more important than...'

'How dare you! How dare you tell me what to do! How dare you decide what is important for England and what is not.' Lord Armstrong shook with rage. 'It seems to have escaped your notice that my wife has already given birth to four healthy boys without complication or drama.'

'Father, it is different this time. Bella has been most unwell.'

'And whose fault is that? I have no doubt at all that you have been encouraging her to think herself worse than she is. Mountjoy had no real concerns when he examined her, or he would have informed me of them. My wife has expressed no real concerns either, until today, and no doubt that is thanks to your encouragement. She has not once written to me of any serious complaints, have you, my dear?' Lord Armstrong demanded, turning suddenly on his wife, who seemed to be trying to bury her bulk into the depths of her armchair.

She shook her head. 'I did not wish to worry you, Henry. I know how important—'

'There, you see!' Lord Armstrong declared. The obvious note of triumph in his voice, however, made him rein in his emotions. When he spoke again, it was in his more usual tone, and most pointedly directed only at his wife. 'Despite your reluctance to burden me, I was worried, my love. Which is why I have arranged for Sir Gilbert to attend you every month until your date. Though he is almost as much in demand as I, he has graciously agreed that he will take up residence at Killellan Manor for your lying-in. You see how much of a care I have for our child.'

For our child! Not for his wife. The nuance would before today have been lost on Cressie, but Giovanni had helped her to look at her world in a very different light. She fully expected Bella to be reassured, however, and was as unprepared as his lordship for her response.

'No!' Bella struggled to sit up, casting cushions and shawls aside. 'I will not have him here. I don't want him here.'

'Sir Gilbert?' Lord Armstrong looked puzzled. 'But he has attended the births of every one of our sons. He is the best in his field.'

'*No!*' With a supreme effort, Bella rose from her seat. 'I won't have him, Henry, do you hear? I want a midwife. I want a woman. I will not have that man prodding and poking me with his cold fingers and telling me not to make a fuss in that finicky voice of his. "Come, Lady Armstrong, show a little restraint. Do you hear the cows calving in the field bellowing so loud?" I'd like to see him give birth to such great strapping boys as mine without a bellow or two. I'd like to see him managing to be stoic, faced with those dreadful instruments of torture of his. I will not have him. I shall make my own arrangements, Henry, since you will not be here, and that is the last I have to say on the matter. I am retiring to my bedchamber now. Since your visit is to be of such short duration, I will make no further calls on your time. I do not expect to see you until morning.'

With as much dignity as her rippling flesh and swollen ankles shuffling in their tight slippers could muster, Bella left the drawing room. Cressie, dumbfounded, also decided a strategic retreat was much the best tactic. It had been quite a day and she had much to reflect upon.

Cressie recounted the events of the drawing room to Giovanni the next morning. 'I feel such an idiot. I was so taken up by resenting poor Bella that I completely failed to realise that she is just as much a victim of my father's selfishness as my sisters and I. She really does care for him, and he really does care naught for her. You were right,' she whispered, for her brothers were all four of them seated at the table working, George and Freddie on their letters, James and Harry at their geometry. 'My father is no more interested in what Bella wants than he is in what I want. You should have seen her face last night when she realised that he was only here to make sure we all behaved ourselves while he swans off to Russia with Wellington. I actually felt sorry for her.'

Giovanni paused in his work, frowning over at Freddie, whose hands he was painting. He was finding Cressie's pacing presence far too distracting. It had seemed only practical to move the schoolroom to the portrait gallery, to allow Cressie to teach the boys while he worked, with only occasional breaks necessary to have them in the formal pose. The arrangement meant that he had made excellent progress on the portrait, sufficient to free him in the afternoons to work on Cressie's picture without impacting on the commission. But today, he could not concentrate.

She was different. It was as if she had changed overnight. Having cast off her resentment, her anger on Lady Armstrong's behalf seemed fresher, had somehow lost its previous debilitating quality and turned into a positive force. Penthiselea, the warrior queen. There were no half-measures with Cressie. She was on Bella's side now, and would not waste time bearing a grudge for how she had been treated by her stepmother in the past. He wondered fleetingly what Lady Armstrong would make of this turnabout. From what Cressie had recounted of last night's denouement, it seemed that she too was beginning to resent his lordship's high-handed treatment. They would make unlikely allies, Cressie and her ladyship, but it seemed probable that allies was what they would become.

Giovanni smiled to himself. He'd like to see the outcome of the revolution in the Armstrong household that he had played a part in igniting. Sadly, it was unlikely, for this commission would take him only a few more weeks. An ache like a hunger pang gripped his belly, but he dismissed it. It wasn't so much that he would miss Cressie, it was more that he was worried he would not have enough time to finish painting her. He'd have to work like a demon.

He tried to concentrate on the work in front of him, for which Lord Armstrong was paying, but he was far more interested in Cressie's change of attitude towards her father. He doubted very much it would be so easy for her as she thought right now, to cast off the habit of obedience. He knew from his own experience that it was a durable and persistent habit which required constant vigilance to suppress. The important thing was that Cressie had made a start.

She had confided the small morsel of praise Lady Armstrong had bestowed upon her last night. The effect it had on her seemed out of all proportion, for it sounded to him like the most grudging of compliments, voiced as much to irk her sire as to bestow approval on her stepdaughter.

How little Cressie required to make her blossom. It had been obvious to Giovanni, how much her brothers had come to enjoy being with her, simply by the significant decrease in disruptions to his work. Harry, in particular, had a head for numbers, and had earned James's fury by finishing the exercises in Cressie's primer well ahead of his older brother, then demanding more difficult sums. James, a boy made in his dear papa's image, had not taken well to this evidence of superiority, but Cressie had ignored his tantrum, and there could be no better tactic.

If only Giovanni could ignore Cressie, but he was horribly aware of her as she paced restlessly behind him, stopping every few moments by his easel and preceding almost every remark with 'and another thing' as she replayed last night's scene for him, or recalled another incident from her past in which her father had put his own needs over others. There were a great deal of these, a bottomless well of examples which she had obviously, unwittingly, been storing away in that clever brain of hers with every detail intact.

He abandoned his attempt to complete his depiction of Freddie's hands. The expertise with which he rendered hands was one of the things for which he was most praised, one of the techniques he had worked hardest to master, but he was not in the right frame of mind today. Picking up another brush, he began to paint in the boy's shirt instead.

'It is extraordinary how many shades you use to portray something which looks simply white to me. Watching you paint makes me realise the enormity of your skill. I cannot believe I ever suggested you were merely a craftsman.'

Cressie stood by his shoulder, gazing at the canvas. One of her curls tickled his cheek. She smelled of chalk and lavender and rather deliciously of strawberries, which Giovanni traced to the sticky patch of conserve on the sleeve of her gown where one of her brothers had grabbed hold of her. They were always grabbing hold of her. Though she was not naturally tactile, it was another change he'd noticed, her willingness to join in their rough and tumble and lately, to administer cuddles and even the occasional consoling kiss. His hand tightened on the long handle of his sable brush, thinking of those consoling kisses. He swore quietly under his breath. What, was he envious now, of a few childish kisses? Ridiculous. But yesterday, just before

Harry burst in on them—that had been a kiss so very far from consoling, he'd been quite unable to think about anything else since.

He was thinking about it now, as Cressie's skirts brushed against his trousers. She was asking him about shading. He had to find something to distract his thoughts. 'Here, you can apply the next pigment. I will guide you.' He loaded his brush with lead white, and handed it to her.

'Giovanni!' She looked as if he had given her a diamond necklace—or at least, as any other woman but Cressie would look, upon receipt of diamonds. 'You can't mean—I would not dare. You saw my attempt at a horse.'

It touched him unbearably, her glowing gratitude, the genuine admiration it implied, which meant so much more than any other because there was no one else, not in England, not in Italy, who understood his work so well. So little it took to please her, and so much she deserved. If she were his to please…

He strangled that thought at birth. Cressie was staring at him uncertainly. 'I can see you've changed your mind. I don't blame you,' she said, obviously swallowing her disappointment.

Giovanni shook his head decisively. 'The beauty of oils is how easily any mistake can be repaired, for they take so long to dry. But you will not make a mistake. Come here.'

He pulled her backwards against him, holding her still with one hand on the curve of her hip, which was another piece of her anatomy which had kept him awake at night, before covering her hand which held the paint-brush with his. The nape of her neck was warm, so delicate. Her fingers trembled under his. She had been making an effort not to pick at the skin around her nails of late. He had refrained from commending her, knowing she would prefer that he didn't notice. 'Gently,' he said, meaning the reprimand just as much for himself as for her. 'The lightest of strokes, but keep the brush steady. Don't press down too hard. See.' He guided her hand over the outline of a shirtsleeve on the canvas.

'I'm painting! I'm actually painting. Imagine, in a hundred years' time when some expert looks at this portrait, they will frown over these very brush strokes, and wonder if you have allowed an apprentice to work with you.'

Cressie's fingers fluttered under his. Giovanni told himself she was simply nervous. And the way she was pressing her delightful bottom against his thighs, that was just for balance. He struggled against the rush of blood to his groin which was his instant response. Her breathing seemed to have quickened. Nerves again, he told himself. He would not look down over her shoulder at the rise and fall of her breasts. Such sensitive breasts, her nipples the same dark pink as one of the roses which grew in the gardens at Palazzo Fancini. He tried instead to think of the pigments he would use to create the exact shade, but it was too late. Unbidden, his hand had slid up from Cressie's thigh to span her ribcage, just under the swell of her breast. Appalled, he made to remove it.

'Don't!' Her voice was no more than a ragged whisper. 'I mean,' Cressie said, 'please do not move, lest the brush slips. I would not like Freddie's shirt to be ruined.'

He refrained from pointing out what he had already about the nature of oils. Relying on the fact that the easel and the large canvas obscured them from the view of the boys, he let his fingers drift upwards to cup her breast. She shuddered. His erection stiffened. The paintbrush wobbled. 'More,' Cressie whispered. 'I think we need more paint.'

The palette was on a side table. A stretch away. She leaned forwards, her bottom rubbing against him, and this time he knew it was deliberate, for she glanced over her shoulder at him with a smile that was both mischievous and sensual, before she loaded the brush and managed to nestle even closer against him on her return.

'Papa, have you come to see our new schoolroom?'

'Papa, have you come to look at our picture?'

'Hell and damnation!' Cressie exclaimed rather loudly. Fortunately, the scraping back of chairs and the delighted squeals of her brothers meant that no one other than Giovanni heard her.

He caught the paintbrush just before it spattered the polished oak boards of the gallery's floor with lead white. He was on the point of assuring her that her father would have noticed nothing untoward when he caught Lord Armstrong's assessing gaze and abruptly changed his mind. These last few weeks, he had come to think of the man, whom he had met only once, as an ignorant buffoon. He had forgotten the salient fact that Lord Armstrong was one of the most respected diplomats in England, if not Europe. Such a man did not achieve success without having acute powers of observation, the ability to assess a situation accurately. Judging from his expression, those powers were telling him that something was not as it should be. His eyes, which Giovanni was disconcerted to note were a faded version of Cressie's, were not focused on his sons but on his daughter.

'Why was I not informed that you had abandoned the schoolroom?'

'Come, Father, you know you have no desire to be bothered with petty domestic detail. I thought you would commend my arrangements, for they are most efficient, allowing me to teach and Giovanni—Signor di Matteo—to paint at the same time.'

Cressie was flushed, but she seemed remarkably unflustered. In fact, she seemed almost to be relishing the situation. Giovanni suppressed a smile, and made a very small bow. 'Lady Cressida is most resourceful,' he said.

Lord Armstrong's eyes narrowed. He was patently puzzled, but was fortunately so entrenched in his view of his daughter as undesirable and lacking in desires of her own that the reason his suspicions had been aroused did not occur to him. He made no attempt to return Giovanni's bow and turned his attention to the canvas. 'Hmm.'

'Signor di Matteo has made excellent progress, do you not think, Father?'

'Better part of the canvas is still to be covered.'

'Yes, but he has completed all of the faces, and most of the hands. These are the most time-consuming and important elements. They are excellent likenesses, do you not agree?' Cressie persisted.

'Yes, not too shabby,' Lord Armstrong admitted grudgingly, 'but I'd expect nothing less for the kind of fee he demands.' He turned away from the canvas after the most cursory inspection, ignoring the various pleas of his sons, now clustered around him, to agree that their particular likeness was the best. Swatting and patting indiscriminately at his offspring, for he hated to have his clothing pawed, he turned to Giovanni. 'I had hoped to be here when the portrait was completed, but that will not be possible now. I am needed in Russia on important matters of state.'

As ever when he mentioned his calling, the diplomat seemed to puff up his chest. If he had feathers, Giovanni thought, Lord Armstrong would have preened them. He said nothing, however, refusing even to pretend to be impressed, though it was his normal custom to pander to his clients' vanity.

'I shall have my man of business pay half your fee on completion,' Lord Armstrong continued. 'You will understand that the remainder will be held until I have returned, and can signify my acceptance of the piece.'

Giovanni sensed, rather than heard Cressie's protest, and quelled it with a quick shake of his head. He picked up the cloth and covered the easel and then began to gather together his brushes.

'What on earth do you think you're doing?' his lordship demanded.

'You pay me half my fee, I leave you half a painting. When you return, and are available to *signify your acceptance*, I will complete it. Until then, my work here is done.'

'I say! That is most unreasonable.'

Giovanni shrugged. Across from him, he saw Cressie cover her mouth with her hand. She knew he was bluffing. It surprised him, that she could read him so well. He continued to pack up his painting equipment.

'You are being most unprofessional,' Lord Armstrong protested.

'We agreed on the terms of my commission. I happen to know that you—how do you call it—pulled strings—in order to gain precedent.'

'I don't know what you mean.'

'Sir Gareth McIlroy was to be my next client. He informed me that he would cede his place in my schedule to you. I know how desperate he was to have a portrait of his wife, who has consumption, completed as a matter of urgency. I must therefore deduce that the favour he owed you was significant.' Giovanni permitted himself a small smile. 'But if you wish to call a halt to proceedings I'm sure Sir Gareth would be most grateful and relieved.'

Lord Armstrong, quite disconcerted, made a show of consulting his watch. 'I cannot be wasting the morning haggling over a picture. Very well, Cressida shall authorise full payment to you when the portrait is finished.'

'Not Lady Armstrong?'

His lordship's eyes narrowed. He was fairly certain that he was being disrespected, but he had no idea how. He closed his watch with a brisk snap of the gold case and returned it to his pocket. 'My wife has more important matters to concern herself with. My daughter, on the other hand, has nothing better to do. Which puts me in mind.' He turned towards Cressie. 'I have left a list of instructions for you to follow in my absence, but there are two other things I want to mention. Firstly, Sir Gilbert. You will prevail upon your stepmother to let him attend to her when he visits. All this stuff and nonsense about midwives is just that. Secondly, Cordelia. Your Aunt Sophia is, naturally, authorised to accept any suitable proposal while I am away. She knows my preferences.'

'What about Cordelia's preferences, Father?'

'Cordelia will prefer whomever her aunt directs her to prefer. Cordelia knows her duty. Sophia knows all about the business of launching a girl, none better,' Lord Armstrong said, quite forgetting the misalliance his sister had failed to prevent Cassandra from pursuing. 'You will leave her to it, and you will refrain—*refrain!*—from interfering, do you hear me, Cressida?'

'I do, Father. Though why you should be concerned about any influence I may have with Cordelia when you are so sure that she knows her duty…'

'Impudence is a vice that is tolerable in the very young. In a woman of your age, it is quite misplaced. I will bid you farewell, Cressida, for I aim to spend the rest of the day with my boys, and must leave before dinner. You may write me with news of my wife when her time comes.'

With a dismissive nod to Giovanni, Lord Armstrong departed with his gleeful sons. 'And I am willing to bet that within the hour he will have had quite enough of their angelic company and will be calling for me to take them back,' Cressie said to his retreating back.

Giovanni laughed drily. 'I hope that you will make a point of being unavailable, since he so summarily dismissed you.'

'Not just me. He was barely civil to you.'

'Do not apologise on his behalf. I do not care this much for the man's opinion.' Giovanni snapped his fingers to demonstrate, a gesture which Cressie thought peculiarly Italian. He began to clear away his brushes.

'Aren't you going to carry on with the portrait?'

'I find I am no longer in the mood for painting.'

Cressie picked up the brush of lead white and drew it over the back of her hand, leaving a faint trace of paint. 'Can you only paint when you feel inspired?'

'If that were true I would have produced nothing in the past decade. It is many years since I felt inspired to paint any subject. Until I met you, that is.'

'What is so different about me?'

'I don't know. It is a mystery, and therein, perhaps, lies the answer. You are fascinating, unfathomable and quite unlike any woman I have ever met. It would appear that you are also my muse.'

Cressie flushed. 'An object of obsession? That doesn't sound at all like me.'

'To obsess does not seem at all like me. And yet…'

Seconds passed in silence, the atmosphere crackled with tension like the moments before a thunderstorm breaks. What he had left unspoken hung between them like overripe fruit ready for plucking. Cressie blurted out the first thing that came into her head. 'I can help you with that.'

Giovanni stared at her in dumb incomprehension.

'The brushes,' she faltered, pointing vaguely, 'would you like me to help you clean the brushes?'

Bemused, Giovanni agreed. She followed him down a service staircase to the basement scullery which he had requisitioned for his own. A dank room no longer used by the kitchen staff, it was lit only by an oil lamp. He had left his coat up in the gallery. She watched him at the sink, admiring the lean lines of him, the way his forearms flexed as he worked his brushes free from paint.

Cressie felt restless. Tense. Exhilarated. She felt as if she were looking at the world anew, with a clarity that was almost painful. It made her want to behave outrageously, to make up for years of compliance. For the first time, facing up to her father made her feel better, not worse. She was buoyed with confidence. The way Lord Armstrong had looked at them, she and Giovanni, in the gallery, he had known that there was something amiss, but it had not occurred to him that his daughter, his obedient, mousy little daughter, could have been behaving so outrageously.

'Here, let me see your hands. You have white paint all over them.'

Giovanni pulled her over to the sink and began to wipe her hands clean with a rag dipped in turpentine. His touch was firm and sure. He had been working all morning, but his hands had barely a spot of paint on them. He was always so neat and pristine. Save for yesterday, in the attic. Remembered pleasure rippled through her, settling low in her belly. When he had touched her—heavens, the way he had touched her. And then this morning too. She really thought she might melt. He, in contrast, had been so—well, hard, there was no other word for it. Perspiration beaded in the small of her back. Really, really hard. And she had been the one who had made him so.

The turpentine-soaked rag had been replaced with a clean cloth. Giovanni seemed to be taking an unnecessarily long time to dry her hands. She watched him, fascinated by the slender length of his fingers stroking the cloth over her skin. Her heart began to thump as she caught his gaze on her, eyes dark in the dim light, but unmistakably glistening with awareness. He dropped the cloth. He pulled her to him, touched her forehead, her cheeks, her lips, as if he were painting her with his fingers. A wild excitement fluttered through her.

His kiss was darker even than his eyes, drawing her into a sultry, sensual whirlpool of emotions. Desire was sharpened by a hunger she had not known she possessed, made urgent by its newness, strengthened by its illicit nature. Forbidden fruit. She for him, he for her. Cressie dug her fingers into Giovanni's buttocks and kissed him deeply. Mouth. Tongue. Lips. She drank him in, inhaled him, devoured him.

And he kissed her back as if it were not enough, not nearly enough. He groaned, hauling her so tightly against him that she almost lost her balance, flailing against a wooden door set low into the wall of the scullery. The latch dug painfully into her back. 'Ouch!'

'*Dio!* Every time I kiss you something or someone intrudes—what is that?' Breathing raggedly, Giovanni pulled her away from the wall. 'I have not noticed it before. Are you hurt?'

'No.' Cressie put her hand up to her hair. As she suspected, it was in a wild tangle, bits of it hanging down over her cheeks. Thank goodness the light was dim. The strength of her response to him was frightening. He would be thinking her one of those women who threw themselves at him, if she was not careful. Which was exactly what she was doing, wasn't she?

Distracted, confused, she turned her attentions to the door. 'Where does this lead to?' she asked, already lifting the latch.

'I have no idea.'

Giovanni seemed to be having as much difficulty as she in controlling his breathing, Cressie was relieved to notice. His hair was standing up in spikes. The tail of his shirt was hanging out of his trousers. Had she done that? Cressie peered through the open door. A steep set of stone stairs disappeared into the gloom. 'A cellar of some sort, it must be part of the foundations of the original house. I had no idea it was there.'

'Shall we take a look?'

Cressie looked doubtfully into the gloom. 'It's very dark down there.'

Giovanni picked up the oil lamp. 'You are surely not afraid?'

She tossed her head back and glared defiantly at him, though she knew it was exactly what he expected her to do.

'Let me go first,' Giovanni said. 'Take your time, these steps look dangerous.'

Not as dangerous as the uncharted waters she was already swimming in, Cressie thought, treading carefully down into the darkness.

They found themselves in a passageway which led, as Cressie had suspected, to the cellars of the original manor house. It was to make sure she did not slip that Giovanni held her close to him, she told herself, the same reason she clung to his arm.

There were several chambers, each with a low vaulted roof forming a shallow dome. It was surprisingly warm. 'We must be directly below the kitchens,' Cressie whispered.

Intrigued, Giovanni held the lamp high, inspecting the herringbone brickwork of the ceilings. 'The family who built this place must have been wealthy. These are almost Roman in style.'

Cressie's eyes were alight with wonder. 'I had no idea. The mathematics of the arch are most fascinating, you know. In fact, there is a most excellent work on the subject by another of your countrymen, the Abbé Mascheroni. Our own Robert Hooke explains the specific equations behind the dome at St Paul's Cathedral. I came across his work at the Royal Society.'

'The Royal Society? How did you gain entry to that august, and I believe exclusively male, bastion?'

'I…' Cressie hesitated. She had no doubt at all that Giovanni would be intrigued and amused by the story of Mr Brown, but it suddenly struck her how much more astonished he would be by the sudden appearance of Mr Brown in the flesh. He wanted to paint the private Cressie—what better way than to have Mr Brown captured in oils? It was an inspired idea! She shook her head, smiling enigmatically at him. 'Later,' she said. 'I'll tell you later. Trust me.'

'Trust you. I cannot deny I owe you that.' Giovanni's broadest smile, so rarely seen, was all the more delightful when it appeared. It made him seem so much younger. It made her realise how stern his usual expression was. It was not that he lacked humour, but he looked at the world even more darkly than she did.

They were standing at the juncture of two of the domed vaults, by a set of supporting pillars. Giovanni held the oil lamp high, peering up at the stonework. 'Look at this, Cressie.'

Cressie. Cressie. Cressie. She jumped, startled by the sound. The echo was eerie, bouncing round the vault, as if spirits were whispering her name. 'Giovanni,' she said softly, crying out with delight at the result.

Giovanni laughed. 'It is a whispering gallery. Astonishing. In the church of Santa Maria del Fiore, when I was a child, my father—the man I called—never mind. Let us experiment.' Leaving the lamp on the floor beside Cressie, he retreated to the next gallery before crouching down in the darkness against a pillar. 'Cress-i-da,' he whispered.

She giggled. 'Gio-vaaa-ni.' She waited until the echo, which seemed to reverberate for ever, finally died down. *'Don Giovanni,'* she trilled, completely off-key, following her rendition of the line from Mozart's opera with a clap of her hands to produce a most satisfactory crack of thunder. She was rewarded with a guffaw of very masculine laughter, followed by an even more off-key rendition of the next line. 'That was terrible,' she called.

'*Si.* Now you know something else about me that no one else does. I sing like a donkey with haemorrhoids.'

The peals of her laughter rung around the room like church bells. She was becoming accustomed to the strange effect. Cressie settled down on the cellar floor. The whispers, the dark, made the mood intimate without being stifling. Dangerous. And exciting. 'Tell me something else,' she said, keeping her voice low.

'I don't like dogs.'

'I am afraid of dogs.'

'My favourite cheese is pecorino.'

'I like to eat honey from the comb.'

'Your lips taste of honey.'

'Oh.' His words gave her goose bumps. The whispering gallery brought out Giovanni's Italian accent. 'Say that in Italian.'

'*Le tue labbra sanno di miele.* You have the most delightful *fondoshiena*,' Giovanni said. 'Last night, I dreamed of your *fondoshiena*.'

The acoustics of the cellar made it sound as if he had whispered in her ear, as if his words had brushed her skin. 'Fondo...?'

'The French word is *derrière*. The English word...'

'Is bottom.' Giovanni thought she had a delightful bottom. It was a shocking thing to say, and Cressie felt intoxicated. 'Tell me,' she whispered, tempted by the dark, by the spiralling of tension inside her, tempted by temptation itself. 'Tell me exactly what it was you dreamt.'

Chapter Six

Cressie heard the sharp intake of Giovanni's breath as her question swirled around the confined space. She waited, heart pounding, for his answer. When he spoke, soft as a sigh, the words washed over her like a caress. 'In my dream, I was watching you undressing,' he said. 'You knew I was watching. As I watched, you started touching yourself.'

She slumped back against the wall of the cellar. It was cool, but her skin was burning hot. 'Where? How? What was I touching?'

'Your breasts at first. When you pulled your chemise down over them, your nipples were budded, hard. As they were when I touched them yesterday. Do you remember?'

'Yes.' She closed her eyes. Imagined and remembered. His fingers. His tongue. His lips. She slid her hands inside the neck of her dress, and touched herself, pinched her nipples, stroked them, as he had done.

'Are you touching them now, Cressie?'

'Yes.' Circling them with her thumbs as he had done.

Imagining it was him, his hands. 'Yes,' she said, and the echo made her voice hoarse and guttural, which she found she liked, for it made her feel like the kind of woman who would enjoy being watched as she touched herself. A shocking, wanton woman. She wanted to know more, and he seemed to be able to read her mind.

'When you bent over to remove your stockings...' A pause. 'The line of beauty. I wanted to taste you. To kiss the skin at the top of your thighs. The softest of skin. Touch it, Cressie. Tell me, is it the most delicate of skin?'

She arched back against the wall, rucking up her skirts. She had no thought of where she was or what she was doing, lost in the intimate world of touch and sensation, no room for thinking or questioning. Parting the two halves of her pantalettes, she slid her hand between her legs. 'Soft,' she whispered. 'The softest,' she said, stroking herself, her fingers sliding of their own volition inside her, where the tension was focused. 'Wet,' she whispered, already beginning to lose herself, 'hot.'

Giovanni's voice was harsh now. 'I bent you over. I slid inside you,' he said, his words and his dream echoing what she was already doing.

She could almost feel him, feel the thick shaft of his manhood, which this morning had pressed so insistently against her. It was easy to imagine him inside her. Cressie's fingers slid over the damp hot mound of her sex. She was knotted tight. It was not the first time, but it was the first time she had imagined, wished, fantasised, that it was someone else doing the touching. 'Giovanni. Giovanni. Giovanni.' Almost unaware, she said his name to a rhythm, stroking and dipping, stroking, not wanting it to be over—another new departure, not wanting it to end. 'What next?' she panted. 'Giovanni, what next?'

'Slowly. Do not rush. I—I did not rush.'

'Slowly,' Cressie repeated but she no longer wanted slow.

'You tightened around my shaft. So tight.'

'Hard. Tight. Oh, yes. Oh, please. Oh sweet…' She climaxed with a violence that threw her, hot pulses raged inside her, twisting her, tossing her up into the air, spinning her from the inside, pulsing and throbbing, until she slumped, panting, breathing hard, cast adrift.

Slowly, she came back to herself. Blinking she saw her legs sprawled, her skirts rucked up, her hand… She peered out into the gloom, but there was no sign of Giovanni. He had not stolen up on her, though he could have. She should have been mortified, but felt only a wafer-thin floating bliss, not a release, but a shifting of her axis, as if she had shed her skin. Or another skin.

Standing up and shaking out her skirts, she called his name tentatively, but there was no reply. She didn't know whether to be glad or disappointed. What did one say on such an occasion—thank you?

Cressie struggled against a wholly inappropriate and slightly hysterical desire to laugh, but as she picked her way slowly back through the cellars to the stairs which led to the scullery, the strangeness of what had just occurred began to puzzle her. Sitting down on the bottom step, she distractedly picked at her thumb, a habit she had recently managed to cure herself of. Since yesterday, when she had finally faced the truth about herself, since last night when she had confronted her father, since this morning, when Giovanni had made his desire for her quite plain, the things which had been niggling in the back of her mind had begun to solidify. Questions left unanswered. Doors determinedly closed. Giovanni wanted to know all about her, but he gave away little about himself. There were secrets lurking there, and there was definitely pain too, she was sure of it.

Thinking right back to the first time they had met, she counted the occasions when he had deflected a question, the occasions when he had claimed to understand something but refused to explain how. For a mathematician, she had been remarkably remiss in pursuing proofs from him. For one who prided herself on her thirst for knowledge, she had been very easily rebuffed. He told her he wanted to free her, he told her he wanted to help her, but he refused consistently to tell her why.

'Damn!' Her thumb was bleeding. Giovanni, it seemed to Cressie, gave her only so much as she needed, and no more. She was grateful, but she was also insulted, for though he had helped her look anew at the world, though he had helped her take pleasure in her own body, he had remained detached even from that.

'It's all wrong!' Cressie told the oil lamp. 'Plain wrong. What the *devil* is he hiding? And as for his claim that he somehow protects his artistic integrity by remaining unengaged by anyone or anything—what is he, some sort of artistic Samson, afraid he'll lose his ability to paint if he gives up on his vow of determined isolation?' She scrambled to her feet and picked up the lamp. 'I have to make him reveal himself, just as he did me. I shall probably have to make him angry, to provoke him into it, just as he did me. Because if I don't, let me tell you,' she told the lamp firmly, 'I doubt very much he will ever be the great artist I believe he is destined to be.'

Alone in the attic studio where he had hastily retreated, Giovanni stared at the portrait of Lady Cressida and tried desperately to focus on the mundane technicalities of his craft. Background. Glaze. The hands needed some rework.

It was useless. The aching throb of his persistent erection demanding release erased any hope of concentrating on work. He had never craved a woman as he did Cressie. Had never, with any of the many women he had made love to, felt such a deep, almost tangible connection as he had felt with her. And he had hardly touched her. Though he had wanted to. *How* he wanted to.

Giovanni turned his back on the canvas. The existence of those other women in his past, especially the circumstances surrounding those liaisons, made it impossible for him to explain to someone like Cressie. He did not want her to think of him as the kind of man he had been. He wanted her, he wanted her so much, but he *would not* destroy what existed between them. He would have to find a way, somehow, of explaining how impossible it was for him to make love to her. A way to persuade himself as well as Cressie, without poisoning her with the whole, unpalatable truth.

Posing in her evening gown the next afternoon, Cressie seemed to Giovanni quite distracted. It was as well that all he was painting today was her dress, for she seemed incapable of holding any pose, twitching the folds of velvet and gauze first one way and then the next as she fidgeted constantly.

'I cannot work unless you sit still!' He had not meant to sound so harsh, but frustration of every sort had him in its vice-like grip.

Cressie jumped to her feet. 'I cannot! I cannot sit still. I cannot hold my tongue. I cannot let another moment pass without demanding an explanation.'

'Of what?'

'Of everything!'

Under other circumstances, Giovanni would have laughed at this. Cressie had a flair for the dramatic quite at odds with the literal, logical part of her nature. The way she threw back her head, making her breasts tremble, showing off the line of her throat, she was quite magnificent at times like this—though he doubted she would care to be told so. And today, he was in no mood for drama. Yesterday he had come too close to losing his self-control to contemplate any further drama. Since he had decided, quite unfairly, that this was Cressie's fault, he resorted to icy sarcasm, even though he knew she did not deserve it. 'I am afraid you overestimate me. Even I do not claim to know everything.'

'Do not mock me, Giovanni.' Cressie stormed over to the window, leaning back against the frame. 'You have known me—how long?'

'Several weeks.'

'It is almost seven since we first met.'

'I see the mathematician is back.'

She ignored this quite unnecessary jibe. 'For seven weeks, you have made it your business to point out the error of my ways. No, do not interrupt, Giovanni, for once you will listen to me. I am not complaining. I see that you were right. I did not want to listen, but I did listen eventually. You gave me no option but to listen.'

'Because I understand. Because I know what it is like. Because I wanted you to learn from my experience. Because I recognise in you, Cressie, a lot of myself,' Giovanni exclaimed in exasperation. 'Surely you realised that?'

'How could I when you've never told me that before. Don't you see? I cannot learn from your experience if you will not share it with me. I cannot recognise our similarities if you will not reveal them to me.'

'I have no idea what you're talking about.'

She sashayed across the room, her train gathering dust, walking just as seductively as the borrowed gown demanded. It made him wary, this abrupt change in her mood, no longer angry but very confident and very determined.

'It is time for me to know you a little better,' she said, coming far too close for comfort. 'We have established the public personas of both Cressida and Giovanni. If you wish to see the private Cressie then you must also reveal a little of the private Giovanni. *Quid pro quo*, as your ancestors would have said.'

'What do you want to know?'

'Why will you not speak of your father? Why will you not talk of your family? Blood and beauty. It is your credo. Why are you so obsessed by both? Why are you alone? Why are you so scared of the very notion of sharing human contact of any sort? Why do you dismiss my questions? Why do you close yourself off from me? You have helped me see. You have made it possible for me to view the future with hope rather than dread. I want to do the same for you.'

She recited her questions with cool calm, but he was not fooled. There was a determination in her eyes that made him very wary. 'I admit, there were things in my past—but they are exactly that, in my past,' Giovanni said.

Cressie shook her head, just as he expected she would. 'I will not be fobbed off so easily this time. You recognised my discontent, you saw the unhappiness at my core. I now see that you recognised it because you share it. You said you see a lot of you in me. You are not happy, Giovanni, are you?'

'Cressie, this is arrant nonsense. I will not—'

'Oh, for goodness' sake!' She dropped her pretended air of calm as abruptly as she had assumed it and grabbed his arm, pulling him bodily over to the easel. 'Look at that! It's damned perfect. It's a polished, technically brilliant, mathematically beautiful painting, but it's not art. You said that yourself. It's cold, it's lacking emotion and it's utterly self-contained and sure of itself. Just exactly like you.'

She was right, but no one, not even Cressie, was permitted to take such critical liberties with his art. It was the one thing to guarantee his instant loss of temper. 'How dare you to presume so!' Giovanni snarled.

She flinched, but did not turn away. 'I dare because I

know you, I presume because I know you can be a truly great artist not just an extremely successful painter. You want to paint emotion. You want to capture passion. How on earth can you do that when you are so— what is it you called me?—buttoned-up! Well, you are so buttoned-up that it is just possible you will suffocate yourself.'

'You are not even making sense. What has brought this on?'

'You! Why did you kiss me, Giovanni? Why do you touch me, why do you look at me as you do? Yesterday evening, here in this very studio, you touched me, you kissed me, you were the one who started it. Yesterday morning, when you allowed me to paint with you, you deliberately provoked me into—you know what you did. And after that, in the whispering gallery. You initiated all of those things. Is it some sort of game, to show me that I cannot resist you, to prove that you can resist me?'

'Stop it, Cressie! You don't know what you're talking about.'

'You're right. In one sense I don't, because you have locked the door on me. But in another—Giovanni, if we are so alike as you maintain, can you not trust me?'

He considered it. For a few seconds, he really did think about confiding in her. But to do so would be to admit that there was just cause, that his life, which he had worked so hard for, was not as perfect as he wished it to be. He was at the peak of his profession. He wanted for nothing and he wanted no one. He need explain himself to no one! 'If you leave the dress up here, I can fin-

ish the portrait without your having to pose any further,'
Giovanni said starkly, turning back towards the easel.

'You don't even need me for that, then, is that it?'

'That is it,' he replied, picking up his brush and turning his shoulder.

The door of the attic closed behind her. Giovanni
dropped to the floor and put his head in his hands. He
didn't want to think about what she'd said, didn't want
to consider the accusations she'd thrown at him. Yesterday morning, in the whispering gallery, it had taken
all his strength of mind not to surrender to the urge to
take pleasure in her pleasure, to take his pleasure with
her. He wanted her in a way he had not thought possible,
after years of abusing his charms, the subsequent years
of denying them. It would be different with Cressie, he
was sure of that, but that made him all the more certain
that it would be wrong.

It would be wrong, even though every time he
touched her it felt right. It would be wrong, even though
he could barely sleep for thinking of her. It would be utterly wrong because he did not deserve her and she most
certainly did not deserve to be tainted with his past.

Giovanni rubbed his eyes with his knuckles and got
to his feet. She probably hated him now. The chances of
her allowing him to paint the second portrait were slim.
She would not be his muse, because he would not allow
himself to feel the passion that smouldered between
them, but she could not see as he could, the risk they
would take if he cast off the artist and became the man.

He thumped the floor in frustration. His life was not
perfect. Even before he'd met her, the sense of frustra-

tion, of suffocating, was there. And almost from the moment he saw her, he'd known. He needed to paint her. The urge was stronger than ever. He needed to re-claim himself with this painting, reclaim the artist he had buried inside the society painter. He could not bear this particular canvas to remain blank. But years of isolation, of deliberately cutting himself off, could not make him view even the smallest of explanations with-out a shudder of disquiet. He would have to think hard about how best to make good the damage he had done.

Cressie paced the empty schoolroom. The boys were outside with Janey. For the second day in a row, she had forced herself to stay away from the attic studio. Two days of being coldly polite to Giovanni downstairs in the gallery while she taught her brothers and he painted them. Two days, alternating between fury and frustra-tion that she had so signally failed to break down his reserve. Two days of waiting it out in the vain hope that he would change his mind, in the slightly more likely hope that he would say he needed her to sit for the com-pletion of her portrait.

She tried to work on her second children's primer, taking the invaluable experience she had gained in teaching from the first into account, but she could not concentrate. Work on her thesis was impossible, and even when responding to written questions raised by readers of her articles, she found her mind wandering.

There were two globes standing on top of the cup-board where she stored the boys' books, slates and chalks. One celestial, the other terrestrial, they were beautiful objects made by Carey's. Cressie's enthusiasm for the stars meant that the former was put to much more use than the latter. She rubbed at a fingerprint with the cuff of her gown. She really must persuade her father to invest in a telescope. Perhaps if she could get James to write him a letter...

'Cressida! Here you are. I have been looking all over for you.' Bella burst into the schoolroom, her face crimson.

Cressie ushered her stepmother towards a chair. Bella sank down, fanning herself with the letter she held in her hand. She was now quite pale, with perspiration beading on her brow, and looked to be on the brink of a swoon.

'Why did you not send a servant to fetch me?' Cressie asked, wondering if she dared leave Bella to search for smelling salts.

'I could not—I wanted you to see—here, read this.'

Bella thrust the letter at her. With a sinking feeling, Cressie recognised her Aunt Sophia's spidery scrawl. 'Cordelia?'

Bella, somewhat recovered and breathing more evenly, managed to nod.

Retiring to the window seat, Cressie read her aunt's missive. Cordelia, it seemed, was setting the *ton* alight. Already, Aunt Sophia had had to reject five completely unsuitable requests for her hand. *My personal belief is that Cordelia is set upon amassing as many offers as possible*, Aunt Sophia wrote. *Rumour has it that she has actually had her name entered in White's betting book, in competition with Valeria Winwood's daugh-*

ter. The scandal of such a wager pales in comparison to the very low birth of her adversary. Everyone knows exactly how Valeria Winwood acquired her husband.

There was worse to come. Cordelia's penchant for fast company had resulted in several minor scandals, including her attendance at a boxing match of all things. Aunt Sophia, that stalwart of society, seemed to be genuinely afraid that Cordelia's vouchers for Almack's would be withdrawn. Reading between the lines, Cressie was much more concerned that her sister might, whether of her own volition or not, make a dreadful misalliance.

'She demands that I come to town,' Bella said waveringly. 'She says that she cannot be responsible for the consequences if I do not. What am I to do, Cressida? Your father has only just departed for Russia—why did Sophia not raise these issues with him?'

Cressie scanned the letter again. It would be a mistake to underestimate her aunt, who was one of the few people capable of outmanoeuvring Lord Armstrong. Which meant that this letter was a deliberate ploy. 'I wonder,' she mused, 'do you think that my aunt simply wishes to be rid of the burden of Cordelia's come-out?'

Bella pursed her mouth. 'Sophia has the gout, and she is past sixty, for she is several years older than your father, so it would not surprise me if she was a reluctant chaperon—especially given the friskiness of her charge who, as I know all too well, would wear out a whole battalion of chaperons.'

'I must confess that I'm still surprised that Cordelia would take such advantage of the situation.'

Bella looked sceptical. 'Really? I am not.'

'What do you mean?'

'Cordelia is no more interested in marrying a man of your father's choice than any of you have been, save for Caroline. And I suppose Celia—that foolish man who was her first husband, the one who got himself killed, he was your father's choice I believe. But as for the rest of you...' Bella made a sweeping gesture. 'First Cassie, then you, and it seems obvious to me that now Cordelia too is set on defying your poor father, though why, I do not know.'

Cressie's jaw dropped, making Bella titter. 'You think because I am fat and frumpy that I notice nothing. You think because you are all so clever that I am incapable of simple observation. Despite appearances, I *do* see what goes on under my nose, Cressida. I am aware, for example, that you are allowing that charming and rather delicious portrait painter to take your likeness. I hope you know what you are doing?'

Cressie was too dumbfounded to speak. Her cheeks flooded with colour. She was mortified, not that she had underestimated her stepmother, but that she had judged her so callously, and had indeed assumed her foolish as well as fat. 'I did not know—we did not mean—indeed, Bella, it is simply...' She stuttered to a halt under her stepmother's critical gaze.

'Let us at least have some truth between us, Cressida. We will never be bosom friends, and I have no interest in playing the mother to you any more than you are interested in allowing me to. It would suit me very well to have every one of you married and gone, for then perhaps your father would pay a little more attention to me and my boys. I don't care who you marry. I don't give a fig whom Cordelia marries either, so long as you both marry.'

'And if I don't choose to find myself a husband?'

Bella shrugged. 'Then choose to find a way of quitting my household.'

'Would you support me if I asked my father for an annuity?'

'My dear Cressida, you may play the blue-stocking spinster with my blessing, but you must know how little real influence I have with my husband. He wants nothing from me save a succession of sons. You will have to find your own way of persuading him, if that is the road you choose to take.'

Cressie examined her ragged thumb. Deciding it was quite bloody enough, she tucked her hand out of reach under her skirts. Her stepmother's candidness had excused her from some of the guilt she felt, for she knew deep down that not even a desire to make amends would bring about a genuine attachment between them. It was a relief to know that Bella felt the same, though not such a relief as to make her feel anything other than dreadful about her own behaviour over the years since her father's second marriage.

She got to her feet, folding her Aunt Sophia's letter up. 'I am glad we had this talk, Bella.' Cressie kissed her stepmother's cheek. The skin was cool, with some of the bloom of youth upon it still. Bella was not so very much older than she. Lost somewhere in the layers of fat and insecurity, there must be a Bella who regretted what she had become, who perhaps longed for escape, just as Cressie did. 'You look better today,' she said. 'Has the sickness eased?'

'Not really.'

Bella placed a hand on her stomach which, Cressie noticed, was not nearly as distended as it had seemed a few days ago—nor nearly so swollen as it ought to be. From the very earliest days of her previous pregnancies, Bella had been vast. 'You know that my father has insisted that Sir Gilbert Mountjoy visit?'

'I shall not see him, and your father is not here to make me do so.'

'But perhaps—forgive me, Bella, I know very little of these matters, but surely you should not still be so sick?'

'It is a girl, that is why. Everything about this confinement is different, and I am sure it is because it is a girl.' Bella heaved herself to her feet. 'What am I to do about that letter?'

'Obviously, you cannot go to town. I believe my aunt exaggerates matters in order to try to goad you into action. My father has only recently left London. If Cordelia really had been so outrageous, he would have heard about it. I shall write to my sister and demand the truth from her. Until we hear back from her, I think the best thing we can do is ignore this.'

'Very well, but if something happens in the meantime…'

'It shall be on my head,' Cressie said with a wry smile. 'I have nothing to lose in terms of my father's goodwill, but you do. I understand that.'

With a satisfied nod, Bella sailed out of the schoolroom. Left to her own musings, Cressie stared out of the window, where her brothers were fishing from the bridge. She would write to Caro as well as Cordelia. Since her marriage, Caro had become quite withdrawn, visiting Killellan Manor only rarely, London even less. But of the five sisters, Caro was the most intuitive. It would be interesting to read her views on Bella's revelations.

She must have drifted off to sleep, perched on the window seat with her cheek resting on the pane, because Cressie woke with a start, to find Giovanni standing in the schoolroom doorway, a most forbidding expression on his face. She jumped up, automatically putting a hand to her hair, which was pressed flat on one side, a tangled mess on the other. 'You startled me. What do you want?' Her voice was flat and unwelcoming, to compensate for that unchecked moment of being pleased to see him.

'I came to apologise.'

It was as she expected—he wanted to finish his painting, nothing more. 'This is quite a day for unparalleled events,' Cressie said coolly.

Giovanni flinched. He was, as usual, dressed entirely in black, save for his white shirt and a waistcoat of alternating navy and sky-blue stripes. 'I was unforgivably rude. I lost my temper. I said things I should not have—I am very sorry, Cressie.'

'What you mean is, will you please still pose for me.'

'That is not what I mean. I want to explain why it is so crucial to me to paint you,' Giovanni countered. 'Will you listen?'

Cressie sighed. He seemed genuinely contrite, and

she was genuinely pleased to see him. The silence between them these last two days had made her realise how much conversation they normally shared. She'd been lonely without him. 'Yes, of course I will. Indeed, with the ample evidence I have just been given of my lack of perception and quickness to judge, I would be happy to listen. No, don't ask for I have no intentions of explaining right now.' She sat back down on the window seat and patted the cushion beside her.

Giovanni, however, chose to remain standing. He seemed unsure of himself, less composed than usual. And now that she looked at him closely, which she had not permitted herself to do since their quarrel, she saw that there were dark shadows under his eyes. 'You have been working too hard.'

'Not at all.' His denial was automatic, but he caught himself almost immediately. 'Yes, I have. I often work at night when I cannot sleep. I have been trying—experimenting with form.'

'Thank you. For not brushing me off, I mean.'

'You are welcome. You see, I do listen, but it does not come naturally to me, the urge to explain.'

Cressie laughed. 'Nor to me, as you well know.'

As he sat down beside her, she was granted one of his rare, true smiles. 'I did not mean to be so—overbearing. I must have seemed to you every bit as much of a tyrant as your father at times, trying to browbeat you into my way of thinking.'

'Good grief, Giovanni, please, you are nothing like my father.'

'I am extremely relieved to hear you say so, but...' He

took her hand in his, and kissed her wrist. 'I am sorry. I wanted only to help you.'

His lips had the usual effect on her pulse. Only now that he was here, actually contrite, did Cressie allow herself to admit how upset she had been by their disagreement. 'You have helped me, but now you must allow me to help myself, if I can.'

'And to help me too, if you will. I want to prove that I can produce something more than just a *polished, technically brilliant, mathematically beautiful painting*.'

'Did I say that?' Cressie made a face. 'Sorry.'

'It is the truth, that is what I do paint, but I am capable of more. With your help.'

Giovanni leaned over to touch her face, tracing the line of her forehead, her cheek, her throat. Such a familiar touch, one she had not thought she'd feel again. It made her skin tingle, it roused memories of all the other times he had touched her, and it brought with it too a melancholy, a prelude of the time when he would not be here, when her portrait would be done, and Giovanni would be done too, with her. But for the moment, he was still here. And that was enough. 'When will we start?'

'You are still willing to sit for me, Cressie?' She laughed at his eagerness, at the way he clapped his hands together and leapt to his feet. 'We can begin tomorrow. I have finished the other portrait, the first one, save for the final glaze.' His smile faded. 'But I need to tell you first—explain something.'

Frowning, Giovanni began to spin the Carey globes, just as she had done earlier, first one then the other. 'You asked me why I must always retreat from you, why I

am so buttoned-up, as you put it. You've awoken in me
what I thought was dead, Cressie, the desire to create,
to paint from the heart. You have rekindled my passion.
And the reason I cannot—the reason I will not—I am
afraid. No, I am terrified that if I allow myself to…'

He spun the terrestrial globe so viciously that it
rocked on its stand, then turned to face Cressie square
on. 'I am afraid that if I allow us to become close, if
we make love, I am afraid it will destroy the magic between us. I am afraid it will prevent me painting you.
I don't want to destroy what I have only just rediscovered. Do you see?'

She saw that his words were irrefutably from the
heart. She saw that he believed them, though she could
not understand why. Cressie was afraid to speak, lest
she say the wrong thing. 'Thank you. For explaining.
For trusting me with your—thank you.'

He seemed both relieved and just a little bit uncomfortable. Was he still holding something back from her?
She agreed to sit for him the next day. It was only later,
as she lay awake in her bed replaying the conversation,
that the exact words he used tempered her euphoria. *I
don't want to destroy what I have only just rediscovered.*

He had once had another muse. Of course he had,
and it was a very stupid and illogical thing to be jealous
of her, whoever she was, especially since she was obviously no longer in Giovanni's life. Had he made love to
her? Certainly. Had he loved her?

'That,' Cressie told herself, laying aside her transla-
tion of Legendre's *Exercices de Calcul Intégral*, 'is absolutely none of my business.' But logic and emotion

were, she was discovering, rarely in alignment. The idea of Giovanni in love sat very ill with her.

'You are late.' Giovanni was standing in front of his easel, his drawing board covered in charcoal sketches, when he heard the door slowly open. 'I have been working on some ideas, but I am not sure—aren't you coming in?'

Cressie hovered in the doorway of the attic, clutching her mother's evening cloak around her. 'Have you set your heart on Penthiselea?'

He scored his charcoal impatiently through something. His cravat dangled over a chair, on which were also his coat and his waistcoat. He had a smudge of charcoal on his forehead. She could see a smattering of hair peeping out from the open neck of his shirt. Cressie's throat went dry. The light in the attic was bright, with the sun shining directly through the dormers. Through the billowing folds of his cambric shirt, she could quite clearly see his nipples, could see that the hair arrowed down towards the dip of his belly. She shouldn't be looking but she couldn't drag her eyes away. She reminded herself that in order to inspire him she must allow him to keep his distance, but what she wanted was to rip the shirt clean off his back and run her hands over the lean, hard muscles she was certain were underneath, to feel the contrasting roughness of his hair and smoothness of his skin, the sinew and tendon ripple as she touched him, to hear him groan as she tasted him. She wanted to...

'Cressie, are you coming in or not? Why are you wearing that cloak?'

She closed the door behind her, and leaned against it. 'I had an idea. It is a surprise.'

He was looking at her now, no longer distracted by the drawing board. 'I don't, as a rule, like surprises. I rarely find them to be pleasant.'

She didn't want to let Giovanni see how nervous she was, for it would quite spoil the effect. It had seemed such an inspired idea but now that it came to it her resolve began to falter. Would she look preposterous? Would he ridicule her? Standing up, she began to unfasten the cloak, her trembling fingers fumbling with the clasp. 'Turn around,' she commanded. 'Don't look until I say so.' She dropped the cloak to the ground and slipped the hat she had been hiding beneath it on to her head. 'Giovanni?'

'Si?'

'You can turn around now. I want you to meet…'

'Penthiselea,' he guessed.

'Mr Brown.' Cressie swept her hat back off her head in a movement she'd practised for hours last night in front of her mirror, and made a bow she was rather proud of.

She was rewarded with an astonished bark of laughter. 'What on earth…?'

'You remember you asked how I managed to attend meetings at the Royal Society? Well…' Cressie did a little twirl, her coat tails flying '…this is how. You were right, I would never be admitted as a female, no matter how impressive my scientific achievements, but some of the great minds of the age lecture at the Society and I go to great lengths to hear them.'

Giovanni laughed again. 'I never doubted your passion for your studies, but this is something else entirely. Am I to understand that you actually travelled about London dressed in these clothes? Did they know, the august members of the Royal Society, that a woman had penetrated their hallowed rooms, disguised as a man? They must surely have guessed, for you seem to me a very feminine man.'

'Do I? I am not aware that my disguise was detected. Save by Mr Babbage, of course. A friend, who facilitated my attendance.'

'And has Lord Armstrong met Mr Brown?'

'Good heavens no! No, no, he must never know. No one knows, other than Mr Babbage. And now you.'

'I am honoured. And really very impressed, Cressie. But why did you take such enormous risks? Were you discovered, the consequences could be catastrophic.'

'I know, but not so catastrophic as never being able to—can you not see, Giovanni, how stifling it is to be a mere woman? I cannot deny that each time Mr Brown and I go out into the world I am in a constant state of terror, but it is also so—exhilarating. Such freedom as these breeches give me. And I must admit, there is too a certain *frisson* in knowing that I am fooling the world. Is that so very difficult to understand?'

'Not so very difficult, knowing you. You are a remarkable and very brave young woman, Cressie.'

'Young man, if you please, just at the moment,' she replied with a toss of her head.

Once again, Giovanni laughed. 'Mr Brown, it is a genuine pleasure to make your acquaintance,' he said, bowing extravagantly. 'I kiss your hand, Mr Brown—you are quite, quite perfect.'

And he did kiss her hand, his mouth lingering on her palm, though he dropped it immediately at the resultant *frisson*, making a show of inspecting her costume. 'Well?' Cressie demanded. 'Will you paint me as my alter ego?'

'I can think of nothing better. So very delightfully seditious, you look. There is something about the clothes which brings out all of your curves. I cannot believe that any red-blooded man was taken in by you. Your English intellectuals must all be blind.' He had been circling her, but now he stopped in front of her. 'This is wrong,' he said decisively, pulling out her hair pins and casting them carelessly onto the floor. 'The trick will be to show you as Mr Brown and Cressie at the same time.' More pins flew in all directions until her hair tumbled down over her coat. 'Now, put the hat back on so—but at this angle, like a coquette. Yes. And the coat like this. Yes, yes. Once more I commend you, Cressie—this is inspired.'

Giovanni kissed her hand again. Cressie closed her eyes, the more to relish the touch of his lips, and wondered how much more of this she would be able to endure without losing her self-control. He stood her on a box and paced around her, adjusting her clothing, her hair, her breeches, her boots. He smelt of charcoal, turpentine and linseed oil, faintly of sweat and overlaying it all, something definitively male and quite definitely Giovanni. Was there such a thing as eau de Cressie? She tried to distract herself, wondering what it would be.

Chalk definitely. Her soap, which was scented with lavender, that was good. Jam or chocolate or barley sugar, depending upon what particular treat her brothers had been indulging in—not good, but not so bad. The other day, though, Freddie had spilt the contents of a whole jar of dead frog spawn over her. She hadn't smelled very nice at all then. One of the pigments Giovanni used smelled rather like that, now she came to think of it. Which colour was it?

'You can stand down now. I think we should try another pose.' Giovanni pulled a gilded chair into the middle of the room. It was Egyptian in style, rosewood inlaid with brass, the legs turned and fluted, the black velvet seat saggy and faded.

'Oh, I remember those chairs. There was a full set and a table to match in the small dining parlour. My mother loved everything Egyptian. She was prone to saying that she'd liked to have been Cleopatra.'

'Your mother does not sound at all like the kind of woman your father would have married.'

'You'd think not, to see him now, but I believe in the early days, when they were first married—well, you've seen the kind of dresses she wore.' Cressie giggled. 'At least, I assume she wore them for my father. Oh, that is a terrible thing to say.'

'But you wish it was a little true, no?'

'A little. I mean no! We are discussing my mother, for goodness' sake, Giovanni.'

'Motherhood does not automatically invest a woman with virtue.'

'Well, no, of course not. In fact, motherhood is often

the result of a lack of virtue,' Cressie agreed, 'but I have
no cause to think that *my* mother—I mean, they are all
so alike, my sisters—except for me, and—Giovanni!
Do you think that is it? Do you think perhaps I'm not
my father's child?'

She didn't mean it. Much as she hated to admit it,
Cressie could not deny the resemblance between herself
and Lord Armstrong, especially around the eyes, but
she was in a skittish mood, and dressed as Mr Brown
she felt a reckless confidence, quite freed from normal
proprieties. She had meant it as a joke, but her jest had
somehow gone awry. 'Giovanni? What have I said?'
He had been smiling, teasing, light-hearted but at the
same time wholly focused on her guise, on his painting. Now his face was dark, his brows drawn tight together. His satyr look.

'It is nothing.'

'I thought we were going to have no more lies between us.'

'I do not lie.'

'Not lies, then. Avoidance of truth. Stop prevaricating. What on earth have I said to upset you? I did not
mean it, about my mother playing my father false, that
is.'

'I do not care one bit for what your mother did or did
not do. I want you to sit in this chair sideways, like this.'

Cressie suffered him to adjust her, crossing first one
leg then the other, facing one way then the other, resting
her chin on her hand, clasping her hands, with her hat
on and with her hat off, while all the time trying to pin-
point the exact part of the conversation where his smile

had turned sour. Not the first mention of her mother. Nor at the shocking notion of her possibly having an *affaire*. But after that. Something about motherhood. That was it! 'I said motherhood is often the result of a lack of virtue,' she exclaimed. 'Do you—were you…?'

Giovanni threw himself away from her. 'Always you must pick and pick. I feel sometimes as if I have no skin left. Yes, I was referring to my own mother. Now you have your answer, can we please concentrate on the task in hand?'

'Yes, we can,' Cressie agreed. Partly because his tone brooked no argument but mainly because she had just managed to breach, ever so slightly, the walls he had built around himself, and she did not want to press her luck too far.

'Mr Brown awaits Signor di Matteo's pleasure,' Cressie said. Which on reflection was probably an unfortunate turn of phrase.

Chapter Seven

It had been Cressie's idea for the boys to build a kite, the notion being spawned after reading of the American Benjamin Franklin's use of them in his research into the nature of lightning. Unfortunately, Mr Franklin did not see fit to explain the method of construction, and Cressie had only the vaguest idea of the practicalities. Having fired up her brothers' imagination with the project, she was at a loss as to how to progress it until Giovanni stepped in. With a few rough sketches, he explained the mechanics and sent the four boys off, with James in charge, in search of the various components.

Cressie was astounded when they returned, all four of them in unusual harmony—though when she thought about it, she realised that they did argue a lot less these days. Only when their father was at home had their bickering and jostling for position resumed, their individual demands for attention and precedent, which her father seemed to relish, in the manner of a king and his fawning courtiers. James, Harry, George and Freddie treated Giovanni as if he were not their king but their general, jumping to obey his every order, anxious to execute it to the best of their ability, quietly pleased rather than gloating when they earned his praise. Which Giovanni gave unsparingly, but justly, as he did his reprimands.

Unlike Lord Armstrong, who tended to blame whoever was convenient, or whoever was his current victim of choice. There was one particular time, when Cressie was twelve or thirteen. Caro it was, who had broken the Chinese figure which had been a gift to their father from the British Ambassador to that far-off country, but it was Cressie who was sent to bed for being discovered in the same room as the pieces, despite Caro's noble protests of guilt. Caroline, their father had insisted, was simply trying to cover up for her clumsy sister.

The memory was startlingly vivid. There had been many of these little pastiches of recollection popping into Cressie's head these last few days, long-forgotten, usually trivial things, which caught her by surprise with their freshness. Had she tucked them away because they were too painful, or because they would have made her attempts to conform too painful? Both, most likely. The surprising thing was that they didn't hurt now. They made her sad, often wistful, but neither regretful nor resentful. There was no point in railing at her past, and now that she was starting to understand herself more, she could see that each memory was part of her, and each one could be turned to a more positive effect. It might be fanciful but she felt as if she were evolving and in doing so growing stronger.

Her brothers had scorned Cressie's inept attempts to help them build their kite, demanding Giovanni's assistance instead. She'd been happy to step out of the fray and more than happy to watch the kite take shape under Giovanni's expert guidance—though he disguised his efforts so well, her brothers were convinced the finished product was entirely their own work. He was patient when it came to decorating the kite too, sketching in fantastical Chinese dragons and samurai warriors for the boys to colour, making sure that none of them were aware when his quick hand fixed their childish mistakes.

It was a blustery day, and perfect for the first launch. Cressie perched on the stone wall of the field, watching Giovanni instruct her brothers in the art of kite-flying, another subject about which she had been clueless. The breeze blew the skirts of her emerald-green pelisse around her legs. She wore no hat, but had tied her hair back with a green silk ribbon, which seemed to be holding for the moment. The skirts of Giovanni's coat flew out behind him, giving her tantalising glimpses of long, muscular legs clad in his customary tight trousers. He wore boots today, black of course, and highly polished, though now spattered with mud, which he didn't seem to mind at all.

The boys were taking turns with the kite in pairs, James with Freddie, Harry with George. 'Your turn to launch her,' James said, handing the kite carefully over to his youngest brother. 'Here, hold her high above your head by the struts.'

'Like as if she is a fluttering butterfly,' Freddie shouted encouragingly at his twin. 'You have to be careful not to tear her wings, doesn't he, Gio?'

'A fluttering butterfly,' George shouted delightedly, 'a buttering flutterby.'

'A buttery, fluttery, utterfly.' Freddie clapped his hands together gleefully, jumping up and down, spattering his nankeen breeches with mud.

'Watch out—it's trailing in that puddle.' James grabbed the beribboned tail, catching it up and gathering it carefully together before handing it to Harry. A few weeks ago, such a silly thing would have resulted in a fight and a broken kite, Cressie marvelled.

'Ready, Harry?' Giovanni asked.

'Ready,' the boy replied solemnly, taking the spool as if it were the crown jewels.

'Do I run now, Gio?' George shouted.

'When Harry gives the order. Harry, you must remember to feed out the line slowly.'

Frowning hard, Harry did as he was told. James, the veteran of one successful flight already, impatient as usual to show his superiority, made to shout out instructions, only to find himself silenced by Giovanni's hand over his mouth. He looked so surprised that Cressie couldn't help laughing. For a moment, James looked upon the brink of a tantrum, but a quirk of Giovanni's eyebrow stopped him in his tracks.

Harry called out the command to launch. George ran as fast as his chubby legs could carry him across the field. Unfortunately, he was so intent on holding the kite aloft that he first splattered himself with a wet cowpat, then tumbled head first over a large boulder. Boy and kite went flying, the one down the other up. A gust of wind yanked the kite high, and would most likely have lifted Harry off his feet had not Giovanni lunged and caught him just in time.

Cressie ran to George, who was lying flat out on the grass, but by the time she reached him he had staggered to his feet. 'He's just winded,' Freddie assured her solemnly.

'And smelly. What on earth…?'

'I smell like a cow's bottom,' George announced.

'You always smell like a cow's bottom,' Freddie said with a snigger.

'Never mind that—look!' George exclaimed. 'Up, up, up high. Higher than yours.'

'Not higher.' Freddie frowned up at the kite, which was soaring above their heads, the rich colours of the dragons and the warriors like exotic jewels against the blue English sky. 'Well, perhaps *as* high.'

Harry was struggling to control the kite with the whole string played out. Bright red in the face, his fair hair blowing wildly, cap askew, the tail of his shirt hanging out like a flag where it had come loose, he really looked as if he might take off himself.

'Harry's going to fly, Harry's going to fly,' the twins called, holding hands and spinning round and round, their ecstatic faces turned to the sky. 'Gio, Gio, Harry's going to fly.'

'Giovanni, I think he might need some help.'

'What do you think, Harry? Can you hold her?'

Harry said something that sounded like a strangled affirmative. Cressie, now thoroughly concerned, protested. 'He's not a baby,' James said, jumping to his brother's defence. 'Why do girls always fuss, Gio?'

'I think your sister is jealous. I think she would like to fly the kite for herself, wouldn't you, Cressie?'

She would. He knew she would, but one look at her brothers and she knew she could not spoil their fun. 'I am not nearly strong enough,' Cressie said graciously, though she would dearly have loved to have flown the kite, Giovanni standing close behind her, guiding her hand just as he had done when he allowed her to paint a little of the canvas.

She retreated to the wall once more, contenting herself in her role as spectator, watching a very different Giovanni from the one she knew, laughing, entirely at ease. He was every bit as athletic as she had imagined him as he ran across the field with the boys and the kite, his lean body showing to admirable effect as he hoisted James into the lower limbs of a tree to free the flapping toy.

'So this is the kite I have been hearing so much about.' Bella, in a claret pelisse topped with a Paisley shawl, picked her way carefully towards Cressie. 'I heard the boys' shrieks from the salon window. I don't think I've ever seen them laughing so much. Look at Georgie, waving his hands like a windmill. And James. I had not noticed how tall James had become these last few weeks. Why, his breeches are several inches too short for him.'

'Janey has let the seams out several times, but I fear he is about to burst out of them,' Cressie said, smiling.

'They seem to bicker so much less these days. Henry—your father—told me that it was in a boy's nature to fight constantly. "It's how the lads assert themselves," he said. "Encourages their competitiveness," he insisted.'

Taken aback, not so much by the accuracy of Bella's mimicry as by the mocking tone behind it, such a contrast to the tender way she had spoken of her sons, Cressie was forced to laugh. 'My father believes that competitiveness is one of the ultimate virtues. For a man, that is.'

'Your father loves to compete provided he can be sure to win. I meant what I told him, Cressie. You have been a very good influence on my sons.'

'Thank you. You will not take offence when I tell you that your compliment means all the more, coming from you.'

Bella laughed. Not her usual tinkle, but a gurgle which sounded positively girlish. 'Because it is so grudgingly given, you mean.'

'Because you are such a stern critic, is how I would have worded it.'

'Same difference.' Bella leaned her bulk against the stone wall, shading her eyes against the sun. 'Signor di Matteo is quite the most beautiful man I have ever seen, I must say. Not handsome, but beautiful. I confess, I thought him a cold fish, but one would not think so, seeing him like this. I saw the drawings he did for the boys. He understands them very well. Unlike…'

Bella trailed off into silence, looking suddenly older and sadder. Feeling uncomfortably as if she were intruding, Cressie returned her attention to the kite flyers. James was helping Freddie with the spool now, Giovanni standing with his hand resting casually on

Harry's shoulder, the pair of them laughing at some private joke. She hadn't seen Giovanni with his guard so completely down before.

'He would make a good father, though I doubt he will ever choose to become one.' Bella too was watching Giovanni. 'For all his attractions, he is a man who avoids human contact. Yet he obviously likes my boys. Perhaps it is because they are no threat to him.'

'What do you mean?'

'Ask yourself why a man who could have any woman, if his reputation is to be believed, chooses to have none. It is not that he is the type who likes men, that much is obvious—though it is obvious too that men of a certain sort would find him most appealing.' Bella smiled her tight little smile. 'I may live out of the world, but I once lived very much in it and I still keep up with the latest gossip, Cressida, do not look so shocked.'

'Gio—Signor di Matteo—I believe he was in love once.'

Bella snorted. 'Is that what he told you? I doubt it is true. Or if he was, it was more likely a hundred times than once. Poor Cressida, I detected you had developed a fondness for him but I had not realised things had gone so far. Take my advice. Do not set your heart on a man like that. He will freeze the life out of you, for he has not a heart to give you in return. Trust me on this, I know about these things. Now, I think I have had my annual allocation of fresh air and exercise. It certainly makes one peckish. I hope cook has been baking today. '

With an airy wave of the hand, Bella began to pick her way delicately back across the meadow. As she watched her go, Cressie decided that Bella was wrong on any number of scores. For a start, Giovanni was not in the least like Lord Armstrong. It was merely that Bella was hurting, and wished to lash out. You only had to look at the way Giovanni was with Freddie, George, James and Harry, to see that he was not the selfish, self-centred man her father was.

Bella was simply jealous. And she was wrong about Giovanni's reserve too. It was nothing to do with him being cold. Quite the reverse. He had been hurt, hurt so badly that he had lost his muse. And yes, perhaps his decision to turn his skill to commerce was a cold and calculated one, but what was wrong with that? He was the best—he deserved to be recognised as such.

But the thing Bella was most wrong about was her assumption that Cressie—Cressie!—could possibly be imagining herself in love with Giovanni. The thought hadn't even crossed her mind. Would *never* cross her mind. She was the muse he had lost. She was proud to be his muse, and honoured, and in addition, it meant that she could see at first hand whether she had been wrong about art and mathematics and beauty and—and all that stuff which was important, very important, even if she had lost sight of it.

Cressie jumped down from the wall and ran over to join the boys, who were gathering in the kite, flushed from their exertions. 'If you could capture them like this,' she said to Giovanni, 'it would make a painting much more like the truth than the one in the gallery.'

'And far less valuable, sadly. I could sketch them for their mother, though, if you think she would like it?'

'I think she would adore it. That is very thoughtful of you.'

'They are actually quite nice boys, when you get to know them.'

Giovanni handed the kite to Harry and picked up Freddie, throwing him over his shoulders, much to the little boy's delight. 'Gee gee, Gio is a gee gee,' he giggled.

Cressie lagged behind, watching Giovanni gallop across the meadow with Freddie on his back. Bella was right about one thing—he would make an excellent father. It took her by surprise, the sadness that gripped her. Thinking that she would never marry was one thing. Realising what she would be sacrificing, that was quite another.

Giovanni had finally settled upon a pose. Cressie sat sideways on the Egyptian chair, her breeched and booted right leg crossed over her left, one arm resting casually on the chair back, the other on her crossed leg. She looked full on at the painter, her beaver hat provocatively tilted over one eye, her hair wild and hanging free. The tails of her coat hung down almost to the floor, her neckcloth carelessly tied, the buttons of her waistcoat undone.

'I don't look a bit like a man,' she said, when he showed her the preliminary sketches.

'Do you wish to?'

She twisted a strand of hair around her finger, her latest attempt to stop herself biting her fingernails. 'I thought I did. I thought I wanted to *be* a man.'

'I remember you told me you wished just that.'

'But I don't now. I think I like this. It's…'

'Subversive, I hope. I want to show you peeping out from your disguise. You have a very mischievous sense of humour. I want to demonstrate that. And I want to use the clothing to show—I am not sure how, but I want your man's clothes to show more of the woman.'

Cressie giggled. 'Perhaps if you combine Mr Brown with Penthiselea you can achieve that effect.'

'That is it!' Giovanni threw down his charcoal and threw his arms around Cressie. 'You are a genius!'

Smiling and shaking her head in bewilderment, Cressie tried not to notice the instant response of her body to his. 'I am more than happy to be called a genius but I have no idea why you do so. I meant it as a joke.'

'But no, it is perfect. It is outrageous. It will be…'

He kissed his fingertips. The gesture was so dramatic and so typically Italian and so untypically Giovanni that Cressie laughed. 'I don't understand. How can it be so outrageous? Oh!' As realisation dawned, her smile faded. 'You mean that I will have to…'

'Bare your…'

'Breast.' Cressie swallowed. Her throat was dry. She licked her lips. She looked at Giovanni to find that he was staring at her chest.

'You have beautiful breasts. Speaking as an artist, that is,' he added quickly.

'Do I?'

'Si. Bellissimo.'

Colour slashed Giovanni's cheeks, emphasising their sharpness, giving his face a hungry look. He led her back over to the chair. 'Let me show you. It can be done tastefully.' She sat statue-still as he arranged her coat and waistcoat, as he untied her neckcloth. His fingers were cold, shaking slightly as he undid the six little pearl buttons on the bib of her shirt. She wore only her corsets underneath. When his fingers brushed her skin, she breathed sharply in.

Giovanni loosened the laces. His hand hovered over her breast. Her nipples hardened in anticipation. She could see, from the angle at which his head was bent over her, that his hair grew in a little circular whorl at the back of his head. Heat radiated, from him, from her, from both of them. Her skin was on fire. Sweat prickled at the base of her spine.

Giovanni stood up. 'Then—when we come to paint— then we will…'

Disappointment made her rash. Cressie dragged her corset down, twisting the open neck of the shirt so that the vee shape where the buttons stopped supported her bare breast. 'There, is that what you meant?'

Giovanni simply stared. Her nipple looked a much darker pink against the white of the man's shirt. Cressie hadn't really paid much attention to her nipples before. It seemed to her that it was defiantly pert. She straightened her back. She felt defiantly pert herself. She placed her open palm over her breast, cupping it lightly, shivering as her fingers grazed her aching nipple. His breath came out in a low hiss. His eyes went dark. He was swallowing repeatedly. Desire and power surged together. 'What do you think, Giovanni?'

'I think…' It was his dark smile, the one that made

her feel as if she were being twisted tight from the inside. 'I think,' he said, 'that you know perfectly well what I think, Lady Cressida. I just hope you can hold the pose.'

She could not decide whether to be glad or sorry when he disappeared behind his easel again and began to sketch. He drew no grids this time, his movements seemed freer, his concentration much fiercer than before, as he sketched and muttered and scored lines through what he'd drawn, tearing page after page of drawing paper from the board and casting it on to the floor.

It felt like a day had passed, it might have been as little as an hour, when he looked up and smiled triumphantly. 'I have it.'

Her nipple was stiff with cold and nothing else by now. She had no thought but to move before her muscles seized altogether, and to cover herself. 'May I see?'

She hadn't expected him to agree, but he beckoned her over, another change from the previous portrait. 'Well?' he demanded impatiently.

Cressie shook her head in amazement. 'You don't need me to tell you.'

'I do, Cressie.'

'Giovanni, it's brilliant.' She grinned as she stared at herself, roughly outlined in charcoal but nevertheless fully realised. There was no careful symmetry evident in this portrait, though she could see that the angles, of her face to the front, of her body in profile, were quite deliberately chosen. It was the contradictions which she liked best though. A female in man's clothing. A manly pose and a womanly breast. Her face, serious and yet mischievous. And the overall effect, it was strangely sensual, though she could not say how. She looked out from the drawing defiantly, confidently, herself, but not as she had ever seen herself. 'It is—confusing though. I don't know what to think.'

Giovanni smiled with deep satisfaction. 'That is it exactly. Confusing. Inflammatory. Anarchic. Not one thing or the other.'

'It doesn't—I mean I can see that there are some rules, but it seems to me that you have quite deliberately broken many.'

'Poor Cressie, what will your theory say of this painting?'

'I really have no idea.'

'I will prepare the canvas tonight. We can start painting in oil tomorrow. No more today, you must be tired.'

'I was not the one who spent all morning running about with four obstreperous boys. You must be exhausted.'

Giovanni shook his head. 'I enjoyed it, to tell the truth. I had forgotten how exhilarating it is to be young and carefree. I envy them their innocence.'

'Watching you all today—I have achieved at least one of the things I hoped from my time here. I have come to love them for themselves, and not because they are my brothers.' Cressie picked up her cloak and began to smooth out the folds. 'I ought to go and write to Cordelia now. I promised Bella I would, but I confess I have been putting it off.'

'Why?'

'My Aunt Sophia wrote—oh, it's complicated. You wouldn't want to know.'

'Sit down. Tell me about it, I do want to know. Cordelia is the sister who is in London, yes?'

Giovanni took the cloak from her and placed it on the Egyptian chair, guiding her over to the window, where he had placed a rather tatty *chaise-longue* in the embrasure for him to rest on between bouts of painting. 'I am all ears,' he said, 'as you English bizarrely like to say.'

It was a relief to pour out her concerns, and a relief to laugh too, for it was true, Cordelia might lack judgement, she was rash and unthinking and often very selfish, but she was always amusing company, she had a knack for making sure no one could ever be angry with her for too long, and really some of her exploits were very droll. 'Though why she should wish to watch two men beating each other up with their bare fists, I cannot imagine,' Cressie finished. 'I will have to find a way of making her heed our aunt before she puts herself beyond the pale, though I have no idea how.'

'From what you have said, Cordelia will do exactly as she wishes, whether you intervene or not.'

Cressie smiled. 'You are quite right, and I can't help but admiring her for it. She is like a cat, my youngest sister. You can throw her from the highest of windows and she will always land on her feet.'

'You love your sisters very much.'

'Yes, I do. We are all so different, but I never doubt they would come to my aid if I really needed them. Perhaps it is a result of growing up without Mama. When we were younger and all living here at Killellan, we were very close. Now—well, you know what the situation is now. But I wouldn't be without them. Or my brothers. I can't imagine what it was like, growing up an only child as you did.'

Giovanni shifted uncomfortably. He had become used to suppressing the unwonted urge to confide in Cressie, accustomed to reminding himself that the past was in the past. But the more he denied himself, the more he had begun to realise how isolating was his silence. It was not so much that he wished to talk about it, more that he wished Cressie to know him better. He found he wanted to share some of himself with her. It mattered that she understood him, even just a little. And sitting here so comfortably in the privacy of their studio, with the daylight waning, and the outline of what he hoped would be his magnum opus on the drawing board, with Cressie so relaxed and at her ease sitting beside him, he would never get a better opportunity. Her remark, that their relationship was entirely one-sided, had hit home. It had just taken him a long time to acknowledge that fact.

'You have that look.' Cressie was managing to frown and smile at the same time. 'The look that tells me I've said something you don't like, and you're not going to tell me what it is.'

'You are wrong this time. I am going to tell you. I was just—steeling myself.'

Cressie had kicked off her top boots. Now she folded her legs up underneath her and turned side-on to face him. 'Is it so bad?'

'I do have a family, many sisters and brothers, though none of them are full-blood. Some are known to me, some not, and those who are known will not acknowledge me for the same reason that my mother will not acknowledge me and why my father had me raised by a fisherman's family until he needed an heir. The man who fathered me is Count Fancini. An ancient and extremely wealthy family, with a bloodline which can be traced back until before there were records. I am Count Fancini's bastard. Illegitimate. His baseborn son.'

Cressie actually reeled with shock. Her eyes were huge as she covered her mouth with one hand, the other reaching for his. He ought not to allow her to take it, he did not need the words of pity which she was obviously trying to swallow, but he twined his fingers in hers all the same, and it felt—right. Not pity, but sympathy—he could bear that.

'Oh, Giovanni, how awful.' She was blinking furiously. 'I cannot imagine—I shall never, never complain about my family again. No wonder you were hurt when I joked about wishing my father was someone else. I am so, so sorry. Did you say that your father—your real father—he had you adopted?'

'*Si.*' Giovanni tightened his clasp on her hand. 'For twelve years, I thought myself the son of a fisherman. My father—the man I thought was my father—was a rough man, but kind. He—it was he who took me to Santa Maria del Fiore. You remember I told you, the church with the whispering gallery? And he taught me to swim. And of course to fish. I was teased by the other boys in the village for the way I look.' He winced, and smacked his forehead. 'This face, it was not at all like the face of the people I called *Mamma* and *Papa*, but I never questioned, and they never breathed a word, my parents. I thought they loved me.'

'Giovanni, of course they did.'

It was like a weight around his heart, this truth. Like a heavy stone he never tried to move, for how could he when the facts were so clear? 'They handed me back to him, Cressie. I was just a child and they gave me back without protest.'

'No. I am sure—that cannot be true, Giovanni. No one who has raised a child as their own could simply hand them over. It would be too painful. Your memory must be playing tricks.'

'I was twelve years old. I remember it perfectly, as if it was yesterday. I remember they made no move to hug me when the carriage came to take me away. I remember the one answer to all my letters was a request to stop writing. My father—my real father—told me he had been paying them to look after me.' Giovanni swallowed, but the lump in his throat would not budge, the stone in his heart seemed heavier than ever. No matter how many times he told himself it didn't matter, he could never quite make himself not care. He dug the knuckles of his free hand into his eyes so hard that he saw red. It didn't help.

Cressie shuffled along the *chaise-longue* and put her arm around his shoulders. She stroked his head, a strange little movement, as if she were trying to tuck a lock of hair he didn't have behind his ear. It was intensely comforting. 'You told me once,' she said softly, 'that what we think and how we feel are often quite different things. You said there was a big gap between logic and instinct. I remember it so well because it struck a chord with me. I know you think you ought to hate them for giving you away, those people. But for twelve years, the better part of your childhood, you thought they were your parents. It would be quite unnatural for you not to love them, even if they did hurt you. Look at me, for goodness' sake. I don't respect my father, I don't like him, there are times when I hate him, but I still love him, and I know that won't ever go away, no matter how hard I try. I've stopped trying to hate him. It is a relief, I promise you.'

Cressie kissed his temple, then resumed her rhythmic stroking. She was warm against him, soft and pliant, contradictorily more feminine than usual in her man's clothing. Giovanni allowed himself to relax against her, just the tiniest bit. It felt good. 'I don't hate them,' he said. 'They were poor people, they needed the money. I understand that.'

'That's just arrant nonsense.' Cressie stopped her stroking and put her face up so close to his that their noses almost touched. 'You loved them. You were obviously happy with them. They clearly loved you—your father did not have to teach you all those things, swimming and the like. He did not have to take you to that church with the whispering gallery. They cared for you and you loved them as all children love their parents. It must have been awful, beyond awful, for all of you, when they had to give you up. At the very least, you must feel hurt. Your real father is obviously a man of great influence. If he desired your return, I doubt there would have been much to be done to stop him. I am sure they did not abandon you, Giovanni, though I can understand it must have felt like it. I can see why you think you hate them.'

Cressie's truths had always been uncomfortable. Her way of seeing through things to the nub of the matter, it was one of the things he most admired in her, but it was painful to be on the receiving end. Such clarity of thought made it impossible to avoid confronting the truth. And how much worse would it be if he told her the whole unadulterated truth? *Never!* Giovanni pushed her away gently. 'I don't hate my parents,' he said, which was true.

He could almost see the wheels and cogs in Cressie's mind working. He saw the very moment when she decided not to pursue the matter. For a split second, he was relieved. 'Then tell me about your real father,' she said. 'The one you really do hate.'

He was forced to laugh, a hollow sound which made Cressie shiver. 'Blood. My real father is the man who taught me the significance of blood. He is the reason I understand you so well. He is very, very like your own father in character.'

Cressie shuffled back along the sofa and nestled up against him. 'Tell me the whole story,' she said, draping his arm around her shoulders.

Her curls tickled his chin. 'It is a sad story. The sort of story someone else would have turned into a fairytale. I have never told it before.'

'I have often thought fairytales tend towards the

tragic. Celia used to read us *Cendrillon*, it was Cassie's favourite story. She loved the romance of a poor little ragged girl marrying a prince, but I always thought what Cendrillon would have preferred would be to have her mama back. We didn't have a wicked stepmother ourselves at that point, of course,' Cressie added with a grin. 'I think Bella would have put quite a different slant on that story. But I am interrupting yours. Please, go on.'

He couldn't think with her so close. Giovanni untangled himself from her embrace and laid his head back against the *chaise-longue* and closed his eyes. 'Once upon a time,' he began, for it was easier to think of this as a story than to relive it, 'there was a rich Italian count. His name was Fancini.'

Cressie shifted round on the seat, the better to watch his face. Shocked beyond measure by what he had thus revealed of his childhood, she could now see quite clearly why Giovanni appeared so cold. To have been abandoned not once but twice—no wonder he was determined no one else would hurt him. As for that woman who had been his lover and his muse—how could she have hurt him when she must have known—no, she did not know, for Giovanni said he had never told anyone. Cressie was to be his first and only confidante. That counted for something, even if he didn't love her as he had the other woman. Not that that was relevant in any way. She was not in love with Giovanni. The very thought of it was—was—not to be thought of!

But she did find herself thinking of just that as she listened, wrapping her arms around herself, mostly to stop herself wrapping them around Giovanni. She could not possibly be in love with this man. This strange feeling, a sort of tightness, a dawning awareness like a light flickering in the dim recesses of her mind, waiting for her to turn the corner and discover—no, that wasn't love. And the ache in her heart, that was sympathy for the pain he had suffered, nothing more.

'Count Fancini was of impeccable birth,' Giovanni continued, 'from a long line of blue-blooded Tuscans and who counted the Granducato di Toscana amongst his closest relatives. The count has a child from his marriage, that all-important thing, a male child, a son and heir to the vast country estates and the palazzo in Florence. The Countess Fancini produces many more children, but all die or are still-born. The count, a man of lustful appetites, has several more healthy children, born, as they say, on the wrong side of the blanket, but all are females and therefore unworthy.' He opened his eyes momentarily. 'You see,' he said with a wry smile, 'it is the same the world over.'

Cressie touched his hand briefly, but said nothing. He closed his eyes once more, speaking as if he were far away, talking of another world, of other people, as if none of it were connected to him. Which was completely understandable. How many times had she herself escaped into the fantasy life of Mr Brown? How alike they were in their experiences. An affinity, that was what they had. That was *all* they had. She smoothed her waistcoat down over her shirt. Affinity was a most logical explanation. She couldn't understand why it felt such an unconvincing one.

'One day,' Giovanni was saying, 'Count Fancini met

a girl, a beautiful young lady in actual fact, as well born as he, quite a different sort altogether from his other amours. Though he had no business wooing her, being a married man, woo her he did. And Carlotta, for that was the young lady's name, most foolishly imagined herself in love. Her parents had the highest hopes of her making an excellent match—blood and beauty again, you see. These hopes seemed dashed when Carlotta discovered herself with child, but between them, her parents and the father-to-be, Count Fancini, hushed up what could have been a major scandal. Carlotta gave birth in secret. Six months later, still apparently fresh and virginal, she was married off. The boy—for it was, unfortunately, a boy—was given to a childless family of humble origin as their own, and thus, the story ended. Or so thought Carlotta and Count Fancini.'

'And then?' Cressie asked with a sinking feeling. This was a fairytale without a happy ending.

'And then,' Giovanni said, his voice becoming icier in his efforts to maintain his air of detachment, 'the count's only legitimate son tragically died. And the count was by now, for reasons associated with his having been so eager to indulge his lustful appetites, unable to father another child of either sex...'

'Let me guess,' Cressie said fatalistically. 'The count decides an illegitimate son is better than no son at all and has him summarily recalled from his foster parents.'

'Exactly.' Giovanni's smile faded, to be replaced by his satyr look. 'Like your Cendrillon, who in Italian is known as Cenerentola, our poor little fisherman's boy was granted great riches. He was given the best of tutors, taught how to fight with a sword, how to converse politely, how to bow and how to eat with his mouth closed. He was taught how to be a gentleman. He worked hard at his studies, he wanted very much to please his most intimidating and most powerful new father, but the count was a difficult man to satisfy. Giovanni was forbidden all contact with the people he still thought of as his real family. Their names were beaten out of him, and—as I said, finally he was given proof that they had no wish to see him. He knew he ought to be happy living in such luxury, but the truth is that he was lonely. He was still much too rough around the edges to be exposed to society, and he was not permitted to find friends among his father's servants and tenants. Where once he had had the run of the village and the freedom of the sea, now he was confined to the family estate. Beautiful as it was, Giovanni came to think of it as a prison.'

'I don't know what to say.' Cressie was struggling not to cry, all the more so because Giovanni was so determinedly unemotional. Whereas she was feeling—what? She didn't know what to think either. She couldn't allow herself to think. Not about that. Not about him or her feelings for him.

Oblivious of the turmoil raging in her heart, Giovanni shrugged her hand from his arm. 'There is nothing to say. I was never hungry. I had an excellent education. I was still a bastard, but I was as close to being a legitimised bastard as it is possible to be. My father formally recognised me and had his will changed. I should have felt privileged.'

'But?'

'I tried, just as you did, Cressie, to do what was expected of me. I tried to be grateful, I tried to pay back what was being given with obedience. I was miserable.'

'Which is why you recognised it in me?'

'Exactly. Like you, I fooled myself into thinking that if only I tried harder I could want what my father wanted for me, but I could not. The one thing I had of my own was my art. I'd been drawing since before I could read or write. When he saw how much it meant to me he had my paints taken from me. Drawing, you see, is a hobby for women. Painting is carried out by artisans. Neither are acceptable activites for the son and heir of a count.'

'Like mathematics for the daughter of an earl,' Cressie said. 'At least my father merely discourages me. I shall never think of him as a tyrant again.' She uncurled her legs and wriggled her toes to rid herself of the pins and needles which had taken hold. 'Was it then your mother, Carlotta, who encouraged you to paint?'

Giovanni swore. 'I met her only once. She did not want to know me. Her reputation was of far more import than her first-born. It was when Count Fancini decided to send me off to the army to finish my education that I finally rebelled. He said he would cut me off. I told him I could make my own way in life without him. He told me I would return with my tail between my legs. I have not seen him since. It has been fourteen years.'

This last part of his story was told in a flat voice, without pretence of distance or objectivity. Giovanni looked drained and horribly close to defeated. It was clear there was more, much more, that he had not told her, but to ask him now would most likely send him into the darkest of tempers or the deepest of depressions.

'So you cast off your blood and made a living out of beauty,' Cressie said.

She could restrain herself no longer. Jumping to her feet, she pulled him with her, putting her arms around his waist and resting her head on his chest. She could feel his heart beating, slow and steady. Her senses were alight, attenuated, alive with an awareness of him. She couldn't fool herself any longer. This wanting, this dragging, drugging insistent wanting, she ought to have known it could be nothing else.

She reached up on tiptoe to smooth his hair, unable to stop herself fluttering kisses over his forehead, his eyes, the sharp planes of his cheeks. 'I'm so sorry, I'm so sorry,' she whispered over and over. Sorry for him. Sorry for her own stupid self. 'Sorry,' she said, pressing herself more tightly against him, as if burrowing into him would bring comfort, telling herself that was all she wished, while at the same time her hands stroked his head, his neck, shoulders, and her mouth sought his and her heart wished for so much more.

When their lips met, she felt his resistance. She closed her eyes and pressed tighter into him. Kissing. Little tiny kisses to comfort and reassure and to take away the pain. Kisses that soothed, then kisses that slowed as he began to respond. Kisses that became a kiss. Her lips clung to his as tightly as her hands, her body. She felt as if she were pouring her heart out in her kiss. And it was that, not the salt taste of her tears, which made her stop lest she betray herself.

'I'm sorry. I'm so sorry,' Cressie said, tearing herself free. 'I doubt you feel better for having unburdened yourself right now. My own experience with such confessions as you have drawn from me is that all you will feel is exhausted. But you will feel the benefit of it soon, Giovanni, and see things more clearly.'

Loath as she was to leave him, she knew him well enough. He would not like to have the details picked over or analysed. Besides, she needed time alone with her own thoughts, time to reconcile herself to *that* thought. She touched his cheek, almost overwhelmed by what she was feeling, desperate now to get away before she broke down. 'You will create a new sort of beauty here, with me as your model, yes? I must go and write to my sister now. Thank you for trusting me with your story.'

She kissed his other cheek, then draping her cloak around her made for the door. Giovanni stood still, his eyes blank. Cressie felt as if her heart were being squeezed, seeing him so. She loved him so much. There, it was said.

Chapter Eight

'I categorically refuse to see him. You have to get rid of him, Cressie, I beg of you.'

Bella gripped at the sleeve of her stepdaughter's dress plaintively. Pink silk striped with grey, the gown had a plain round neck, puffed sleeves which tapered to end just past the wrist and a pretty design of scroll-work around the hem in the form of waves. It was one of Cressie's favourites, but it crushed very easily. She tried to unpick her stepmother's fingers, but Bella refused to let go.

'Sir Gilbert has travelled all the way from London; surely you can at least grant him a short audience. It would be a most sensible precaution. You must think of the health of your unborn child. There is no disputing he is considered the pre-eminent man in his field.'

'No!' Bella threw herself across the salon and dropped dramatically on to a sofa. 'No, no, no! I told your father, I was most plain with him. I simply will not have that horrible man touch me again. His fingers are like—like frozen twigs. And his nails are far too long for his calling. They are positively sharp, Cressie. You cannot imagine.'

Cressie could, unfortunately, imagine very well thanks to Bella's graphic description. She shuddered and pressed her knees together. 'Could you not simply consult with him, discuss your symptoms without subjecting yourself to the rigours of an examination? You have been quite unwell, after all.'

'Because this child is a girl. I have been sick, that is all.'

Bella folded her arms protectively over her stomach. Her really very small stomach. In fact Bella herself, Cressie thought, seemed to be shrinking. Was she losing weight?

'Please, Cressie. Don't force me to see him. His head looks like an egg peeking above a bird's nest. He has one eyebrow permanently raised and a way of looking at one—he makes me feel as if I have committed some sort of heinous crime. And his voice. It is cadaverous, all whispery and monotone and cold. I tell you, he would not look out of place in a graveyard. He makes me feel as if *I* shall not be long in taking my own place there. As for his hands—but I have told you about his hands.'

Bella was now wringing hers together tragically. Her feet, no longer swollen but clad in blue satin slippers, were dancing a frantic little two-step, thanks to the way she was jiggling her legs, something of which she seemed to be wholly unaware. Why, if she disliked the surgeon so much, had she allowed him to attend her at all three of her confinements? Cressie rolled her eyes. The answer was obvious. Lord Armstrong must have insisted. It was wrong of her, but she couldn't help thinking that it would be gratifying to help thwart her father just once. Telling herself that she did so only for Bella's sake, Cressie nodded. 'Very well. I am sure you exaggerate—the poor man cannot be so grotesque as you describe but I will send him away. I have to admit that you are looking much improved these last few days.'

'The sickness has gone, certainly.' Lady Armstrong sank back on to the sofa with a huge sigh of relief. 'Thank you, Cressida. I very much appreciate this, I truly do.'

The words seemed to be genuinely heartfelt. Cressie was touched and rather pleased at this latest development in their relationship. As Bella said, they would never be bosom companions, but there was honesty and an understanding between them which meant they could exist, if not in harmony, then at least in peace. Even the two oldest boys seemed to have noticed the thaw in their relationship. James and Harry rarely played the obnoxious brat when in their mother's and Cressie's company, whereas before they had misbehaved terribly, feeding off the enmity between the two women. Which meant that Freddie and George no longer followed their lead with their own childish tantrums. Rarely did Cressie wish, as when she first took on her role to teach them, to tie them up and gag them, or to run screeching from the room tearing at her hair in frustration. Her brothers would never be angelic but they were nearly always biddable, and indeed likable, these days. She supposed that Harrow would soon change all that, if her father and the excruciating man he called his friend, Bunny Fitzgerald, were anything to go by.

She paused in front of a looking-glass in the hall-way. Her hair was a mess, as usual. She had stopped pinning it up during the day, for she had to take it down each time she sat for her portrait, and so instead tied it back with a ribbon. Today's was dusky pink like her gown. Giovanni said she suited this particular colour but should never wear a paler shade. She could sort of see what he meant when she saw how well this gown suited her, but she had no idea why.

The ribbon dangled from her fingers as she stared at her reflection. It had been almost a week since she'd started posing for the Mr Brown portrait. Almost a week since Giovanni had told her the story of his past. And almost a week since she'd realised that she was in love with him.

She'd hoped the feeling would go away of its own volition. Melt away in the same way as it had crept up on her. The wild elation she felt every time she looked at him, the warmth that enveloped her when she thought about him, the ache in her heart when she reminded herself that every day that passed was another closer to him leaving. But she didn't really wish it would go away, and it had not. The opposite in fact. Every time she saw him, it seemed to expand, this feeling, filling her with a longing which was physical and more. Each moment she spent apart from him was a moment lost. Each little fact she managed to extract from him was a treasure, to be stored up and added, like pieces of tes-serae, to complete the mosaic of him. Not that she believed she'd ever have the complete picture. There was no time, and in any event, Giovanni was a man who would never give all of himself to anyone. That he had given her so much already, so much more than he'd ever given anyone before, that was one of the things which made it easier for her to bear the thought of his absence.

She loved him. In one sense it made no difference at all. There was no point in contemplating any sort of future with him. She knew for a fact that Giovanni had no interest in any sort of alliance, sanctified by the church or not. Of her own wishes, she was not so certain, but she was beginning to conclude that marriage, even if it was to a man of her own choosing rather than her father's, was one of the things she'd been silently rebelling against all her life. She didn't want to be someone's wife. She wanted to be herself. She still had no idea what that meant, but she did know it didn't require a change of name.

In another sense, though, being in love changed everything. Time took on a strange quality. When she was with Giovanni it accelerated, the hours flew past unnoticed. When apart it slowed inexorably, almost seemed to stop altogether. The relationship between love and time. Maybe she could occupy herself with a new theory in the long endless days after he was gone, she thought wryly.

For the moment, everything had taken on a new meaning. She saw and heard things differently. Her mood swung wildly from exhilaration to despair in seconds. The stupidest things made her cry. Or laugh. She was in a constant state of awareness. She wanted, passionately wanted, to have everything and all of Giovanni that she could. She wanted to know him inside and out. She wanted him. She really, really wanted him. But ever since he had begun on this second painting, ever since he had named her his muse, he had steadfastly refused to surrender to the smouldering tension which fired each portrait session. He would not make the first move for fear of breaking the spell. Cressie was certain that the chemistry between them could only enhance it. Which meant she would have to make the first move. And so far, she had been unable to pluck up the courage to do so.

A solicitous cough behind her made her jump. 'Sir Gilbert Mountjoy wishes me to inform Lady Armstrong that he must leave for another urgent appointment in fifteen minutes, my lady,' Lord Armstrong's butler said. 'I informed her ladyship, but she said that you had the matter in hand.'

'I do.' Cressie hurriedly tied her hair ribbon. 'Lead the way, Myers.'

'I tell you, Giovanni, I had been convinced that Bella's unflattering description of Sir Gilbert could only be much exaggerated,' Cressie exclaimed an hour later, sitting in the attic studio, 'but in fact it was nigh on perfect, possibly even understated. He is a veritable death's head of a man. I cannot blame her at all for fleeing from his ministrations. He really does have fingers like icy twigs. I shuddered when he shook my hand. Why any woman with child would let that walking cadaver anywhere near them is quite beyond me.'

Giovanni smiled over the top of the easel. 'So the

venerable surgeon has been despatched, never to return. What will Lord Armstrong make of that, I wonder?'

'I could not care less,' Cressie said impatiently. 'Bella has an excellent point. If my father cannot make the effort to be in attendance, he has no right to dictate arrangements for the birth. After all, *he* is not the one who has to suffer the privations. Do you think she is looking better, Giovanni?'

'I think she is certainly looking thinner. Has she ceased to devour half a patisserie shop each afternoon?'

'She's not eating much at all, but she seems to be much the better for it.' Cressie lapsed into silence. She loved to watch Giovanni at work. He had a special painting frown which was not at all like his satyr look. When he was happy with something, he smiled lopsidedly and tapped his brush on the edge of his palette three times. When he wasn't happy, he pressed his thumb hard into his forehead. For some reason known only to himself, he had abandoned his normal custom and was painting this portrait in his shirtsleeves, discarding his waistcoat as well as his top coat. As a result he had managed to get paint or oil or pigment or charcoal, sometimes a mix of all, on his shirt by the end of each session. When she suggested a smock he laughed scornfully. He seemed to have an infinite supply of snow-white shirts anyway, for he turned up each morning to paint her brothers looking as immaculate as ever. Only here, in their attic studio, did he relax both his dress code and his behaviour.

'I had a letter from Cordelia today.' Cressie rolled her neck and stretched her legs as they took a short break, an hour or so later. 'She says that Aunt Sophia is exaggerating matters. She denies any knowledge of a wager on the number of her suitors, and informs me that there is absolutely and positively no need for either Bella or myself to come to town. Were it not for that last remark, I would be a little reassured.'

Giovanni stood frowning at the canvas, obviously unhappy with some element of the painting. 'But you are not reassured?'

Cressie wandered over to stand beside him. 'I think Cordelia is scheming. I suspect all these silly things my aunt has herself in a tizzy over are a ruse to deflect attention from Cordelia's real indiscretions, and I think Cordelia knows perfectly well that I would smell a rat the moment I saw her. What I don't know is what I should do about it.'

'You said yourself that your sister will do as she wishes whether you intervene or not,' Giovanni said distractedly.

'Yes, but…'

'I think it is the hair. I cannot capture the exact way it falls over your eye just here.' Giovanni swept a long curling tress of her hair over her forehead. 'I wonder if you tilted your head a little more like this—so. Or tucked your hair behind your ear, perhaps. Let me demonstrate, if I may.' Cressie stood quite still, concentrating on breathing. 'Yes, that is better,' Giovanni said. 'If you had perhaps a pearl earring that would be…yes.'

His fingers were tangled in her hair. His thumb caressed the lobe of her ear. Did he realise he was doing it? She could feel his breath as he leaned towards her. His

fingers were stroking in delicious little circling movements, the area just behind her ear. Was it accidental,
this feather-light touch in this most sensitive spot, or
was he just thinking about the painting? She risked a
glance. Dark eyes. *That* look, the flaring-heat one. Not
the painting then. The knot of excitement which was
permanently present when she was with him, when she
thought of him, which was only temporarily unravelled
when she touched herself at night in the dark thinking
of him, the knot began to tighten.

'I have a pearl drop,' Cressie said.

She meant an earring. It didn't sound as if she meant
an earring. It didn't look as if Giovanni thought so either. His eyes flickered closed. 'You have a pearl drop,'
he said softly, making the words sound even more erotic.

His mouth hovered over her ear. His fingers played
up and down the line from her ear to her neck, thread-
ing and unthreading through her hair. Though she had
pulled her shirt closed when he had called a break, she
had not bothered to pull her corsets back into place. The
cotton of her shirt was abrasive on her nipples. They
were stiff and engorged.

Giovanni kissed her earlobe, taking it gently into his
mouth and sucking. He licked his way around the contours of her ear, as if he were painting it with his tongue.
His thumb stroked the pulse at the base of her throat.
His other hand crept around her waist and slid down to
cup her bottom. She knew he would come to his senses
any moment. She knew that if he did, she would most
likely lose hers. She had to find the courage. Cressie

slipped her arms around Giovanni's waist and lifted her head up to kiss him full on the lips.

He did not resist. She slid her arms up his back, flattening her palms along the ridges of his muscles, feeling the heat of his skin through his linen shirt, opening her mouth to him, silently pleading with him not to stop.

He didn't. His kiss was languorous, his lips clinging to hers, not with a violent thirst but drinking from her as if she were nectar. Slowly, his tongue licked across her bottom lip. She dug her fingers into his back and arched into him, flattening her breasts against him. His kiss deepened. His fingers tightened on her bottom. His breath was warm on her face as he kissed her, and kissed her, and kissed her.

Slowly, like a dreamer awakening, he stopped and began to disengage himself from her embrace. What to do? She didn't know what to do. And then she did. For they were the same, she and he. That's what he had said. Kindred spirits. 'I dreamt of you last night, Giovanni,' Cressie said in the barest whisper.

Her words instantly arrested his retreat. 'What did you dream?' he asked. Her words from the whispering gallery. He understood. And now she must turn his words into hers. 'I was watching you undressing. You knew I was watching.' She hesitated. 'I was touching myself.'

His pupils were huge. She had his entire attention, fixed unwavering on her. But he did not move towards her. 'Cressie…'

'Like this,' she said, pushing back her coat and waistcoat, sliding one hand inside the open neck of her shirt, cupping her breast. Her heart was pounding. She was hot, but she was not at all embarrassed. 'I was touching myself like this, Giovanni.'

He moaned. A low guttural sound, it found an echo in her own sigh as she circled her aching nipple. His hand reached for her breast then dropped. He stared as she touched herself, fascinated. It was empowering and extremely arousing, the way he looked at her, the way she could make him look at her.

'I dreamt you saw me,' Cressie whispered. 'You were pulling your shirt over your head, and you turned around to look at me. I dreamt that when you saw me, you called to me. "Help me, Cressie," you said. And I did.' She let go of her breast and pulled his shirt from his trousers. Up slid her palms on his skin, finally on his skin, as she pulled the folds of his shirt until he tore it off and threw it across the room.

His skin was not tanned but a beautiful olive colour. The dip from his ribs to his abdomen was clearly defined, almost hollow. Black hair ran in a thin line up from his navel spreading out over his chest. His nipples were dark brown. She touched them, rubbing her cheek against the rough hair of his chest. Don't say beautiful, she told herself, don't say it. But he was. Truly beautiful.

'What happened next, Cressie?' he said, his breathing shallow.

He seemed mesmerised by her. He would do as she bid, but only if she bid him. He wanted her, though he was terrified to break the artistic spell. But he wanted her to break it. She could see that, in the way he looked at her, in the tension which made him seem coiled, every muscle tight, poised. *What next?*

Echoes in the whispering gallery. She dragged her shirt over her head, mirroring his movement. 'You touched me here,' she said, taking his hands and laying them on her breasts, which had escaped from her corset. 'You touched me.'

He did. As he had before, as she had imagined that day, and each night since. He cupped her breasts, lowering his mouth he hungrily licked around their contours. He sucked hard on each nipple then circled with his tongue. Heat, fiercer than any she had felt before, engulfed her. Every part of her seemed to be connected. Her nipples, her fingertips, her ears, her toes. Even the backs of her knees tingled. *What next?*

'The softest of skin,' she whispered. 'I wanted you to find the softest of skin.'

'Softest,' he repeated, slipping his hand inside her breeches.

There was not enough room. Hurriedly she undid the buttons. His hand found the gap between the legs of her pantalettes. Cressie gasped. How could his touch be so different from her own? She had imagined him touching her there, but she had never dreamed it could be like this. The way he touched her, so gently, like the fluttering of a feather over her skin, and yet it seared.

'What next?' he asked, his voice ragged against her ear.

'I needed to know if we were the same,' Cressie answered. 'I needed to touch you. "Let me touch you," I said. And you unfastened your trousers. You took my hand, and you guided me, you taught me.'

She prayed that he would, since she was beginning to lose confidence, and her prayers were for once answered. Giovanni took her hand and slid it inside his trousers. Soft hair at the top of his thigh. Then rougher. His groan was louder and less restrained when she cupped him. Heavy. Warm. He contracted in her hand.

'Cressie. I don't think…I can't think. Cressie, what next?'

What next? 'Show me,' she said. 'I asked you to show me how to touch you. And you touched me too. Show me, Giovanni, show me now as you did in my dream. Show me how to do to you what you did to me in the whispering gallery.'

She could sense his hesitation. He knew she was playing an erotic game. This was no mere recounting of a dream but a form of seduction. He lifted his head to look at her, tilted her chin to look deep into her eyes, searching. She did not know what he found there, only that it was pivotal. The shift was almost tangible, from doing her bidding to his taking control.

Giovanni's smile was entirely sensual. 'In the whispering gallery,' he said, 'I have never so much in my life wanted you to touch me. Wanted it to be me touching you.' He was kissing her neck now, his fingers stroking her thigh, with his other hand easing her breeches down. She had taken off her boots when she broke her portrait pose. 'In the whispering gallery, I wanted to be with you like this,' Giovanni said, lowering her to the floor, quickly kicking off his shoes, discarding the rest of his clothing to kneel before her, between her spread legs, completely naked.

'I wanted to do this.' When he leaned over her to kiss her, her breasts brushed his chest, the most delightful *frisson*, but not nearly enough. His mouth was hot, his kisses dark, drawing the tension up from deep inside her like water from a well. 'You were aflame in the whispering gallery,' he said, 'you were slick and wet, weren't you?' His fingers slid slowly inside her, and Cressie gasped. 'And I was hard,' Giovanni said, his voice so low it vibrated. 'Feel how hard I was, Cressie.'

He took her hand and wrapped it around his erection. She couldn't help noticing how different he was from Giles. Darker skin. Thicker. When she clasped her fingers around him, he pulsed. When he slid his fingers deeper inside her, she cried out.

Her cry released any vestige of restraint in both of them. Giovanni pulled her hard up against him and began to stroke her, his fingers sliding over her, circling her, slipping into the heat of her then back over, sliding, sliding, like his tongue sliding inside her mouth now. She knew she should be returning his touch, but it was all she could do to hold on to him as he touched her, fingers and tongue, her mouth, her sex, bringing her to a height she had not thought possible to climb, pushing her mercilessly on until she climaxed, feeling as if she were splitting, pulsing around his fingers, her mouth pressing hot, wild kisses into his throat, his shoulders, his heaving chest. But it was not enough this time, her own completion. Not nearly enough. She wanted to share it with him. 'Show me,' she insisted, 'Giovanni, tell me what you want, show me.'

She thought he would resist her. She saw the effort there in his eyes. Then she began inexpertly to stroke him, and he arched his back, his hand sinking into her flank. 'Like this?' she asked. He muttered in Italian. Something that sounded like a plea. Then he kissed her again, putting his hand over hers to slow her, showing her how to hold him. 'Like this?' she asked again. But even as she did, she felt him tighten, felt the pulse of blood and the rush of seed, and heard him cry out, a painful cry as if she had released the very devil, as he spent himself over her hand.

The speed of his climax, the unstoppable nature of it, swept Giovanni into a strange vacuum, a world where he floated in wholly unaccustomed bliss for the longest, sweetest moment. It was not that he had forgotten, he was certain of that, even though it had been years. This felt different. Completely different. Apart from anything else, he had never, in the past, had any difficulty in controlling his release, for those women he had pleasured had expectations. Expectations he had not only met, but surpassed.

His face was buried in Cressie's hair. Her breasts were pressed against his chest. He could feel her heart racing. His own was pounding heavily. He ran his fingers down the perfect curve of her spine. The line of beauty. He should be ashamed by how quickly he had unravelled, of his lack of restraint, but he was not. He felt none of the things he had felt before—no ennui, no sadness, no sense of emptiness nor even the slightest hint of the disgust which had seized him when he had been forced to sell himself in order to survive until his artistic success made it no longer necessary. It had become a habit, performed like the most perfunctory of tasks. But this, this was very different.

Cressie's arms were wrapped tight around his waist. The salty, musky scent of sex mingled with the familiar smell of her, lavender and chalk and freshness. Her face was pressed into his chest. Her breath was soft on his skin. It only now occurred to him how bold she had been. She was no experienced woman seeking amusement, nor was she one of those women seeking the relief of a fresh male body from the tired, familiar one of her husband. But she had been determined, nevertheless, despite her very limited experience, to seduce him. Not for her own pleasure, but for his.

It was that, Giovanni realised, which made it so very, very different. She wanted to please him. Her pleasure was in pleasing him. She had given herself to him unselfishly, encouraged him to take what he wanted and demanded that he show her what he desired. No woman had ever done that before. All they had been interested in was what his body could do for theirs. Cressie wanted him for himself.

As if he needed further proof, she stirred and sat up, smiling shyly, blushing, as she pushed her hair back from her face. 'I hope my lack of expertise did not spoil things for you.'

Giovanni winced. 'Rather it was my lack of control which—Cressie, why did you do that?'

'I wanted to show you that surrendering to passion will make you a greater painter not a lesser one.'

'So you did it to prove a point?'

Cressie dropped her eyes and tugged self-consciously at her corset, pulling it back up over her breasts. When she looked at him again, her blush had deepened. 'That is not the real reason. I—after the whispering gallery—I needed to know, Giovanni, that it was not just me who felt—this. To prove something to both of us, I suppose.'

Disarmed by her frankness, he was also uneasy, for he sensed that she was nevertheless holding something back. Giovanni got to his feet, pulling her up with him, and picked her shirt and breeches up from the floor, hastily pulling on his own trousers. The sense of euphoria which had thrown him high in the air vanished, dropping him abruptly back down to earth like a kite which suddenly loses the wind. Angry with himself for having even half-formed the thought that he would give anything to be able to make love to Cressie properly, for even starting to imagine her response, Giovanni grabbed his own shirt and pulled it quickly over his head. She was sitting on the Egyptian chair pulling on her boots and looking horribly forlorn. The twisting in his gut warned him too late what he had risked. That she had risked so much more, and all for his sake made him feel quite sick with guilt. Yet he could not make himself regret it. That feeling, the aftermath of his climax, that feeling of bliss, of real ecstasy, of completion, he would not regret that.

Dio, what a self-centred bastard he was. As if anything was possible between them with his past. As if he would ever inflict his sordid self on such a unique creature. He did not deserve to even fantasise about her. He had to put an end to this somehow, without hurting her feelings and without revealing the shameful facts behind the necessity to end it. He had nothing to offer Cressie save her portrait. It sickened him, knowing how close he had come to ruining her. The taste of what might have been was bitter, but he swallowed it down as he knelt in front of her, taking her hands between his. 'I say nothing because I don't know what to say,' Giovanni said, trying for once to speak as candidly as she deserved. 'I have no words to thank you for being so—so brave and so—to take such a risk—you have great courage.'

'Giovanni, I have not—'

'No, let me speak. What you did for me, it was beautiful, but I cannot allow it to happen again. It was my fault. No, I will not let you take the blame, Cressie. I knew exactly what I was doing. I could have stopped, but I did not—do not pretend that you think differently.' He touched her forehead, the soft plane of her cheek which he loved for being so very different from his own, the sweet curve of her lips which from the moment he saw her he had wanted to kiss. 'Despite your years, you are an innocent. And I am not. It is not right, for me to take what you offer. Not for any reason, and especially not in the name of art. I will not pretend that I will find it easy, but I won't take advantage of you. You deserve far more, far better than me.'

'You're not taking advantage of me.'

'Are you angry?' Giovanni asked, puzzled by the mulish note in her voice.

'I won't be patronised.' Cressie pushed his hand away and got to her feet. 'You're not using me. If anything, I was using you. I wanted to see what it would be like, and now I know. Perhaps now that we have brought this—tension—between us to some sort of conclusion, we will be able to focus on the task in hand. Which, I may remind you, is the completion of our little experiment.'

'You think I was patronising you? In what way was I patronising you?' Giovanni asked, struggling to understand her sudden change in mood. How could she have misconstrued what he said?

Cressie strode over to her favourite position at the window. *'It is my fault. I will not let you take the blame. You deserve better.'* She threw herself down on the window seat, and almost immediately jumped back up again. 'I am six-and-twenty years old. I am an intelligent woman and contrary to what you said, not without experience. I knew perfectly well what I was doing, Giovanni, and if—and I say *if*—I chose to do it again, then it would be because I wanted to, and not because you have somehow put me under your spell. I can make up my own mind, as you have spent the past two months telling me.' She strode over to him, standing with her hands on her hips, her eyes bright with temper. 'If you wished to put your mind at rest as to my expectations, you had only to ask.'

'Cressie, that is not—'

'Take your hands off me!' She pushed his chest so forcefully that he staggered back. 'Did you think that one touch from the Adonis of the art world would make me fall at your feet as no doubt hundreds of other women have? Or worse, being your muse, did you worry that I'd fall in love with you? Well, I've done neither of those things.'

She dashed a hand over her eyes and took several deep breaths. Her hair covered her face. Her shoulders were hunched. She was obviously trying hard not to cry. He wanted to put his arms around her, but suspected she would strike him if he did. *Inferno! This is what he got for attempting to be honest!* His conscience pricked him. Not wholly honest. Nowhere near wholly honest, but he could never sully Cressie's ears with the unadorned, unpalatable truth.

She had pushed her hair back from her face again. Her cheeks were streaked with tears. He hated to see her cry, knowing how much she hated it herself. 'Cressie, I swear, it was not at all my intention to upset you. I only wanted…'

'To warn me off.' She sniffed. 'There was no need, Giovanni. You have made it absolutely clear that you have no wish to share your life with anyone, and my own plans for the future don't include any man,' she said with a toss of her head.

It was ridiculous, but it was as painful as if she had stabbed him. 'You have plans? You haven't mentioned any plans.'

'Why should I? You form no part of them, nor wish to.' Cressie took a deep breath. When she continued, the hard edge had disappeared from her voice. She looked deflated. 'That was unkind of me, Giovanni, I beg your pardon. I did not tell you my plans because they are only half-formed. I am thinking of writing to my sister Celia in A'Qadiz. She has established a new system of schooling there, which educates girls as well as boys. For some time she has been endeavouring to increase the number of schools but has been struggling to find suitable teachers. I believe I have a talent for teaching. I have come to enjoy it, and I think that in A'Qadiz Celia would give me the freedom to experiment with new methods. I don't know what she'll say, but if her reaction is positive—well, it means that I am no longer dependent on my father. And it means I could have finally found my true calling.'

'Arabia! That is halfway round the world. Could you not teach here in England?'

'In a ladies' seminary you mean? I cannot embroider, you know I cannot draw, and I have no wish at all to spend my days beating the basics of arithmetic into the heads of a clutch of girls who see its only application in calculating the annual income of their future husband.' Cressie clapped her hand over her mouth. 'Now *I* am being patronising, but even if there are young women out there who wish to learn what I can teach, they will not be permitted to do so. In A'Qadiz, Celia's husband, Prince Ramiz, is very forward looking and wants the best for all his people. He supports Celia's desire to see girls educated in the same subjects as boys. It is revolutionary, and in some parts of their kingdom it is being resisted, but—you see what a challenge it would be?'

What he could see was that the evangelical sparkle was back in her eyes. He could see that she meant it when she said she hadn't considered him at all as part of her future. Which was exactly what he wanted. So why did it hurt? 'I see that it is a challenge you would relish,' Giovanni said tightly.

His own contrariness angered him. He'd thought his future perfectly mapped until he met Cressie. He wandered across the room to stand in front of the easel. Mr Brown peered out at him from the canvas, mischievous and sensual and subversive, just as he'd hoped. The colours were vibrant, the brush strokes clearly visible, the portrait itself less defined, more like a sweeping impression of Cressie than a precise mirror-like representation. It would not sell. It was too different. He thought it was good, he thought it was innovative, but he'd been wrong before. If this was his future, then his future was going to be a struggle.

A struggle he would have to make alone. How ironic. Alone, free of demands and obligations, free of the need to sell himself for his art, that was what he'd dreamt of back in the early days. Alone. The word took on a different meaning now that he had surrendered himself to passion. Alone meant being without Cressie. Alone no longer meant safety, security, success. It meant loneliness.

What an idiot he was! He should be glad that Cressie had her own plans. Glad that she was looking forwards to a future of her own choosing, glad that she saw no place for him there. It was a mistake to imagine what had happened between them was in any way profound. A release of pent-up desire, that is all it was. And this absurd wish to divest himself of all his secrets, to confess all—what the devil was he thinking?

'What about you, Giovanni? What does your future

hold?' Cressie stood at his elbow. How many times had she stood there beside him, inspecting his canvases, speaking her thoughts which were almost always a reflection of his own, and even more often taking him aback with her insights, for she seemed able to see behind the paint to his intentions. Would he be able to develop this new di Matteo style without her? He had no option.

'I will finish this portrait of Mr Brown,' Giovanni said brusquely, 'and that is the only part of my future you need concern yourself with.'

Cressie picked up her cloak. Giovanni clearly wanted her to leave, no doubt already wishing what had passed between them undone. She would not allow him to spoil it for her. For those precious moments, he had been hers and hers alone. For those precious moments, she had allowed her heart free rein and given him all of herself. But he didn't want her, and now she ought to be very glad indeed that she had not betrayed herself. She would not add her broken heart to the burden he already carried around with him. Wrapping the cloak around her, she managed a bright and completely false smile. 'Very well. Since you have no need of me, I shall go and progress my own plans.'

Closing the door of the attic behind her, Cressie bit the inside of her cheek hard. She would write to her publisher. Mr Freyworth could not fail to be impressed by the results she had achieved with her brothers. And if he was not, she would find another publisher. That, at least, was something she could control. Her stupid, contrary heart, now that was something else entirely.

Chapter Nine

It was a beautiful English late-spring day, the sky cobalt blue, the hedgerows bursting into life, studded with cow parsley, celandine and campion. Primroses huddled in bright yellow clumps in the lee of the stone walls which bordered one side of the road. The woodlands were bright with bluebells, fluffy white lambs gambolled in the rolling fields and the trees were awash with fresh green foliage. 'It is as perfect an English idyll as you could wish for, if you were that kind of artist,' Cressie said, glancing over to Giovanni, who was sitting beside her on the gig.

'Thankfully I am not. Flowers tend to be painted by flowery painters,' he replied witheringly.

Cressie smiled. 'I can think of no adjective less applicable to you than flowery.'

Giovanni bowed. 'I will take that as a compliment. Tell me, why are you so eager for us to take tea with your neighbours today?'

'Aren't you tired of being cooped up at Killellan?' In fact, it was she who was feeling claustrophobic. In the aftermath of what might well be her one and only experience of making love to the man she loved, even if they hadn't technically made love, Cressie had discovered yet another example of logic and instinct being at war. There could be no future for them, that was plain, so it would be futile to waste any more time being in love with him. Except she was in love with him, and she couldn't persuade herself not to be. He kept his distance, as promised. She kept hers. Except that every time they were alone together the distance narrowed to nothing in the glances they exchanged, the looks quickly disguised, sometimes just in the way they talked to each other. It hung there, unacknowledged but palpable like a spectre at the feast, the attraction between them. Giovanni at least had the diversion of his painting to occupy his thoughts. Cressie—Cressie was plain frustrated most of the time. She'd thought getting outside, away from the studio and the portrait and all the attendant emotions and memories, would dissipate the tension. But it was still present in the way he sat as far away from her on the bench of the gig as possible, in the way his hand seemed always to be in the process of avoiding her.

Cressie forced her attention back to the road, though the horse was so familiar with the journey, on account of Lord Armstrong's housekeeper being the daughter of Lady Innellan's butler, that she really had no need to do more than keep a loose hold on the reins and point him vaguely in the right direction. 'You have barely been over the door since you arrived, save that one day kite-flying in the park with the boys,' she prompted Giovanni, who seemed distracted, lost deep in the recesses of his complex mind. 'I thought you might appreciate a change of scene.'

'I will have a change of scene soon enough when I return to London,' he replied tersely.

He'd been mentioning his departure more and more. Was he managing her expectations, or his own? Cressie wondered. One positive effect it had. The desire to tell him how she felt was well and truly under wraps. She would be horrified if he guessed the depth of her feelings for him and therefore made every effort to ensure he did not, sometimes wittering inanely for hours about Celia and teaching, even though it was much too early for her letter even to have reached A'Qadiz, far less for her sister to reply. 'I have a confession to make,' she said with forced brightness. 'I accepted the invitation to tea not just to get away from Killellan. I had another motive.'

'That sounds ominous.'

'It was meant to be a surprise, a nice surprise, for you. Don't spoil it by making me tell you.'

'Cressie, I have told you before that I don't like surprises. I have had enough of them in my life and none of them have been remotely nice. Which is why I cannot abide surprises.'

'Oh very well, then.' Cressie sighed. 'I discovered from Bella that one of the Innellans' guests is someone I thought you might be very interested to meet.'

Giovanni frowned. 'Why?'

Cressie hesitated, wondering if she had been a little rash. After all, Giovanni had not actually said he intended to paint anything other than this one portrait in his new style. But he was so passionate about it, he surely could not mean to return to his perfect pictures, even if they did earn him pots of money. Could he?

'He is apparently something of an expert on the latest vogues in art,' Cressie confessed in a rush. 'I thought you might like to talk to him about—about your new—I thought it might be useful if you—talked to him,' she finished lamely, for the satyr look had given way to something quite thunderous.

'And what makes you think you have the right to take such a liberty with my work? Do I send off your mathematical primers to a publisher and tell them perhaps he might like to print them? Would I have the temerity to write to your sister in Arabia and suggest she offer you a post in one of her schools?'

'They're not all schools as such. Some of them are no more than glorified tents. But I take your point,' Cressie said hurriedly, for Giovanni looked as if he might throw her out of the carriage. Or more likely himself. 'I'm sorry. I didn't think it was taking a liberty. I thought that if you could speak to him, explain...'

'Explain what, precisely?' Giovanni cursed. 'One portrait, Cressie. I have painted one portrait—and that unfinished. I don't even know myself what I think of it. And besides that, are you sure you would wish me to be displaying it to all and sundry, given the subject matter? Do you wish the world to see you dressed as a man and baring your breast?'

'I hadn't really thought of that.'

'No, you hadn't really thought at all, had you?'

'But I would do it, Giovanni,' Cressie said, rallying, 'if it meant…'

'That I was provided with the means to expose myself to ridicule for a second time.' Giovanni dropped his head into his hands.

The horse, spooked by their angry tones, encouraged by Cressie's unwittingly tightened grip on the reins, lumbered into a trot which went quite unnoticed by the carriage's occupants. 'A second time?' Cressie repeated slowly. 'What do you mean, a second time?' she asked with something much worse than a sinking feeling. Drowning?

'You think I always intended to paint the depictions of perfection that made my reputation?' Giovanni said bleakly. 'I started out believing in inspiration, in creativity, in truth. And that is how I used to paint, from the heart. But my muse deserted me, I told you that.'

Belatedly reining in the horse, who took another unnoticed liberty and pulled over to crop at the verge, Cressie thought she might actually be sick. 'I remember,' she said miserably, 'the woman who broke your heart.'

'What woman?' Giovanni stared at her, dumbfounded. 'You think that a woman—that I had a lover…'

'She was your muse, this woman. And then she left you. And you were devastated and couldn't paint properly any more without her in your life. Until you met me that is. And obviously,' Cressie said, sensing his bafflement, her face burning with mortification, 'I got completely the wrong end of the stick. Oh God!'

It would be no exaggeration to say that Giovanni looked as if he was wearing a thunder cloud as a cloak.

Rage and something darker, more dangerous, emanated from him in waves. The last thing he would welcome was further questions, but she had to ask them. She would not allow him to make her afraid of him. And besides, she had meant well. Plus, he had an incredible talent, even she could see that. 'Giovanni, what did you mean, a second time?'

He was staring at the floor of the carriage. The planes of his face were stark, his skin pale, the coldness of his expression stripping him of his beauty. He took a deep breath and spoke in a monotone. 'When I walked out of my father's house, I became an apprentice to one of the Italian masters and began to learn the skills which would eventually bring me fame and fortune. But at the same time I was also trying to create a style of my own. Something unique and revolutionary. I was so excited when some of my work was chosen for an exhibition. It was savaged by the so-called experts. A humiliating and very public failure which naturally came to Count Fancini's attention. *You will come back with your tail between your legs. No one will buy those pretty jottings of yours. Mark my words, you will be back. And I will be waiting.* Those were his last words to me when I left. I have never forgotten them—they are seared on my mind. I knew he was patiently waiting for me to fail, but I would not allow him to win. That is when I decided to make a living out of the depiction of beauty and to defy my blood heritage. My father killed my muse, not some woman.'

His words had knocked the wind out of her. Cressie hated the unknown Italian count for his mindless destruction of the son he was so reluctant to acknowledge and so determined to bend to his will. And she was furious at Giovanni for being so very blind. 'You said you would never allow your father to win. But by sacrificing your artistic integrity for commercial expediency, Giovanni, you are doing just that. You are letting him win. You told me you painted in order to prove to your father that you could succeed on your own terms. But you haven't succeeded on your own terms, you've succeeded on his. When will you have earned enough money to be free of him? When will you have produced enough of those mathematically perfect portraits of yours to finally return to your true calling? I'm guessing never.'

A long silence greeted this tirade. Cressie was crying, the tears blinding her eyes. When he tried to hand her his handkerchief, she shook him off, wiping her eyes with the backs of her gloves, fumbling for the reins, which she had dropped on the floor of the gig.

'What are you doing?' Giovanni asked as she set about, most ineptly, trying to turn the horse and carriage around.

'Taking you back to Killellan.'

'No.'

'You have a portrait of my brothers to finish. You have to go back.'

'No, I mean don't turn around, Cressie. Take me to this tea party of yours.'

'What?' Cressie let the reins fall again. The horse, the most even-tempered of beasts under normal circumstances, snorted and tossed his head in frustration.

'You are right,' he said simply. 'About all of it. You are, unfortunately, in the right of it. You have a way of presenting the facts with the precision of a mathematical instrument,' Giovanni added with a ghost of a smile. 'For some time now, I have been ignoring this feeling of...' He gestured with his hands, something like a shrug, which made him seem very Continental. 'I don't know the word. I wasn't unhappy, but I knew there was something wrong. I was beginning to hate every blank canvas, could see nothing of interest in the people I painted because I had stopped looking. I was arrogant, but I told myself that I had the right to be. Like my father, you will tell me.'

His expression was stark, lost, uncertain. He was looking at her as if she had all the answers he sought. Cressie was overwhelmed with love for this man. A tearing tenderness, a fierce, visceral reaction gripped her, to gather him to her, to keep him safe, to tell him it would all be fine, all of it, even though she had no idea what she was talking about. 'Giovanni, you're nothing like your father.' She shuffled over the seat and took his hand between hers. Long fingers, immaculate nails, not a trace of paint. She couldn't resist the most fleeting of kisses. 'We really are very alike, you and I, trying to play our fathers at their own game, and not realising what we actually need to do is break free from them. You don't have anything to prove to Count Fancini, but you have a lot to prove to yourself.'

He laughed. 'You see. Like a precision instrument.'

He touched her forehead. She knew before he did that his fingers would move on to her cheek, her throat.

Cressie closed her eyes, trying to memorise the way his touch made her skin tingle, her muscles clench in anticipation. She could not bear for there to be a time when she would have to imagine and not experience. When his lips met hers, she was so surprised that she almost flinched. He had been so very careful to keep his distance. His kiss was the gentlest of touches. His lips were like silk. His hand cupped her jaw, his thumb stroking her throat. She thought she might truly melt, had barely slipped her arms awkwardly around the bulk of his greatcoat, when he let her go.

'*Grazie*, Cressie. I am sorry I lost my temper. What you have done—it was—*grazie*.' He picked up the reins and handed them to her. 'I will miss you when it is time for me to go,' he said, 'but in future, when I am in any doubt about something, I will say to myself, what would Cressie think, and I am sure you will keep me on the right path. What is the name of this expert that I am to attempt to impress today? Is it Granville? Sir Magnus Titmus perhaps?'

'I don't actually know. All Bella could tell me was that he was from the Continent and was the up-and-coming man. Which was why I thought—but there's no point going back over all that again.'

Cressie took up the reins once more and coaxed the patient horse back into a plodding walk towards the Innellan estates. For a wild moment she'd thought that kiss had signified a turning point, for if Giovanni could finally shed the shadow of his father, perhaps he could also make room in his life for her. For a few heart-breaking seconds, she'd thought she could even in time make him love her. She bit the inside of her cheek hard to stop the foolish tears from flowing, telling herself it was enough that she had helped him, a blessing that she had not blurted out her feelings and turned him from her for ever.

'Lady Innellan seems to have invited half the county,' Cressie said, surveying the packed drawing room. 'Those who are not in London for the Season, that is. Her son, Sir Timothy Innellan, has just returned home from the Continent to claim his title, as I told you. Rather belatedly, in fact, for his father passed away over a year ago.'

She nodded over at the prodigal son. Giovanni saw a heavily bearded man dressed in a flowing robe and turban with a crescent-shaped sword dangling from his waist, holding court in the middle of the room. 'Goodness,' Cressie muttered, muffling a giggle, 'one must assume that his travels have taken him to Arabia.'

'What dangers do you think he fears to encounter in his mother's drawing room?' Giovanni asked, also smiling, though rather at Cressie's face than the new baronet with the bayonet.

'Scheming dowagers with marriageable daughters for a start,' she replied promptly. 'I am glad my father is not in the country. I am sure he would have no qualms in throwing me in Sir Timothy's path. "Take her with my blessing, even if you have the look of a Whig,"' Cressie said in a very fair imitation of her father's pompous mode of speech. 'Though actually, Sir Timothy has more the look of those strange men who stand guard outside the harem in Celia's palace. I saw them when I visited. Most intimidating. Now I come to think of it, Celia told me that traditionally they were *castrato*. I wonder how far Sir Timothy has taken his admiration of the East.'

'I wonder what his mother would say if she discovered you were speculating about such matters in her drawing room while taking tea,' Giovanni said. 'You have a most unconventional sense of humour.'

'My Aunt Sophia is always telling me to put a guard on my tongue.'

'Don't ever do so on my account.'

There was no time for Giovanni to dwell on the dwindling number of days left for her to heed his words, for Lady Innellan descended upon them at that precise moment. A stately woman who had, according to Cressie, worn her blacks dutifully and cast them off promptly a year to the day upon which her husband had departed this earth, she was an old friend of the Aunt Sophia Cressie was so fond of. Her first words following her introduction to Giovanni were to enquire after the aforementioned lady. 'For I believe that her health is somewhat in decline,' she said to Cressie. 'She is bringing out your sister Cordelia, is she not? Quite a charge, for a woman of her years. I am surprised Bella did not take on the responsibility. How is your stepmother, by the way? I have not seen her in an age.'

'Unfortunately she too has been unwell, though she is a little better now.'

'Do not tell me she is increasing again! Does your

father intend to match every one of his daughters with a son?' Lady Innellan asked with a titter.

Giovanni watched with amusement as Cressie struggled between a desire to ridicule her father by agreeing, and the urge to defend Bella. The grudging respect she had for her stepmother clearly got the upper hand. The smile Cressie returned was just as false as the one her hostess had given. 'Oh, I think my father is more than content with his four boys. An heir and several spares, as they say. It is a pity that not everyone can be in such a fortunate position.' She looked pointedly at Lady Innellan's single heir. 'Bella wishes for a daughter this time. I am sure she will be up and about directly, when you would be most welcome to call, but in the meantime I shall pass on your good wishes, shall I?'

'I wonder that you are not in town with your sister, Cressida. Your father must be most eager to see you suitably attached. It has been—what—eight seasons now?'

'I am needed at Killellan,' Cressie said, and Giovanni noticed her hands curled into fists beneath the long sleeves of her pelisse.

She did not need his protection, she was more than a match for Lady Innellan, but he couldn't help standing a little closer all the same. 'Lady Cressida is taking her brothers for lessons while her stepmother finds a suitable new governess,' Giovanni said. 'I have been commissioned to paint the boys' portrait and thanks to Lady Cressida's extraordinary ability to control her brothers, the task of taking their likenesses is proving surprisingly straightforward.'

Throughout the conversation, Giovanni had been

pointedly ignoring the fact that Lady Innellan was bat-
ting lashes like a hummingbird's wings at him, casting
him smouldering sideways glances. Now, he saw with
resignation that the smile she turned on him was very
different from the one she had bestowed upon Cressie.
'Your reputation precedes you, *signor*,' she said. 'It is
quite an honour to have you here in my modest pro-
vincial drawing room, for you are quite the recluse, I
believe. There are several of my guests most eager to
make your acquaintance.'

Several ladies, no doubt. He saw that thought flit
across Cressie's mind too, as she glanced around the
room, smiling wryly over her shoulder in recognition
of the coyly admiring looks being cast his way. 'I begin
to understand,' she whispered, 'what you mean when
you say that beauty can be a burden. Shall I make our
excuses?'

He was tempted, but her earlier challenge would not
allow him to turn away. *You don't have anything to
prove to Count Fancini, but you have a lot to prove to
yourself.* She was right. He would have to face the bas-
tions of the art establishment at some point. Why not
make a start with this newcomer? Giovanni shook his
head and turned to Lady Innellan. 'I am told that you
have an art expert visiting you. Will you be so kind as
to introduce me to him?'

'Indeed. My son met him on the Continent where
it seems they became very good friends,' her ladyship
replied, reluctantly ceasing her blatant inventory of his
person. 'Where—oh, there he is, hugging my son's side

as ever. They are very good friends indeed, you know. Quite inseparable.' She raised a beckoning hand.

As the man picked his way daintily across the salon in answer to Lady Innellan's summons, Giovanni felt a sick feeling of recognition.

'Signor di Matteo,' Lady Innellan said, 'may I present…'

'Luigi di Canio,' he said heavily. 'We are already acquainted.'

'Well, well. If it isn't the illustrious Giovanni di Matteo.' Luigi's smile dripped with a venom many years in the fomenting. 'How very—interesting—to find you here.'

Luigi had been a well-built youth, but now he was inclined towards the corpulent. His hair was still the colour of ripe wheat, but it was receding from his high brow at a rate which he was obviously self-conscious about, for he had attempted to disguise it by having it combed out, Giovanni noticed. Vain and extremely effete were the first impressions he projected, with his thinly sneering mouth and his ridiculous pointed beard. His clothes had all the flamboyance one would expect from an Italian artist too. A bottle-green coat, a waistcoat embroidered with pink cabbage roses and a cravat tied in a monstrous bow. He looked rather like a precocious over-large child, though Giovanni was not fooled. Luigi's grip was limp, his palms damp but his pale blue eyes were extremely astute and cold, like the eyes of a reptile.

As Luigi bowed low over Cressie's hand, it was no consolation to Giovanni to see her repress a shudder.

Nausea gripped him, and fury, though it was directed more at himself than at Luigi, that vindictive, malicious figure from his past who would not be able to resist making trouble. And Luigi could make plenty trouble, for he had observed Giovanni's rising star with the meticulous attention of one whose own star was falling. Luigi, that most expert bearer of grudges, would be unable to resist dropping enough hints to reveal the truth in the most tarnished and tawdry of ways. The truth that Giovanni should have told Cressie himself.

He gave himself a shake. They were in an English drawing room taking tea. Luigi was an honoured guest. Why would he sully the occasion with the past which did neither of them credit?

But his unease refused to be calmed by logic as Luigi began to inspect Cressie from head to foot in a way which made Giovanni's hackles rise. 'Lady Cressida,' he said. 'Charmed. You must be the latest subject of Giovanni's attentions.'

Cressie was on her guard, and rightly so. Giovanni would not trust Luigi any further than he could throw him which, looking at his ample girth, would not be far. 'I beg your pardon?' she said.

Luigi tittered. 'In oils, my dear. In oils.'

'Oh, I see,' she said, looking unconvinced. 'No, that privilege falls to my brothers.'

Cressie knew something was awry. Giovanni wanted to drag her away from the polluted air around Luigi. He wanted to wrap his hands around the salacious slug's throat and throttle him. He knew, with sick certainty, that what he ought to have done was told Cressie the whole truth. He knew too that the truth Luigi would imply would be much, much worse than the reality. He had to get out of here. Yet still he did nothing, frozen into inaction by their surroundings, by the vain hope that he had underestimated his fellow Italian.

'How do you come to know Signor di Matteo?' Cressie was asking now.

'Luigi and I were apprenticed at the same studio,' Giovanni intervened curtly.

'You are a fellow artist?' The disbelief in her tone would have been amusing under any other circumstances.

'Sadly,' Luigi said with a bitter little smile, 'I found I did not possess enough talent to earn the right to call myself that, unlike my friend Gio here. But I do find, dear Lady Cressida, that a little practical knowledge is most helpful in my current calling as an arbiter of taste. As such, I would have to admit that our man here has done very well for himself. Have you not, Gio? After that—debacle?—yes, I fear it really was a debacle. Did he tell you, Lady Cressida? A most unfortunate exhibition, as I remember...'

'I know all about it,' Cressie interrupted.

Luigi raised his brows in surprise. 'He told you, did he? How interesting.'

It was her obvious dislike which sealed Giovanni's fate. Cressie had no other intention than to defend him, he knew that, but her words had implied too much between them. He had always thought it a lie, what they said about drowning men's lives flashing before them, but that is exactly what seemed to be happening to him.

He saw a montage of beautiful faces, and floating sneeringly above them all, his Nemesis.

Luigi was unable to disguise his delight at having discovered what he undoubtedly thought was an *affaire*. He had a nose for scandal and a taste for revenge which he would not be able to resist. Giovanni clenched his fists, but made no move to use them. A part of him was resigned. A part of him thought he deserved his fate. A part of him wished desperately that he could undo the past. Cressie was looking distinctly upset now. She wanted him to speak. She wanted him to explain. But how could he?

Luigi too was eyeing him askance, but he would not give him the satisfaction of showing how he felt. 'You really do surprise me,' he was saying to Cressie. 'That is not the sort of thing one confides in just anyone. Though perhaps you are not *just anyone*. Giovanni's taste in women, like his taste in art, has changed significantly, if that is the case,' he added with a waspish smile. 'Back in the old days, our Gio was really rather more renowned for the beauties he bedded than his paintings. So eager those ladies were, to lend both their faces and their fortunes to help a poor starving artist on his road to success. Though of course, Lady Cressida, you will know all about that particular aspect of our Gio's success too, since he has taken you into his—er—confidence.'

Giovanni's muscles tensed. Finally he spoke, his voice a menacing growl that didn't sound at all like his own. 'I warn you only once, Luigi. You will mind that vicious tongue of yours, or tea party or no tea party I will…'

'You will beat me with your fists for my insolence, the way you used to when we were apprentices.' His eyes alight with malice, Luigi tossed his head disdainfully and turned to Cressie. 'Gio never could endure being teased about his many lady friends.'

'Giovanni has painted many beautiful women, that is no secret,' she responded. Her voice was flat as if she didn't believe her own words. 'I don't know what you are implying, but...'

Luigi laughed, a brittle little sound like the crystals from a chandelier tinkling in a draught. 'He did a lot more than paint them, my dear. How do you think he survived, in those years when he scrabbled about for commissions? I concede he possessed a raw artistic talent, with the emphasis on raw. He did not leap, fully-fledged, from that tragic exhibition to the higher echelons of portraiture in a matter of days. Or even months. But our friend has more than one string to his bow, as you already know, I am sure. This beautiful face, this so very, very attractive body of his, they were quite an asset back in those days when he was struggling in his artistic garret.'

'Stop it!' Cressie pleaded. 'Stop saying those wicked things. You say them only because you are envious of his talent.'

Luigi simpered. 'Oh, I do not deny I am envious, my dear Lady Cressida. Back in the old days, I would go so far as to say that I was even just a tiny bit jealous. I am not short of personal charm myself even now. As a young man—well, I considered myself at least as worthy of Gio's attentions as those ladies, and Gio—'

'Stop!' Cressie reeled as if he had brought her world tumbling down, though Giovanni knew it was rather his own which crumbled. *You deserve better*, he'd said to her. Now she could see that he had been right. He was aware of her drawing Luigi a look of disgust before bestowing upon him something more forlorn. He was aware of Lady Innellan making her way towards them, her son in his ridiculous outfit in tow. He was even aware of the look Sir Timothy bestowed on Luigi di Canio. Not of a friend but that of a lover. He saw Cressie recognise that too. On the way back in the carriage, she would have enjoyed speculating about that look. But now she picked up the skirts of her pelisse and ran for the door.

It was Giovanni's cue. With a vicious snarl, he smashed his clenched fist smack into the middle of Luigi's astonished face.

Cressie had the gig halfway down the carriageway of the Innellans' manor house, sobbing, almost blinded by tears, and tempted to try the unlikely feat of urging the horse into a gallop when Giovanni leapt into the carriage. He looked every bit as devastated as she felt. Cressie steeled herself. She would not allow herself to feel sorry for him. She would not speak. She would not utter a word. The one thing she had not done was give herself away completely, and she absolutely would not do that now!

'Cressie.'

'I don't want to talk about it.'

'*Si*. I understand.'

He lapsed into silence. The air between them had the heaviness of a pending thunderstorm. Cressie focused hard and quite unnecessarily on the road ahead, which the horse took at his usual sedate pace. The hedgerows were still in full blossom. The trees were still luscious green. The bluebells were still blue. Not just blue. Cerulean? Too dark. Cornflower? Not pink enough. Lilac? Teal? Cobalt? 'Oh for goodness' sake, who cares!' she exclaimed.

'I do.'

'I wasn't talking about you,' she snapped.

'Cressie...'

'How could you! How could you, Giovanni? How could you *sell* yourself in such a way. Why, you are nothing short of a *gigolo*!'

He flinched, but did not deny it, which made her feel much worse instead of better. 'The first time you kissed me I remember wondering if seduction was part of your technique. When I got to know you better, I felt guilty for having thought so.' Cressie attempted a derisive snort. It sounded pathetically like a sob.

'I have never kissed you for any other reason than that I could not resist you.'

'Very good, Giovanni, that is excellent. If you would relieve me of the reins I would applaud you. The fact is that you *did* resist me, despite my attempts to throw myself at you.' And the fact was that this was the most mortifying thing. All those women, and Giovanni had made love to them casually, easily and regularly! So many others he had made no effort to resist, yet he had gone out of his way to resist her. 'What is wrong with me?' she demanded, too hurt and too angry to care at how needy she sounded and how pathetically jealous. 'Why not me?'

Once again he flinched. Did he turn paler? It looked as though the blood had drained from his face. But she would not feel sorry for him. And she would not feel sorry for herself either! 'Do you know, I was actually envious when I thought you'd had another female muse,' Cressie continued remorselessly, determined to whip her anger into a fury lest she break down into hysterics. 'What an idiot I am. I didn't realise you'd had hundreds. I didn't realise I was just the latest in a very, very long line. Who will be next, I wonder? Lady Innellan? A little old, perhaps, but she is very wealthy and made her interest in *you* obvious enough. Though perhaps you are more fussy these days, now you are in such high demand.'

'Enough!' Giovanni grabbed the reins and pulled the horse over to the side of the road. A pulse beat at his temple. 'I told you, I have not been with a woman in years. I do not lie, Cressie.'

'But you are obviously very sparing with the truth, Giovanni.'

'*Si*. That is true. But I have never lied to you.'

He dug the heels of his hands into his eyes. His shoulders were hunched. The sound he made was very like a dry sob. Was he crying? It took everything in her to refrain from touching him. She couldn't bear it, to see him so dejected. If only he could explain. Mitigate. Make it not true.

'There were not hundreds, but there were many.'

Giovanni sat up, holding himself rigidly. He had himself under control again. And he was not avoiding her eye. She could see the resolution written in the stark planes of his expression. The stripped look she'd seen on one occasion before today. The look that told the blunt, unvarnished and horrible truth. She didn't want to hear it, but she knew she had to. Cressie gripped her fingers together tightly.

'It is as Luigi implied. I was desperate, not so much for success at first, as simply to prove my father wrong. I would make my art pay. I knew I had the skill, but I needed time and I needed willing subjects and they needed to be...'

'Beautiful.'

'I could not make my name painting anything other than perfection. At least, not the name I wanted to make.'

'I know how it is,' Cressie said dully, 'you don't need to explain.'

'It was easy. Far too easy. This,' Giovanni said, pointing at his face, 'this face, this body made it easy. I knew it was wrong, but to me if felt so much less wrong than forcing myself into the mould my father had created for me. I told myself that at least this way I could use my talent. And I was not wholly lacking in morals. I took only what was offered freely. And I did not take from those...' He swallowed several times. When he spoke again, his voice was low, filled with self-disgust. 'There were men as well as women willing to pay.'

Cressie stared at him in horror. 'You mean they— did Luigi?'

'Once again, I commend your perception. As you saw, he is not someone who takes well to rejection, of any sort. You have to believe me, Cressie,' Giovanni said earnestly, 'I never—not with men, not with any woman who wanted more from me than a few afternoons' pleasure. They paid what was at the time an inflated fee for their portraits. I asked nothing more. But I will not deny it, I sold myself. My performances—for such they were—were polished, skilled, technically brilliant but emotionless. Just like the paintings I produced.'

'And when your portraits began to be in demand, you no longer needed to sell your body, is that it?' Cressie said tightly.

'That is it. I will not pretend that it disgusted me at the time, Cressie. What young man would find taking a beautiful woman to bed a chore? It was only afterwards that I began to find myself repellent. There is a pleasure, a different kind of pleasure, to be had in sacrifice, in cleansing. Until I met you, that too was easy. Since I met you—but what is the point in talking about it? I will not taint you with my sordid past. You…'

'Deserve better,' Cressie finished for him quietly. 'So you said.'

'And meant it.'

Giovanni made to take her hand, but stopped himself. She should have been glad he did so, but it was this simple gesture which nearly broke her. He would always stop himself. And though his revelations were appalling, what was even more appalling was that she still loved him. 'Will Luigi talk?' Cressie asked.

'Not for some time.'

'What do you mean?'

'When I last saw him he was flat out on Lady Innellan's drawing-room rug with a small crowd gathered round him. He seemed to be missing some teeth and there was, I confess, some blood on that ridiculous bow of his.'

Cressie put her hand over her mouth. 'You should not have,' she said, though actually, she could not pretend to be anything other than glad.

Giovanni shrugged. 'You can take the boy from the fishing village, but you cannot take the fishing village from the boy—or so they say. I expect I have created quite a scandal. I am sorry for that.'

'I am sure Lady Innellan will be secretly delighted. Notoriety is the next best thing to popularity. Besides, the incident will be put down to the tempestuous nature of Italian artists. Giovanni, are you sure that Luigi will not make mischief?'

'He has much more to lose than I. His reputation is still relatively new and he knows I could easily ruin him if I chose to reveal some of what I know about his own sordid past. He will also know that if he did so, I would hunt him down like a dog. Not that I care. I am done with living my life this way, Cressie. You are right. I must make my own way on my own terms.'

It was small comfort now, but it would feel more significant in the future. Right now, she was completely drained. It felt as if her bones had been removed. She wanted nothing but to lie underneath her bedclothes in the dark and howl. Resolutely, she picked up the reins.

'There is just one more thing.' Giovanni touched her

arm, snatching his hand back immediately. 'It was different with you. I want you to know that. When I told you I was afraid of the passion between us, I meant it. I was not just afraid that surrendering to it would destroy what inspired me to paint you, I was afraid I would destroy you. I have never before been with a woman who cared for how I felt. When you touch me, it is as if no woman has ever touched me. You always ask me for proof. I can provide none but it is the truth none the less. It was different with you. You will simply have to trust me on that.'

Tears clogged her throat, but she was too raw to do any more than nod and set the horse in motion. 'Thank you for being so honest with me but I can't talk about this any more, Giovanni. I just can't.'

They completed the short journey in silence. Cressie held herself in, gathering tightly together, counting the minutes until she could be alone. The one thing she didn't feel was disgust. Stealing a glance at him, sitting ramrod straight, staring sightlessly ahead, obviously lost inside the morass of his jumbled thoughts and emotions, she knew that the one thing she did feel was love. Despite all, she loved him and was resigned that she always would.

Chapter Ten

'I'm afraid her ladyship requires your presence urgently, Lady Cressida. She is most anxious to speak with you.' Myers's words of greeting were the last thing Cressie wanted to hear as she pulled the gig up at the front door. 'I'll have the carriage taken around to the stables, my lady. Lady Armstrong awaits you in the small salon.'

The image of the sanctuary of her darkened bedchamber which had sustained her during the last few miles of the drive home, vanished in a puff of smoke. What else could go awry on this most inauspicious of days? Cressie jumped down from the gig, brushing away Giovanni's proffered helping hand, and wearily trudged through the reception hall.

Bella was lying prostrate on her favourite *chaise-longue*, her sal volatile in one hand, an ominous-looking missive in the other, but upon Cressie's opening the door, she scrambled to her feet. 'This came by express not long after you left for Lady Innellan's,' she said, waving the letter in the air. 'I wanted Myers to send someone to fetch you straight away, but he managed to convince me it would be futile since it would be too late by the time you returned for you to leave for London tonight. Only if you wait until the morning I fear it will be too late. According to this letter, it is already too late. I told you, Cressida, I told you it was on your head if anything happened, and now—what are we to do? Your father will *kill* me.'

Cressie took the letter, eased Bella back on to the *chaise-longue* and waved the sal volatile under her nose. 'I can think of nothing less likely than my father turning to murder. Do not be ridiculous, Bella, and I pray you please do not work yourself up into hysterics. It cannot be good for the baby, and if something happens to that…'

'There you are wrong. This baby is a girl— your father will not care one way or the other if anything happens to her,' Bella replied tartly, patting her stomach.

Which was probably, sadly, true, Cressie thought abstractedly, dropping into a chair opposite her stepmother. She had already noted that the hand which had written the letter belonged to Aunt Sophia. She was already, following receipt of Cordelia's last missive, prepared for bad news. Her aunt's frantic note confirmed the worst. Cordelia had apparently eloped, though with whom and whence were details conspicuous by their absence. 'I should have known. I suspected all along that Cordelia was leading my aunt and everyone else up the garden path with her wild behaviour,' Cressie explained in answer to Bella's questioning look. 'A ruse to mask a far deeper game, and it seems I was right. Though what my aunt expects you to do about it, I have no idea.'

'Me!' Bella shrieked, dropping the bottle of smelling salts.

'The letter is addressed to you.'

'Cressida Florence Armstrong, you know perfectly well that we agreed…'

'Stop! Bella, please stop. It was an attempt to lighten the mood. A feeble attempt at a joke.'

'Very feeble.'

Cressie rubbed her brow. 'I suppose I must go to London to see what can be done to retrieve the situation.'

'You do not look well, Cressida. Is something amiss?'

'I have a headache.'

'You never get headaches.'

'Bella, it's been a long day, and I'm tired and the very last thing I wish is to go traipsing off on a wild goose chase after Cordelia, who is very likely hiding out somewhere not too far away laughing up her sleeve at the chaos she has caused.'

'How went your visit to Lady Innellan? Did you make the acquaintance of that man you seemed so keen on introducing Signor di Matteo to?'

Cressie winced. 'The only way to describe the tea party is that it was unforgettable.'

'I am not surprised,' Bella said with a hungry look in her eye. 'I had heard a rumour that her ladyship had recently appointed, at great expense, a London cook.'

'I was not referring to the food. There was an altercation between Giovanni and his fellow-Italian art expert over… It does not matter. You will no doubt hear a wildly exaggerated version of events once the servants start talking but for the record, Giovanni was much provoked.'

'I cannot say I am totally shocked. Your father says the Latins, despite their bold claims about being the cradle of civilisation, are the most obstreperous, ill-disciplined and rash nation on earth. He says he would rather deal with a Berber horde than mediate between two Italians with a grievance. He says—'

'Lady Innellan was asking kindly after you,' Cressie interjected, unable to listen to another syllable of her father's guide to diplomacy.

'What was the son like?'

'Let us say that there is absolutely no chance of him being interested in becoming a candidate for my hand.'

'Aye, his tastes do not run in that direction,' Bella said with her sharp little smile. 'I'd heard that too.'

'Did you? Goodness, I had no idea you were so very well informed,' Cressie said tartly. 'It is a pity your contacts cannot give us some clue as to the whereabouts of my sister.' She thumped her forehead with the heel of her hand. 'I beg your pardon, that was quite uncalled for.'

'Are you sure it is a headache you are suffering from? Has that man been taking liberties? I warned you about him, Cressida.'

'You did, and let me assure you again, Bella, that you need have no fears in that direction. None whatsoever.'

Bella pursed her lips, noting the catch in her stepdaughter's voice. 'This trip to London may have come at timely juncture, it seems to me. A little distance will bring some perspective.'

'I suppose I must go.' Cressie got to her feet. Her legs felt like lead. 'I think after all it would be best if I left straight away. The days are getting longer. We may get as much as halfway there before nightfall.'

Bella got to her feet looking remarkably recovered, Cressie thought uncharitably. 'You will take two of the stable boys as outriders as well as the groom. And your maid, of course. Myers will arrange it all. I will call for him forthwith.'

Less than an hour later, Cressie was seated in the Armstrong travelling carriage on her way to the capital. She had not seen or spoken to Giovanni, not even to explain her sudden departure. There had been no time, and it was probably for the best. When she returned, when time and distance had placed some perspective on today's revelations and she had perhaps made a start on the dismantling of her love for him, then she could finish sitting for him, for she was determined that he would complete the portrait. Else all would indeed have been lost.

Giovanni stood in front of the two portraits of Cressie. Thesis and antithesis. The public Cressie and the private. A representative painting and an interpretive one. The former was classically beautiful and highly polished. Lady Cressida, totally lacking in any of Cressie's real character. Mr Brown, Cressie's alter ego, on the other hand, was a rougher piece of work all together. This version of Cressie had her fierce intelligence, her impish sense of humour and a hint of her sensuality. This version was subversive, an image intended to unsettle the viewer, but looking at it now, it still did not seem to be exactly the Cressie that Giovanni had wished to depict.

There was something missing. Or lacking. An authority, a certainty. Art as truth, that's what he wanted to paint, but this did not represent the whole truth. This was a painting which spoke as he had—in half-truths, to disguise the reality. Truth was not one but two-sided. It showed not just the truth of the sitter but the truth of the painter. The emotion which was missing was not Cressie's but his. There was no avoiding it. Giovanni dropped on to the bare boards in front of the portraits and groaned, slumping back against the wall and banging his head heavily in the process. If he could bang it a little harder and achieve blessed oblivion, then he would be happy.

He cursed inwardly. Who was he trying to fool! He would never be happy. Not with his work, not with his life. Something was missing. Lacking. And the source of that void was the same as the missing element in the portrait. Cressie.

Giovanni swore again, this time in the guttural dialect of the fishermen among whom he had been raised. He was in love with Cressie. That was the truth lacking in the Mr Brown portrait. He had not acknowledged his love for her and it showed in the work. The empty space in his heart which he had become accustomed to think would never be filled was now overflowing. He was in love with her. Cressie had taken up residence there.

Giovanni pulled his drawing board towards him

and began to sketch quickly. The forms took shape almost unbidden. Cressie laughing. Cressie furiously biting back the tears. Cressie beaming with pride at some minor accomplishment of her brothers. Cressie frowning over one of her mathematical tomes. Cressie, eyes closed, head thrown back, back arched in ecstasy as she climaxed under his touch. He wanted to paint all of those Cressies, a portrait of a woman with every one of the elements which made her so essentially her, the woman he loved and whom he had lost irretrievably, thanks to the many he had not loved who had gone before her.

If he could only reclaim his innocence. If he could only undo the past. As his hand raced over another blank sheet of paper, he remembered something she had said to him. Something about the past being the thing which made her herself. All of it, she'd said, describing some trivial incident which she'd only just remembered—*if I undid any of it I would be a different person.*

Would he undo his past if he could? Giovanni's hand stilled. He remembered a summer morning, a sea the colour of Cressie's eyes. He was four, perhaps five years old. He remembered the fish, a large coral-pink snapper, far too heavy for his line. He remembered being determined to haul it into the boat without his papa's help. He stood up to heft the line and fell head first into the sea. He remembered the water closing over his head, and then a pair of arms around him, the feeling of safety, of sanctuary. Papa. The swimming lessons began the next day. He remembered Mama smiling with pride the day she watched him swim from the boat to the shore for the first time, with Papa by his side, under solemn oath not to help him.

It was a cliché, but it was also true. Like a floodgate opening, the memories tumbled their way into his mind, bright with primary colours, warm as the heat of the Tuscan sun, silly things long forgotten. He *had* been happy. He *had* been loved. It was because it had been so that it had hurt so much, the forced separation. Might it have been because it would have been too painful for them that they had severed contact with him so brutally, his adopted parents? Too late now to discover that truth. That memory was in sepia, of his return to the village by the sea, the year he left Italy for good. They were both dead. Papa's boat lost in a storm. Mama lost to a cancer left too long untreated.

He had run out of drawing paper. The light was fading when there was a cautious tap at the door. Giovanni jumped to his feet, trying to smooth down his hair with his hand. Cressie. He reminded himself that it was hopeless, but still he hoped. Foolish, foolish, foolish, he told himself as he turned the drawing board with its revealing sketches to the wall. She must not see those. They said something she must never hear. She had most likely come to tell him she would not sit for him again. It would be like her, not to leave things unfinished between them. Cressie liked her facts straight and ordered. But still, as he hurried over to the door and turned the key in the lock, Giovanni's heart gave a strange little leap.

'Harry told me I'd find you up here.' Bella's face was flushed with effort. 'I need to talk to you, Signor di Matteo.'

* * *

Bella swept past him and into the room, stopping dead in her tracks in front of the two portraits. Her face, as she stared at first one and then the other in a bizarre reflection of the stance Giovanni himself had taken a few hours before, was comical in its variety of expressions. 'Does my husband know about this? I cannot believe that he actually commissioned these—these images of his daughter.'

'No commission. I have been painting them for my own pleasure and entertainment.'

Bella nodded. 'I am sure you have derived much pleasure from painting them, Signor di Matteo. What is the meaning of this one, if you please?' she asked, pointing to the unfinished portrait.

She knew nothing of Mr Brown, of course, and Giovanni was not about to enlighten her. He shrugged. 'I thought it would be amusing, to depict Cressie—Lady Cressida—dressed as a man. Given her interest in mathematics,' he added disingenuously.

'A semi-naked man, in point of fact. I would like to hope that at least some elements of this portrait stem from your vivid imagination and are not representative of reality, *signor*.'

'As you say, Lady Armstrong. I have taken some artistic liberties.' One of those half-truths at which Cressie said he was too adept, but in this case he could see no alternative.

It seemed to have the desired effect. Bella pursed her mouth but did not challenge him. 'What do you intend to do with these canvases? The first, I will grant you, is a very pretty piece. I am sure Lord Armstrong would be happy to find a space for it with the family collection, were you to present it to him. But the other—there is something lascivious about it. Real or imagined, I cannot permit you to expose my stepdaughter to public ridicule.'

He had never intended to exhibit it, had never intended to show it to anyone, no matter what Cressie said, but Giovanni was not inclined to have Lady Armstrong dictate to him. 'That is Lady Cressida's decision,' he said stiffly. 'I painted it for her. The painting is hers to do with as she wishes. I will let her decide.'

'That may be problematic.'

'Indeed. Why so?'

'Because she has gone.'

'Gone?' Giovanni repeated stupidly.

'To London. She was summoned there on urgent family business.'

Cressie was gone. She had left without telling him. She could not have made her feelings clearer. 'By family business you mean Lady Cordelia, I assume,' Giovanni said dully.

Lady Armstrong narrowed her eyes. 'What, may I ask, do you know of it?'

'What? Nothing, save that Cressie—Lady Cressida was concerned her sister would act rashly.'

'It is a pity, then, that Cressida did not choose to act more pre-emptively herself, and thus spare us a very embarrassing situation. Your discretion, *signor*, I assume I can count on it?'

'In every respect, my lady.'

'Which brings me to the point of my expedition all the way up here, Signor di Matteo. Cressida will be detained in London for at least a week. It looks to my untutored eye as if my sons' portrait is nearing completion. You will oblige me by making every effort to finish it before she returns.'

'You wish me gone?'

Lady Armstrong tittered. 'You Italians, why must you be so dramatic. I have no wish to cast you from my door, I merely desire you to complete your commission as quickly as possible.'

'Before Cressie returns.'

Her ladyship smiled at this slip. 'Indeed,' she said, 'before *Cressie* returns.' Her smile faded as she made her way across the attic to the doorway. 'Let us call a spade a spade, *signor*. Despite what she may claim, Cressida is no woman of the world. I, on the other hand, am precisely that. I strongly suspect you have been taking liberties. Indeed, anyone would, who saw these paintings. And one merely has to see the way that Cressida looks at you, hear the way she speaks your name, to know that she is setting herself up for a fall. I am not her mother, but nor am I the wicked stepmother she and her sisters labelled me. I would not like to see Cressida hurt any more than she has been already, Signor di Matteo, and if you remain here then that is almost certainly what will happen. Do we understand each other?'

'Well enough, Lady Armstrong.' The whole truth this time. Giovanni nodded curtly. 'If it is any consolation, hurting Cressie is the last thing in the world I would wish to do.'

'It is no consolation, *signor*, for the deed is already partly done.'

Without giving him time to respond, Bella swept from the room as suddenly as she had entered it. Sick at heart, overwhelmed by the cascade of harsh truths which had flowed his way today, Giovanni lit two oil lamps and arranged them on the table by his easels. Removing the completed canvas from one, he replaced it with his drawing board and studied his sketches of Cressie. Later, he would stretch a new canvas. Tomorrow he would begin the third painting. If he worked at it day and night, he could complete it and be gone before she returned. A triptych—Lady Cressida, Mr Brown and Cressie. 'Three Aspects of Lady Cressida,' he would title it. An arc that encapsulated her. He was so inspired by the concept he had to force himself not to start painting straight away.

In the days which followed, night blurred into morning and into night again. Giovanni worked furiously. The portrait of the Armstrong boys required only the final touches and the glaze. The boys were subdued in Cressie's absence. He took them out each afternoon, to fish and to climb trees and to fly their kites—for they had each one of their own now.

There were moments, usually in the smallest hours, when he stood before the third part of his triptych, his eyes gritty with the oil light and lack of sleep, when he asked himself if it would not be possible for them to forge a future together. As the painting took shape, all the arguments against this possibility solidified. He took to reciting them in an effort to dispel the most foolish of hopes before it could take a grip of him and torture him.

Though he had from the first been at pains to help her free herself from her father's tyranny, Giovanni was not so cruel as to wish Cressie to become estranged from her family. Despite all, she loved her father, and though it was a love that would likely grow stronger the more distance she put between herself and Lord Armstrong, he had no doubt that the diplomat would make every effort to ensure that she suffered if she went so spectacularly against his wishes by taking up with Giovanni. He would be apoplectic, and would undoubtedly extract revenge. He could probably not tear the sisters asunder, but he could make sure that Cressie never saw her brothers again, nor her home, nor indeed the mysterious Aunt Sophia whom Cressie seemed so fond of.

Giovanni's past lovers and his abuse of his own body, he saw as such an obvious barrier as to be barely worth mentioning. The look of disgust on Cressie's face when she called him a gigolo was something he would never forget. He would not inflict such a man upon her.

As if this was not enough, there was the simple fact that she was not actually in love with him. She was not the type to become infatuated, but she did not talk like a woman in love. She talked, on the contrary, like a woman with very clear ideas about deciding her own fate. *I've finally found my calling*, she had said to him. She was excited about the future—she must be, for she talked about it all the time. Her future lay in a far-off land where she could be with her two dearest sisters. She had no thought of making a place for him. She didn't love him. How could she?

The third painting was almost complete. It was like nothing he had created before, the brush strokes wild and instinctive. In places he had resorted to using a palette knife to apply the pigment directly to the canvas. The lines of the figure blurred and seeped into each other as did the colours. The background was almost organic, a part of the subject rather than an accessory. Nothing about it was clearly defined. Yet as Giovanni looked at it in the grey light of dawn, he knew finally he had created something true, something from the heart. This was how he would paint in future, and damn what anyone else thought of it. Cressie, his muse, his heart's desire, had given him back his calling. That was her parting gift to him. This painting would be his to her.

Giovanni lined up the three portraits to form the triptych, Cressie in the middle, flanked by Lady Cressida and Mr Brown on either side. Who knew, he might in time become a true artist and not a mere painter. Here was the map of his progress. Here, in the centre, was the pinnacle of his art to date, the foundation for his future.

You are letting him win. Giovanni caught himself looking over his shoulder at the door, then gave himself a shake. Too many sleepless nights. Cressie was not here, only her words whispering like ghosts in his head. He had spent the last ten years painting the kind of work whose success he thought his father would admire to prove him wrong. But as Cressie had so rightly pointed out, by doing so he was allowing his father to control his actions even now. Ever since he had been lifted from his life with Papa and Mama, he had been fighting Count Fancini in one way or another. He had not seen his father for fourteen years, but still he knew the count was waiting, patiently—or more likely impatiently—waiting. Giovanni's failure to confront the man had prolonged that game, allowed the illusion that he might return to be maintained. Perhaps even given his father hope.

To make a fresh start, he must lay his demons to rest. It seemed so obvious. He would cancel all his commissions and return to Italy *pronto*. Giovanni put down his palette and pulled a large cloth over all three paintings: Lady Cressida, the last of a kind; Cressie, the first of a kind; and Mr Brown, the pivot. Making his way down to the scullery to clean his tools, he could not pretend that leaving without seeing her again filled him with anything other than misery. He loved her, would always love her, and would never love another woman. But she had given him the gift of his art. He would not repay her generosity by abusing it again. And that required an audience with Count Fancini.

'I fear there is nothing more to be done, Aunt Sophia.' Cressie sat carefully down on the chair beside her aunt's day bed, for the skirts of her new gown were much fuller than she was accustomed to wearing. It had been delivered by the modiste this morning, and she had been unable to resist trying it on. Cream silk striped with the shade of dusky pink Giovanni most admired her in, the dress had puff sleeves with long under-sleeves in soft pink wool. The neckline was trimmed with pink velvet, as were the three flounces which formed the hemline, and though the dress hung straight at the front from her waist, at the back it was pleated and swung out behind her when she walked. She was pretty certain that Giovanni would like this effect, for it emphasised the curve of her bottom—something she had ascertained after much squinting over her shoulder and contorting in front of the mirror.

'Henry will have to be informed.' Aunt Sophia spoke in a pale imitation of her usual stentorian voice. Cressie had been dismayed to discover her so frail-looking. If they ever did recover Cordelia, along with her reputation, it was inconceivable that Aunt Sophia could continue to act the chaperon. Like it or not, Cordelia would have to cut short her Season and return to Killellan until next year, when Bella would be well enough to bring her out herself.

Cressie pressed her aunt's hand, the skin dry and papery. 'I shall write to my father myself, Aunt, do not fret.'

'If we could but find a clue. It is the not knowing that is the worst. For all we are aware, Cordelia may be dead.'

Cressie chuckled. 'Now I know that you must be much more seriously ill than you appear, Aunt Sophia, for that is the most ridiculous thing I've ever heard you say. If Cordelia were dead, her body would have been discovered.'

'Not if she were at the bottom of a cliff. Or tied up in an attic. Or…'

'What about bricked in behind a fireplace? You sound just like Cassie.'

'I most certainly do not.' Lady Sophia struggled upright. 'Did I tell you that I saw that poet of hers recently? Augustus St John Marne, that was his name. Didn't speak to the man, of course. Quite down in the mouth he looked too, wandering in the wake of that carrot-haired wife of his and a clutch of brawling brats.'

'Thus are the mighty fallen,' Cressie said. 'Cassie had a lucky escape.'

'You may not remember, but he more or less abandoned her at the altar. She had not the sense to realise—but she was ever a flighty piece. I fear Cordelia is another such. Have you really been unable to find any trace of her at all?'

'She took a hackney carriage when she left Cavendish Square, but she took care not to let her direction be overheard. I don't know how many hacks there are in London, but short of interviewing every single driver—it would take months, and goodness knows how much in bribes, by which time I am very sure Cordelia will have informed us herself of her fate, one way or another.'

'You do not hope this will turn out well for her, Cressida?'

'No, I don't, Aunt,' Cressie said gently, 'and I think you are far too sensible to rely on hope either.'

'No, I do not. I am feeble of body but not yet of mind,' Aunt Sophia said with a glimmer of her customary wit. 'You should return to Killellan, Cressida. It has been more than a week—Bella will have need of you. There is nothing more we can do until your sister shows her hand.'

'I am more concerned about my brothers' lessons. I suspect they will be making hay in my absence,' Cressie replied, forcing a smile.

Her aunt drew her a piercing look. 'You do not fool me, Niece. Something is amiss with you. You are quite—changed. Were it anyone else, I would say there was a man behind it, but in your case—what is it, Cressida?'

'Nothing.' Cressie caught herself just before she began to pick at her thumb.

'Rubbish. You think because I am sick and abed that I need to be mollycoddled, but I know there is something wrong, and I am sure I can help. Is it Bella?'

'No.' Cressie opened her mouth to deny once more that anything was amiss and faltered under her aunt's gimlet stare. 'It is nothing for you to worry about. Trust me,' she said, borrowing Giovanni's words.

Aunt Sophia did her the honour of heeding her wishes, though her parting words were to reassure her of her support should Cressida require counsel. Sitting in the carriage a few hours later, dressed in a comfortable travelling gown with her new purchases safe in her portmanteau, Cressie heaved a sigh of relief at having to no longer put up a front, and gave herself over to her anxieties.

She missed Giovanni terribly. She had not thought herself lonely when he came into her life, for she had Cordelia. But Cordelia, she now realised, was as self-contained in her own way as Cressie. Six years between them, and Cressie having assumed the position of elder sister when Cassie married, meant that there would always be a distance between them. And besides, Cordelia had never understood her quite as Giovanni did. No one had.

'He sees me as no other does,' she recalled Celia saying of her husband. Cressie hadn't understood that until now. 'And I see him in the same way,' Celia had added. That hateful little man Luigi di Canio had forced Giovanni to strip himself bare. The revelations had been so shocking that Cressie had for the first few days when she arrived in London been unable to think beyond the hurt they caused. That he could have so carelessly given himself to those other women. *Sold* himself. The very thought of it made her shudder. Shamefully, shudder not so much with disgust, as with simple jealousy, for he had given them so easily what she had never had from him.

It was a conversation with Aunt Sophia, a discussion of all the prospects which Cordelia seemed to have thrown away with her mysterious elopement, which had given Cressie pause for thought. Was not her own father in the business of selling his daughters, trading their bodies and their bloodline in order to achieve what he wanted, what Cressie called his dynastic web? For Lord Armstrong, his daughters were a means to an end. Truly, was this so very different? Or perhaps even worse, for at least Giovanni sold his own flesh and blood to his own advantage, not someone else's.

It amused her to imagine having that conversation with her father. Cressie smiled bitterly out of the window of the coach as the countryside flashed by. Was she so desperate to persuade herself that she could accept Giovanni's past, that she was resorting to sophistry? That was what Lord Armstrong would accuse her of.

Sophistry or not, what mattered was whether she could come to terms with those other women in Giovanni's past. Asking herself this question made Cressie realise she had already decided that she wanted to. Which raised the question of what Giovanni wanted. She had no idea how he really felt about her, and had given him no chance to tell her after Luigi di Canio had put his vicious spoke in the works. Loathsome man. She was glad Giovanni had punched him. She would like to punch him herself. Better yet, lock him in a room with the worst possible art she could find and force him to look at it every day until he begged for mercy.

Through the window of the coach, the countryside was becoming familiar. 'Not far to Killellan now, my lady. No more than an hour,' her maid said.

Cressie nodded distractedly. An hour, not much more, and she would see Giovanni again. She would tell him— no, not that she forgave him, it was not her right to forgive. Actually, now she came to think about it, it was Giovanni who was far more disgusted than she by his past. Sordid, he'd called it. He hated his body, the instrument of pleasure he had sold. It was different with her. He'd said that too, but she had been so angry and so hurt. *It was different with you. I want you to know that.* He thought he was so tainted he would destroy her, but had he not also implied that she could remake him?

When you touch me, it is as if no woman has ever touched me. Cressie shivered. He had not once mentioned Giles, never reproached her for her lack of innocence. That too had not occurred to her until now. It was not the same, but it was not so very different, her giving herself in return for a name, a position, for the sake of her father's approbation. When she had confessed this truth of her past, Giovanni had been angry, not *at* her but *for* her. He had not judged her. He had made her see that she must stop judging herself. It was not the same, but it really was not so very different at all.

When you touch me, it is as if no woman has ever touched me. Yes, that too was the same. He made her feel as if he were the first. Was it too fanciful to imagine that they could start anew? If he loved her as she loved him, she had no doubt they could. But did he? As the coach trundled up the carriageway to Killellan Manor, Cressie allowed herself to hope. Not for the conventional happy ending of orange blossom and blessings. She had no interest in either. But for something new, something which she and Giovanni could create together. And the first step was to see him, talk to him, tell him.

She sprang out of the carriage before the footman had a chance to let the steps down, and was in the reception hall struggling with the ties of her bonnet when Bella opened the door of her salon. 'No news,' Cressie told her stepmother hurriedly. 'No trace of Cordelia. I will write to my father tonight, but first I must—forgive me, but I must see Giovanni. Do you know where he is?'

It was the expression on Bella's face rather than her words which stopped Cressie in her tracks. Pity. 'Gone?' she repeated, trying to take in the meaning of the word. 'Gone where?'

'Italy, apparently,' Bella told her.

One's hopes being utterly dashed was actually akin to being flayed alive, Cressie discovered as she dropped her bonnet on to the marbled floor. She felt like a child, opening the wrong present on her birthday. Or no present. Or—for God's sake, what difference did it make how she felt! Cressie ran up the stairs at full tilt, hurled herself into her bedchamber, locked the door behind her and howled like a baby in an agony of pain and frustration.

She did not discover the portraits until the next day. Bella it was who told her to look in the attic. 'He left them for you.'

'You've seen them?'

'What were you thinking, Cressida? I cannot believe you allowed things to go so far.'

'Things did not go far enough, as far as I am concerned,' Cressie replied, too worn out and depressed to prevaricate. 'I love him, Bella. I love him.'

If she was in search of comfort, she was to be disappointed. 'More fool you,' her stepmother replied. 'Did I not warn you about such men?'

'You said he was heartless, but he is not.'

'Did he compromise you, Cressie? Because if you are with child, I can help. I believe there might be a way—are you with child? All those headaches you have been complaining of lately, I was thinking that was a sign that you might be—are you?'

Confused by the change, the strange note—was it eagerness?—in Bella's voice, Cressie did not answer directly. Bella had lost more weight since she last saw her, she noted. In fact, the amount of weight she seemed to have lost these last few weeks was quite dramatic. The voluminous flowing gown she wore made it difficult to tell, but if she did not know for certain that Bella was increasing she might think… *Did* she know for certain? 'When you first told my father about your pregnancy, he said Sir Gilbert Mountjoy had examined you,' Cressie said.

'That man!' Bella waved a dismissive hand. 'I told him about my sickness. He told me to rest.'

'So he didn't actually examine you?'

Bella was beginning to look uncomfortable. 'There was no need.'

'Are you really expecting, Bella? Is there a child?''

Her stepmother took a faltering pace backwards, clutching at her stomach protectively. 'If it is your father you are worried about, you need not,' she said. 'He won't be back for many months. By the time he next deigns to pay us a visit, you would have already given your baby over to me. It's bound to be a girl. Both Cassie and Celia had girls first. Henry would never know the difference.'

'Bella, what on earth are you talking about?'

'I saw the paintings, all three of them. After he'd gone, I went up to the attic to take a look. There is no way he could have painted you like that unless you had—but it doesn't matter.' Bella stretched out a pleading hand. 'It doesn't matter, Cressie. I will take your baby. Your little girl. I'll take her as my own and I'll never tell, I promise you.'

'Bella, I'm not with child,' Cressie said gently, 'and I don't think you are either, are you?'

A large tear rolled down Bella's cheek. 'I thought I was, I truly did. All the signs were there. My courses stopped. Then there was the sickness, all the time the sickness. And my stomach swelled. And my breasts. And you saw my feet, Cressie.'

'I did.' Cressie put her arm around Bella's waist and steered her towards the *chaise-longue*. 'I did see.'

'I wasn't lying.'

'No. No, of course you were not.'

'Only it all stopped. And then my courses started. And I feel so empty. So very empty. But she was never there, my little girl. Janey said—she said that I—she said that sometimes when a woman wants something too much, that she can imagine it is true. I couldn't contemplate telling your father the truth—you can imagine his reaction—so I just sort of carried on pretending and hoping, not knowing what else to do.' Tears trickled down Bella's rouged cheeks.

'Please don't cry, we are all of us capable of deluding ourselves by wanting something too much,' Cressie replied gently, thinking of the clearly misplaced hopes and plans she had concocted in the carriage, remembering with fresh pain that Giovanni was gone. Gone!

'I thought if you had been so foolish as to allow that man—are you sure, Cressie?'

'Bella, I wish I had been so foolish. Truthfully, I would gladly have been so foolish if he had allowed me. But it was Giovanni, not I, who would not—not—he would not.'

'Oh.' Bella's fingers tightened around Cressie's. 'I know it's a terrible thing to say but I confess I wish he had.'

Cressie laughed, a bereft little sound. 'Not as much as I wish it.'

She handed her stepmother over to the tender ministrations of Janey, eventually. The nursemaid took her aside to apologise. 'I wanted to say something, my lady, but I did not quite know *what* to say.' Telling her not to worry, Cressie asked Janey to take good care of Bella, and made her guilty escape.

Three paintings. Bella had said three paintings. She eased open the door of the attic, holding the oil lamp high, for it was past dusk. No easels. No palette. No brushes. Only the smell of linseed oil and turpentine hung faintly in the air. Giovanni was not there. Of course he was not, but it took her a moment to stop looking for him.

The paintings stood in a row along the *chaise-longue* by the window. True enough, there were three canvases. *Lady Cressida*, the printed label by the left-hand painting said. *Mr Brown*, read the label on the right-hand portrait. The finished painting had a wittiness to it she had not noticed while it was a work in progress. It made her smile, and it set her off balance ever so slightly. So many contrasts, the portrait asked far more questions than it answered. How could she have been so pompous as to think she knew anything about art? Her stupid theory, so logical and so precise, explained nothing about how real art played on the emotions.

Turning to the middle portrait, her visceral reaction

felt like a punch to the stomach. *Cressie*, said the label. Just Cressie. Stretched quite naked, gloriously and provocatively naked, across the canvas, her arms over her head, making no attempt to hid her breasts, her sex. Her smile was all the more wicked for its being shameless. *Cressie.* Simply Cressie, revealed and naked. This was how Giovanni saw her, defying every rule, and innately beautiful in a way she could not explain but did not need to. The truth. The unadorned truth. And it was beautiful, *she* was beautiful.

She understood finally, staring at herself as she had never seen herself before, but with a recognition that was incontrovertible. Giovanni's art showed the truth about her, the sitter, and about himself too, the painter. He could not have been clearer if he had written it in bold capitals. This, Giovanni was saying, is the woman I love.

Chapter Eleven

Firenze was as beautiful as he had remembered. Giovanni walked along the banks of the Arno as the setting sun cast a warm glow on the soft stone of the impressive buildings on the river bank opposite, light and architecture combining to dazzling effect. The jewellery shops lining the Ponte Vecchio were closed for the evening, but the sun's dying rays caressed the old stone, mellowing it from ochre to burnt umber. The reflection of the arches on the water was so crystal clear it could be another bridge, upside down and quietly drowning. It was a melancholy thought, but he shook it off. He had no intention of quietly drowning, not any more. He had come here, to Florence, to ensure just that.

He had tried to paint this scene many times, but his work had always lacked lustre. Beautiful as the city was, he was never going to be a landscape artist. It was people who interested him, not places. And at this moment, as his feet found their way of their own accord to the Palazzo Fancini, one person in particular.

The palace, built by the Fancini family during the

Renaissance, was modelled on the palazzo built by the
notorious Medicis. Roman in style, it was classically
proportioned, presenting a stuccoed frontage to the
street, facing on to beautiful gardens to the rear. The
servant who opened the vast oak door to him was unfamiliar. The ring of Giovanni's footsteps on the cloistered
inner courtyard as he made his way to the count's private apartment was, on the other hand, only too familiar.
He could hear the echoes of his boyhood self playing
alone here. He could see the ghost of his adolescent self
too, sheltering from the heat of the summer sun with
his drawing board perched on his knee, his concentration almost comic in its intensity.

Count Fancini's rooms opened out one from the other,
presenting a series of salons of increasing grandeur.
In the old days, the count had told him, the status of a
visitor was easily demarcated by the progress he made
through the various echelons towards the inner sanctum.
In the old days. Giovanni's father was wont to speak as
if he himself had lived through the Renaissance, had
had the ear of the Medicis, had wielded influence and
the power of life and death. Which he did, which he
had, over his son, until the day Giovanni had left the
palazzo for ever.

No, that was a lie. Count Fancini's grip had remained
tight around his son for all the years he had thought that
he was free. Cressie had been right about that. Today
that state of affairs would end.

As the servant threw open the last of the double
doors, the ones leading into the grandest of the salons
where the ceilings were embossed with gold leaf and the

tapestries which covered the vast space of the walls had been embroidered many centuries ago, Giovanni halted in his tracks. Memories assaulted him, brutal in their clarity. Beatings and tears, then as he grew older and his resentment and stubbornness grew, beatings stoically endured dry-eyed. Punishment and reward was his father's credo. He had tried. Despite the resounding sorrow of his forced separation from Papa and Mama, Giovanni had tried to please his father. But nothing he did had ever been good enough for the count, and there is nothing like repeatedly telling a boy he is a failure to make a rebel of him.

The servant coughed politely. Giovanni stepped into the salon. Count Fancini was seated at the far end by the window which overlooked the gardens. He did not rise, but as he approached, Giovanni saw that this was due to infirmity rather than lack of inclination. The old man sat in a wheeled chair.

'Conte.' Giovanni bent over his father's hand. It was liver-spotted, the veins knotted through the translucent skin.

'Mio figlio. So, you come at the last. They told you I was dying, I suppose.'

'No, padre.' Though it would have been obvious to even a casual observer. Giovanni took the seat opposite his father. The count had always been a robust man, as tall as Giovanni but much more heavily built. The old man before him had the gaunt, wizened look of one close to death. He could not feel anger towards a man so tragically reduced. All the things he wished to say, the recriminations and accusations, all fled from his

thoughts. What was the point? It had happened. It was part of him. It was over. Giovanni took his father's hand. 'I came to say goodbye, *padre*,' he said gently. 'Not because you are dying, but because I must live.'

There was to be no tender death-bed reconciliation. The count was too stubborn and too accustomed to having his own way for that. There could never be love between them, nor even affection, but a mutual parting was finally, reluctantly, agreed. The papers which would free Giovanni from his heritage would be drawn up the next day. The count refused to discuss who would inherit now that Giovanni had confirmed he would not. With an echo of his old self, he cackled derisively when his son suggested the establishment of a suitably worthy charity might be an appropriate solution. 'Bribe my way into the Almighty's good books, you mean? It is a little late for that I think.' Giovanni resigned himself to ignorance. His father was stubborn but not a fool. He had had fourteen years to form an alternative plan for the continuation of his name.

'So, you will return to England?' the count asked as he rose to take his departure.

'I have no fixed plans.'

'I heard that you were much in demand. Do you not have a list of anxious clients awaiting you?'

Giovanni shook his head. 'I have no fixed plans,' he repeated. He was mid-bow when Count Fancini made the astonishing request. 'You want me to take your likeness?' he repeated in disbelief.

'A parting gift,' the old man said with a toothless smile, 'I do not want to be remembered like this. Do you think you can make of this withered visage a thing of beauty?'

Giovanni laughed. 'Still, you doubt me. I shall prove you wrong.'

'Do not expect to be paid. It is a father's last request of his errant son.'

'Then I shall honour it. And in doing so perhaps I might finally please you.'

But Giovanni never did get the opportunity to find out if he had, for the count died before the portrait was completed, and in any case, it was a painting done to please himself. This canvas had all the truth of the one he had left for Cressie. An old man, once powerful now fallen, admired but bereft.

One gift the count granted him. Not his final words, but his last words to Giovanni. 'It was a lie that those fisher-folk washed their hands of you,' he told his son. 'They wrote many times begging to visit, to see you just once more. I forced them to write, saying that they wanted you to cease communication.'

'Bastardo!'

Count Fancini laughed. 'Look at you. When I see you like that, I know you are indeed my son. Unclench those fists, boy, you can do nothing to hurt me now. I am already dead.'

'But my letters? I wrote to them…'

'Every week. And every week, I had them burned.'

'Knowing you, I should have guessed.'

Count Fancini's smile was as vicious as Giovanni remembered it. 'You were always too trusting.' His smile faded, his mouth settling into its usual sneer. 'You never took my name,' he said. 'Di Matteo. The name of those commoners. That is how you are known, not Fancini.'

'I did not think you would wish such a venerable name as yours associated with such a menial trade as mine.'

'I did not think you would make such a success of it.'

Did the count really think him a success? Giovanni had framed the question when he saw the look in his father's eye. His silence denied the count a last opportunity to deride his profession. Whatever were the old man's true thoughts on the subject, he took them to the grave. When next Giovanni returned to the palazzo, his father was unconscious.

He took the unfinished canvas back to his lodgings and completed it there. He attended the funeral, keeping a discreet distance from the other mourners as the count's body was interred in the magnificent family crypt. Taking his customary evening stroll along the banks of the Arno at the end of that momentous day, idly speculating about the path his future might follow, Giovanni realised with a start that for the first time in his life he was truly free. Free of his past. Not exactly washed free of his sins, but cleansed all the same. He had done what he had done. He had been wrong. He had paid a heavy price. Now he was free to choose his future. And he could not contemplate any future which did not involve Cressie.

Cressie, who deserved better than he, but whom, he also realised with a blinding flash as bright as the sun's rays on the stained glass of Brunelleschi's Duomo, he had not actually allowed to choose for herself. He had decided for her by leaving. He had nobly decided he would not inflict himself on her, but what if he was wrong? He had not asked her. *Dio*, what if he was mistaken?

He ran through the narrow streets of Firenze towards his lodgings. He must pack. He must return to England. *Pronto*. He ran as if his very life depended on it. Which in fact it did.

The late afternoon sun cast its golden rays through the dormer windows of the attic, a dimple in one of the glass panes sending shards of light shimmering on to Cressie's dress. In the weeks since Giovanni had left Killellan, summer had arrived, Bella had continued to grow thinner, Cordelia had remained incommunicado save for a brief note to reassure her sister that she was quite well, and Cressie had tried very hard not to pine. Giovanni was gone. At times she was angry at him, but most often she simply felt regret. He loved her. She had only to look at the *Cressie* portrait to see that but loving her and wanting to be with her were two different things. He had been gone months, without a word. Being in love did not necessarily mean being together. It was a tragedy, but she had to accept it for reality. She had her proof in his silence. She was, after all, a mathematician.

Looking up at the wall above her writing desk where the drafts for her soon-to-be-published geometry primer lay waiting to undergo final corrections, for her practical experience had paid its dividends in persuading Mr Freyworth to publish, Cressie studied the framed triptych.

She had been tempted to have them hung in the portrait gallery, but not even the anticipated horror on her father's face, if he ever returned from Russia, could persuade her to make them public. If Giovanni had wished them to be seen by anyone other than her, he would have taken them with him, or told her so. This, rather than embarrassment, was why she had decided after much thought not to submit them to the Royal Academy on his behalf. The portraits told their story, hers and Giovanni's. So she had hung them here in the studio where they had been painted, where their story had been played out, and claimed the attic for her study. She had thrown herself into her work, for there was nothing else for it.

The boys' new governess had taken up her position last week. Cressie had insisted that Freddie, George, James and Harry have a say in the selection process, and her brothers had taken to Miss Langton, who had five brothers of her own, immediately. She was teaching them from Cressie's newest primer. The publishing firm, which would print the first, was already clamouring for the second. It seemed that Cressie had hit upon quite a gap in the market for school books. Lord Armstrong knew of none of these developments. He would return expecting a new son, to find instead a new governess, two departed daughters and most likely a newly independent wife. Almost, she wished she could be here to see it. Almost.

Cressie pushed her chair back and roamed restlessly over to the window. The arrangements for her visit to Celia were also in train. Her eldest sister made no promises, but she was encouraging. And touchingly, lovingly eager to be reunited with Cressie.

The crunch of gravel through the open window alerted her to the arrival of a carriage. Most likely Lady Innellan, who had become quite a bosom-bow of Bella's. Looking out, she saw not the Innellan barouche, but a travelling coach. The door of the coach was thrown open and a familiar long, trousered leg appeared. The occupant leapt to the ground without waiting for the step to be lowered. Cressie felt faint. The blood thrummed in her head. It couldn't be, it simply couldn't, could it?

He was tanned. His hair had grown. Abandoning what little decorum she possessed, Cressie leaned precariously out of the dormer window and cried out to him.

'Giovanni!'

He looked around in confusion.

'Gi-o-vann-i!'

He looked up. He smiled, that particular smile he saved for her. And then he ran across the carriageway, up the steps and into the house.

She met him at the door to the attic and threw herself at him. He didn't hesitate, he didn't recoil or make the least show of resistance. He swept her up into his arms, carrying her over the threshold of the attic as if she were a bride. He had not shaved. His chin was blueblack with stubble. He looked tired, but also different somehow. She couldn't put a name to it. She stopped trying when he set her down and pulled her tight against him, and kissed her.

'Cressie.' He kissed her again. 'Cressie, Cressie, Cressie.'

He kissed her again. His stubble grazed her skin. His lips were soft on hers, his mouth warm. She stood on her tiptoes to twine her arms around his neck. He smelt of dust and travel. Of the lemon soap he always used. Of sweat a little and of Giovanni a lot. She closed her eyes and breathed him in, saying his name.

He was kissing her forehead now, her eyelids, her brows, her cheeks. He was kissing her ear, pushing her rebellious hair back to nibble on her lobe. She wanted to climb inside him, wrap him around her, make of them one skin which could never be separated again. 'I missed you,' she said, almost laughing at the inadequacy of the words. 'You never sent word, and I missed you terribly.'

'Cressie, I have so much to tell you, so much I need to say.'

'You came back, that's all that matters.'

Giovanni lifted his head to look deep into her eyes. 'But there is one thing of paramount importance I need to say.'

'You have already said it. You said it there, though I would very much like to hear the words.' She pointed at the triptych. Giovanni gazed at the framed paintings as if he had not seen them before, then he smiled again, a slow, sensual smile that wound its way around her heart.

'I did not realise it was so obvious.'

'I am very glad it was,' Cressie said. 'It is all I had to cling on to.'

'I love you, Cressie.' Giovanni pulled her back into

his arms. He touched her forehead. Her cheek. Her throat. She almost cried with the bliss of it. 'I love you more even than that painting can say. I don't deserve you, but...'

'Don't say that, Giovanni.'

'What I was going to say, if you would let me finish, *tesoro*.'

'*Tesoro*? What is that?'

'Darling. My darling Cressie, I know that I don't deserve you, but I am asking anyway. I went to Italy to—to confront my past. I saw my father. No, later I will tell you all. I saw him, I made my peace with him and with myself.' He took her hands and placed them over his heart. 'This is yours if you will take it, Cressie. *Ti amo*.'

She could feel his heart beating beneath her hand. She could see now what was different about him. He no longer carried the long shadow of unhappiness with him. 'I don't care about the past, Giovanni. We have both done things we have regretted. We've both wasted a lot of time trying to be what others wanted from us. I would not wish it undone, for I would not change you, and really, I don't care. All I'm interested in is the future.' Cressie took his hand and placed it over her own heart. Feverishly beating, it fluttered in her breast as if trying to escape. '*Ti amo, tesoro*. I love you so much, Giovanni.'

This time his kiss was crushing, his lips hungry, famished, feasting on hers. Their tongues touched, igniting the fierce flame of passion which had smouldered between them too long unsated. His hands framed her face, his fingers tangling in the wild curls of her hair, tugging it free from its ribbon, spreading it out over her back.

He gathered her close, sinking his face into her hair and breathing deeply. 'Lavender. And Cressie. How I have missed that.' He kissed her mouth again, tenderly this time, then with increasing passion. His hands were feverish, on her back, on her waist, on her bottom, on her breasts. He was trembling. 'I don't know what to do,' he said, with a lopsided smile. 'I feel as if—it is stupid. I feel as if this is the first time. I don't know what to do.'

His words, the way he looked at her, heated, loving, and yet almost bashful, she thought she might actually faint with the depth of her love for him. She felt like laughing hysterically, like crying, like declaiming her love from the attic window. 'Make love to me, Giovanni,' she said, 'that's all I want. That's all you have to do.'

With a confidence she was far from feeling, Cressie locked the door of the attic and led Giovanni over to the Egyptian chair and pushed him down on to it. She glanced over at the image of herself hanging on the wall. *Cressie.* Fingers shaking, she wrestled with the hooks of her gown. It was not the most elegant of undressing, but she had no doubt of how it was being received. Giovanni was riveted as she shrugged herself out of her dress. Standing in her undergarments, she played his words from the whispering gallery over in her mind.

'Corsets,' she said, placing herself before him. His breath was warm on her nape as his fingers struggled with the ties. When she turned around, his pupils were almost black. Colour slashed his cheeks. His breathing was ragged. She slipped out of her petticoats. Turning sideways, she propped one leg on a footstool, and leaned over, feeling her pantalettes stretch tight over her bottom, rewarded by Giovanni's sharp intake of breath. The line of beauty. She slipped off her shoe and rolled down her stocking. She had never seen a face so stark with passion. It made her feverish, damp with anticipation. The knot in her belly was aching. She turned to repeat the process. Bend. Shoe. Stocking.

She had only her chemise and pantalettes now. Quickly, she dispensed with them. A glance at the portrait—not that she needed to be reminded. He caught her looking, and a smile dawned. Cressie lay down on the *chaise-longue*. She stretched her arms over her head. She arched her back. Her nipples were hard. She turned her head to smile. Cressie's smile. It came to her so easily, looking as she was at the man she loved. Seductive. Provocative. Confident.

Giovanni was on his feet now, casting clothing wildly across the room, yanking so hard at his shirt that the buttons flew. Cressie held out her hand to him. Naked, his chest heaving, his eyes wild, his erection jutting up thick and heavy, he looked at her as if she were...

'Beautiful,' Giovanni said, kneeling before her. '*Tesoro, sei bellissima.* I do not think I have ever seen anyone so beautiful as you. Cressie. My very own Cressie.'

She thought she had never seen anyone so beautiful as he as he leaned over her to kiss her. She thought she had never been so happy as she was now, as his lips touched hers, as she opened her mouth to him. She was so hot and so tense and every bit of her tingled and throbbed, she thought she would climax, just from him kissing her. Then he kissed his way down to her breast and took her nipple in his mouth, sucking slowly, a gentle tugging pull that made her cry out, and Cressie stopped thinking altogether.

An aeon he spent kissing her breasts, stroking them, cupping them, crushing his face between them. She was writhing, struggling to hold herself in, when he kissed his way down her stomach. 'Softest,' he murmured, reverently parting her legs, pulling her over on the *chaise-longue*, tucking his hands under her bottom to lever her towards him. 'Softest,' he said again, his voice husky with passion as he kissed her thighs, licked the yielding flesh.

Heat built inside her. She thought she had experienced passion with him before, but this was quite different. His touch inflamed her, made her want to scream her frustration, to surrender to the fire which he was kissing into an inferno, and yet she didn't want to surrender to it just yet. When his tongue touched the damp folds of her sex, she whimpered. Though he was gentle, a mere whisper of a feather-light touch, she could hardly bear it. She arched her back, dug her heels into the chaise, her hands into his shoulders. 'Giovanni.' His tongue was rougher now. 'Yes. Please. Oh, Giovanni.' And yet more. She came like a tempest, great rolling waves gripping her, squeezing her, shaking her, turning her inside out.

She could hear herself crying out, but it was such a strange sound and she was so far away, riding the crest of her orgasm, that she couldn't associate it with herself.

As she shuddered, he licked her again, until she thought she could bear no more. Sliding on to the floor beside him, twining her legs around him, her arms around him, she pulled him on top of her, panting, pleading.

He kissed her hard. He angled himself against her. Then he hesitated. 'I'm afraid,' he said in a strangled voice. 'I have never wanted anything so much. Just watching you, I am so…I'm afraid I won't be able to…I don't want it to be over.'

'Giovanni, it's never going to be over until we die. Please,' Cressie said desperately, 'make love to me.'

'Cressie, in truth I think I may die if I do not.'

He kissed her swiftly and entered her slowly. Delightful. Delectable. Delicious. Luscious. Nothing was sufficient to describe it, the slow penetration as he slid into her, gradually merging his body with hers. Braced above her, his chest glistened with sweat, heaving with the effort of restraint, she thought she had never seen him more beautiful. He kissed her again, holding himself still inside her. She could feel the blood pulsing through his shaft. It made her muscles pulse, an echo, a summons. They were the same. The same.

He withdrew slowly, breath rasping. She gripped him tight. He pushed his way into her again. Stars exploding. They couldn't be, but they were, right behind her lids. She forced her eyes open. His face was starkly beautiful, his eyes focused on her face. She arched up. He swallowed. He thrust. Not so slowly this time. Then he thrust again. Harder. *Frisson.* Friction. She hadn't ever. 'Haven't ever,' she gasped in a vain attempt to tell him what he was doing to her. He thrust again and she shuddered. It was different but the same, this climax. More violent. Not just hers. Claiming. It rolled over her, gripped her, made her grip him, made her clutch at him, cry out his name wildly as he thrust one last time and fell on top of her with a harsh cry just as wild as her own.

'I painted his portrait, before he died,' Giovanni said much later, when they had wrapped themselves in each other and were sprawled on the *chaise-longue*, their bodies dappled with the light of the sinking sun and he had told her of the reunion with the count which was not a reunion. 'I will show you it later. I think it is good.' Giovanni stroked her hair. 'He asked me, but I didn't really paint it for him, I painted it for me.'

'You don't regret it, turning down such a huge inheritance?'

'I could not keep it, Cressie. I know that it is the one thing which would have reconciled your father to our...'

'Liaison?' Cressie said with a chuckle.

Giovanni's hand stilled. 'There is nothing temporary about what I feel for you. I will give you my name, I will give you all that I have if you will take it, but even if you don't, I will never let you go.'

Cressie rolled over to prop herself on his chest. She touched his forehead. His cheek. His throat. He smiled at her in recognition of the gesture. 'I have no intentions of going anywhere far from your side.'

'You don't think I made a mistake, turning down the count's estates?'

'You would have made a serious mistake, let me tell

you, Giovanni di Matteo, if you had come here bearing riches with which to bribe my father. Of course you didn't make a mistake.'

'But your father—it is not him so much as what he can do.'

Cressie nodded. 'I know. He could forbid my seeing my brothers, but I doubt very much if Bella would allow it. She knows how fond they are of me, and though she seems to love my father, she loves her sons more. As to my father—to be frank, I think the less I see him the easier it will be for me to love him.'

Giovanni gave a bark of laughter. 'My thoughts exactly.' His hand moved down her spine to stroke the curve of her bottom. 'Do you want to marry me, Cressie?'

'I don't know. I want to be with you always, I know that much.'

'I won't have my children called bastards.'

'They will be our children regardless. But if we are lucky enough to be blessed, then you may most certainly do me the honour of bestowing your name upon me.'

'*Grazie, signorina.* You have a very naughty smile, did you know that?'

'I did not, until you painted it.' Cressie wriggled her bottom, and felt a most satisfactory response from beneath her. She smiled again, quite deliberately, and equally deliberately brushed her breasts across his chest. 'Giovanni, do you still believe we are kindred spirits, you and I?'

'I am certain of it.'

Another wriggle. He was definitely hard. She was definitely ready. 'Does that mean you like what I like?'

'Yes, it does.'

Cressie smiled, her new-found seductive smile. She kissed his mouth. Then she slid down on to the attic floor between his legs. 'Good, then let me show you exactly what I like,' she said.

Historical Note

The inspiration for writing a heroine who was a mathematician was sparked when I read Benjamin Woolley's biography of Lord Byron's only legitimate child, Ada. Estranged from her husband almost immediately after her marriage, Byron's wife, Annabella, was terrified that her daughter might have inherited her father's wild temperament, and introduced a strict regime of formal studies, including philosophies based on reason and logic, in an attempt to counter any such tendencies. My heroine was born thirteen years before Ada, but the two have read many of the same textbooks and share an acquaintance in Charles Babbage, whose counting machine is credited with being the progenitor of the computer.

The idea of having Cressie write a mathematical 'theory' of beauty which mirrored the technique which Giovanni used in his portraits came from two sources. I first came across William Hogarth's 'line of beauty' when I took an arts foundation course with the Open University. Jenny Uglow's excellent biography of the artist, *Hogarth: A Life and a World*, taught me a bit more on the subject, which I filed away, vaguely thinking that it might come in useful some day. Then, on a recent visit to Hampton Court with one of my sisters (sisters do tend to play a vital role in my life and my books), I saw Sir Peter Lely's paintings of the 'Windsor Beauties' and was much struck by the theory that he'd actually painted each of the individual women using a sort of 'template' of beauty in order for the portraits to be more acclaimed. It was here, in Hampton Court, that the idea for Giovanni's side of the story was born.

At the time Giovanni was painting, ready-mixed oils would have been unavailable. He may have made his own pigments, but would most likely have ordered them from a catalogue and mixed them himself. Much of the technical detail of his craft I gleaned from reading about the English artist Turner. Giovanni's travelling box of oils is actually based on the one found in Turner's studio. There are 'models' for the three paintings which Giovanni does of Cressie: *'Lady Cressida'* is based on one by the portraitist Thomas Lawrence, *'Mr Brown'* takes its inspiration from Goya and *'Cressie'* is inspired by Goya's famous painting *'The Naked Maja'*, reputedly the first portrait to depict pubic hair. Though Giovanni precedes the Impressionists by some years, I've tried to show his artistic journey from the glossy, idealised style of portraiture popular during the Regency to the more 'impressionistic' style which took hold towards the end of the nineteenth century. However, I'm no artist, so any mistakes I've made in describing Giovanni's painting technique are most definitely all my own work.

Finally, for those who are interested, a few historical facts and figures and slight historical liberties I have taken. Though it was not exactly common, there is a precedent for Giovanni's father, Count Fancini, making his illegitimate son his heir. Guilio de' Medici was the Earl of Florence's natural son, for example. Lord Armstrong's trip to Russia to discuss the problem of Greek independence was actually made by the Duke of Wellington in 1826 and not 1828. Killellan Manor is based on Pollok House in Glasgow, which lies within the country park housing the amazing Burrell Collection, and which is very familiar territory for me. There is no whispering gallery in the cellar there—that particular piece of architecture was inspired by New York's Grand Central Terminus. If you wish to know still more about the inspiration behind this book, please do check out my *Pinterest* page.

* * * * *

MILLS & BOON

THE HEART OF ROMANCE

A ROMANCE FOR EVERY KIND OF READER

MODERN

Prepare to be swept off your feet by sophisticated, sexy and seductive heroes, in some of the world's most glamorous a romantic locations, where power and passion collide.
8 stories per month.

HISTORICAL

Escape with historical heroes from time gone by. Whether yo passion is for wicked Regency Rakes, muscled Vikings or rug Highlanders, awaken the romance of the past.
6 stories per month.

MEDICAL

Set your pulse racing with dedicated, delectable doctors in t high-pressure world of medicine, where emotions run high passion, comfort and love are the best medicine.
6 stories per month.

True Love

Celebrate true love with tender stories of heartfelt romance the rush of falling in love to the joy a new baby can bring, a focus on the emotional heart of a relationship.
8 stories per month.

Desire

Indulge in secrets and scandal, intense drama and plenty of hot action with powerful and passionate heroes who have it wealth, status, good looks...everything but the right woman.
6 stories per month.

HEROES

Experience all the excitement of a gripping thriller, with an romance at its heart. Resourceful, true-to-life women and st fearless men face danger and desire - a killer combination!
8 stories per month.

DARE

Sensual love stories featuring smart, sassy heroines you'd wa best friend, and compelling intense heroes who are worthy o
4 stories per month.

To see which titles are coming soon, please visit

millsandboon.co.uk/nextmonth